MARRYING
Olivia

TRUE PLATINUM SERIES

MORGANA
BEVAN

Cover Design by: Pretty Little Design Co.

Editing by Dayna Hart

Proofread by Amy Rooney

ISBN: 978-1-916719-14-9

CONTENT ADVISORIES

<u>Tropes:</u>
Rock star romance, secret relationship, instalove, teenage crush, one of them is famous, drunken Vegas wedding, accidental marriage, forced proximity, opposites attract, rock stars on tour, steamy backstage encounters, found family, British hero, small-town heroine, angst

<u>Triggers:</u>
Death of a parent, cancer, suicide (mentioned, past memory), anxiety.

<u>British English</u>

To all my American readers, I'm a **British** author and this book is written in **British English**. There are variations in the language between the US and British English. That means some words are spelt differently. Hell, we speak differently.

Happy Reading!

Morgana x

For anyone who's ever had a poster of their celebrity crush on their bedroom wall and dreamed of marrying them someday. Never say never.

MARRYING OLIVIA PLAYLIST

1 - She Had Me At Head's Carolina - Cole Swindell
2 - So High School - Taylor Swift
3 - I melt with You - Modern English
4 - Slow Hands - Niall Horan
5 - Sparks Fly (Taylor's Version) - Taylor Swift
6 - Speechless - Dan + Shay
7 - Girls Like You - Maroon 5 ft. Cardi B
8 - Til My Last Day - Justin Moore
9 - Tennessee Whiskey - Chris Stapleton
10 - Carry You Home - Tim Hicks, Hanna Reid
11 - a million pretty pieces - Nightly, Fleurie
12 - Meant to Be - Beba Rexha (Feat. Florida Georgia Line)
13 - Country Girl - Luke Bryan
14 - Can't Do Without Me - Chayce Beckham, Lindsay Ell
15 - My Girl - Dylan Scott
16 - Take Me Out - Carrie Underwood
17 - Beautiful Things - Benson Boone
18 - Make You Feel My Love - Adele
19 - Good As it Gets - Little Hurt
20 - All of Me - John Legend
21 - Waking Up in Vegas - Katy Perry

22 - Mess is Mine - Vance Joy

23 - mixed signals - davvn, chillary

24 - it's Quiet Uptown - Kelly Clarkson

25 - Easy to Lie - Forest Black

26 - Dream in a Little Less Colour - Lacey

27 - I Won't Give Up - Jason Mraz

28 - Bad Life - Sigrid, Bring Me The Horizon

29 - Stay Awake - Dean Lewis

30 - If Your Light Goes Out - The Maine

31 - Need You Now - Lady A

32 - Satellite - Nickelback

33 - I'll Be - Edwin McCain

34 - I Don't Want to Miss a Thing - Aerosmith

35 - Supermarket Flowers - Ed Sheeran

36 - Die A Happy Man - Thomas Rhett

Listen to the Playlist on Spotify here.

CHAPTER ONE

LEWIS

"*H*ey, Ben. Got anything good for me tonight?" I shouted, the sound almost lost to the strum of a guitar and the chatter of the crowd in the next room.

Alex and Tom stopped behind me, waiting not-so-patiently while Alex continued whining over his ex-girlfriend playing hard to get.

"Couple new acts. One or two might have something." He pursed his lips as he scanned the lineup for the showcase.

Whenever I visited LA, I always stopped at Rhymes. Not out of some need to be a mentor—I mean, I'd been in the music business for going on thirteen years now and let me tell you, I'd seen some shit. I'd make a fucking excellent mentor. But I digress.

No, the hours I spent at this tiny, no-frills venue located down an alley near Sunset and Vine were some of the most inspiring.

I'd walk in with a heavy weight on my shoulders, an ache in my bones that said the time to call it quits was fast approaching.

Couple of beers and a few acts later and the ideas were coursing through me faster than I could track them. My fingers itched to pick up my guitar and join the acts on stage.

For a few fleeting hours, the joy returned.

Don't ask me when it faded. I'd tried to trace it, to find the exact moment my brain checked out and the music became nothing more than a job. But I couldn't find it. It all blurred into one messy, chaotic disaster.

Even with Alex's moaning, I needed this.

In two weeks, we'd ship out for the longest tour of our careers. Two years, hundreds of stadiums, and five continents. Somehow I had to refill the well and keep it full.

The alternative if I failed didn't bear thinking about.

I refused to let my friends and bandmates down.

"That one act you liked last time just finished twenty minutes ago." Ben grimaced apologetically. "Sorry, man. If you'd let me know you were coming in, I would have sent over the schedule."

"No need." I waved his apology off. "I wasn't planning to stop by. I'm sure there'll be some great music anyway."

"If you consider that off-key strumming great, you and I need to have a conversation," Alex grumbled. He frowned at the doorway that led to the main bar and the stage. "Who the fuck taught this guy to play?"

Tom and I shared a look. When Alex wasn't trying to win Ceri back, he treated us to this... grumpy man child act.

"Let's get some drinks, yeah?" Tom slapped his hand down on Alex's shoulder and shoved him towards the doorway. "Hopefully, it'll mellow you the fuck out before one of us decides we don't need another guitarist and glasses you."

Alex laughed but Tom threw me a dark, raised-brow look. It screamed 'Did I say I was joking?'

"There is this one chick," Ben said before I followed them. "Singer-songwriter from South Carolina. The voice on her." He shook his head, a look of pure peace in his eyes. I wanted it. "You'll love her, I'm sure of it."

I thanked him and followed Tom and Alex into the main room. It didn't take me long to find them at the bar, and to Alex's delight, the guy who couldn't play guitar finished up his set to a cold audience.

"Do you remember what it was like for us getting on a stage in the beginning?"

Alex's attention snapped to me and his brow furrowed. "Of course I do."

"Oh really?" I drawled, unable to stop the smirk claiming my lips. "What was it like?"

"Nerve-wracking." He cut a sly look to Tom. "Tom threw up like three times."

"Like fuck I did. That was you, you dickhead."

We'd been fourteen-year-old, cocky kids who thought they were destined to be rock gods. Turns out we weren't half wrong, but that didn't absolve us from the time-freezing moment when that first spotlight hits, and suddenly we're blind, with too many expectant eyes on us to count.

I look back on those early days with a bittersweet nostalgia, but I wouldn't wish to relive them.

Alex crossed his arms, a beer bottle dangling from his fingers. "What's your point?"

"You don't need to be an asshole to a stranger learning the ropes." I stared at him, searching for a sign that the message got through. "This isn't you, Al. We know you're frustrated but taking it out on other people isn't going to make Ceri like you any more."

"If anything, you're fucking up your only chance to win her back," Tom added, his tone severe. "You've got three months to prove her wrong. Once you're divorced, you probably won't get another opportunity."

I snorted. "She'll move and change her number without a second thought."

In Ceri's situation, I would.

Alex glared at me, but for the first time in weeks, he looked like he was listening. His expression lost some of its fire and he nodded.

Rehearsals had started already, but there was only so much the band could do when our lead singer kept hopping across the pond.

All of that changed tomorrow. We were meeting our opening acts and Lily landed later tonight. Things were finally starting to heat up and as much as I dreaded spending two years on the road, anything would be better than this perpetual waiting.

Part of me also hoped it would give Alex something else to focus on, other than driving Ceri mad.

The lights dimmed before any of us could say more.

"Please welcome to the stage the incredible Olivia Monroe," the announcer said, his voice amplified by the sound system.

The crowd clapped and screamed, a surprising contrast to the last act. People jostled for the best view of the small stage and the single stool and mic stand sat in the middle. String lights wove through Rhymes' logo in the background, casting a warm glow in the darkness.

The spotlight turned on as she settled herself on the stool with a coy yet nervous smile. Everything about her captivated me instantly—from the loose strand of chestnut hair she tucked behind her ear to her ripped jeans, bohemian-style top, and beat-up Converse.

"Good evening Los Angeles! I'm Olivia, and we're going to have some fun for the next twenty minutes," she said, her voice lyrical. "I hope you enjoy the show."

I was transfixed, and she hadn't played a note yet. The guys chattered amongst themselves, about what I couldn't say. I only had eyes and ears for her.

Her fingers strummed the guitar, setting an upbeat tone, building with percussive taps on the guitar's body. She leaned towards the mic, her foot tapping gently on the stool rung, and then she started to sing.

The whole room stilled, all focus zeroed in on her as that

voice flowed out like honey. Sweet yet complex, with an almost ethereal quality that left me enthralled.

"Hey! Where are you going?" Tom grabbed my arm, pulling me back. I tore my gaze from her—from Olivia—and blinked at him like I was coming out of a dream. I couldn't remember taking a step. "Are we getting a table or what?"

"Sure." I shrugged off his grip and turned back to the most captivating woman I'd ever seen. "I'll find you."

Their protests were swallowed as her voice rose and I kept moving forward, pushing through the mesmerised crowd until I found myself front and centre. I was helpless, pulled by some invisible force to be as near as possible to this siren on stage.

Her voice was incredible, but that wasn't all that drew me. The way she seemed to glow under the soft stage lights, eyes closed as her fingers caressed the smooth neck of her guitar, stole my breath.

She had it. That joy I'd lost.

Utter happiness radiated from her, and it made me grin but also ache at the loss. I remembered it so clearly; the way it used to feel, the way I could close my eyes and be swept away into my own world despite knowing there were hundreds, thousands, millions of eyes on me and one badly timed twitch could ruin the song.

Her eyes fluttered open and green officially became my favourite colour. Our gazes locked for a moment and I felt a spark of connection so real it left me reeling. At that moment, I'd have done anything for her, gone anywhere with her.

How was it possible to feel so drawn to a stranger?

Her full lips curved into a smile made for much more than performing. It was made for lazy Sunday mornings tangled in sheets, for stolen kisses in the back of a tour bus, for heated whispers in the dark of night.

I couldn't remember wanting those things, but now, listening to her, watching her, they consumed my thoughts.

She held my gaze for I don't know how long, seeming to sing directly to my soul. When she shot me a sly look, almost like we were sharing some secret, I couldn't help but reciprocate. Then she glanced away, taking a piece of me with her.

Alex and Tom sidled up on either side, jostling me from my daze. I barely stopped myself from scowling at them.

Couldn't these fuckers see I was having a moment?

"She's incredible, mate!" Tom said.

"Of course she is, we only pick the best." Alex took a swig of his beer.

Wait! What?

Unfortunately, his attention was still on me when the realisation struck and my eyes widened. A shit eating grin spread across his face. "You didn't know she was our opening act, did you?"

I might have tuned out when all those decisions got made. What? I was a musician, not a businessman. Plus, Lily had found her, and if our lead singer said she was perfect for us, then she was perfect.

And had you been paying attention, you would have found her sooner.

Shit.

I stayed silent, still struggling to wrap my head around the strength of my reaction. Her voice had awoken something in me. It had energised me yet shepherded me to a peace I hadn't experienced in a long time.

CHAPTER TWO

OLIVIA

*D*o you think anyone would notice if I started fangirling on stage? Yeah, it probably wouldn't go over too well. But Lewis Davies was staring at me like I'd fed him my grandmother's county fair award-winning cobbler.

I'd adored The Brightside forever. I'd been in high school when they'd hit it big. I'd fallen in love with their music. Then my mother surprised me with tickets to their Savannah show. She had never told me how she got them, but I didn't care. I nearly lost my mind with excitement.

Seeing them live changed everything for me.

I'd wanted to make music ever since I could remember thanks to my granddaddy. Nearly every memory I had of him involved a guitar. He'd made it look so easy and seeing my fascination, he'd made it his mission to teach me.

Only it wasn't easy in the slightest.

My impulsive nature nearly outdid my drive to learn, but thankfully, my grandaddy was a stubborn man. Because of him,

I spent the majority of my childhood and teenage years fiddling with guitar chords and filling notebooks with snippets of lyrics.

Then I'd seen The Brightside live and something had clicked.

Hope seeped beneath my skin and refused to let up.

They were only two years older than me, and they'd not only made incredible music, they'd broken out.

They were from a small Welsh town on the other side of the ocean. If they could make a real career out of music and hit it big in another country, then surely this small-town South Carolina girl had a reason to hope. That concert lit a fire in me, a burning determination to chase my own musical dreams no matter the odds.

It hadn't been easy. I moved to Nashville, wrote every free moment, played every showcase, worked every shift I could as a waitress to support myself and keep myself flexible for the moment my big break came. I poured my heart and soul into every note, every lyric, hoping someone would hear the truth in my words.

And it would come. I knew it in my bones.

I just didn't think it would take ten years, or come directly from Lily Tyler, The Brightside's lead singer. When that unknown number flashed up on my phone, I almost didn't answer. It was right in the middle of a busy shift, but I'd spent so long waiting for that call that I'd scrambled into the kitchen and answered while the cook shouted at me.

He shouted some more when I quit on the spot and walked out. I didn't even bother taking off my apron.

She'd given me a month to prepare, but nothing was going to stop me from living this dream of mine as soon as possible.

To anyone else, the speed at which I'd packed up my Nashville apartment, found a replacement for my roommate, and moved all my stuff back to Jasmine Bay would be depressing. They'd think it meant I hadn't lived, but I saw it differently.

To me, it meant I'd achieved my goals. I'd been ready to

leave on a dime when the moment came, and I did. I'd been prepared.

But this? I wasn't prepared for this.

To be playing my second open mic in Los Angeles within a week and find myself staring at my teenage crush. For that guy, a super successful musician, to be watching me like I'd blown his mind... how was I supposed to react to that? My teenage self was screaming inside.

I'd braced myself for meeting him tomorrow. I'd given myself the pep talks, reminded myself not to stare at him like a lovesick teenager. I'd practised my introduction in the mirror, trying to strike the right balance between professional and friendly.

With my heart racing and my mind spinning, I knew none of it had worked.

The crowd cheered and applauded when I finished the set. The melody still hummed through my bones as I stepped off the stage and packed up my acoustic guitar. Exhilaration buzzed inside of me. I was drunk on the euphoric rush that always came with playing to an engaged audience, but it didn't have a chance in hell of drowning out the nerves. My belly did somersaults worthy of an Olympic gymnastics team.

Should I walk up to him? Or should I sneak out and pretend I haven't seen him?

I winced at the last idea. If I wasn't allowed to be a lovesick teenager, I definitely couldn't pull any of that high school bullshit.

This was the start of my music career, and he was part of the reason I had it. The least I could do was say hello. I owed him that much, even if the thought made my palms sweat and my mouth go dry.

I weaved my way through knots of people, exchanging grateful smiles and the occasional high-five. All the while, those damn nerves twisted in my gut and threatened to choke me.

It was nothing. Just saying hi to a normal guy I've never had a crush on and whose band wasn't responsible for my entire career.

I scanned the room, rising up on my tiptoes to try and see over the shoulders of people much taller than me. The longer I looked, the more disappointment pinched my insides. It settled like a lead weight in my belly, dragging down the corners of my hopeful smile.

Maybe he'd left.

He didn't owe me anything. I was just another opening act, a blip on his radar. Nothing special.

The host announced the next act. I'd get a drink and enjoy the rest of the night. Or, you know, drown my sorrows in a whiskey or three and chalk it up to another crazy LA experience.

I glanced over my shoulder, giving the room one final scan. When I still couldn't spot him, I bit my lip. Disappointment dug deeper and I silently chastised myself for being so ridiculous.

Sighing, I turned back to the bar and slammed into a hard surface. It grunted and hands gripped my shoulders as I stepped back, blinking at the Super Mario image filling my vision.

"Maybe you should work out less," I muttered. I rubbed my head, expecting a bump, but that would be ridiculous. I'd run into a person, not a wall.

"You alright?"

I froze. I couldn't tear my eyes from what I now realised was a band t-shirt with 'Hey Mario' on it. If there ever was a moment when the ground needed to swallow someone, now was it.

Slowly, I dragged my gaze up his buff chest, over his stubbled jaw until his hazel eyes captured mine. They were even more mesmerising in person, flecks of gold catching the dim bar light.

He smiled and it creased his eyes, somehow making him hotter. That smile could've powered a small country. It certainly made my heart rate skyrocket and my brain short-circuit.

Photos really didn't do him justice.

The thought should have worried me, but all I could do was stare at him, my tongue stuck to the roof of my mouth and my mind running off down a road it had no business going. One where we weren't in a crowded bar, neither of us wore a stitch of clothing and I didn't need to feel guilty for getting lost in his eyes. Where I could trace the lines of his tattoos with my fingertips, explore the planes of his body with my hands and lips...

"I'm Lewis Davies."

"I know."

I stared at him, dawning horror burning up my neck.

Way to make a stellar first impression.

He smirked. "And I know who you are." He ducked his head, his eyes glittering with amusement. "But I figured you'd appreciate me not being the big-headed asshole that assumes his reputation precedes him."

Despite the flush of embarrassment, I laughed. "Yeah, you might be right about that."

He glanced briefly at the stage and then those captivating eyes landed back on me, stealing my breath all over again.

"You were incredible up there."

"Thank you."

"That last song gave me goosebumps."

I fought the urge to pinch myself to check if this whole thing was nothing more than a dream.

"That means the world coming from you."

I just about swallowed my tongue as the words fell from my lips. What in the world was I thinking? Might as well have asked him to sign my bra while I was at it.

"From a member of The Brightside, I mean."

He nodded. "I didn't..." he blushed and my insides squealed at the sight of it. He cleared his throat and tried again. "I come here whenever I'm in LA. I didn't expect to find you, in case you thought—"

"That you were checking up on your investment?" My brows quirked and he laughed, the sound surprisingly nervous. It humanised him somehow.

"Yeah, that." He turned, beckoning to the bartender at the nearby bar. "Would you fancy joining me for a drink?"

I opened my mouth to say yes—what else?—but then I spotted two of his bandmates at a table in the corner, watching us with amused grins.

"What about your bandmates?"

"Ignore them." He shifted a step and blocked my view. "They're big boys. They can look after themselves."

"And I can't?"

"No—I didn't mean—ah fuck." He dragged a hand through his hair and laughed. "Do-over?"

I couldn't say a do-over would make me forget that even he wasn't immune to making an ass of himself. But I wasn't about to torture the poor man. Not when he looked so adorably flustered.

"A do-over sounds perfect," I said with a smile and held out my hand. "I'm Olivia Monroe, but my friends call me Liv."

His shoulders relaxed and his lips curled. "It's nice to meet you, Olivia. I'm Lewis Davies, bassist for The Brightside. My friends call me Lewis, but I'm pretty sure I'd let you call me anything you want." He bit his lip and eyed me with a question in his eyes.

Oh lord, is that a flirty look? It is, isn't it? That little quirk of his lips, the mischief dancing in his eyes… yep, definitely flirting.

Holy shit, Lewis Davies was flirting with me.

It was surreal, exhilarating, and absolutely terrifying all at once. He was even more gorgeous in person, all tousled hair and scruffy jawline and eyes that could make a girl forget her own name. And those lips… I could write a whole album about those lips alone.

Say something. Anything. Before he thinks you're having a stroke.

"Yes, you can call me Liv," I managed to say, my voice coming out breathier than I intended.

"Thank you." His warm hand engulfed mine, his slightly calloused fingertips dragging across my skin, sending a tingle up my arm. His eyes sparkled with mischief and something else I couldn't quite place. Something that made my belly clench and my thighs press together.

"Well then, Liv," he said, his voice low and inviting. "How about that drink?"

I nodded, not trusting myself to speak again. He guided me towards the bar, his hand resting lightly on the small of my back. The simple touch sent my heart racing and my barely-under-control thoughts spiralling to forbidden places. Him pressing me up against the bar, his body flush against mine as his lips claimed my neck. His hands, those talented musician's hands, skimming under my shirt, tracing the curve of my waist, the dip of my spine. Me hooking a leg over his hip, drawing him closer, feeling the evidence of his desire hot and hard against me. I imagined his fingers dipping into the waistband of my jeans, teasing, exploring, making me gasp and arch and beg for more.

Heat burned my skin when I shook it off. Lewis stared at me, an amused but intrigued glint in his eyes. I ignored it and focused on the bar and the array of bottles that promised to cure me of these nerves.

As we approached, the bartender set two drinks down in front of us.

"To serendipitous meetings." Lewis clinked his glass against mine.

I eyed the amber liquid, a silly part of me wondering if it was fate that he knew my drink of choice. I took a sip, the smooth whiskey warming my throat. It burned going down, but in the best way. Like the first touch of a lover's hand.

"Do you make a habit of buying drinks for unsuspecting opening acts?"

He laughed, the sound rich and genuine. "Only the incredibly talented ones who nearly knock me on my ass."

I ducked my head, my cheeks heating. "Flattery will get you everywhere, Mr Davies."

"Please, call me Lewis. Mr Davies makes me feel like I'm in trouble."

"Aren't you? Are you supposed to be fraternising with the newbie?" I teased, emboldened by the whiskey and his easy charm.

"If this is trouble, I'll gladly take the punishment." His gaze raked over me appreciatively, setting my skin on fire. "How did you get from South Carolina to opening for us? Where did Lily find you?"

"That's two questions." I took a sip of my whiskey, the liquid courage warming my veins. "Where do you want me to start?"

"The beginning," he said without so much as a beat of hesitation. "I have this overwhelming desire to know everything about you."

I blushed again. I had to get a grip on my reactions to him, and fast.

"It all started with a dream and a beat-up guitar."

The same guitar my granddaddy taught me on, the one with the scratch on the body from when I'd dropped it trying to master my first G chord.

He chuckled, nodding in understanding. "The best things always do."

I told him about my granddaddy and his stubborn-as-an-ass attitude, how he held me to my fleeting wish to learn and wouldn't let me stop. Not even when my fingertips were raw and bleeding, when I wanted to throw that guitar out the window and never look at it again.

That is until he died not long after I turned fourteen. Grief nearly drove me to put the guitar down for good, but with my mother's unwavering encouragement I pushed through. She'd sit with me for hours, listening to me stumble through chords, never once complaining about the noise.

I didn't tell him about The Brightside's part in my journey.

"I moved to Nashville as soon as I graduated high school." The memories flooded back. My mother crying buckets as she helped me load my stuff into the beat up truck my granddaddy left me. The truck I sold as soon as I got to Nashville to help with rent. "Figured if I was going to make it, that was the place to be."

"I've spent my share of time in Music City. Played some of my first U.S. gigs in those honky-tonks on Broadway. It's a special place." His expression softened, a look of understanding shining in his gaze. Those hazel eyes seemed to see straight through me, to the heart of my hopes and aspirations. Like he knew, bone-deep, the hunger that drove me, the need to pour my soul out in lyrics and melodies.

"It wasn't easy, making a go of it." I shrugged. "I worked at just about every bar and restaurant in town, trying to make ends meet while I chased my dream."

"I know that grind all too well. The late nights, the endless hustle…" He groaned. "We did it while in school. Didn't make us all that popular with our teachers, but I'm sure they've changed their tune by now."

"I have a long list of ex-bosses." My smile slipped and my voice quieted, the words almost getting lost beneath the new artist performing on stage. "I can't tell you how many open mics I played, hoping for my big break. Sometimes to a packed house, sometimes to an audience of one very drunk, very uninterested patron." I shuddered at the memory. The stale smell of spilled beer, the drunken heckles, the soul-crushing indifference. It was enough to make anyone question their life choices.

"But you kept at it," he said, his tone laced with admiration.

I shrugged, a small smile tugging at my lips. "Giving up wasn't an option. Music… it's all I've ever wanted to do. All I've ever needed to do."

"I can relate."

We stared at each other, silence stretching between us as we —or at least I—got lost in each other's eyes. My fingers itched to touch him, to find out if his facial hair would tickle like I imagined or whether it would be soft.

I caught myself leaning forward and slammed back into my chair, my pulse racing. "So…" I glanced away and cleared my throat while that annoying burn of embarrassment coloured my skin.

Don't do it. You'll give yourself away.

But curiosity got the better of me.

"What about you? How did The Brightside go from playing small-town Welsh pubs to headlining world tours?"

A wistful smile danced on his lips, his eyes taking on a faraway look. "Similar story, different accent. It wasn't a straight shot to success, that's for sure." He tapped the bar, keeping time with the singer crooning a love song on the stage behind me. "I started playing in pubs when I was a kid, barely strong enough to lift a bass, let alone tall enough to reach the mic. But I knew, from that first rush of performing, that I'd found my calling."

"And the rest is history?"

"Hardly. They say we were an overnight success." He laughed, the sound warm and rich. "We played every dive bar, every festival, every birthday party that would have us. Slept in the van more nights than I can count, lived off petrol station sandwiches and the kindness of strangers." He shot me an amused look, but the edges were frayed. He seemed to brace himself before continuing, "But every step, every struggle… it was all worth it, to be able to do what I love, to share my music with the world."

I probably imagined it or it was nothing more than the play of the stage lights, but I could have sworn something haunted flashed in his eyes. "But you made it in the end. You broke through."

He nodded. "That we did." His hand found mine on the bar, his rough, guitar-string calloused fingers lacing with my own. Sparks danced across my skin and an ache bloomed low in my belly. I squeezed my knees together, a futile attempt to ease the growing throb of desire, but the intensity in his gaze stole my breath and made me forget why I needed to fight it. "But something tells me the best part of our journey is just beginning."

"Oh?"

"Yeah," he said, his voice low and intimate. "I have a feeling this tour, meeting you… it's the start of something special." His thumb traced maddening circles on my wrist.

My heart thundered, my skin tingling with anticipation it had no right to feel. I let the way he looked at me sink in, the way his hand felt in mine… it was electric. Magnetic. Like standing on the edge of a cliff, exhilarated and terrified and so, so alive.

"I think you might be right," I managed, my voice hushed.

His thumb continued its torturous dance on my wrist, sending shivers cascading down my spine. "It's like… like we were meant to find each other." His eyes widened and for a second horror flooded his expression. "That's not a line. I don't… I've never said that to anyone before."

Butterflies took flight in my belly. "Why would I believe a good-looking Grammy winner with legions of adoring fans hasn't hit on a woman before?"

For the second time tonight, I wished the hardwood floor would open up and swallow me whole. He stared at me, a slow smirk unfurling on his face.

He leaned forward, invading my personal space until I was drowning in the earthy, spicy scent of him mingled with a hint of whiskey, until I couldn't mistake the naked hunger in his eyes. "You think I'm good-looking?"

My heart slammed against my ribs, my mouth going dry. How was I supposed to answer that? The truth was obvious—he was the most gorgeous man I'd ever laid eyes on. But admitting that felt dangerous.

"I mean…" I stammered, my cheeks catching fire. "Doesn't every woman?"

He didn't let me off the hook. Instead, he leaned even closer, his nose almost brushing mine. I could count the flecks of gold in his mesmerising eyes, could feel the heat radiating off his body, and practically taste the whiskey on his breath.

"I'm not asking about every woman," he murmured, his

breath ghosting over my lips. "I'm asking about you, Liv. Do you find me attractive?"

There was no hiding from the intensity of his stare, from the raw, undeniable hunger simmering between us. With alcohol buzzing in my veins and his proximity clouding my judgement, I threw caution to the wind.

"Yes," I breathed, the confession escaping on a sigh. "I find you incredibly attractive, Lewis."

Something wild and reckless flared in his eyes.

"Good." His gaze dropped to my mouth, his tongue darting out to wet his lips. "Now what are we going to do about it?"

My pulse kicked into overdrive, my skin suddenly too tight, too hot. This was dangerous territory. The rational part of my brain screamed at me to back off, to put some distance between us before I did something I couldn't take back. But the part of me that had been drawn to him from the moment I saw him, the part that craved his touch, his attention... that part was rapidly winning out.

"Lewis..." I started, my voice shaky. "We're going to be working together. Closely. For the next six months. Maybe we shouldn't..."

"Shouldn't what?" he challenged, his hand coming up to tuck a strand of hair behind my ear. His fingers lingered, tracing the delicate shell, sending a shiver racing down my back. "Shouldn't act on this connection between us? Shouldn't explore whatever this is?"

I swallowed hard, my resolve crumbling under the heat of his gaze. "It's risky. If things didn't work out..." If I let myself fall and he didn't catch me...

"Who says they won't?" He cupped my cheek, his thumb caressing my cheekbone, leaving a trail of sparks in its wake. "I know we just met. I know we're about to go on this wild, intense journey together. But what I feel... it's real. It's powerful. And I don't want to ignore it."

His eyes bored into mine, dark with promise and sincerity. Every cell in my body was screaming at me to lean in, to close the distance and kiss him like I'd been dreaming of doing for half my life.

"I'm not suggesting we elope. I'm just asking for a chance. One night, to see where this leads."

He leaned in closer, his lips a whisper from mine. "Here's what I propose. We have one more drink. We talk, we laugh, we enjoy each other's company. And then we walk out of here together, catch a cab to my hotel... and let the night take us where it will. No pressure, no expectations. Just you and me, exploring this fire between us. What do you say?" His voice was rough, gravelly with restrained desire, his eyes molten pools I wanted to drown in.

My mouth went dry. It was a tempting offer, the promise of a night with him, no strings attached. A chance to indulge the fantasies I'd harboured for so long, without worrying about the consequences.

"What about the tour? What about tomorrow?"

"We'll figure it out," he assured me. "One day at a time. But I don't want to look back and wonder 'what if?' I don't want to regret not taking this chance, not seeing where this could go." He brushed his thumb over my lower lip, his touch searing, branding me with possibilities.

His words struck a chord. How many times had I held myself back, let fear dictate my choices? How many opportunities had I let slip by, too afraid of the risks to reach for what I wanted?

Not this time. Not with him.

"Okay," I whispered, my voice steady with newfound resolve. "Let's do it. One more drink. And then... let's see where the night takes us."

CHAPTER THREE

LEWIS

One more drink turned into two, then three, as the minutes stretched into hours at Rhymes. The bar grew quieter as the night wore on, but we hardly noticed, too caught up in each other.

The world beyond our little bubble faded into irrelevance. All that existed was Olivia—the sparkle in her green eyes as she talked, the musical lilt of her laughter, the way her knee brushed against mine under the table, sending sparks racing up my thigh.

We'd been talking for hours, the drinks before us long forgotten, our voices growing hoarse. But I couldn't bear to let the night end.

"My sister hated me for a while when the buzz started growing around us."

Liv laughed. "I doubt that."

"No, she definitely did," I said, my voice taking on a more sombre tone. "She was thirteen. It didn't last long, but it wasn't all that surprising."

She leaned forward, an elbow resting on the bar, her eyes filled with genuine interest. "What happened?"

"Tegan was one of my biggest supporters from the start." I sighed, the memory playing out in my mind as if no time had passed. "She was always there, cheering me on at every gig, telling anyone who would listen that her big brother was going to be a star."

"That's sweet."

My sister's excited face filled my mind, her eyes shining with pride as she watched me from the front row of those early shows.

"But then, almost overnight, it was like a switch flipped. She got moody, started snapping at me for no reason. It was so out of character for her, and I couldn't figure out what I'd done wrong."

Liv's brow furrowed in sympathy. "That must have been tough, especially with everything else you were dealing with at the time."

"It was." I paused, swallowing around the lump that had formed in my throat. Even after all these years, my memories of that time were still a mixed bag of bittersweet and painful emotions. "Turns out, she was jealous." I shook my head, forcing a laugh I could barely feel.

She smiled, but the edges were brittle as she watched me with shrewd eyes, no doubt seeing through me.

"I'd been invited to my first BAFTA show. I was going to meet all of her favourite celebrities, and she hated that she was being left out." I twisted my glass on the bar top, my attention fixating on it, unable to look at her as I said, "On top of that, she was convinced I was going to forget about her once I became famous."

The idea of it was laughable then and now. Even after her death, she was never far from my thoughts. To think I could ever forget my family.

"I couldn't let her think that. Tee was my world, y'know?" I said, my voice hoarse. "So I did the only thing I could think of —I made her my plus-one."

Liv laughed.

"You should've seen her face when I told her. It was like I'd handed her the moon on a silver platter."

"I bet she was ecstatic." She reached for my hand, prying it away from my empty glass and lacing her fingers through mine.

"She was. Spent weeks planning her outfit, practising her 'I'm so excited to meet you' speech in the mirror." I shook my head, a fond grin tugging at my mouth despite the sadness creeping in at the edges. "The night of the show, she was practically vibrating with excitement. I thought she might actually combust when we got to the red carpet."

Liv laughed, the sound melodic and soothing. "I can only imagine. Thirteen-year-old me would've been the same way."

"It was a great night. We laughed, we danced, we tried to spot all the celebrities. She was in her element, charming everyone she met with her endless enthusiasm." I paused, my throat tightening as the memory played out. Tegan's smile, her laughter, the way she'd hugged me so tightly at the end of the night, whispering 'thank you' over and over.

"Lewis?" Liv's gentle voice pulled me back to the present. "Where'd you go just now?"

I blinked, surprised to find my eyes stinging with unshed tears. "Sorry, I just…" I cleared my throat, trying to find the words.

I could see the questions in her eyes, the curiosity warring with hesitation. But she didn't push. I'm not sure what I would have said if she did. I didn't want to go down that road, not tonight.

Instead, she smiled, a mischievous glint entering her gaze. "Y'know, all this talk of childhood memories has got me thinking about the summer I discovered my one true love."

I raised an eyebrow, intrigued. "Oh? And who might that be?"

"Not who, what." A playful smile teased her lips. "I'm

talking about the flakiest, most irresistible pastry to ever grace my taste buds—the incomparable baklava."

"Can't say I saw that one coming."

"Nobody ever does." She shifted in her seat, shaking her head like that was a great oversight. "It all started when I was about five years old. Our town librarian, Delphine Broussard, had just gotten back from visiting her sister who moved to Turkey."

The gleam in her eyes as she spoke was captivating. I couldn't help but imagine her as a child, all wide-eyed wonder and insatiable curiosity.

I'd give anything to see that look on her face every day for the rest of my life.

"Back then, I had no idea what baklava even was. All I knew was that Delphine walked into the library one morning with this big white box, and the smell..." She closed her eyes, inhaling deeply as if she could still smell it. "It was like nothing I'd ever smelled before. Sweet, heavenly."

The way she closed her eyes in bliss had me shifting in my seat, adjusting my suddenly hardening erection while trying to keep my mind out of the gutter. Not-so-helpful images of other things that might make her react like that filled my mind, her eyes closed, lost in pleasure.

"I was curious as a cat, of course. I pestered Delphine with questions—what was in the box? Where did it come from? Could I have some? She just laughed and told me to be patient, that she'd share her treasure with the whole town at storytime that afternoon."

"Storytime?"

Liv nodded. "She was always travelling, always bringing back stories and souvenirs from her time away from town. She would gather everyone who cared to listen to her in the town gazebo the day she returned and basically hold court over us all." She chuckled. "Not that it took much for her to captivate me and my big imagination. Waiting was nothing short of torture for me."

My sister had been exactly the same. She wanted everything right then and there. If they'd have invented teleportation, she would have been the first person offering herself up as a test dummy.

"By the time three o'clock rolled around, half the town had squeezed into the gazebo, all of us eager for a taste of whatever was in that mysterious box."

"And then she opened it?"

"And then she opened it," Liv confirmed, her voice hushed with remembered awe. "And I swear, Lewis, I've never seen anything so beautiful in my life."

She groaned and yet again I had to adjust myself.

"It tasted like a dream. The second that pastry touched my tongue, I knew I'd found my soulmate in pastry form. It was everything good in this world." She sighed happily, lost in the memory. "From that day on, I was hooked. I begged my mama to learn how to make them, scoured every cookbook in the library for a recipe."

"Did you find one?"

"Yes, but no matter how much I tried, I couldn't recreate it." She continued to smile, unfazed by her inability to master the pastry. "Mama, seeing how frustrated I got with my failure, talked Hattie, our local baker, into taking a whack at it."

"And did she succeed?"

"Well, of course." She looked almost affronted at the question and I covered my mouth to hide my amusement. "Hattie Mayfield fails at nothing."

"I'm sure."

"She doesn't." Liv's eyes narrowed.

"I believe you." I squeezed her hand and her smile returned.

"Anyway, from that day on, they were all I would order when I went into Mayfield's bakery. Right up until the day I left town."

"A creature of habit, I see," I teased, enjoying the way her nose scrunched up.

"Hey, when you know what you like, you stick with it," she

defended, pointing a playful finger at me. "You know what's funny? The whole town knows when I'm back home, just by my mama's bakery order."

"Oh?"

"Yep. My mama, she usually gets a croissant delivered every morning. But when I'm in town? She switches it up to baklava. Says it's her way of letting Jasmine Bay know their songbird has returned to the nest."

"That sounds…" I shook my head, unable to form words with the image of an entire town abuzz with excitement, all because of a pastry order.

"Laugh all you want, but in a small town, that's big news," she said, her eyes dancing with mirth. "I swear, it's like a real-life Stars Hollow sometimes."

"I'll have to visit sometime, see this magical baklava for myself."

Surprisingly, I meant it. I'd never been attracted to the small-town America image. Hell, I had run from my small-town Valley life as fast as I could.

"Is that so?" she asked, her voice dropping an octave, her gaze locking with mine.

"Mhmm. I mean, after all this build-up, I think I deserve a taste, don't you?" I knew we weren't just talking about pastries anymore, and from the way her breath hitched, she knew it too.

"I think that could be arranged," she murmured, leaning in until our faces were inches apart. "I'd be more than happy to give you a personal tour of Mayfield's… among other things."

I swallowed hard, my eyes dropping to her lips, my mind conjuring all sorts of images of her 'personal tours.' "I'll hold you to that, cariad."

She smiled, slow and sultry, her fingers tightening around mine. "Oh, I'm counting on it, rock star."

The air between us crackled with tension, the anticipation building with every shared breath, every brush of skin on skin. It would be so easy to close the distance, to taste those tempting lips, to see if she was as sweet as the baklava she praised.

"Last call!" the bartender announced, shattering the moment like a hammer to glass. "You don't have to go home, but you can't stay here."

I blinked, the spell momentarily broken.

"Wow, guess we closed the place down, huh?" Olivia glanced around, seeming as surprised as I was.

"Guess so," I agreed, though every fibre of my being rebelled against the idea of letting her go. "Time flies when you're in good company."

She ducked her head, a pleased flush colouring her cheeks. "I'll say. I can't remember the last time I talked this much. My voice is going to hate me tomorrow."

"Worth it though, right?" I raised a brow, hoping I wasn't alone in feeling the undeniable pull between us.

Her gaze met mine, soft and warm with promise. "Definitely worth it."

I settled the tab and we gathered our things, the air heavy with unspoken questions. What now? Where did we go from here?

She turned to me as we stepped out into the balmy Los Angeles night. The street was alive with energy, strains of music and laughter floating on the breeze.

"I'm not ready to say goodnight just yet." Her hand found mine, fingers lacing together like it was the most natural thing in the world. "Walk with me for a bit?"

"I'd love to."

"I love this city at night," she said, her head tipped back to take in the towering buildings, the palm trees swaying in the breeze. "It's like anything is possible, you know? Like magic could be waiting around any corner."

I watched her, mesmerised by the play of city lights across her face, the way her eyes sparkled with wonder. She was right

—there was magic in the air tonight, a sense of possibility that crackled like electricity.

I'd never get enough of looking at her.

"I've lived here for a decade, and the city still finds ways to surprise me."

She turned to me, her smile soft and knowing. "But it's different, isn't it? Seeing it through someone else's eyes?"

"It is." I nodded, my gaze locked with hers. Her fresh perspective was like a portal back to my eighteen-year-old self, still free of the scars and pressure that came with being at the top.

We walked on, the comfortable silence broken only by the occasional comment or observation. Liv was endlessly fascinated by everything, from the street art to the buskers serenading the passers-by.

"I can't believe I'm really here." Pure awe filled her voice. "In Los Angeles, about to go on tour with The Brightside. It's like a dream come true."

I chuckled, charmed by her enthusiasm. "Believe it, cariad. This is just the beginning."

She grinned, bumping her shoulder against mine. "And what a beginning it is. I mean, teen me would be losing her mind if she could see me right now, strolling the streets of LA with Lewis Davies."

I raised a brow, a smirk tugging at my lips. "Teen you, huh? Should I be flattered or concerned?"

She laughed, the sound bright and unrestrained. "Oh, definitely flattered. You were plastered all over my bedroom walls back in the day. I used to dream about moments like this."

Something warm and possessive unfurled in my chest. "And? How does reality measure up?"

She looked at me, her eyes dancing with mischief and something deeper, something that made my blood heat. "The reality, Lewis Davies, is blowing my teenage fantasies out of the water."

I swallowed hard, my grip on her hand tightening. "Good to know."

We came to a stop at a street corner, waiting for the light to change. Liv turned to face me, her free hand coming up to rest on my chest. The heat of her touch burned through the thin fabric of my shirt—as if I needed to be any more aware of this woman.

Her gaze dropped to my lips, her tongue darting out to wet her own. My breath caught, my heart pounding a furious rhythm beneath her hand.

I searched her face for any hint of hesitation or doubt but found none. Her eyes were bright with desire, her cheeks flushed. Every line of her body radiated want, need, an aching hunger that matched my own.

I knew I should be cautious, that kissing her here on a public street was a risk. Anyone could see us, snap a photo, start the rumour mill churning.

She rose up on her toes while I ducked my head, capturing her mouth with mine, pouring every ounce of the desire, the longing, the need that had been building between us all night into the kiss.

She responded with equal fervour, her arms winding around my neck, her body moulding to mine like it was made to fit there.

I lost myself in the taste of her, in the feel of her soft curves pressed against my body. She was intoxicating, addicting, and I knew I would never get enough. My tongue swept into her mouth, tangling with hers in a dance that left us both breathless.

When we finally broke apart, chests heaving and eyes glazed, I rested my forehead against hers, a smile playing at the corners of my kiss-swollen lips.

"Wow," she breathed, her fingers playing with the short hairs at the nape of my neck.

"Wow indeed." I stole another quick, hard kiss, unable to help myself. "That was…"

"Even better than I imagined." She grinned, nipping at my bottom lip.

I groaned, my hands flexing on her hips. "Keep talking like that and I might just have to take you home with me."

She leaned in, her lips brushing the shell of my ear as she whispered, "Promise?"

Blood roared in my ears, my body tightening with need. "Oh, I promise. But only if you're sure that's what you want."

She pulled back, her gaze locking with mine, clear and certain. "I'm sure. I've never been more sure of anything in my life."

CHAPTER FOUR

OLIVIA

*T*he taxi ride to Lewis's hotel was far too long. I'd never known desperation like that, stuck in traffic in a confined space with the man I just *needed* to jump, but all I could do was sit on my hands before I gave the poor taxi driver a free show.

The elevator wouldn't have been much better, but the second the doors closed, we were blissfully alone, so the ride passed in a blur of frantic, urgent kisses and wandering hands, our desire building with each passing level.

By the time we stumbled out onto his floor, giggling like teenagers, I was practically vibrating out of my skin with need. He fumbled with the key card, cursing under his breath as it took a few tries to get the light to flash green. The anticipation was delicious torture, but lord, how I needed it to end!

Finally, it clicked open and we practically fell inside, a tangle of lips and limbs. The door slammed shut behind us and suddenly, it was just us, cocooned in our own private world.

"Fuck, I've been wanting to do this all night," Lewis growled against my lips, his hands sliding possessively over my curves. "You have no idea what you're doing to me, Liv."

"I reckon I have some idea," I teased, giving his bottom lip a playful bite as I pressed myself closer, feeling the solid proof of his desire. "Seems like I ain't the only one who's been... stirred up."

He chuckled darkly, the sound sending shivers down my spine. "Stirred up is an understatement. I've been half-hard since the moment I saw you on that stage."

I whimpered, the idea that I had such an effect on him sending a fresh wave of heat through my already over-stimulated body. "Lewis..."

"Shh, I've got you." He walked me backwards, never breaking the kiss, until my back hit the wall. The contrast of the cool surface and his warm, hard body made me gasp. "I'm going to take such good care of you tonight."

And then his mouth was on my neck, his teeth and tongue lavishing attention on that sensitive spot just below my ear, and coherent thought fled. I fisted my hands in his hair, keeping him right where I wanted him.

"Oh lord, yes," I moaned, my head falling back to give him better access.

His hands weren't idle, busying themselves with the buttons of my blouse until it fell open, revealing my black lace bra. He groaned his approval, his fingers tracing the scalloped edges.

"You're so fucking beautiful," he murmured, almost reverently. "I can't believe this is happening."

"That makes two of us, sugar." I took advantage of his momentary distraction to tug at the hem of his t-shirt. "Off, please. I need to feel you."

He obliged, yanking the shirt over his head quick as a whip. And lord...

I'd seen him shirtless in magazines, in music videos. I thought I knew what to expect. But nothing could have prepared me for the reality of Lewis Davies bare-chested and panting with desire. For me.

His body was a masterpiece, all toned muscle and smooth, inked skin. I yearned to trace every line of his tattoos with my tongue, to memorise each dip and plane like an old country road.

"Like what you see?" he asked, a self-satisfied grin tugging at his kiss-swollen lips.

"You... you're perfect," I sighed, letting my hands roam over his tattooed chest, feeling the muscles quiver beneath my touch. "Absolutely perfect."

"Hardly. But I'll happily be your canvas to explore." His voice dropped low, heavy with want.

I leaned in, planting a tender, open-mouthed kiss over his heart. I felt it hitch beneath my lips, betraying his composed front. My tongue darted out, tasting the salt on his skin, and he sucked in a sharp breath.

"Fuck, Liv..."

Emboldened, I ventured lower, peppering kisses along the inked wings of the bird tattoo on his ribs. His hands found their way into my hair, clenching and unclenching as I explored.

When I reached his nipple, I flicked it with my tongue before closing my lips around it and suckling softly. He jerked against me, a ragged moan escaping him.

"Christ, your mouth..." He tugged at my hair, pulling me back up to claim my lips in a searing kiss. "It's dangerous."

I grinned against his mouth. "You have no idea."

He reached behind me, unhooking my bra with one practised hand. It fell away and I was bared to his heated gaze. A twinge of self-consciousness had me wanting to cover myself, but the look of pure hunger in his eyes stopped me.

"Stunning," he murmured, cupping my breasts in his large, calloused hands. "Absolutely stunning."

He brushed his thumbs over my nipples and I arched into his touch, already addicted to the way he made me feel. Like I was cherished, desired... worshipped.

His head dipped, taking one pebbled peak into his hot mouth. I cried out, my fingers digging into his shoulders as he suckled and nipped, sending jolts of pleasure straight to my core.

"Lewis, please…"

He hummed around my taut nub, the vibrations making me squirm. His hand slid down my belly, popping the button on my jeans. He lifted his head, his eyes dark and questioning as his fingers toyed with my zipper.

"Can I?"

"God, yes. Touch me, please." There was no coyness, no shame. I needed him with a desperation I'd never known.

He wasted no time, sliding my jeans and panties down my legs in one go. I stepped out of them, kicking off my shoes in the process, leaving me completely bare before him.

He took a step back, his gaze raking over me hungrily. I resisted the urge to squirm under his intense scrutiny, instead letting him look his fill.

"Fucking hell… you're a vision, Olivia Monroe." His voice was gravelly, strained. "I'm going to take my time with you, worship every inch of this glorious body until you're begging for release."

I shuddered at his words, at the dark promise in his eyes. "What if I'm already begging?"

He smirked, dropping to his knees in front of me. "Then I better get to work."

He lifted one of my legs over his shoulder, opening me up to him. I braced myself against the wall, my heart pounding in anticipation of that first intimate touch.

But he made me wait, ghosting his lips along the inside of my thigh, his beard scratching deliciously against the sensitive skin. I squirmed impatiently, silently pleading for more.

He chuckled, his breath hot against my soaked core. "Patience, cariad. I'll get you there. Eventually."

And then, finally, he gave me what I craved. His tongue

parted my folds and I moaned, my hips bucking against his face as pleasure rocketed through me.

"Yes! Just like that," I panted, my head falling back against the wall as he repeated the motion, setting a steady, relentless rhythm that had me seeing stars.

He groaned against me, the vibrations adding a new layer of sensation. "You taste fucking incredible. I could spend hours just devouring this pretty pussy."

His words, filthy and reverent, only stoked the fire burning in my veins. I ground against his face shamelessly, chasing the release that hovered just out of reach.

He slid two fingers inside me, curling them just so as his tongue flicked rapidly over my clit. It was almost too much, the dual stimulation pushing me to the brink embarrassingly fast.

"Lew... I'm gonna... I'm so close," I whined, my thighs trembling around his head.

"That's it. Let go for me. Come all over my tongue," he commanded, sucking my clit between his lips and humming.

It was my undoing. The coil in my belly snapped and I shattered, wave after wave of ecstasy crashing over me as I cried out his name. He worked me through it, gentling his touch but not letting up until I was a boneless, satisfied puddle.

He eased my leg off his shoulder, pressing a tender kiss to my inner thigh before rising to his feet. He pulled me into his arms, supporting my weight as I caught my breath.

"That was..." I trailed off, still lost in the haze of my orgasm.

"Just the beginning," he promised, claiming my mouth in a slow, thorough kiss.

I could taste myself on his tongue and it sent a fresh spark of desire through my sated body.

"I'm nowhere near done with you yet."

He scooped me up, carrying me further into the suite. I clung to his neck, nuzzling into his throat as I let him lead us to his bed.

It wasn't until he laid me down on the mattress, hovering

over me with lust-darkened eyes, that it hit me. I was in Lewis Davies's hotel room. In his bed. About to make love to the man I'd fantasised about for half my life.

A giggle bubbled up in my throat. "Pinch me."

He cocked a brow. "Come again?"

"Pinch me. Because this can't be real. Things like this don't happen to girls like me."

His eyes softened, his hand coming up to cup my cheek. "Oh, I assure you this is very real, cariad. And you're not just any girl. You're everything I never knew I needed."

Emotion clogged my throat at his words, at the raw sincerity in his gaze. I didn't know what to say, how to express the magnitude of what I was feeling, so I did the only thing I could—I pulled him down into a bruising kiss, pouring everything I couldn't verbalise into the press of my lips.

He met me with equal fervour, his body settling over mine like it was made to be there. The rough fabric of his jeans abraded my sensitive core and I hissed, breaking the kiss to tug at his waistband.

"Off. I need to feel all of you."

He nodded, rolling off me just long enough to shuck his jeans and boxer briefs. He fished a condom out of his pocket and rolled it on. Then he was back, his glorious naked body aligning with mine, skin to skin from head to toe.

We both gasped at the contact, the air crackling with the intensity of it. He felt incredible, his hard planes fitting perfectly against my soft curves. Like two puzzle pieces clicking into place.

"I knew you'd feel like this," he murmured, trailing his lips along my jaw, down the column of my throat. "Like silk and sin, heaven and temptation all wrapped up in one gorgeous package."

I arched into him as his words and touch ignited me from the inside out. "Lewis… please…"

"Shhh, I've got you," he soothed, reaching between us to

position himself at my entrance. "I'm going to make you feel so good. Gonna claim this pretty pussy, make it mine."

I moaned at his indecent promise, spreading my legs wider in blatant invitation. He accepted, pushing forward slowly, inch by delicious inch until he was seated to the hilt, stretching me in the most exquisite way.

"Oh god," I whimpered, my nails biting into his shoulders as I adjusted to the sweet invasion. "You feel... you feel incredible."

He groaned, his forehead dropping to mine as he fought for control. "Nothing has ever felt this good. You're perfect, Liv. So fucking perfect."

He started to move then, withdrawing almost completely before surging back in, setting a deep, deliberate rhythm that had me seeing stars. He angled his hips just right, hitting a spot inside me that made my toes curl and my back bow off the bed.

"Yes, yes, yes... right there," I chanted mindlessly, meeting him thrust for thrust. "Don't stop, please don't ever stop."

"Never," he grunted, swivelling his hips in a way that sent sparks rushing through me. "Could stay buried in this heaven forever and never get enough."

He kept up that steady, measured pace, stoking the fire slowly, building me up towards a peak that promised to eclipse anything I'd ever known.

With every push and pull of our bodies, every heated gaze and whispered endearment, I imagined something deeper taking root. A connection, a bond I couldn't name but also couldn't deny.

It terrified me, even as it thrilled me. Because as desperately as I wanted to hold onto this feeling, to believe in the pretty words he was murmuring into my skin, a small, cynical part of me couldn't help but wonder...

Was this real? Or was I just another notch on a rock star's bedpost, a convenient way to blow off steam before the tour?

The thought was like a bucket of ice water, threatening to extinguish the heat building between us. I tried to push it away, to lose myself again in the magic of his touch, but it lingered, an unwelcome spectre in the back of my mind.

If he noticed my momentary distraction, he didn't let on. He just kept moving, kept claiming me with his body and his words, driving me closer to that elusive edge. His hand snaked between us, finding my clit and rubbing in tight, urgent circles.

"Come for me, Olivia. Let me feel you fall apart around me," he demanded, his voice strained with his own impending release.

"I... I can't... it's too much," I whimpered, even as my body coiled tighter, preparing for the inevitable snap.

"Yes, you can. Let go. I've got you," he urged, his thrusts becoming erratic as his own control slipped. "Come with me. Please..."

It was the please that did it, the desperate edge to his voice. I shattered, my orgasm hitting me like a freight train, stealing my breath and my sanity in one fell swoop.

I was vaguely aware of him following me over, my name a reverent chant on his lips as he lost control. But I was too lost in the maelstrom of sensation, of pleasure so intense it bordered on pain, to fully process it.

We clung to each other as we rode out the aftershocks, our sweat-slicked bodies heaving in tandem. He peppered my face with soft, sweet kisses, murmuring words of praise and affection into my skin.

"That was... fuck, that was incredible," he breathed, rolling onto his back and pulling me into his side. I went willingly, draping myself over his chest as I struggled to catch my breath. "You're incredible."

"So are you," I murmured, tracing idle patterns on his damp skin. "I've never... it's never been like that for me before." It was a confession, a secret whispered into the darkened room.

He tipped my chin up, forcing me to meet his gaze. There was a softness there, a tenderness that made my heart clench. "Me neither. This... this is special, Liv. You're special."

I wanted to believe him. Desperately. But that nagging voice of doubt wouldn't be silenced, growing louder with each passing minute.

What if this was just a line? What if, come morning, he regretted this? Regretted me?

I didn't think I could bear it, having this taste of perfection only to have it ripped away. It would break me in ways I wasn't sure I could recover from.

CHAPTER FIVE

OLIVIA

"*I* can't believe I slept with him. What was I thinking?" I paced around my hotel room, my phone pressed to my ear and my heart racing a mile a minute as I dodged the clothes I'd been meaning to clean up since I'd arrived and the suitcase that took up most of the available floor space. "I wasn't thinking at all!"

Soft morning light filtered into the room, the type that I rarely saw because I didn't normally make a point of getting up at dawn. Today, I'd made an exception to not be in Lewis's bed when he woke up.

"Liv, honey, take a deep breath," Ashley said, her warm, familiar voice coming through the line, a soothing balm to my frayed nerves. "I'm going to need you to start from the beginning. What exactly happened, and who's the 'him' in this situation?"

I took a deep breath, trying to gather my thoughts. The memories of last night flooded back—the electric connection at the bar, the spark of chemistry, the way his touch set my skin on fire, the intimate conversation that led to us shutting the place down, and the searing kiss we shared on the street.

"The 'him' is Lewis Davies," I said, my voice shaking.

"Isn't he the one you had a poster of on your bedroom wall in high school?" she asked, a note of surprise in her voice.

I groaned, sinking down onto the edge of the bed. "Don't remind me. This is a disaster, Ash. How could I let this happen?"

"Okay, slow down. What exactly *did* happen? How did y'all end up in bed together?"

I filled her in, starting from the moment I laid eyes on him in the crowd, the doubt that it could even be him. I mean, what were the chances that he'd walk into the same bar I'd be playing?

When I got to the part where he outright admitted that he wanted me and made me promise to go back to his hotel with him, she let out a low, amused whistle.

"A man who knows what he wants. Is it bad if I kinda approve?"

"That is not helping."

I sat up and started wearing a path in the carpet again, too restless to stay still as I recounted absolutely everything.

"So what's the problem?" She asked when I was done. "Sounds to me like you had yourself a magical night with a man you have chemistry with. I fail to see the downside."

I gnawed on my bottom lip, my belly knotting with doubt. "The problem is I snuck out on him at sunrise, like some guilty one-night stand!" I said, the words rushing out of me filled with shame. "One minute I was blissfully tangled up in his arms and the next I was wide awake, completely freaking out about what this meant."

"I'm sorry, go back. You did what?" she sniggered.

"Ash."

"No, no. You don't get to drop that in my lap and not let me react." She laughed, the sound disbelieving. "Liv Monroe, the woman who hasn't gotten out of bed before 9 AM since high school, got up with the sun to sneak out on a rock star she just had earth-shattering sex with." She tutted. "I'm not sure if I should be amused or concerned. These two versions of you don't align at all."

I flopped backwards onto the bed, staring up at the ceiling. "I know, I know. It was a cowardly move. But I freaked out!" My pulse picked up speed again just thinking about it. "All I could think about was how this might screw everything up. We have to work together now! What if he thinks I'm some crazy groupie?"

"Whoa, slow your roll!" Ashley cut in, her voice firm. "First of all, you are nobody's groupie. You're a talented musician in your own right and don't you forget it."

Her conviction bolstered me, quieting some of the self-doubt swirling in my head. I took a deep breath, trying to centre myself.

"Now, as for Lewis, did he give you any indication that this was just a casual hookup for him?"

I paused, thinking back. The way he looked at me. Like I was the only person in the room. "No... it felt like more than that. And the way he touched me, kissed me..." I shivered at the memory, my body lighting up all over again.

"Exactly. So give the man some credit. Maybe he's just as nervous as you are." Her voice softened, understanding seeping through. "Honey, I know you. It's not like you to back down from what you want. You're not a quitter and you've never been one to run from your feelings."

Tears pricked at the back of my eyes, her words hitting a little too close to home.

"I know, but this is different."

"How is it different?"

"I'm scared, Ash," I whispered, my voice cracking.

"Scared of what?"

"Of everything," I admitted, my voice small. "Of how this will affect our working relationship, of making a fool of myself, of getting my heart broken."

"Oh Liv..." Ashley let out a long breath.

I sighed, collapsed back onto the mattress. "I can't afford to get distracted by some guy, even if that guy is Lewis freakin' Davies."

"You won't," she assured me, her tone leaving no room for argument. "You're Olivia Monroe, rising star and total catch. If he can't see that, it's his loss."

I couldn't help but smile at her unwavering support. "You have to say that. You're my best friend."

"And as your best friend, it's my job to tell you the truth. Even when you don't want to hear it."

I sat up, my brow furrowing. "What truth?"

"That you have a tendency to catastrophise. You let your fears run away with you. Remember when you were terrified to move to Nashville? You almost talked yourself out of it a hundred times."

I bit my lip, the memory washing over me. She was right. I did have a habit of getting in my own way, of letting my doubts overshadow my dreams.

"But I didn't," I said softly. "I pushed through the fear, and I did it anyway."

"Exactly. And look where it got you. On the verge of everything you've ever wanted."

I took a shaky breath, trying to absorb her words.

"That was different."

"It wasn't."

"What did you tell me when I was worried about hanging out my design shingle in Jasmine Bay?"

"No risk, no reward."

"Exactly." Her voice hardened. "There's no reward without a risk so if you want that man, you're gonna have to face a little emotional turmoil and uncertainty."

A watery chuckle escaped me. "Using my own words against me, huh?"

"If the boot fits…" she muttered. "I'm not saying you should go declaring your undying love for the man. Lord knows it's too soon for that nonsense. But don't count yourself out before you even get to bat."

"I know, you're right. I just... what if I screwed everything up by running out on him like that?"

"Then you apologise and explain. He's a grown man, Liv. I'm sure he can handle a little morning after awkwardness." Ashley's voice was gentle but firm. "The question is, what do you want? Do you want to explore this thing with him, see where it leads? Or do you want to chalk it up to a crazy night and keep things strictly professional?"

I gnawed on my bottom lip, considering her question. For a second, I lost myself in memories of the previous night—the way our laughter mingled together, the secrets we shared in hushed tones, the electricity that sparked between us with every touch. Could I really walk away from that?

"God help me, but I think I want to see where this goes," I admitted, my voice barely above a whisper. "It's crazy and reckless and so not like me, but I can't shake this feeling that it could be something special."

"Then you owe it to yourself to find out," she said, a smile in her voice. "But Liv? Promise me you'll be careful with your heart, okay? I don't want to see you get hurt."

"I promise." I took a deep breath, resolve settling over me. "No more running. It's time I woman up and face this head on."

"Good, now..." She sniggered and I groaned. "More importantly... did you get a picture?"

"Picture of what?" I asked, playing dumb.

"Of him? You sneaking out? I'm not really sure."

We both laughed. Then reality smacked me in the face, and all that confidence I'd found drained away.

"Oh god, I have to see him later today for an icebreaker thing."

"Perfect timing then. Get it sorted before you head out on tour." She missed the note of fresh panic in my voice. "Think you can keep your hands to yourself until then?"

"I make no promises."

"Well if things do heat up again, at least make sure you have protection. Safe sex is great sex and all that." I could practically hear her wink through the phone.

"Ashley Dawson, you scandalous woman!" I gasped in mock outrage. "Such a thing for an unmarried Southern Belle to suggest!"

"Pshh, you're hardly a blushing virgin. And I'd like to keep you disease and baby free, thank you very much!"

We both dissolved into laughter.

"I needed that." I sighed happily once I caught my breath. "What would I do without you, Ash?"

"Crash and burn, most likely."

By the time we said our goodbyes, I felt lighter, more centred. Ready to face whatever came next.

CHAPTER SIX

OLIVIA

$\mathcal{T}$he muffled sounds of conversation and laughter filtering through the rehearsal studio door did nothing to calm my jittery nerves. I hesitated outside, trying to talk some sense into myself. I'd earned my place here, through countless late nights, endless rehearsals, and more rejections than I cared to remember. Lily Tyler hadn't chosen me on a whim; she'd seen something in me, something worth investing in.

There was absolutely no reason I should be frozen to the spot staring at the door handle like it would bite me.

I ran my clammy palms down my jeans, squared my shoulders, and reached for it. Now or never. I wrenched the heavy door open. The rich scent of coffee and the sugary sweetness of pastries immediately hit me. My belly churned, too knotted with anxiety to even consider eating.

The room was a hive of activity, people milling about, chatting and laughing in small clusters. My gaze skittered over them, trying to take it all in. So many new faces, so many names to learn. It was overwhelming.

And then I saw him.

Lewis stood off to the side. He looked tense, guarded. So different from the man who'd captivated me last night with his easy smiles and magnetic charm. Had I done that? Or was last night an act? In all the interviews and fan videos I'd seen of him, he'd never looked like that. Before I could spiral into self-doubt, a voice cut through the chatter. "Liv!"

I turned. Lily Tyler, lead singer of The Brightside and current reigning queen of the music industry. She was even more gorgeous in person, all tousled blonde waves and sparkling blue eyes.

"I'm so glad you're here!" She engulfed me in a warm hug, her enthusiasm contagious. "Everyone, gather round! I want you to meet Olivia Monroe, our insanely talented new opening act. These are my guys."

She gestured to four guys I would know anywhere: her bandmates Alex, Andy, Tom, and finally Lewis, who still hung back despite the converging crowd. Faces blurred together as Lily rattled off names and introductions. "Lover's Knot are joining us in a few weeks." She waved to a team of people huddled in a corner, their voices low but their hands gesturing and their mouths moving a mile a minute. "You'll meet that lot in a bit. This is Ryan, lead singer of Rhiannon. Absolute dream to work with, you'll love him. And here we have Dan, James, Jared - the rest of their merry band of troublemakers." She winked at them and they laughed, easy and familiar.

I stared at all of them, desperately trying to commit their names and faces to memory. Ultimately, I knew it was hopeless.

"Don't let her fool you," the red-haired one said, eyes twinkling with mirth. "We're angels, the lot of us."

"Uh huh, sure," Lily drawled, her tone dripping with affectionate sarcasm. "And I'm the Queen of England."

More laughter, more inside jokes I couldn't begin to decipher, a stranger amongst friends.

Ryan stepped forward first, his whole demeanour screaming

lead singer. He flashed a broad smile and pulled me into a hug like we'd been friends for years. "Ryan. Welcome to the madhouse. You won't regret joining us."

"That's debatable." Dan playfully bumped Ryan out of the way and offered me his hand to shake. "We've been known to drive people to the brink of insanity, but the music makes it all worth it."

Their guitarist laughed and clapped me on the back. "Ignore him. Compared to his kid, we're a walk in the park." He thumbed at Dan who glared at him. "I'm James, resident guitarist extraordinaire and if you ever want to jam, I'm your man."

"Resident pain in my ass more like," Jared said, rolling his eyes but his lips quirked in amusement.

I laughed, a little overwhelmed but charmed despite myself.

"If anyone's the resident guitarist extraordinaire, it's me." Alex shook his head, his tone teasing. "Jesus, give a man an inch…"

While they all bantered like old friends, talking over each other, I was acutely aware of Lewis, still hanging back, still watching with that inscrutable expression. Our eyes met and it was like a bolt of electricity, the air suddenly thick with tension and unspoken questions. I wanted to go to him, to pull him aside and explain…

But I couldn't.

Not here, not with everyone watching.

LEWIS

If it weren't for the fact that I knew they were all madly in love with their fiancées and girlfriends, I'd be grinding my teeth to dust or staking my claim.

And it would get leaked to the press in less than twenty-four hours…

"Yeah, thanks for joining us on such short notice." Andy, our rhythm guitarist and long-standing voice of reason, offered Liv a kind smile. "We're not always this... enthusiastic. I promise we'll tone it down, once the novelty wears off."

Since when was three weeks short notice?

I wanted to laugh, but that would just draw attention to me and the fact I wasn't acting like myself. How was I supposed to act natural when everything about this was the opposite?

"Or we won't, and she'll have to learn to love us, warts and all." Tom grinned at her and Liv laughed. "But anything you need, just say the word." He slung an arm across her shoulders and I tamped down the urge to rip it off.

"It's great to meet you all. I have to admit, I'm a little intimidated, but mostly just excited to be here."

Her gaze flicked to me and electricity crackled across the space between us, raising every hair on my body. Surely she felt it too.

I opened my mouth to say... something, anything, but the words died in my throat. What could I say in front of everyone that wouldn't give us away?

I'd started to worry she wouldn't come.

Some of the pressure had let up at the sight of her. She was here, not a figment of my overactive imagination. Chestnut waves, sun-kissed skin, coy smile. A vintage band tee skimmed her curves, and ripped jeans hugged her legs. Gorgeous in an effortless, girl-next-door way that made my palms itch to touch her.

"Now that that's over..." Lily took Liv's arm and guided her out of the crowd we'd turned into. "Coffee and refreshments are over there." She gestured to the craft table. "Grab some fuel before we dive in!"

Liv flashed her a grateful smile and made a beeline for the coffee.

Tom snorted, elbowing me. "What was the deal with you and the new girl last night?"

I bristled. "Sod off. I was just being friendly."

"That what we're calling it these days?" Alex quirked a

brow. "Right. Maybe I should try that line on Ceri. Do you think she'd buy it?"

"Try it." Tom clapped him on the shoulder, amusement creasing his eyes. "I'll get the camera ready to document the results."

I rolled my eyes but didn't dignify them with a response.

When I found my bed empty this morning, something had seized in my chest. Doubt crept in. Maybe I'd imagined the sparks flying between us, the effortless conversation, the mind-blowing sex. Maybe she regretted it.

Maybe I'd fucked everything up before it even began.

Only no matter how I tried, I couldn't shake the memory of her falling apart in my arms. Or the way she'd been last night, eagerly leaning into me at every point.

Before I could second guess myself, I followed. I stopped next to her, willing my muscles to relax. My hand brushed against hers as we reached for the mugs, sending a jolt straight through me. Her cheeks coloured, and she snatched her hand back.

"Sorry," she said, her voice shaky. "Didn't see you there."

She peeked at me from beneath her lashes. The air between us crackled with tension as we both searched for the right words. I could feel curious eyes on us, watching, speculating. She seemed to sense it too, her gaze darting around the room before landing back on me. She shifted her weight, trying to appear casual, but the tightness in her jaw betrayed her.

"Nice to meet you, Olivia," I managed. I shot for casual but probably missed by a mile. "Heard great things about your music."

"Thank you." Her voice was bright but there was an under-current of strain. "I'm looking forward to touring with The Brightside."

I lowered my voice, acutely aware of the eyes on us. "About last night—"

"Not here," she hissed under her breath.

A wave of relief washed over me at her words. So, she

wanted to keep this between us, too. It was a small comfort, knowing we were on the same page about the need for discretion. The last thing either of us needed was for our private life to become fodder for public speculation.

"Then when? You snuck out without a word—"

"I had an emergency. With a friend." Her gaze slid away from mine.

Bollocks.

I let it drop and we wandered to the circle of chairs, coffees in hand.

As we took our seats on opposite sides of the circle, our eyes locked, a magnetic pull that was almost impossible to resist. I could drown in her gaze, in the depth of emotion swirling there.

Andy's voice broke the spell, his tone casual but curious. "I didn't see you last night. What did you get up to?"

I opened my mouth, ready to respond on instinct. Then I caught Alex's gaze from across the circle and a twinge of suspicion hit me in the gut. His brows rose, a knowing smirk playing at the corner of his lips. They were tag-teaming me, trying to catch me off guard.

I schooled my features, keeping my expression neutral. "Nothing too exciting." I shrugged.

Andy nodded, but I could see the wheels turning in his head. He exchanged a quick glance with Alex, silent communication passing between them. They weren't buying it, but for now, they'd let it slide.

Jack Tyler, Lily's father, stood at the front of the room, patiently waiting for everyone to take their seats. The hum of chatter died down as he cleared his throat.

"As you all know, we're embarking on our biggest tour yet. Seventy cities across the U.S. and Canada. Now I'd like to introduce our stellar team who'll be making sure everything runs smoothly…" He turned to Kevin, our manager, with a pointed look. "Some of them are new positions and brand new faces."

Kevin's jaw tightened but he nodded, rising to his feet. "Yes,

in light of the scope of this tour, we've brought on a few addi-
tional personnel to handle more of the day-to-day tasks. Mia
Johnson will be our Production Manager." He gestured to a
blonde woman with a no-nonsense air about her. She gave a
curt nod of acknowledgement. "And you all know Riley Clark.
Apparently, we didn't scare him off two years ago because he's
agreed to continue as your Tour Manager."

"We also," Jack cut in, his voice carrying a note of steel,
"have decided to hire a Tour Bookkeeper. To keep track of
merchandise sales and finances at each venue." His gaze locked
with Kevin's in a silent battle of wills. "I'm sure you understand
the necessity, given the scale of this operation."

Kevin's nostrils flared but he pasted on a tight smile. "Of
course. We want everything above board and accounted for."

The tension hung thick in the air and I exchanged a
confused glance with Alex. What the hell was that about? But
Jack quickly moved on, introducing the rest of the team—sound
engineers, lighting technicians, roadies and techs, lots of people
we'd worked with on previous shows. As he rattled off names
and roles, my attention kept straying to Liv. I couldn't seem to
stop myself from sneaking glances her way, and more often than
not, I caught her doing the same. It was magnetic, this unspoken
pull between us. Like we were connected by an invisible tether.

Slowly, subtly, I arched a brow at her. She bit her lip. I jerked
my chin at the door in a silent "Can we talk?"

She shook her head minutely, flicking her gaze meaningfully
to the others.

I sighed and mouthed "Later."

She gave a tiny nod.

This dance continued throughout the meeting, a private
conversation conducted entirely through meaningful looks and
furtive gestures. I caught snippets of the debrief: the band
rehearsal schedule that rarely changed, the dancer rehearsals
that had increased in hours and difficulty. I'd never ask the question aloud—too concerned that I'd sway my bandmates into
making choices they didn't want—but I had a feeling it was Lily

unconsciously wanting to go out with a bang. We'd all agreed to attend at least one session with the dancers over the next two weeks.

"We learnt our lesson last time. There'll be no bands sharing tour buses this time!" Riley's voice cut through the chatter. "Bus assignments are as follows: The Brightside, you're on Bus 1. Rhiannon, Bus 2. Lover's Knot will be on Bus 3 when they join us. Liv, you'll be on the dancers' bus for now, but we might shuffle things around later depending on how you feel. Any questions? No? Great. Moving on…"

By the time Jack dismissed us, my skin was buzzing with anticipation. Every cell in my body was attuned to her, every nerve ending alive and screaming for her touch. Just being in the same room as her was a sweet, exquisite torture, a teasing glimpse of everything I wanted but couldn't have.

Not yet, anyway.

Because despite her skittishness this morning, I knew what I'd felt last night was real. That connection, that bone-deep rightness… it wasn't something you could fake or force.

She felt it too. I'd stake my life on it.

Now I just had to convince her to take a chance on it, on us. To leap into the unknown with me and see where this thing between us could go.

It wouldn't be easy. She was spooked, hesitant. Afraid, maybe, of the intensity of what we'd shared. I could understand that. God knows, it terrified me down to my bones.

But the thought of letting her go, of never experiencing that rush, that heart-stopping connection again? That terrified me more.

So I'd fight for her, for this. I'd prove to her that what we had was worth the risk, worth facing her fears. I'd convince her to give us a chance.

I just needed to get her alone first.

CHAPTER SEVEN

OLIVIA

"*N*ervous, new girl?" A woman with a platinum blonde bob asked after the meeting ended. She'd spent the last hour watching us all through a camera.

I shook my head, smiling. "But ask me again in two weeks."

"That's good." She chuckled watching one of the Rhiannon guys—so I couldn't remember their names, sue me—break out a set of drumsticks. "They can all be a lot, but you'll get used to it eventually."

"Oh, I'm not worried about that." I stuffed my notebook into my satchel as I followed her to the craft table for one more treat before I tried to find a taxi back to the hotel. "I mean my head is spinning with all the new faces and names, sure, but that's no concern."

"Ah." Her expression softened, reading something on my face. "It's your first stadium tour."

Try first big tour entirely.

"Oh, don't worry, you'll get used to it quickly enough," she said, her tone reassuring. "I'm Nia by the way."

"Liv."

"Well, Liv, you'll be happy to know you're not the only woman on this tour."

"Thank the Lord for small mercies."

She laughed. "Stick with me and my girls. We'll make sure you don't drown in all this testosterone."

"I appreciate that."

My gaze inadvertently strayed. I couldn't help but notice the way his black hair fell across his forehead, the slight scruff along his jawline. He looked tired, but still unfairly gorgeous.

"It's nice to know I'll have some female companionship out on the road," I said, refocusing on Nia before I could get lost in 'what ifs'.

"Oh, we're more than just companionship. We're a full-on support system. Gotta have each other's backs in this crazy industry." Her grin turned conspiratorial. "Plus, we have way more fun than the boys."

My brows climbed and I opened my mouth to ask for details. I'd heard the post tour tales about the endless parties every night and enough alcohol and drugs to take down a horse. I couldn't imagine *more*. But before I could get a word out, a familiar voice called my name from behind me.

My heart leapt into my throat as I spun to find Lewis, hands shoved in the pockets of his worn jeans, a tentative smile playing about his lips. His gaze flicked to Nia briefly before settling back on me, those hazel eyes intense and questioning. Nerves and anticipation swirled in my belly, leaving me as jittery as a June bug on a string.

"Can we have that chat now?" He ran an agitated hand through his styled hair, turning artfully messy into true destruction.

My heart melted a little at his anxious expression. This confident, charismatic rock star was nervous. About me. I bit my lip, indecision warring with the desire humming through my veins. Was it smart to be alone with him so soon after…

Oh, screw it!

I glanced at Nia, an apology on the tip of my tongue, but she waved me off with a knowing smirk.

"Go ahead. We'll catch up later." She winked at me, her eyes darting between Lewis and me with unconcealed curiosity. "Have fun, you two."

Heat crept up my neck at her insinuation, but I managed a nod and a smile. "Thanks. I'll see you around before the tour kicks off, I'm sure."

"Count on it."

Lewis's hand found the small of my back as he guided me away from the table, his touch sending a shiver down my spine. The warmth of his palm radiated through the thin fabric of my t-shirt, the contact both comforting and electrifying.

We walked towards the exit, the silence between us charged with anticipation. As we exited the rehearsal studio and stepped out onto the quiet LA street, a wave of heat hit me. A member of the studio staff popped up beside us, clearly sensing someone was leaving.

"Can I call you a taxi?" he asked, already reaching for his radio.

"Oh, that's okay, I—"

"No!"

Lewis's panicked voice cut me off and I glanced at him in surprise. He cleared his throat, his ears reddening.

"I mean, uh, no need. I've got this. Thanks, though."

The staff member nodded, a hint of confusion in their eyes, but they didn't argue. "Let me know if you need anything else."

"Thanks." Lewis nodded, flashing them a tight smile while his fingers flexed against my spine.

Oh he's definitely nervous.

The thought sent a thrill through me, even as my own belly swarmed with butterflies.

"Do you fancy a short walk actually?" he asked when we were alone again.

I cocked my head, studying him for a moment. The nervous energy radiating off him was palpable, a stark contrast to the easy confidence he'd exuded the night before. It was endearing, seeing this other side of him. It made him more real, more human.

"Lead the way." I smiled, hoping to put him at ease.

We walked in silence for a few minutes, elbows bumping, the electric awareness of his body next to mine making the humidity feel suffocating. I searched for something, anything to say to break the tension mounting between us.

But I got distracted by my own thoughts as we walked down the street towards the busier road, marvelling at the surreal turn my life had taken. A few days ago, the furthest west I'd ever gone was New Orleans. And now I got to walk around the city that had made bigger careers than Nashville.

It was surreal to say the least.

"So, uh, how long have you been in LA?" I asked, wincing internally at the lame question. I'd followed his career, I already knew the answer.

He smiled, but it didn't quite reach his eyes. "A while now. It's a great city, lots of opportunities."

"Right, yeah. Opportunities." I nodded, feeling like an idiot.

Why is this so hard?

Last night, the words flowed so easily between us. Now, I couldn't think of a question I didn't already know the answer to.

But I had to say something. We shouldn't just walk in silence. I'd go crazy, hyperfocusing on the heat of his palm seeping through my thin t-shirt.

"You never did tell me how you ended up at my show last night."

He glanced down at me, a soft smile playing on his lips. "Would you believe me if I said it was fate?"

I arched a brow. "I'd say you've been listening to too many of your own love songs."

He chuckled. "Fair."

He took a deep breath, his expression turning serious.

"Honestly? I needed an escape. I go to that bar whenever I'm in the area and need a little perspective and inspiration. But running into you…" He shook his head, a smile I could only describe as delirious crossed with disbelief claiming his lips. "It was unexpected, but the second I saw you, I felt this connection."

His words sent a flurry of butterflies through my belly. I knew exactly what he meant. That instant spark, the feeling of rightness. Like we were meant to find each other.

"But in all seriousness, last night was…" Lewis trailed off, rubbing the back of his neck as he searched for the right words.

It had only been a few hours since I'd lost my cool with Ashley and I thought I'd buried the fears that came with it. Now they unravelled like I'd never gotten them under control.

I ducked my head, nerves twisting inside of me.

"It was… really something."

I couldn't quite bring myself to look at him, afraid of what I might see in his eyes. Regret? Disappointment?

The silence stretched between us, heavy with unasked questions. I wanted to just come right out and ask him if it meant anything to him, but the words wouldn't form. I chanced a glance at him, only to find him watching me intently, his brow furrowed.

"Do you regret what happened?" he asked, his voice hesitant, almost pained.

"No!" My heart seized and words finally rushed out, "No, of course not. Do you?"

"Not at all." The relief in his tone was palpable. "Last night was… it was amazing. Being with you, it felt right. Really right."

Heat flooded my cheeks and I had to look away, the sincerity in his eyes too much. "Careful, a girl could get used to that kind of sweet talk."

"Maybe I want you to."

My gaze snapped back to his. "Lewis…"

"I like you," he said softly, his voice low and earnest. "A lot. More than I probably should after such a short time. But I can't help it." He stepped closer, crowding into my space, surrounding me with the scent of leather and spice.

My heart raced, a mix of disbelief and elation coursing through me. He liked me. He wanted to see where this could go. I searched his face, looking for any sign of hesitation or uncertainty, but found only earnest sincerity.

"I felt it too."

The connection, the spark... it wasn't in my head.

You snuck out of his hotel room for nothing.

All that worry and panic, absolute wasted energy. I could have had morning cuddles, seen him groggy, his hair adorably mussed and his voice rough with sleep. I could have traced the lines of his tattoos in the early light, shared lazy kisses, basking in the afterglow of our incredible night together.

Still, despite the burn of regret, a weight lifted off my chest.

"I really like you too."

His face lit up and my belly flipped. God, he was gorgeous when he smiled like that. All crinkly eyes and boyish charm. It was almost too much.

"Maybe more than I should considering the circumstances. It could get so messy."

"I'll do messy for you." His smile widened, relief and joy shining in his eyes. "Grab dinner with me tonight? Just the two of us."

That was not what I was expecting. Dinner? Like a date?

"You would really want that after I..."

"Snuck out of my room without leaving so much as a note?"

I winced. "I'm sorry about that. I just... I panicked."

"Why?"

"I got scared. Scared of how much I felt for you, scared of what it could mean if you didn't... feel the same." Because why on earth would an uber successful musician like him feel something genuine and serious for me. "So I ran."

Understanding dawned on his face, his posture softening. "I

get it. It's a lot to process, especially with everything else going on. Don't worry, Liv, I don't blame you."

"You don't?"

He shook his head. "This thing between us, it's new and intense and a little terrifying. But it's also exhilarating." He took a step closer, his fingers grazing mine where they hung at my side. "Exciting. Like standing on the edge of something big, something life-changing."

I nodded, my throat tightening with emotion. "That's exactly how it feels. Like we're on the brink of something incredible, but it's also so daunting."

"I know. But…" He took a deep breath "I don't want to let fear hold us back. I don't want to miss out on what this could be, just because the timing isn't perfect or the situation is complicated."

My heart raced, hope and anticipation rushing through me. "What are you saying?"

"I'm saying…" He licked his lips, nerves and determination warring on his face. "I want to give this a real shot. You and me, seeing where this goes. No expectations, no pressure, just… exploring this connection between us. Figuring it out as we go."

I stared at him, my breath catching. He was offering me a chance, an opportunity to dive into this thing between us, consequences be damned. It was terrifying and thrilling all at once.

And I wanted it. God, did I want it.

"I'm in."

"Yeah?" His smile grew as I nodded. "So, dinner?"

A smile tugged at my lips. "I'd love to."

Relief washed over his face, followed quickly by a beaming smile. "Great! That's great. I know this little Italian place downtown. The pasta is almost as good as the company." He winked, and my heart did a little flip.

"Oh boy, if your criteria for pasta is anything like your choice of t-shirts, then I'm not sure I should trust your judgement," I teased, gesturing to the band tee stretched across his broad chest.

He clutched his heart in mock offence. "Hey now, don't knock the classics. I'll have you know this is a highly sought-after collector's item."

"Is that what they told you when they sold it to you at the thrift store?"

He laughed, the sound warm and rich. "Ouch. You don't pull your punches, do you?"

"Nah, you're too cute to punch," I said without thinking. "But seriously, you better not mean Olive Garden!"

He threw his head back and laughed, the sound rich and warm, curling around me like an embrace. "Give me some credit. I promise, it'll be the best pasta you've ever had."

Given it had been a very long time since I'd gone on a date, I believed him.

"I'll pick you up at seven?"

"Sounds perfect." My cheeks hurt from smiling so much but no matter how I tried I couldn't drop the dopey grin. "It's a date."

"It's a date," he confirmed, his eyes crinkling at the corners. God, he was adorable. And sexy as hell. And interested in me.

Our date. The words sent a giddy thrill through me as we resumed walking. This was really happening. I was going on a date with Lewis.

If only teenage me could see me now...

The giddy combination made me bold. "One condition though."

His brow furrowed. "Anything."

I bit my lip, looking up at him through my lashes. "You let me make it up to you. For this morning."

His pupils dilated, his fingers tightening on mine. "Yeah?" He rasped, his voice gone gravelly. "And how do you plan on doing that?"

I pushed up on my toes, bringing my mouth to his ear, my breasts brushing his chest. I heard his sharp intake of breath and grinned. "Thought I'd leave that up to your imagination..."

He groaned, his other hand coming to my hip, tugging me flush against him. "Keep that up and we won't make it to dinner," he warned darkly.

Satisfaction hummed through me but I forced myself to step back. It wouldn't do to combust on the middle of the sidewalk.

"Down boy," I teased, laughing at his affronted expression. "What kind of girl do you take me for? At least buy me dinner first!"

"Minx," he growled playfully, running a hand through his dishevelled hair. "You'll pay for that later."

"Promises, promises."

We grinned at each other, giddy and heated.

He swallowed. "I should find you a taxi before…"

I laughed and he raised his hand, hailing a taxi coming towards us. It immediately pulled over, the driver eyeing us expectantly.

I should have rushed towards it, the promise of AC making my little Southern heart happy. But my feet wouldn't move, and my gaze returned to Lewis, searching for… something.

I didn't want to leave this little bubble we'd created, not when I'd just started to let myself embrace the way he made me feel. Alive. Desired. Like every nerve ending was alight and attuned to him.

He seemed to feel the same reluctance, his fingers flexing on my waist before dropping away. He reached past me to open the cab door, his chest crowding my back. I closed my eyes, leaning into him for just a moment, memorising the feel of his solid strength against me.

"Seven o'clock," he murmured in my ear, his breath stirring the hair at my temple. "Don't disappear on me again, Liv."

I turned my head, my nose grazing his stubbled jaw. "I won't if you won't."

"Never," he vowed roughly.

Then he pressed a chaste kiss to my cheek and made me wish I'd turned my head.

But as I moved to duck into the cab, his hands landed on my hips, holding me against him. I looked up at him, my breath catching at the intensity in his gaze.

"Liv, I…" He paused, searching for the right words. "I just need to make sure you get it. Really get it."

"Get what?"

"This isn't some casual thing for me. Last night, and now today… I'm in this. I'm all in."

"I'm all in too," I whispered.

His smile was soft, almost wondering. "Then I'll see you tonight."

"See you tonight," I echoed, reluctantly extracting myself from his hold and sliding into the back seat. He closed the door gently behind me, his eyes never leaving mine through the window.

As the taxi merged back into traffic, I twisted to watch Lewis through the rear windshield. He had shoved his hands in his pockets. A small, secret smile played across his lips.

Watching me.

I faced forward, sinking back into the cracked vinyl, an uncontrollable grin breaking across my face. I fished my phone from my pocket, my hands shaking with a giddy mix of adrenaline and disbelief.

It was really happening. I was going on a date. With Lewis freaking Davies.

I pulled up Ashley's contact and began to type.

LIV

You'll never guess who asked me to dinner.

With a final decisive tap, I hit send, watching the message whoosh off into the ether. I slumped back, replaying the last twenty minutes over and over in my head. His smile. His touch. The promise in his eyes when he said my name.

Tonight.

Outside, LA rushed by in a blur of traffic and concrete,

palm trees, and endless blue sky. But inside the cab, I let myself sink into the fantasy.

The fantasy of him. Of us.

Damn the consequences. I was all in.

We'd figure out the rest later.

CHAPTER EIGHT

LEWIS

"*I* sure hope I don't come to regret putting my trust in you, Lewis Davies."

I flashed her a semi-nervous smile and she laughed.

"But seriously, why the alley? What happened to the good old front door drop off?"

"It's a safety precaution," I said, as my bodyguard Anderson opened my door and I slid out.

"Parking in an alley is a safety precaution?" she called after me, surprise colouring her tone. "Right, do I want to know what would happen if we walked in the front door?"

I held my hand out for her and grimaced. "I'm sure your imagination could easily fill in those gaps, Carolina girl."

Her feet hit the concrete, and I knew the second the smell of rubbish hit her.

"Yes, it's feeding me something, alright." She wrinkled her nose, glancing around, her grip tightening in my hand. "I'm not sure this is better than crazed fans trying to take the restaurant door down."

I laughed. "Tell me that again when they're your crazed fans."

Her green eyes glazed over at the suggestion and a blindingly happy smile claimed her lips.

"Shall we?" I gestured to the security door a waitress held open.

A warm glow spilled out into the warm Los Angeles night, breaking up the dreary atmosphere of the alley.

"We shall," she squeezed my hand and took a tentative step towards the door, watching her heeled feet at all times.

With a hand at the small of her back, fingers splayed across the silky fabric of her dress, I guided her to safety. My nerve endings practically buzzed with the thrill of having her all to myself for the evening.

When we reached the door, she glanced over her shoulder, flashing me a smile that stole my breath.

Anderson, my ever-present shadow, trailed after us, watching my back. His shrewd, army-trained eyes scanned every corner. If it moved, he had eyes on it.

Warmth and the aroma of garlic and herbs enveloped us as we stepped right into the kitchen.

"Lewis, caro mio! Welcome back," Toni, the owner, said, his voice booming above the ruckus of the kitchen. He was a stout, silver-haired man who had always treated me like an old friend and today was no different. He clasped my hand firmly, grinning like he hadn't seen me a week ago. "I was starting to wonder if we'd see you again before you left."

"You could never get rid of me, Toni, you know that."

"So you say." His eyes creased, displaying laugh lines so deep they resembled canyons. "But it's always a delightful surprise all the same."

A surprise he received ample warning for, but I never corrected him.

His twinkling eyes landed on Liv. "And who is this beautiful signorina?"

"Toni, this is Olivia." I couldn't keep the note of pride from my voice. "Olivia, meet Toni, the man responsible for the best carbonara in LA."

Liv laughed, the sound bright and melodic. "With an introduction like that, I can't wait to try it."

Toni winked at her. "For you, bella, I'll make it extra special." He turned, waving for us to follow. "Come, your usual table is waiting."

As he led us through the cosy dining room, she leaned into me, her lips brushing my ear. "Your usual table, huh? Bring all your dates here, Davies?"

I chuckled, my hand finding hers and tangling our fingers together. "Only the really special ones."

She arched a brow, a playful smirk tugging at her mouth. "Oh, so I'm special now?"

"More than you know," I murmured, squeezing her hand.

But of course she did know. Or she should. I'd laid all of my fledgling hopes out for her earlier today. It went against every rule in the guy code book. Even knowing that, I couldn't find it in myself to regret it.

Toni led us to a secluded alcove in the back, separated from the main space by a thick red curtain. The table was already set with flickering candles, gleaming silverware, and a bottle of red wine breathing on the white linen. Strains of soft violin music drifted in, setting the perfect atmosphere.

"Your waiter will be right with you. Buon appetito!" He bowed slightly before leaving us.

I helped Liv out of her light jacket, relishing the softness of her skin as my fingers grazed her shoulders. Her sage green dress was even more enticing in the low light, hugging her curves in all the right places. I had to force myself to look away as I pulled out her chair.

We settled into our seats and she glanced around, taking in the intimate setting, the secluded alcove that offered us a measure of privacy. "Fancy digs for a first date. You really know how to make a girl feel special, rock star."

If she thought this was fancy, my other date plans would

blow her out of the water. I planned to make the most of every single night I had with her before the tour kicked off and made it harder for me to hoard her for myself.

I chuckled, reaching for the wine. "Only the best for you, cariad."

I seriously needed to stop calling her that. If I thought there was even a small chance that she understood the Welsh word, I'd try. Couldn't have her realising that I'd been almost telling her I loved her from day one.

Anderson scowled at me as he circled the small room, checking for hidden cameras, recording devices and people. My Rhymes visit was a touchy subject where he was concerned. He hadn't quite forgiven me for sneaking out without him yet.

But we'd done this dance for years at this point. It didn't matter how long we'd been playing the fame game, none of us could get used to someone shadowing our every step. So instead of worrying about it, I focused on Liv.

I grinned, picking up the wine bottle. "Well, I figured our first official date deserved something a little more exclusive feeling."

She tilted her head, studying me in that way she had, like she could see right through to the heart of me. "Is this what dating Lewis Davies is usually like? Lowkey restaurants with VIP treatment?"

I stalled while I poured us both a glass, something Toni would grumble at me for later. My mind raced as I tried to decide how to answer. The truth was, I couldn't remember the last time I'd been on a proper date. My life had been consumed by the band, by the constant touring and recording. Romance had taken a back seat to the relentless pursuit of success.

"Honestly? I wouldn't know. It's been a long time since I've done this." At her questioning look, I shrugged and elaborated. "The whole dating thing, it's not easy with the life I lead. The constant travelling, the scrutiny, the lack of privacy…" I trailed off, my gaze flicking to where Anderson lifted a mirror to check behind it.

Understanding dawned in Liv's eyes. She nodded towards Anderson. "That's why he's here."

"Yeah." I sighed, rubbing the back of my neck. "It's a necessary evil, especially after some close calls with overzealous fans. But it makes it hard to just be normal, you know?"

She reached across the table, laying her hand over mine. "I can only imagine. Why wasn't he with you last night at the open mic?"

I groaned, casting a sheepish look at Anderson. His back stiffened but he didn't turn around. "I may have given him the slip for a few hours." I'd never been hassled at Rhymes. It was one of the many reasons I always went back. I felt like a normal guy there. I might get a double take but no one ever made a fuss. "He's still a bit pissed at me. Doesn't like it when I go rogue."

He grunted in agreement and shot me a glare that could have withered an oak tree.

Liv glanced at Anderson, taking in his stony expression. "I bet. Must be a challenge, trying to keep tabs on a troublesome rock star."

"It's a thankless job but someone's gotta do it," Anderson grumbled, just loud enough for us to hear. He nodded curtly to Liv. "You have my deepest sympathy, miss. This one's a handful."

"Alright, alright, point taken. Go hover menacingly elsewhere, will ya?" I tried to look authoritative but couldn't keep the smile off my face. "I promise no more ditching security." For now.

Anderson rolled his eyes. I had no doubt he'd forgive me eventually. He always did.

"I know it's a lot sometimes, the whole entourage thing," I said, playing with the stem of my glass. "Fame is a fickle bitch. You give up so much privacy, so much freedom. But moments like this..." I reached across the table and took her hand, my thumb brushing over her knuckles. "Make it all worthwhile."

Her fingers laced with mine, warm and sure. "I can only

imagine. I mean, I'm just getting my first real taste of it and it's thrilling and terrifying all at once. Like this wild ride that you're excited to be on but half-afraid you'll fly right off the rails."

I nodded, intimately familiar with that sensation. "And it only gets more intense." I squeezed her hand gently.

She laughed, the sound easing the tension. "Thank you. And I do feel very safe and very special to have warranted the Lewis Davies VIP experience, security detail and all."

Her tone was light, teasing, but I couldn't miss the sincerity beneath it. "You are special. And I want tonight to be about us, not the rock star bullshit."

She smiled, candlelight dancing in her eyes. "Then let's make it about us."

The waiter appeared, deftly pouring water and taking our order. We never even looked at the menus, too caught up in each other to bother.

Liv ended up deferring to me. The waiter vanished as quietly as he appeared, leaving us to our seclusion again.

I turned back to Liv, unable to stop drinking in the sight of her in the candlelight. She was breathtaking, a vision, her chestnut hair cascading in waves over her shoulders. I couldn't quite believe she'd said yes, that this magnetic, talented woman had agreed to a date.

Especially after this morning's uncertain beginnings.

She caught me staring and lifted a brow, a playful smile tugging at her lips.

"That's one interesting look. Care to share what caused it?"

I chuckled, leaning back in my seat. "Some of my thoughts aren't appropriate for public consumption."

She raised a brow, intrigued. "Oh? Do tell. You can't leave a girl hanging like that."

I shook my head, grinning. "Now where's the fun in that? I can't give away all my secrets on the first date."

"Ah, so you're a man of mystery." She propped her chin on her hand, studying me with those keen green eyes. "I do love a good puzzle."

"Well then, you're in luck. I've been told I'm quite the enigma." I winked, enjoying our playful back-and-forth.

"Is that so?" She leaned forward, a lock of hair slipping over her shoulder. "Challenge accepted. I'll have you figured out quicker than a hound dog on a coon trail."

My heart skipped a beat at the idea of her wanting to unravel me, to know me deeper. "I look forward to it. But I should warn you, I'm not an easy nut to crack."

"Good thing I'm stubborn then." Her smile turned sly. "And I reckon I'm pretty darn skilled with my hands, too."

I nearly choked on my wine at the innuendo, blood rushing south at the thought of her hands on me. "Is that a promise or a threat, Songbird?"

She tilted her head at that nickname, curiosity shining in her eyes. I expected her to question it, but instead, a coy smile claimed her lips.

"Guess you'll just have to stick around and find out, won't you?" She traced the rim of her glass with a fingertip, her eyes never leaving mine.

Fuck was I in trouble with this one. The best kind of trouble.

We slipped into easy conversation, the banter flowing as smoothly as the wine. Liv regaled me with tales of her Nashville days, painting a vivid picture of honkytonks and dive bars, of late nights spent scribbling lyrics on napkins and hustling for gigs.

"I once played a set at this hole-in-the-wall joint," she said, swirling her wine. "Stage was about the size of a postage stamp and I'm pretty sure the mic was held together with duct tape and a prayer."

I chuckled, leaning forward. "Sounds like a classy place."

"Oh, the classiest." She grinned. "But you know, those are the gigs that really test you. When you're playing to a crowd of half-drunk, disinterested barflies and you still gotta pour your heart out like it's a sold-out stadium."

I nodded, intimately familiar with that feeling. "Those early days, they shape you. Toughen you up for the road ahead."

"Amen to that." She gently knocked her glass against mine in a toast.

Our food arrived, a mouth-watering array of Italian delicacies. Her eyes widened as the waiter set a plate of gnocchi in front of her, the delicate dumplings nestled in a creamy pesto sauce.

"Oh my lord, this smells divine," she breathed, inhaling deeply.

I grinned, picking up my fork. "Wait until you taste it. Toni's gnocchi is legendary."

She took a bite and let out a moan that sent liquid fire rushing through my veins. Her eyes fluttered closed in bliss. "Sweet Jesus, you weren't kidding. This is sinful."

The candlelight danced over her features, casting her in a golden glow. She was the most beautiful thing I'd ever seen.

"You keep looking at me like that, you're gonna make me blush," she murmured, her eyes opening to meet mine.

"Can't help it," I whispered. "You're stunning, Liv. Inside and out."

Her breath hitched and she ducked her head again, a smile playing about her lips. "You sure do have a way with words, Lewis Davies."

"Only speaking the truth, cariad."

We tucked into our meals, the conversation flowing easily between bites.

"Oh, I've got a good one," Liv said, setting down her fork. "So, when I was about eight, my cousin Cooper convinced me it would be a brilliant idea to sneak into Farmer Johnson's watermelon patch and liberate a few of his prized melons."

I leaned forward, already grinning. "I sense this didn't end well."

"Understatement of the century." She laughed, shaking her head. "We were two scrawny kids."

"No. I could never imagine you scrawny."

"I was ten, Lewis, and short, without an ounce of muscle on me. Of course I was scrawny." She waved her hand, brushing my disbelief away. "Anyway, we were struggling to haul these massive watermelons back over the fence. Cooper boosts me up and I'm halfway over, one leg on either side, watermelon clutched to my chest, when who should come stomping out of the barn but Farmer Johnson himself, shotgun in hand."

I barked out a laugh. "Oh no!"

"Oh yes! I was so startled, I lost my grip on that damn watermelon. Dropped it right on Cooper's head." She mimed the motion, her eyes wide. "Knocked him out cold. Meanwhile, I'm stuck straddling this fence, certain I'm about to meet my maker at the hands of a watermelon-crazed farmer."

I was laughing in earnest now.

"Farmer Johnson hauled Cooper up by his overalls, tossed him over the fence, then plucked me off like a misbehaving kitten and set me on my feet." She grinned ruefully. "Made us spend the next week mucking out his stables as penance."

"I bet that cured you of any future watermelon heists."

"Oh, absolutely. To this day, I can't look at a watermelon without getting a phantom twinge in my thighs."

We laughed. The sound echoed in the small space, blending seamlessly with the soft strains of violin music. I couldn't remember the last time I'd laughed this much, or felt this light. I wanted to bottle this moment.

"Alright, rock star, your turn," she said, pointing her fork at me. "Spill. What kind of mischief did young Lewis get up to in Wales?"

I thought for a moment, casting my mind back to my childhood in the South Wales Valleys. "I was thirteen, obsessed with music, and desperate to see my favourite band live. Problem was, the venue has a strict fourteen and up policy."

Liv's eyes sparkled with interest. "What did you do?"

I grinned, the memory playing out vividly in my mind. "It honestly wasn't that brilliant or original an idea, but the lot of us, Alex, Tom, Andy, and Lily hatched this plan." I shook my head, smiling ruefully. "We'd sneak in through the back, blend in with the crowd, and pray no one asked for ID."

"How'd you manage to get past security?"

"Well, that's the thing. We didn't." I chuckled, shaking my head. "We made it as far as the backstage door before this burly bouncer stopped us."

"Oh no! What happened?"

"Alex happened." Even at thirteen the fucker knew how to lie through his teeth and make it believable. "He tried to convince the bouncer that we were on some backstage VIP list."

Liv bit her lip, her eyes shining with amusement. "Did he buy it?"

I shook my head. "He crossed his arms and stared us down, waiting for the truth."

She leaned in, fully engrossed. "And then?"

"And then," I said, drawing out the suspense, "Lily started belting out the band's hit song, right there in the alley without a care in the world."

She clapped a hand over her mouth, stifling a giggle. "She didn't!"

"If I'd done it, I would have sounded like a drunken karaoke champion, but Lily…" I shook my head.

"Please tell me this story has a happy ending."

"'Course it does." I picked up my wine glass and took a drink, delaying the suspense.

"Stop stalling and put me out of my misery."

"Alright, alright." I chuckled and put the glass down. "Lucky for us, the lead guitarist was having a pre-show fag break in the alley and heard the whole thing. In the end we weren't lying at all." I bit my lip as her mouth dropped open. "He put us on the VIP list and shepherded us into the green room with a look of absolute shock still on his face."

"Then what?" she asked, her voice hushed.

"They landed us our first support tour."

Liv's eyes widened, her mouth forming a perfect 'O' of surprise. "No way! That's incredible, Lewis. What a stroke of luck."

I chuckled, running my thumb over her knuckles. "Luck,

fate, whatever you want to call it. That night changed everything for us. Set us on the path to where we are now."

She smiled, squeezing my hand. "It's amazing how one moment can alter the course of your whole life. Make your wildest dreams come true."

"Tell me about it." I shook my head, marvelling at the twists and turns that had led me here, to this table, to her. "Though I have a feeling my wildest dreams are just getting started."

A pretty blush stained her cheeks and she ducked her head, a smile playing about her lips. "Smooth talker."

We fell into a comfortable silence, savouring the last bites of our meal. As I watched her, a thought occurred to me.

"Did you mean what you said last night?"

She glanced up, her fork poised halfway to her mouth. "Which part?"

"That this tour is going to be your first time playing outside the US?"

She nodded, setting her fork down. "Yeah, it's kind of surreal. I mean, I've barely been out of the South, let alone the country." A nervous laugh escaped her. "I had to get my first passport for this gig."

I grinned, excitement bubbling up inside me. "Well you're doing it with the right guy. I'll show you all the best spots."

Her eyes softened, warmth radiating from their green depths. "I'd like that."

I held her gaze, a frisson of excitement and possibility thrumming between us. This woman was something special.

I was already falling for Liv Monroe.

And I was pretty damn sure there'd be no coming back from it.

CHAPTER NINE

OLIVIA

*T*he door clicked shut behind us and before I could take another step, Lewis's arms wrapped around my waist, pulling my back flush against his chest. His lips brushed the shell of my ear, sending a shiver down my spine.

"No escaping now," he murmured, his voice low and rough with desire. "I've got you right where I want you."

I tilted my head back, resting it against his shoulder as his hands skimmed down my arms.

"Is that a promise or a threat, rock star?" I asked, aiming for coyness but missing by a mile. My voice was breathy, betraying my desire.

"Oh, it's a guarantee, babe." He nipped at my earlobe, soothing the sting with his tongue.

I arched against him, relishing the way his breath hitched. "And what exactly are you guaranteeing?"

He dipped his head, his stubbled jaw rasping against my cheek as he brought his lips to my ear. "By the time I'm done with you, you won't even remember your own name, let alone have the strength to walk out that door. That I'm going to keep you here all night, exploring every inch of this gorgeous body until you're trembling and begging for mercy."

Need shot through me, hot and bright, his words branding me.

"You sound awfully confident. You sure you're up for the challenge?" My attempt at sassiness was half-hearted at best, my focus split between the wicked dance of his fingers along my collarbone and the press of his erection against my ass.

He spun me around to face him, his eyes smouldering with promise. "I've never been more certain of anything, cariad. I'm going to take you apart, piece by exquisite piece."

His gaze held mine, the intensity in those hazel depths stealing my breath as he backed me against the door. The playful edge was still there, but it was tempered by something deeper, something that made my heart stutter and my pulse race.

His hands bracketed my head as his body pressed into mine. I could feel every hard plane of him, the heat radiating through his clothes. He leaned in slowly, his lips a hair's breadth from mine, his breath ghosting over my skin. But he held back, hovering just out of reach, a teasing smile playing at the corners of his mouth.

"Lewis…" I whispered, half plea, half prayer.

"Shhh, let me savour this. Let me savour you." His thumb traced the bow of my lip, his touch feather-light and electric. "I've been dreaming about this moment all night, waiting to have you all to myself."

My breath hitched, my lips parting on a sigh. His words wound around me like a caress, sultry and seductive, igniting a wildfire inside of me.

Instead of kissing me like I craved, he brushed his mouth along my jaw, his stubble rasping deliciously against my skin. I let my head fall back against the door, giving him better access.

He took full advantage, trailing kisses down my neck, his teeth grazing my pulse point.

"Please." I threaded my fingers into his dark hair, tugging at him.

He hummed against my throat, the vibration sending sparks of pleasure through me. "Please what?"

"Kiss me," I demanded breathlessly.

He pulled back just enough to meet my gaze, a wicked grin playing about his lips. "Bossy, aren't you?"

"Normally I'd argue, but right now…" I tugged him closer, our breath mingling. "Yes, so very bossy. Kiss me or Lord help me—"

And then, just when I thought I might combust from the anticipation, his mouth crashed onto mine, swallowing my words. I moaned into the kiss, opening for him immediately. His lips were firm and insistent against mine. His tongue swept inside, tangling with mine in a dance that set my blood on fire.

I melted into him, my hands fisting in his hair as I poured every ounce of my pent-up longing into the kiss.

He tasted like whiskey and temptation, hot and heady on my tongue. I couldn't get enough, couldn't pull him close enough. The world beyond this room ceased to exist, narrowing down to the press of his body and the rasp of his stubble against my skin.

His hands slid down my sides, gripping my hips as he rocked into me. I could feel him, hard and insistent against my belly. Lord I wanted him so badly it was like an ache in my bones.

I grabbed fistfuls of his shirt, yanking it free from his waistband. He broke the kiss just long enough to help me drag it over his head, tossing it aside carelessly. Then his mouth was on mine again, hot and demanding.

My palms skated over his bare chest, luxuriating in the warm satin of his skin, the ridges of lean muscle. I trailed my fingers down his sternum, following the path of the tattoo that swirled over his ribs. He hissed through his teeth, his abdominal muscles clenching under my touch.

"Tease," he growled, capturing my wrist and bringing it to his lips. He pressed a hot, open-mouthed kiss to my palm, his teeth grazing the sensitive skin.

I gasped, heat unfurling low in my belly at the erotic scrape.

"Look who's talking, Mr Take-It-Slow."

He smirked, the expression sinful and promising. "Oh, I'll take my time... later. Right now, I need you too damn much for slow."

To punctuate his point, he reached around and dragged my zipper down in one fluid motion. Cool air kissed my fevered skin as the silky fabric of my dress pooled at my feet and I kicked it away impatiently.

Lewis pulled back, his gaze raking over me like a physical touch, his eyes going dark and molten as he took in my matching emerald green bra and panty set. I'd chosen them with him in mind, wanting to feel sexy and confident for our date.

From the predatory glint in his eye, I'd say I chose well.

"Fuck, you're stunning," he rasped, his hands coming up to cup my lace-covered breasts. "The most beautiful thing I've ever seen."

I arched into his touch, my head falling back on a moan as he worked me through the delicate fabric. His fingers plucked and teased, circling my nipples until they pebbled under his ministrations.

"Lewis, please..." I whimpered, my voice thin and needy to my own ears. But I was beyond caring, too lost in the exquisite torture of his hands on my body.

"Please what? Tell me what you need." He pinched my nipple, rolling it between his fingers, sending sparks of pleasure-pain ricocheting through me.

"You," I gasped out, my nails digging into his shoulders. "I need you."

A low, approving rumble vibrated through his chest. "Then you'll have every last inch of me."

He reached behind me, unclasping my bra with deft fingers.

It fell away and he wasted no time, ducking his head to capture one straining peak between his lips.

I cried out, my fingers tangling in his hair to hold him to me as he suckled and nipped, worshipping my breasts with single-minded focus. His mouth was hot and demanding, sending jolts of liquid desire straight to my core.

He switched to the other breast, lavishing it with the same devoted attention, until I was writhing against him, my hips seeking friction, desperate for more.

"So responsive," he murmured against my skin, trailing kisses down the valley between my breasts. "So perfect. I could spend hours just tasting you, learning every secret spot that makes you moan."

"Later," I managed, echoing his earlier promise. "Need you now. Need to feel you."

He groaned, the sound vibrating through me. "Your wish, my command."

His hands slid down, hooking into the sides of my panties. In one swift tug, he had them off, leaving me bare and aching before him.

I watched through hooded eyes as he trailed his fingers up the inside of my thigh, teasing, purposely avoiding where I needed him most.

When he finally, finally brushed against my aching centre, I nearly sobbed in relief. He parted my folds, groaning at the evidence of my arousal.

"Fuck, Liv… you're drenched. Is this all for me?" He circled my clit with the pad of his thumb, the light, teasing pressure making me see stars.

"Yes," I hissed, my hips canting forward, chasing his touch. "Only you. Please…"

"Mmm, I do love it when you beg." He dipped a finger inside me, just barely breaching my entrance before withdrawing. He brought the digit to his mouth, sucking it clean with a low, appreciative moan. "And you taste like heaven. Sweet ambrosia."

I whimpered, a fresh wave of need crashing over me at the erotic sight. My thighs clenched, my body desperate for more of his touch.

And he gave it to me, two fingers plunging deep, curling just so to hit that perfect spot. I moaned as he worked me with expert precision, his thumb circling my clit in maddening counterpoint.

"That's it. Let me feel you." His voice was low and rough in my ear, his words as potent as his touch. "I want to feel you come apart on my fingers, want to feel you squeeze around me as you shatter."

"Lord, Lewis… yes!" I couldn't think, could scarcely draw breath past the waves of sensation surging through me. He was relentless, driving me higher and higher with each skilled thrust and twist.

I came with a wordless cry, my back bowing off the door as ecstasy ripped through me. It crashed over me in unrelenting waves, stealing my breath and my reason, until there was nothing but the blinding pleasure and the anchor of Lewis's body against mine.

He worked me through it, gentling his touch but not ceasing, drawing out my orgasm until I was boneless and trembling in his arms.

"Fucking stunning," he murmured, pressing soft kisses to my temple, my cheek, the corner of my slack mouth. "You're incredible, Liv. I'll never get enough of watching you come apart for me."

I hummed, a sated, languid smile curving my lips. "Mmm, that was…"

"Just the beginning," he finished, his voice hoarse. "I'm nowhere near done with you yet."

To prove his point, he stripped off his jeans. His cock sprang free to jut proudly against his belly. My mouth went dry at the sight of him, long and thick and perfect. I wanted to taste him, to take him into my mouth and drive him as wild as he'd driven me. But that was for another time. Right now, I needed him too badly to wait a second longer.

He fished a foil packet from the pocket of his jeans before discarding them on the floor. My brows rose, a strange mix of amusement and jealousy swirling in my chest. Did he always come prepared?

When he turned back to me, I pushed the thought away. I didn't care how many came before me. All that mattered was here, now. Us.

He gathered me in his arms and hitched my leg over his hip, the blunt head of his cock nudging against my sensitive entrance. I gasped, my over-sensitised nerve endings sparking back to life at the contact.

"Think you can take me? Think this sweet little pussy can handle my cock so soon?" He rocked against me, teasing, painting my folds with the evidence of his arousal.

"Yes," I breathed, tilting my hips in shameless offering. "Yes. I need you inside me. Need to feel you stretch me, fill me up."

He slid home, sheathing himself to the hilt in one smooth, inexorable thrust. I cried out, my fingers scrabbling at his back as I stretched around him, so full, so deliciously stuffed.

"God, you feel incredible," he groaned, his face buried in the crook of my neck. "So hot, so tight. Like you were made for me."

"Move," I panted, wrapping my legs around his waist, taking him even deeper. "Please, I need…"

He silenced me with a bruising kiss, his hips snapping forward to meet my demand. He set a hard, driving rhythm, each thrust sending me rising up on my toes, my breasts bouncing with the force of it.

The room filled with the slap of skin on skin, and our mingled moans and gasps.

But beneath the frantic need, there was something more, something deeper. It was in the reverent way he touched me, the worshipful press of his lips to my skin. It was in the words he whispered against my mouth, filthy praise intermingled with tender endearments.

And it was in his eyes, when he pulled back to gaze at me, his rhythm slowing to a gentle rocking. Those hazel depths held a wealth of emotion, a tenderness that stole my breath and squeezed my heart.

In that moment, lost in his eyes, in the cradle of his body, I felt cherished. Treasured. Loved.

The thought should have terrified me. It was too much, too soon. We barely knew each other, had only just begun to explore this thing between us.

But gazing up at him, I couldn't find it in me to be afraid. It felt right, this connection, this bone-deep certainty that this was where I was meant to be. That he was who I was meant to be with.

Tears pricked my eyes and I blinked them back, over-whelmed by the intensity of the moment. Lewis leaned down, kissing them away with a sweetness that made my heart ache.

"I've got you," he murmured, his lips brushing mine with each word. "I'm right here, cariad. Not going anywhere."

"Promise?" I whispered, hating the tremor in my voice, the vulnerability bleeding through.

"Promise." He sealed it with a kiss, pouring everything he couldn't say into the press of his mouth, the slide of his tongue against mine.

And then he began to move again, slow and deep, stoking the embers of my desire back to a roaring flame. I clung to him, meeting him thrust for thrust, losing myself in the exquisite drag of his body against mine.

The pressure built. It coiled in my core, every nerve ending alight with sensation, a tidal wave poised to crash over me and sweep me away.

"I'm so close…" I panted, my nails raking down his back, desperate for an anchor in the storm.

"Let go, Liv. I'm right there with you." His thrusts grew

erratic, his control slipping as his own climax barrelled down on him. "Want to feel you come on my cock as I fill you up."

I shattered with a hoarse cry, my entire body seizing up as ecstasy consumed me. It ripped through me, a pleasure so intense it bordered on pain, whiting out my vision and stealing my breath.

His cock jolted inside of me and my name became a reverent chant on his lips as he came. We clung to each other as the aftershocks rolled through us, our sweat-slicked bodies heaving. Lewis peppered my face with soft, sweet kisses, whispering words of praise and affection into my skin.

"You're so perfect, Liv. The way you feel, the way you respond to me... I've never known anything like it." His voice was raw.

"Me neither," I managed, still trying to catch my breath, to gather my scattered wits. "That was... God, Lewis. You wreck me. In the best possible way."

He chuckled, the sound warm and content. "The feeling is entirely mutual, cariad."

Carefully, mindful of my shaking legs, he lowered us to the floor. He settled me in his lap, cradling me against his chest as he leaned back against the door. I went willingly, boneless and sated, happy to let him support my weight.

We sat there in silence for long moments, just holding each other, basking in the afterglow. His heartbeat was strong and steady beneath my cheek, his fingers tracing idle patterns on my bare back.

It was peaceful. I felt connected to him, bound by more than just the cooling sweat on our skin and the echoes of our lovemaking.

It was terrifying and exhilarating in equal measure, this depth of feeling after such a short time. But I couldn't bring myself to question it, not when it felt so right, so inevitable.

Lewis tipped my chin up, forcing me to meet his soft gaze. "Where did you go?"

I bit my lip, peering up at him through my lashes. "Is it normal? To fall this hard, this fast?"

"Normal? No, probably not." He shrugged, a wry smile tugging at his mouth. "But whoever said we were normal? We're musicians, Liv. We feel everything harder, faster, deeper. It's what makes us who we are."

"You're not... I mean, this isn't just..." I stumbled over my words, unsure how to voice the insecurity niggling at the back of my mind. The fear that this was just a fling, a tour romance that would fizzle out as quickly as it had ignited.

His brow furrowed, his arms tightening around me. "Just what, Liv? A casual hookup? A way to pass the time on the road?"

"I don't know. Maybe?" I ducked my head, suddenly fascinated by the inked swirls on his chest. "I mean, I wouldn't blame you if it was. You're Lewis Davies, for crying out loud. You could have any woman you wanted."

He tipped my chin back up, forcing me to meet his gaze. The intensity in those hazel depths stole my breath.

"I don't want any woman. I want you. Only you." His voice was low, fierce with conviction. "This is real and I'm in it, heart and soul, for as long as you'll have me."

Tears pricked my eyes, my heart swelling at his raw, honest declaration. "I'm in it too, Lewis. All the way."

His answering smile was blinding, joy and relief and something deeper, something that looked a lot like love, shining through. He claimed my mouth in a slow, thorough kiss, pouring every ounce of his feeling into the slide of his lips over mine.

When we broke apart, I was breathless and glowing, my fears quieted by the certainty in his touch, his gaze.

"As much as I love having you naked in my arms," he murmured, brushing a kiss to my forehead, "what do you say we move this to the bed? Give me a chance to show you just how 'in it' I am."

I grinned, my body already stirring at the promise in his words. "I think that can be arranged."

He stood, scooping me up into his arms as if I weighed nothing. I squealed, laughing as I wrapped my arms around his neck, letting him carry me to the bed.

I couldn't stop smiling, caught in the grip of a lavender haze. He was a once-in-a-lifetime love, the kind of connection most people only dreamed of. And I was determined to hold on tight, to weather whatever storms may come.

Because a love like this, a bond this deep and true...

That was worth fighting for.

CHAPTER TEN

OLIVIA

*T*he Bow Lounge was everything I dreamed a classic Hollywood bar would be—all rich velvets, dim lighting, and the croon of live jazz. I half expected Humphrey Bogart to step out of the shadows with a bourbon in hand. It was the kind of place I could imagine deals being made back in the day, where stars rose.

I followed Lily through the crowd, to a circular booth tucked in the back in a row of others while she whispered names to me, pointing out each of the women who had become her confidants and support system over the last few years.

I'd already met Nia. She sat on the outer edge of the booth, her bobbed platinum hair catching the glow of a lamp hanging above the table. What I hadn't known was just how deep Lily and Nia's friendship went.

"Alys is next to Nia," Lily said, her voice low, indicating the redhead grinning at something the dark-haired woman across from her had said. "She's Ryan's girlfriend. Then you've got Ella and Mel. They're sisters."

The only difference between them appeared to be their age and the length of their hair.

"And Ceri, one of my dancers. Also Alex's ex, but not." Lily sighed.

"How can she be an ex but not?" I asked, studying the raven-haired woman again.

"They just found out they got married while drunk in Fiji a few years ago and he's using it as an excuse to reconnect." She winced, throwing me a warning look. "I wouldn't bring it up. It's a touchy subject."

"There you are!" Nia scooted over to make room on the bench next to her. "We were starting to think you two got pulled into the secret bar they're hiding behind the jukebox in the hall."

"How do you know there's a secret bar?" I slid in beside her, sinking into the buttery leather cushion.

"A little birdie,"—she tilted her head towards Lily as she took a seat opposite me—"might have whispered it in my ear. Apparently, it's where all the real deals go down, away from prying eyes."

Mel leaned forward, her voice dropping to a whisper. "I heard Frank Sinatra used to hold court there back in the day."

"Well that just makes me want to see inside even more!" Ella took a sip of her cocktail. "I wonder what kind of secrets those walls have heard over the years."

"Probably enough to fill a tell-all memoir or two." Lily smirked. "You know what they say—if those walls could talk…"

"We'd all be in a world of trouble." Ceri clinked her glass against Lily's.

My mind conjured images of a dark, smoke-filled room where the likes of Cary Grant, Katharine Hepburn and Bette Davis might have held court once upon a time—making deals, trading barbs and indulging in all the vices 1940s Hollywood had to offer. The thought of being even remotely close to that kind of old-school glamour and intrigue sent a thrill down my spine.

"Sounds like something straight out of a movie."

"Trust me, reality is usually far less romantic than fantasy." Lily signalled a passing waitress to place our drink orders.

"Unless you're Nia, of course." Ceri bumped the photographer's shoulder with her own. "Then every gritty back alley and seedy dive bar is just another opportunity for a killer shot."

Nia grinned, flipping her hair over her shoulder with a dramatic flair. "What can I say? I've got an eye for the extraordinary in the ordinary."

"I don't know how you do it," Alys said, her Welsh lilt warm but tinged with amusement.

The conversation flowed as easily as the cocktails, the girls chatting with the ease of old friends. I sat back, content to listen and absorb, to soak in the camaraderie and the laughter. It struck me how different this was from the solitary life I'd led in Nashville, holed up in my tiny apartment, just me and my guitar. I'd had friends, sure, but nothing like this. Nothing like the bond these women shared.

Once the waitress returned with our drinks and left, Lily raised her glass in a toast. "To Liv, the newest member of our little sisterhood. May she survive the madness with her sanity intact and her liver only slightly pickled."

"Hear, hear!" the women chorused, clinking their glasses against mine.

I took a sip of my whiskey sour, the tart sweetness bursting on my tongue. "I make no promises on the sanity front, but I'll do my best to keep up with you all."

"You'll be fine. We'll show you the ropes." Nia laughed, slinging an arm around my shoulders. "And possibly the inside of a few jail cells, if the night takes a turn."

I nearly choked on my drink, my eyes widening. "I'm sorry, what now?"

"Ignore her," Lily said, rolling her eyes. "She likes to think she's far more hardcore than she actually is."

Nia just sipped her drink, staring at us all over the rim of her glass with a mischievous glint in her blue eyes.

"Though there was that one time in Prague…" Mel said, her brows raising suggestively. "She got close that night."

"Ooh, I remember that!" Ella slapped the table, a smirk claiming her lips. "Wasn't that the night Nia sweet-talked her way into that underground burlesque club that fronted itself as an absinthe bar?"

Alys shot Nia a hard look. "And then promptly got us all kicked out for trying to snap a photo of the owner when there were a million no picture signs."

"In my defence," Nia held up a hand, warding them off, "he had the most amazing face. All weathered and wise, like he'd seen some shit, you know?"

"Haven't we all," Alys muttered into her martini glass.

A tall woman with black hair and dark red tips approached our table, a bright smile on her face. I recognised her from the kick off meeting but her name absolutely escaped me. Who's shocked? She was dressed in a sleek black jumpsuit that hugged her curves, her hair pulled back into a ponytail.

"Ooh, shuffle up, ladies," Lily said. "Our final newbie has arrived."

"Sorry I'm late," she said, leaning in to hug Lily who'd slid out of her seat. "Riley would not stop talking and end the meeting."

Lily waved off her apology. "No worries. We were just getting started." She sat back down and shifted over to make room for her to join us. "Liv, this is Mia Johnson, our fearless production manager."

"It's great to see you again, Olivia." Mia smiled. "I can't wait to see what you do opening night. I've heard great things about your music."

I flushed with pride. "Thank you, that means a lot. I'm excited to be here."

"We're thrilled to have you," she said, settling into her seat. "Lily's been singing your praises non-stop. Says you're the next big thing."

I shot Lily a look, half-thankful, half-mortified. "Flattery will get you everywhere, Tyler."

"Just calling it like I see it." Lily merely shrugged, unrepentant. "Get used to the accolades, because they're only gonna multiply once the world hears that voice of yours."

I busied myself with my newly delivered drink, a blush heating my cheeks.

"So Liv," Nia said, bumping my shoulder with hers. "How are you feeling about all of this? Excited? Nervous? Ready to run for the hills?"

"D, all of the above," I admitted with a rueful grin. "I mean, it's a lot, you know? One minute I'm playing dive bars in Nashville, and the next I'm heading out on the biggest tour of my life with the band I've idolised since high school. It's surreal."

"It's okay to feel overwhelmed." Lily reached across the table and squeezed my hand, her eyes warm with understanding. "This business, it's a wild ride, but we've all been there and any time you need a break or a vent, we'll be ready and waiting."

I smiled gratefully as a knot of tension unwound in my chest. "Thanks, Lily. That means a lot."

"Anytime." She winked, then turned her attention to the waitress who had appeared at our table. "Another round, please. And make Liv's a double. She's gonna need it."

The girls chuckled, and I joined in, the laughter loosening something inside me.

As the waitress hurried off to fetch our drinks, Nia leaned forward, a mischievous glint in her eye. "So, Liv. You and Lewis seemed awfully cosy at the kickoff meeting. Anything you want to share with the class?"

I nearly choked on my own tongue, heat rushing to my cheeks. "What? No! I mean, we just met. We were just talking."

"Mmhmm." Ceri smirked, her eyes dancing with amusement. "Talking. Is that what the kids are calling it these days?"

"Oh, leave her alone," Mel said, though she was fighting a

smile herself. "Can't a girl have a conversation with a guy without it turning into a Crimewatch investigation?"

"Not when the guy is Lewis Davies, who barely bats an eye at all the groupies screaming for his attention," Ella said, her tone dry but teasing. "And the girl is looking at him like he's the last Welsh cake at Cardiff market." Mel tossed a napkin at her, and she dodged, chuckling. "What? I'm only calling it like it is."

I buried my face in my hands, my voice muffled. "Oh my lord, was I that obvious?"

"Only to those of us who know what to look for." Nia patted my arm. "Which is pretty much everyone at this table."

"Fantastic," I groaned, peeking out from between my fingers. "Just what I need, to start the tour with a reputation as a groupie."

"Hardly." Lily rolled her eyes. "Lewis isn't exactly known for being a cad. If anything, I'd say he's the one who looked smitten."

My heart did a little flip at her words. He'd told me how he felt, of course, but there was something about hearing it from other people's lips that made it all the more real.

Belatedly, I remembered his plea for us to keep our relationship secret for now. I bit back a groan. How did I even begin to walk my reaction back and be believable?

"It doesn't matter," I said, aiming for a firm 'don't argue with me' tone, dropping my hands. "I'm here to sing, not to get involved with anyone. Especially not someone in the headlining band."

They all eyed me with varying degrees of disbelief and suspicion. I braced myself for someone to call me on the lie.

"Famous last words," Nia singsonged, but she let the subject drop as the waitress returned with our drinks.

I took a grateful sip of my whiskey, welcoming the burn as it slid down my throat.

"I can't hold my tongue anymore," Ceri said, putting her drink down. She leaned forward and her voice lowered to a stage whisper. "Anyone else noticed a Sanderson brother lurking a couple of booths down?"

Mia and I leaned out of the booth, Nia and Mel lifted themselves up to peek over the top of our booth, and Alys tutted.

"We said no shop talk!" She frowned.

"How is celeb-spotting shop talk?" Ceri shot back.

"It's giving more fuel to the rumour mill, which directly impacts their PR, which is shop talk in my book." Alys raised a brow, her tone brooking no argument. "Besides, they're people too. How would you feel if someone was gawking at you and speculating about your love life in the middle of a bar?"

"She's got a point, but I have zero issues speculating when the celebrity in question is an utter asshole," Mia said, nodding to where one of the brothers leaned against the bar chatting up a redhead. "That is not Chris Sanderson's fiancée. Mark my words, that relationship is faker than botox and there'll be fresh faces on their arms by the end of the night."

"Some things never change." Lily grimaced, shaking her head. "Those two have been playing the field since they hit puberty."

"Hey, nothing to be ashamed of there. At least they're not slinging around wedding rings like Chase Campbell," Mia said, nodding to a dark-haired god laughing with a gaggle of admirers at the other end of the bar. "I swear, that man changes wives like most people change socks. What's the count now, five? Six?"

"Seven, if you count the Vegas wedding that was annulled before the ink was dry," Nia said.

"I don't know how you're spotting these people," Ella muttered into her Old Fashioned. "I can barely keep my year two class straight, let alone cram the faces and names of people I'll never meet into my head."

"It's a skill," Ceri said, smirking.

"Yeah, one she's been practising since we were eight." Lily smiled at her, a fondness in her gaze that made me miss Ashley instantly.

Goodness knows we'd spent our fair share of time poring over gossip rags and daydreaming about rubbing elbows with the rich and famous.

"But there are at least forty people in this room." Alys indicated towards the open bar with her martini glass. "You couldn't possibly get them all right."

"I don't have to." Ceri shrugged before directing a pointed look at Mia. "Mia's local. I'm betting she's spotted more than me."

Mia laughed, scanning the room. "Oh, I see how it is. She's telling you no celeb spotting but it's okay for me?"

"Absolutely." Ceri nodded. "Besides, I'm on this tour against my will. I have to get my kicks from somewhere and it's never going to be Alex."

The more pieces I heard about their relationship the more curious I got. But with the tense set of her jaw, I bit my tongue on every single question. Curiosity didn't need to kill this cat literally five days before she got to play with The Brightside.

Luckily, Mia took the challenge in hand and nodded to a guy in a booth in the opposite corner to us. "That's Aria Campbell. Chase's sister and co-singer in their country band. She was on that reality show, *Married Blind*."

"The one where they marry total strangers?" Mel asked, her eyes wide. "I've heard so many sketchy stories about that show."

Mia shook her head. "I don't know how anyone could agree to marry a complete stranger in the first place. I mean, I love my husband, but it took us years to get to a good place."

"Nah, it's utterly ridiculous. Where's the spark? The chemistry? The butterfly inducing meet cute?" Nia twirled her glass, her brow furrowing. "I could never give that up and I couldn't walk down the aisle for just anyone. It has to be right, and no way did they fall in love at first sight."

Ceri threw a coaster at her. "You watch too many rom coms. There's nothing exciting about marriage." She nodded to Chase. "I don't know what he thinks he's playing at, but one day he's going to find a woman he doesn't want to shake, and she won't trust a word he says."

I couldn't help but stare. I'd followed the media circus surrounding his sister's stint on *Married Blind*, seen the way the tabloids had ripped her to shreds when the relationship imploded weeks after the cameras stopped rolling.

I took a long swallow of my drink, the burn of the alcohol grounding me slightly. Lord, what had I gotten myself into?

"You okay, Liv?" Ella asked softly, her brown eyes kind with concern. "You look like you've seen a ghost."

I mustered a smile, shaking off the catastrophic thoughts. "I'm fine, just… processing. It's a lot to take in, you know? The whole 'fame' thing."

"It's overwhelming, isn't it?" Ella nodded, understanding flickering across her face. "I remember the first time I got papped with Jared. It was just a coffee run, but suddenly there were these cameras in my face, these strangers shouting questions at me. I felt so… exposed. Vulnerable." She shuddered at the memory. "Like I was suddenly public property, my every move scrutinised and judged."

"How do you deal with it?" I asked, my voice small. "The scrutiny, the invasion of privacy?"

She sighed, running a hand through her short hair. "Honestly? Some days are easier than others. But I try to focus on what's real, you know? My relationship with Jared, my work, the people who matter. The rest… it's just noise. You can't let it consume you."

I nodded, absorbing her words like a sponge. It was sage advice, a reminder to keep my priorities straight and my head on my shoulders.

"And it helps to have a solid support system," Mel added, bumping Ella's shoulder affectionately. "People who keep you grounded, who remind you of who you are when the world tries to tell you differently."

Ella's phone chimed with an incoming message. She glanced down, her brow furrowing slightly as she read.

"Everything okay, El?" Mel asked, picking up on her sister's shift in mood.

"Yeah, just Mam asking what time my flight lands tomorrow." She sighed, setting her phone face down on the table. "I was doing my best to ignore it honestly. I love teaching, but I hate leaving Jared for two months."

"Oh, El," Mel murmured, wrapping an arm around her sister's shoulders.

"It'll be fine." Ella mustered a brave smile, but I could see the tightness around her eyes, the flicker of doubt she couldn't quite mask.

"You know," Ceri said, her tone thoughtful. "My cousin's been teaching English online for the past year. She says it's been a total game changer, lets her travel and still do what she loves."

Ella perked up, interest sparking in her gaze. "Really? I've never considered online teaching."

Alys nodded, warming to the idea. "There are so many reputable programs out there now. You could teach from anywhere, even the road, as long as you have a decent WiFi connection."

"And you'd still get those long holidays to spend back home with your family and your man," Mel added with a wink. "Best of both worlds."

"Huh." A slow, hopeful smile spread across Ella's face as she turned the idea over. "I'll have to look into that. Could be a real solution for next year while you guys are working your way through Europe." She bumped Ceri with her elbow. "You might have just changed my life."

Ceri smiled. "That's what I'm here for. Well, that and to make sure Alex gives me the divorce I'm owed."

My gaze drifted to Lily, who had been uncharacteristically quiet throughout the exchange. She was staring into her glass, a pensive look on her face, her bottom lip caught between her teeth.

I tapped the table in front of her. "You okay, Lil? You seem miles away."

"What?" Startled, her eyes snapped to mine, a rueful smile tugging at her lips. "Oh, yeah. I'm fine. Just... thinking."

"About Rhys?" Mel asked, keeping her voice low and gentle.

She winced. "Am I that obvious?"

"Maybe we're just exceptionally perceptive." Ceri shrugged before throwing her a sympathetic smile. "Or maybe we know the look of a woman with a lot on her mind."

Lily nodded, understanding flickering in her eyes. "The curse of dating musicians."

She was silent for a long moment, worrying her lip between her teeth. Then, in a voice barely above a whisper, she said, "Rhys and I only just got back together. I guess, hearing Ella, I can't avoid thinking about what the distance will do to us."

"He's not joining the tour?" I asked.

She shook her head. "I offered, of course, but everything is still so new. I don't think he's ready to turn his life upside down for two years to follow me around the globe." She grimaced. "He's also in the middle of launching an app and hasn't long quit his IT support job to focus on it full time. So I get it, I really do."

But she missed him.

She didn't need to say it. It was written in every tense line of her body.

"But we only just patched things up." She chewed her lip, her gaze dropping to the table. "What if the stitches aren't strong enough?"

"So what if they aren't?" Ceri shrugged when Lily directed her shocked gaze at her. "Do you really think he stands a chance holding you off?"

Lily smirked. "I can be pretty stubborn when I want to be."

Nia snorted. "You're always stubborn, Lily."

A laugh rippled around the table and I found myself joining in. Because yeah, we were a stubborn bunch, the lot of us. Guess you had to be, to make it in the music business.

"But serious, have you heard of this thing called FaceTime?"

Nia asked, her tone gently teasing. "Trust me, with the right angles and strong WiFi, distance is nothing."

Mel nodded. "Seriously. A well-timed sext can work wonders for keeping the spark alive."

"Ugh!" Ella groaned, tossing a wadded up napkin at her head. "I did not need that mental image of my sister, thank you very much."

Lily ducked her head, a watery chuckle escaping her lips. "You guys are ridiculous."

"But we're not wrong." Alys waggled her brows suggestively.

"Okay, but real talk?" Ceri leaned forward, her expression softening into something more earnest. "You and Rhys, you're the real deal. Anyone with eyes can see that. And yeah, it's gonna be hard, being apart for so long. But you know what's harder? Giving up on something beautiful because you're afraid."

Mia nodded, picking up the thread. "Relationships take work, whether you're in the same room or on opposite sides of the world. But if you're both willing to put in that work, to fight for what you have? Then distance is just a minor inconvenience."

Lily stared at them, her expression gradually smoothing out. "You're right," she said at last, sitting up a little straighter, her smile wobbling but genuine. "We've been through too much to let a little thing like distance come between us now."

CHAPTER ELEVEN

OLIVIA

"*A*nd where exactly are you taking me this time?"

"It's a surprise." Lewis's eyes twinkled with mischief as he shut my door.

I shook my head as he rounded the car. Anderson sat in the driver's seat, his body rigid as he watched him. Something told me Lewis had begged him to stay in the car. The only question was why he had agreed when it obviously made him uncomfortable.

I leaned forward, intending to ask the bodyguard exactly that but the other door opened and Lewis slid in. Settling back in my seat, I let it go. For now.

"I could be the kind of girl who hates surprises, you know."

"Are you?" His brows rose, tone dripping with disbelief.

"No, but you didn't know that."

He chuckled. "Would you think less of me if I admitted that I'd still try to surprise you even if you hated them?"

I could never but I didn't say that. I zipped my lips and left him to wonder while Anderson took off into traffic. Amused,

Lewis leaned forward and picked up two takeaway cups that had been waiting in the central console.

"Wasn't sure how you took your coffee, so…" He grinned, holding up the two steaming cups. "I got one with enough cream and sugar to rot your teeth, and one black."

"I'll take the cavity-inducer, thanks."

As I reached for the cup, our fingers brushed, electricity zinging up my arm. From the way Lewis's breath hitched, I knew he felt it too.

We stayed like that for a charged moment, eyes locked, the air humming with possibility and a little bit of regret.

Why did I insist he go back to his own hotel room last night?

For twenty minutes, we sipped our coffees and made small talk while his bodyguard wound through early morning LA traffic and up into the Hollywood Hills. Lewis hummed along to the indie rock playing softly on the stereo, his fingers tapping the door handle. I watched him, a smile tugging at my lips at this relaxed, playful side of the rock star.

Finally, we pulled into a small, nearly hidden parking lot nestled among the trees. Anderson shut the car off and climbed out, his eagle eyes already scanning our surroundings.

"We're here." Lewis threw his door open. "Ready to see the best view in all of Los Angeles?"

"Is that meant to be a hint for what we're doing?"

"Maybe." He hopped out and rounded the car.

I followed at a much slower pace, breathing in the fresh, piney air. "Oh, are we hiking?"

"Maybe," he said again as he grabbed a backpack and cooler from the trunk.

"I don't know what you think you're playing at, but it's pretty obvious right now so just spill it."

"Fine." He slung the pack over his shoulders, handing me a water bottle from the cooler. "Not just any hike. I'm taking you to my favourite spot in all of LA. A place to get away from it all."

Well, colour me intrigued. My mind raced with possibilities.

A secluded beach? A hidden waterfall? Some celebrity-only hideaway? Whatever it was, the fact that he wanted to share it with me launched butterflies in my belly.

We set off up a less-travelled path, Anderson trailing a discreet distance behind. It was narrow and winding, hemmed in by fragrant pines and sprawling oaks. We walked in comfortable silence for a bit, just soaking in nature and each other's presence. Every so often, Lewis would point out a particularly interesting bird or plant, his eyes alight with boyish enthusiasm.

"You sure know a lot about the local wildlife," I teased as he identified a California scrub-jay flitting through the branches.

He ducked his head, a touch of pink tinging his cheeks. "Ah, that's all Mam's doing. She's mad for birds, was always dragging me and my sister out on nature walks as kids. Guess some of it stuck."

I smiled, charmed by this glimpse into his childhood. "That sounds really nice, actually. All my mom's dragging was to church potlucks and bake sales."

"Ooh, I've heard about those." Lewis rubbed his belly appreciatively. "They always look so delicious on TV."

I pulled a face. "I don't know about that but it's like a cure all to some of the people in my town."

He chuckled. "The miracle of casseroles."

I snorted, bumping him with my shoulder. "More like the miracle of Cool Whip and canned cream-of-whatever soup. It was like a competition to see who could come up with the most outlandish combination of processed ingredients."

"Okay, I retract my earlier statement." Lewis shook his head, his eyes sparkling with mirth. "That sounds like a horror show. Bet those church ladies could give Gordon Ramsay a run for his money in the 'what the hell is that' department."

"You're not wrong," I said, giggling. "But you know, for all the questionable food choices, those potlucks were the heart of our little community. Everyone coming together, sharing what they had, catching up on each other's lives. It was nice. Comforting, in its own way."

"I can understand that." Lewis nodded, a nostalgic note creeping into his voice. "Reminds me a bit of my mam's Sunday roasts back home. Gave us a chance to just be a family, you know?"

We continued on, the conversation flowing easily between us, punctuated by the crunch of leaves beneath our feet and the occasional bird call. The steep incline of the trail left me slightly breathless, but I welcomed the burn in my muscles.

"Did you always know you wanted to do this?"

"What? Hike with you?"

I rolled my eyes. "You know exactly what I mean."

"Yeah, I do." He grinned. "But teasing you is entertaining. You either give as good as you get, or your cheeks turn this pretty pink colour and you get this sheepish…"

"Alright, no need for that." I slapped his arm, my face burning. "Just answer the question."

He laughed but quickly sobered as his smile fell away. "Honestly, I can't remember." He adjusted the pack, looking anywhere but at me. He kicked a pebble, watching it skitter down the path. "I used to hole up in my room for hours, teaching myself chords, writing these godawful angsty teenage lyrics."

A self-deprecating chuckle escaped him. His words made me smile, but there was something beneath the surface, an edge of melancholy that didn't belong.

"I think we've all got a few cringeworthy notebooks hidden away. It's like a rite of passage for aspiring musicians."

His lips twisted before he muttered a barely audible "God, I hope no one ever finds mine. I'd never live it down."

He took a deep breath and the tension melted from him.

"Anyway, enough about me." He reached for my hand and threaded our fingers together. "I want to hear more about your delinquent childhood."

I gasped. "I was no such thing."

"Oh, so the watermelon theft was a one off?" He smirked

when I stared at him speechless and unable to deny it. "I thought not. What else did you do?"

I sighed. "Fine, but if any of this gets back to my mother..." I glared at him, trying to be threatening and absolutely failing. "Fourth of July weekend, I was... eight I think, Cooper decided—"

"Cooper again. Did it never occur to you that your cousin was trouble?"

I chuckled. "Every single time I got caught."

"And you didn't stop spending time with him?"

I shrugged. "He was fun until we got caught."

Lewis shook his head.

"Do you want to hear the rest or are you going to keep interrupting me?"

He mimed zipping his lips.

"So it's Fourth of July, and Cooper decided it would be a brilliant idea to set off fireworks from the top of my granddaddy's tool shed."

"Oh no," Lewis groaned, dragging a hand across his face. "I think I see where this is going."

"Do you?" My brows rose. He nodded. "You figured he'd set the roof on fire just from the mention of fireworks?"

He stared at me, shock widening his eyes. "I was expecting a different casualty. Jesus."

"Not so predictable, am I?" I smirked.

Lewis shook his head. "What happened after he set the roof on fire?"

"Why, Granddaddy came running out of the house, hollering and cussing up a storm, of course. Poor Cooper just about pissed himself." I grinned. "We all ended up sitting on the porch, drinking my mama's sweet tea and watching the rest of the fireworks over the lake. It's one of my favourite memories. The telling off and all."

"That sounds really nice." A wistful note entered his voice and he squeezed my hand. "The kind of memory that sticks with you."

Yes, it is.

They also had a habit of sneaking up on me in my low moments, and there had been many over the years, making me forget exactly why I'd been so desperate to leave home. Of course, things always looked brighter the next day, but that didn't stop the occasional pang of homesickness from taking root in my chest.

We turned a corner and the trail opened up to reveal a semi flat clearing. My breath caught, and not because we finally stopped and I could suck in some much needed air. No, nothing could have prepared me for the stunning panoramic view of the city below.

"It's incredible," I murmured. "Like we're on top of the world." Or the last people left on earth.

"That might be part of why I love it up here." He shook his head sheepishly and placed the cooler on the ground.

He whipped a blanket out of his backpack and placed it on the grass while I stared at him in something akin to shock.

"What?" he asked when he caught me staring.

"Do this a lot, do you?"

He shrugged. "Every month or so."

He started unpacking the cooler like it was perfectly normal, spreading out an impressive array of cheeses, fruit, crackers and wine. When it was all done, he sat and stared up at me expectantly.

"You really went all out," I marvelled, settling down beside him.

He shrugged, pouring the wine into plastic cups. "Well, I figured if I was going to drag you up a mountain, the least I could do was provide a decent spread."

I tapped my cup against his. "It's perfect. All of it."

For a while, we just sat together, sipping our wine and enjoying the food, the view, and the simple pleasure of each other's company.

"This is…" I searched for the right words, "breathtaking."

"Worth the hike?"

"Absolutely." I turned to him. "But I have to ask, do you bring all the girls here?"

He chuckled. "I don't know who you think I am, Liv, but I'm really not the serial dater the press claim."

My brows climbed. "Is that so?"

"Yes."

"Then why are there all these rumours about—"

He sighed, the sound loud and frustrated. "Our manager thinks it hurts the band if we're not living up to the stereotypes."

I blinked. "What stereotypes would those be?"

"Somehow I think you know."

"Maybe I do." I shrugged, struggling to hold in my smile. "But then maybe I don't and you should consider it a warning."

"A warning?" He shook his head when I nodded. "The only warning you need is to stay away from Kevin, Carolina girl. If he can figure out a way to exploit you for the band's benefit, he will."

I'd been teasing, but Lewis's tone took such a serious turn that the desire to smile evaporated. "Do I want to ask for specifics?"

"Let's just say he's not above using people's personal lives as publicity fodder." Lewis's jaw clenched, a shadow crossing his face. "He once leaked photos of Alex stumbling out of a club, drunk off his ass, just to fuel the bad boy image. Didn't matter that Alex was going through a rough patch, grieving his grandmother's death. All Kevin saw was an opportunity."

Staring into his sad eyes, a ball of dread settled in my belly.

"You know, this is my favourite part of the job," Lewis said, his voice quiet as he gestured to our little oasis. "Not the picnics, though those are a perk. But the moments like this. Where we get to just... be. No crowds, no cameras. Just the music and the people who matter."

"Is that what I am? Someone who matters?"

The look he gave me could have melted glaciers. "Liv, you... Fuck. You matter so much. More than I even have words for."

Joy expanded inside of me, momentarily chasing away any

grain of doubt or concern. I reached out, lacing my fingers through his. "You matter to me too."

We smiled at each other, a little shyly. Then he took a deep breath, as if steeling himself.

Then his gaze returned to the view, a faraway look settling in his hazel eyes. He fiddled with the stem of his cup, looking for all the world like he was wrestling with something big.

"You okay?"

"Yeah, I just…" He blew out a breath, nodding. "Do you ever feel like…" He paused, searching for the words. "Like you're living a dream, but you're terrified you'll wake up any second?"

"All the time. Especially since Lily offered me this tour. It's like I'm waiting for the other shoe to drop, you know?"

"Exactly." He ran a hand through his hair. "I keep thinking, what if I screw it up? What if I let everyone down? The band, the fans…" His gaze met mine, vulnerable and raw. "You."

I shuffled towards him on the blanket.

Our thighs pressed together, the heat of his body seeping into mine. I pried his fist open to thread our fingers together. He smiled at the contact.

"Hey," I said softly, squeezing his hand. "You could never let me or the band down. You're an incredible musician. An incredible person."

His eyes searched mine. "Yeah?"

"Yeah." I put every ounce of conviction I possessed into the single word. "We're all scared sometimes. It's part of the journey. But I've seen you on stage, I've heard your songs. You were born for this."

A slow smile spread across his face, gratitude and affection warring in his eyes. "How do you do that? Make everything seem brighter?"

I shrugged, a blush heating my cheeks. "It's a gift."

He laughed, the sound warm and rich.

We lapsed into a comfortable silence, our gazes drawn back to the sprawling city below. I leaned into him, resting my head on his shoulder. He pressed a soft kiss to my hair, the simple gesture sending a flutter through my belly.

"Thank you," he murmured after a moment. "For listening. For understanding."

"Always." I meant it with every fibre of my being. "You know, you're not alone in this," I said after a beat, tracing patterns on his knee with my free hand. "The fear, the doubts... I feel them too. Wondering if I'm good enough, if I deserve to be here."

With a finger beneath my chin, he tipped my head back, staring down at me, his brow furrowed. "Of course you deserve to be here. You're phenomenal."

I ducked my head, breaking his grip, a small smile tugging at my lips. "I'm trying to believe that. But it's hard sometimes, you know? To quiet that little voice in the back of your head that whispers 'you're an imposter'."

"I know that voice well. But I also know it lies." He tilted my chin up again, forcing me to meet his gaze. "You, Liv Monroe, are a force to be reckoned with. And I can't wait for the world to see it."

A lump of emotion caught in my throat. "When I'm with you, I feel like I can take on anything."

"Good." He grinned, pressing a quick kiss to my nose. "Because I plan on being there every step of the way, cheering you on."

We settled back into easy conversation, swapping stories and dreams. Lewis told me more about his early days with the band, the dive bars and cramped vans, the thrill of hearing their song on the radio for the first time.

"You know, I... I don't usually talk about my music like that. With such..." I paused, searching for the right word.

"Passion?"

"Vulnerability," I corrected. "Outside, my mama and my best friend, folks back home, they don't really get it. This drive, this need, to make something that touches people."

Lewis nodded, understanding etched into every line of his

face. "It's like breathing. Like your whole heart, poured out in notes and words."

"Yes," I breathed, the single syllable imbued with gratitude and relief. "Yes, that's it exactly."

"Well, then." He brought our joined hands to his lips, ghosting a kiss across my knuckles. "Seems to me this is your time to shine, songbird. To touch those people. To change lives with that voice of yours."

A rush of fear and excitement swirled in my gut at the thought. "God, I hope so. I hope I'm ready."

"You are," he said with bedrock conviction. "And I'll be right there beside you. Your own proud peacock."

Laughter bubbled up, bright and cleansing. "I like the sound of that."

"What about your family?" Lewis asked after a beat, his thumb stroking the back of my hand. "Tell me about them."

I leaned back on my free hand, thinking of home. "Well, it's just been me, Dustin and my mama for as long as I can remember. She's a force of nature. Worked two jobs to support us and put me through music lessons."

Lewis smiled. "Sounds like a hell of a woman."

"She is," I agreed, pride swelling in my chest. "She's my rock. Never let me give up on my dreams."

"And the rest of your family?"

I smiled, thinking of my tight-knit community back in Jasmine Bay. The friends who might as well be family. "It's a small town, so everyone's all up in each other's business. But they show up for you, you know? Potlucks, block parties, cheering way too loud at my high school talent shows." A chuckle escaped my lips at the vivid memory of Aunt Nancy's ear-splitting whistles from the front row.

Lewis grinned. "Sounds like a nice place to grow up."

"It was. Is." I sighed. "Sometimes I worry about losing touch with that, though. My roots. With all the craziness of this new life."

"Hey." Lewis squeezed my hand. "That's a part of you, Liv.

It's in the twang of your voice, the soul in your songs, the kindness in your heart. Nothing can change that."

In that moment, staring into his eyes, I couldn't have turned away even if I'd wanted to. He drew me like a magnet, sparking a bond stronger than music, deeper than attraction. If I believed in soulmates, he would be it.

Slowly, Lewis reached out, tucking a windblown strand of hair behind my ear. His fingers lingered, tracing the curve of my cheek. He leaned closer, gaze dropping to my lips. We'd done this a million times now, but still my breath hitched, heartbeat thundering in my ears.

Just as I let my eyes flutter shut, a strange whirring sound filled the air, growing rapidly louder.

My eyes flew open as Lewis jerked back, eyebrows knitted, head swivelling to locate the source. "What the…"

Lewis stiffened as a helicopter with the local news station's logo crested the treetops, its bulky cameras pointed directly at us.

"Shit," he bit out, his jaw clenched tight.

The sudden intrusion jarred me from the intimate moment. I instinctively pressed closer to Lewis.

"What's happening? Why are they here?" I had to shout to be heard over the noise.

Lewis's arm tightened around me, his body tense. He didn't answer, instead he hauled me flush against his chest, one hand cupping the back of my head to tuck my face into his neck. I squeaked in surprise, my hands braced against the solid wall of his chest, his pine and spice scent enveloping me.

His body tensed as the chopper passed over us, the rumble of its blades filling the air. We stayed frozen, hardly daring to breathe, for a long, weighted minute.

Finally, the whirring began to recede, the aircraft moving off. Lewis remained rigid for a few beats longer before loosening his hold with a shaky exhale.

"I'm sorry about that," he whispered into my hair. "Bloody vultures."

"Does that… happen a lot?"

He sighed, scrubbing a hand over his face. "More than I'd like. The price of fame, or so they say."

"What'll happen if they got a shot?"

"It'll be sold to every tabloid in existence, and their above-the-fold story tomorrow will be about Lewis Davies's latest woman."

I bit my lip, an icy shard of dread lodging in my belly. Would that have been a bad thing?

"Have you… have you told your bandmates? About us?"

He shook his head. "Not yet. I know those wankers. They're the worst at keeping secrets."

A mischievous grin spread across his face. "Plus, it's way more fun watching them try to figure it out."

CHAPTER TWELVE

LEWIS

"*W*hat's the rush?" Tom asked as I started packing up my stuff with a singular focus. "We were going to hit up the brewery one last time before we left, remember?"

With just five days to go until the opening show, we'd been hitting it hard, nailing down every song. Every day between the hours of eleven and six we holed up inside this room, running the set list front to back and back to front until not even one note escaped us. Then Lily would come in after a gruelling session with the dancers and we'd run it again.

Dread and excitement warred inside of me. I'd never dreaded going on tour before.

"Can't," I said, biting back my smile as I picked up my guitar case. I shot him an apologetic smile. "Something came up."

The same thing that came up almost every night. Liv.

Alex chuckled. "I think I know what something looks like."

He leaned against an amp, sweat shining on his skin.

"So do I." Andy crossed his arms and smirked at me. "And it has pretty green eyes and the voice of an angel."

"Funny you're seeing romance everywhere, Andy." I grinned at him, a tiny amount of guilt hitting me for the bus I was about to throw him under. "Wouldn't have anything to do with that date you went on before we left Wales, would it?"

Alex and Tom turned to him, their brows risen and shit-eating grins spreading across their faces.

"Have you been holding out on us, boyo?" Alex asked, prowling towards him.

Andy paled and started backing away. I didn't stick around to find out what lie he'd make up. He absolutely wouldn't admit to Alex's face that he'd taken his baby sister out and hadn't stopped texting her since we'd left LA.

*A*n hour and a half later, I helped Liv into the SUV with Anderson in the front seat.

"Should I bother asking where we're going?" Liv asked.

I shook my head at her, smiling as she rolled her eyes.

"Right, that would spoil the surprise."

"You're getting it, Carolina girl."

I shut her door, cutting off her chuckle and rounded the car. Normally, Anderson would do all of this, but I didn't want to be *that* person with Liv. We had so little time together before the tour, and I needed her to see me beneath the rock star, before the clamouring fans, reporters and constant paparazzi.

"How about a tiny hint?" Liv asked when I slid into my seat. She leaned across the centre seat, batting her lashes at me as her face hovered kissably close.

"Nice try, cariad." I pressed a soft, chaste kiss to her lips and sat back, grinning. "You're going to love it. Pretty sure I've outdone myself this time."

She sat back, shaking her head. "That would be hard to do at this point."

"Just you wait and see." I took her hand, threading our fingers together while I savoured this warm and fuzzy feeling in my chest.

Twenty minutes later, we stood on a rooftop, in our own private dining area. It was like stumbling into a dream, a hidden slice of Southern charm carved out of the LA concrete. Pergolas dripped with twinkling lights, framing intimate seating areas with breathtaking views of the city below.

The city lights sparkled, the views almost unrestricted from our corner table. A partition stood between us, wrapped in sheer drapes that fluttered in the warm breeze. It protected us from the eyes and ears of the rest of the restaurant.

"What do you think?" I asked, tugging Liv beneath my shoulder and squeezing her against me.

"Is that a magnolia tree?" Awe filled her voice.

"We're so close to the tour kick off, I wanted to do something that would help with your homesickness."

She glanced up at me, her vibrant green eyes shimmering with curiosity and something akin to anticipation.

"Lewis, you sly dog!" Sawyer Buchanan said as he stepped onto the patio, his arms flung wide and his smile contagious. He engulfed me in a bear hug, slapping my back. "'Bout time you put in an appearance. We opened weeks ago!"

Sawyer was a bear of a man, all broad shoulders and towering height that must have made manoeuvring around a kitchen galley hard. His dark hair was swept back in a ponytail that looked odd against his chef's whites.

I winced, pulling back. "Sorry, man. The tour prep has taken a lot."

"I can imagine, but I've got my ticket and I'm looking forward to the show so I guess I can't hold it against you."

I chuckled. "Thanks. And I appreciate you making this happen last minute."

"No need to thank me. You're welcome any time." Sawyer waved his hand, brushing the whole thing aside as his attention zeroed in on Liv. "And who might this sweet thing be?"

"Olivia Monroe." She stepped forward, offering her hand. He shook her hand with a calculating glint in his eyes. "And who are you to Lewis?" Sawyer asked, eying me.

Liv glanced at me, biting her lip with clear uncertainty.

"None of that," he said, his blue eyes narrowing on us. "My mouth is like a steel trap. Nothing's getting out and Lewis here knows it."

I sighed. "It's new, Sawyer. Don't pressure us like that."

He grinned. "Not to worry, you just told me more than you know." Then his attention returned to Liv. "Sawyer Buchanan. Welcome to Whiskey and Lace. I consider this place my Southern fusion food baby."

"A Michelin star food baby."

"Too right." Sawyer beamed. "Delighted to be at your beck and call tonight. I hope you'll enjoy my little slice of home."

Liv glanced around again, taking all the intricate details in. "It's lovely."

"That it is." Sawyer ushered us across the patio with a grin. "Now, let's get this party started, shall we? Got a little surprise cooking up just for y'all."

I pulled out Liv's chair, my fingers grazing the nape of her neck as she sat. She shivered and I bit back a smile, taking my own seat across from her. A waiter poured the wine, a rich Cabernet that painted Liv's mouth in shades of temptation.

"To the woman who's already turning my world upside down," I toasted, raising my glass.

She ducked her head, peeking up at me through her lashes. "Flatterer." But she bumped her glass against mine all the same, taking a sip that stained her lips even darker.

The urge to lean across the table and chase that wine with my tongue hit like a freight train. I gripped the stem of my glass a little tighter, forcing myself to focus on the waitstaff streaming onto the patio, arms laden with covered dishes.

"Starting off with a taste of my Louisiana roots," he announced, placing a shallow bowl in front of each of us. "Shrimp and grits, kicked up with Cajun spice and love."

The scent of garlic and cayenne wafted up, making my mouth water. But it was the look of pure bliss on Liv's face as she took her first bite that really did me in.

Her eyes fluttered closed as she inhaled deeply.

"My lord, it smells just like home." Her accent thickened, voice wavering slightly.

I reached across the table, covering her hand with mine. "Figured I couldn't bring you back to South Carolina for a couple of months, but I could bring a little southern to you."

"You figured right." She squeezed my hand. "I didn't realise how homesick I'd been. It's silly, I know, what with the tour starting so soon…"

"It's not silly at all." I rubbed my thumb over her knuckles soothingly. "This is a big change, a big step. It's okay to feel overwhelmed or out of sorts."

"You're too sweet." She dabbed at her eyes. "Goodness, ignore me being all weepy. Let's dig in before this feast gets cold!"

And so we did, with Anderson, ever the discreet guardian, keeping a watchful eye from a distance. My lips curled as the waiters set up another table for him and Sawyer forced him to sit. If you were in his space, you were eating, and refusing was a grave insult he wouldn't forget.

"Now aren't you glad you trust me to surprise you?" I reached out, tucking a stray curl behind her ear. My fingertips grazed the petal-soft skin of her cheek.

"Yes. Not even in my wildest dreams could I have imagined the last week and a half with you." She leaned into my touch, her lips curving into a smile that could outshine the sun. "It's perfect. Absolutely perfect."

Pride and affection burned through my chest as I watched her savour each bite. I'd never met someone who wore their heart so openly, who embraced every experience with such unbridled joy. It was magnetic, intoxicating in a way I'd never encountered before.

"Damn, Buchanan," I said around my own mouthful, the

flavours exploding on my tongue. "If the music thing doesn't work out, I might just have to steal you away to the UK. Open up a Southern joint in Cardiff, yeah?"

Sawyer laughed as he stopped by our table with another dish. "Not a chance, Davies. Gonna take more than your wild ideas to transplant me."

Liv giggled, swiping a hunk of bread through the rich, velvety roux. "Can't blame him for trying though. You've got a gift, Sawyer."

"Well, I do declare, Miss Olivia," Sawyer drawled, pressing a hand to his chest. "You sure do know how to charm a fella."

"Don't let him fool you," I stage-whispered to Liv. "This one's got charm for days. Used to sweet talk his way out of all sorts of trouble before he landed himself a Michelin star."

He just shook his head and left us to our meals without a comment.

"I think this is on a par with Mama Jo's cooking back home." Liv took another bite and groaned. "She's the owner of the diner I used to work at. It's one of my first stops whenever I go back to Jasmine Bay."

"The more you talk about home, the more I want to see it for myself." I reached across the table, tangling my fingers with hers.

She smiled, soft and sweet, giving my hand a squeeze. "Guess we'll just have to go rogue when we get to Savannah."

"I'd like that," I murmured, rubbing my thumb across her knuckles. "I'd like that a lot."

We laughed and joked our way through the first course, the easy flow of conversation warming me more than the food or the wine ever could.

We both sipped, letting the rich wine linger on our tongues. When Sawyer reappeared to whisk away our empty bowls, I caught his eye, mouthing a silent "thank you." He simply winked, disappearing back into the shadows with a knowing grin.

I turned back to Liv, drinking in the way the soft twinkle of the lights played across her skin, the curl of her lips as she smiled at me over the rim of her glass. Every cell in my body strained towards her, pulled by a force I couldn't begin to understand. All I knew was I'd never wanted anyone the way I wanted her—mind, body, and soul.

Leaning across the table, I brushed a smear of wine from the corner of her mouth. Her breath hitched, eyes darkening as my thumb grazed her bottom lip. "Liv, I—"

"Ahem."

We sprang apart like teenagers caught necking.

A startled laugh burst from Liv's throat. "Lord almighty, I'm gonna put a bell on that man."

I chuckled, running a hand through my hair as I tried to gather my scattered thoughts. "Probably wise."

"Hate to interrupt," he drawled, a shit-eating grin spread across his face. He absolutely enjoyed interrupting. "But it's time for your next course." Sawyer set the plates piled high with golden fried chicken, fluffy buttermilk biscuits, and glistening collard greens. "Best hop to it, lovebirds. Night's still young, and the best is yet to come."

"Good Lord, Sawyer," Liv exclaimed, eyeing the spread. "You trying to fatten us up?"

He chuckled, laying a hand over his heart. "Darlin', you know we show our love through food in the South. And I've got a whole lot of love for y'all tonight."

I snorted, picking up a drumstick. "You're one smooth bastard, you know that?"

"Part of my charm." He topped off our wine once more before he sauntered off, whistling tunelessly all the way.

The chicken was crisp and juicy, the seasoning a perfect balance of salty and spicy. I let out an appreciative moan, licking the grease from my fingers.

"Okay, I take it back. You're officially my favourite American, Sawyer!"

"Hey now!" Liv cried in mock outrage. "And what am I, chopped liver?"

I grinned, leaning across the table to swipe a smear of butter from the corner of her mouth. "Oh, you're in a category all your own. Can't even compare."

She blushed, her tongue darting out to wet her lips. I tracked the movement, heat pulsing low in my belly. Christ, the things this woman did to me without even trying.

"Sorry I'm late." A black-haired woman rushed through the patio doors, breathing hard. "I swear no matter how long I live in LA, I will never get used to the traffic."

CHAPTER THIRTEEN

OLIVIA

"*N*o problem, Suze. Glad you could make it," Lewis said, his tone open and friendly. Like he knew her. "We only just finished the second course, so your timing is actually perfect."

Timing for what?

"Oh that's a relief." She gestured to the wide open patio behind us. "Do you want to get started now?"

She was all smiles even though her cheeks were flushed, and her raven hair looked slightly frazzled despite being pulled back into a sleek ponytail. Her clothes gave me pause. Whiskey and Lace didn't strike me as the denim shorts, chequered shirts and cowboys boots sort of place.

"I'm going to be awful at it, but sure." Lewis pushed back his chair and stood, his gaze fixed on me, a little glint there making it perfectly clear that he relished my bewilderment.

Mischief danced in his eyes, a playful smirk tugging at the corners of his mouth. My heart did a funny little flip in my chest. How was it possible to want to smack him and kiss him senseless at the same time?

"Ready?" He held out his hand to me.

"I'd need to know what's happening to be ready for it."

He chuckled and wiggled his hand. "You're not going to find out if you stay there. Or did you suddenly lose your reckless streak?"

"I'm not reckless."

His brows climbed, calling me a liar, and okay, so maybe I'd given him good reason.

I gave in because my curiosity was a vicious bitch. It had nothing at all to do with him goading me. Nothing.

"Liv meet Suze." Lewis gestured between us with a grin that could power the whole damn city. "She's here for your next surprise."

I raised an eyebrow. "Another one? You're spoiling me rotten, sug."

"Oh honey, I've known this one for years and there's nothing he loves more than surprising and/or shocking someone. If you haven't put your foot down yet, I reckon he's just getting started." Suze laughed. "You ready to kick up your heels?"

I stared at her. Was she serious?

"A dance lesson? Here?"

"Not just any dance lesson." He tugged me into his side. "Line dancing. Did you think I'd bring you to a Southern restaurant and end the night there?"

I mean, yes?

"I can't believe you…" I tipped my head back, smiling up at him. "You've truly outdone yourself this time, rock star. Thank you."

"I'd do anything for you, cariad."

Tears burned the back of my throat, happy tears, over-whelmed tears. I blinked them back, determined not to turn into a blubbering mess.

But god, it was a near thing.

Every thoughtful gesture, every sweet word out of his

mouth… it chipped away at the walls I'd built, the armour I wore to protect my heart.

He had a way of making me feel cherished, adored. Like I was the only woman in the world, the only one that mattered.

It was heady and frightening and exhilarating, and another brick fell from the wall, bringing me closer to falling head over heels in love with him.

The band in the section beyond the partition switched gears, the first twanging notes of a familiar tune filling the air.

I swallowed hard, trying to find my voice. "Lewis, I…"

But before I could put my tangled emotions into words, Suze clapped her hands, her face alight with infectious enthusiasm.

"Alright, y'all, let's start with a basic grapevine! Lewis, you just watch Olivia and follow along." She winked at him. "She'll keep you on the straight and narrow."

My body responded on instinct, falling into step with practised ease. I grinned, watching Lewis try to mimic my movements, his brow furrowed in concentration.

"Come on, rock star," I teased, my boots scuffing against the polished wood. "Don't tell me that musical brain of yours can't keep up with a little old country two-step."

He laughed, stumbling slightly as he tried to match my grapevine. "I'm man enough to admit when I'm outclassed. You've got moves I can only dream of."

I preened a little at the compliment, letting the music flow through me as I spun and stepped in perfect time. It felt like coming home, the familiar rhythm settling into my bones and chasing away the last of my nerves.

"That's it, Olivia! You're a natural." Suze clapped along, her eyes bright with approval.

Suze called for a break and Lewis stopped moving with a grateful sigh.

"How'd you get so good at this?" he asked. "Been holding out on me, Carolina girl?"

"I've been line dancing since I could walk. It's in my blood."

Even with Suze calling a break, the live band still played on, and my feet would not stop moving. Lewis watched me with a bemused smile. "Mama used to say I came out of the womb already knowing the electric slide."

He chuckled, low and warm. "Why am I not surprised?"

It wasn't like I'd been out of Nashville long enough to miss it, but getting to show off my skills like this, to let loose and just enjoy the simple pleasure of moving to the music, it would never get old.

"Why did you pick line dancing if you couldn't do it?"

"I'm not really a dancer, so the type wouldn't have mattered, but…" A tiny flush crept across his cheeks. "I knew it would make you happy so…" He shrugged and stole another piece of my heart with ease.

"No one's ever done something like this for me before."

"Then you've been dating the wrong kind of men, songbird."

Understatement of the century.

I huffed out a laugh. "Starting to think that might be the case, yes."

He cupped my face in his hands, his thumbs sweeping over my cheekbones with a tenderness that made me ache. "Get used to it. Because I plan on spending a long, long time showing you exactly how you deserve to be treated."

The sincerity in his voice, the intensity of his gaze… it stole the air from my lungs and set my blood on fire. I wanted to kiss him, to pour everything I was feeling into the press of my lips against his. But Suze's voice cut through the charged moment, pulling us back to the present.

"Alright! Break's over. Let's see if we can't get Lewis up to speed."

I grinned, slightly dazed as I stepped back and held out my hand. "You heard the lady, rock star. Time to show us what you've got."

He took my hand, lacing our fingers together. "Pretty sure we both know you've got me beat in the dancing department. But I'll keep trying if you're willing to be patient with me."

"Always," I promised, something warm and wonderful unfurling in my chest. "We'll take it one step at a time."

And Lord almighty, did we ever. As Suze called out the steps and the music played on, I guided Lewis through the patterns, our laughter mingling with the twang of the steel guitar. He stumbled, his brow creased in concentration as he tried to match my movements. But he never gave up, never stopped trying. And every time he got it right, the brilliant smile that lit up his face took my breath away.

"Look at you go!" I cheered as he nailed a particularly tricky turn. "Reckon you'll be putting me to shame in no time."

"Not bloody likely," he scoffed. "Pretty sure you've got a monopoly on talent in this relationship."

I raised an eyebrow, fighting back a grin. "Oh, is that so? Because last I checked, you're the one with the Grammy. Multiple Grammys, actually."

"Yes, but you're in a league of your own." He shook his head, his expression soft and serious. "Watching you on that stage, hearing your voice... it's like nothing I've ever experienced. You've got a gift, songbird. One that puts the rest of us to shame."

"You really mean that, don't you?" I asked, my voice barely above a whisper.

"With every fibre of my being." He brushed a kiss over my forehead. "Liv, you're extraordinary. In every possible way. And I feel like the luckiest bastard alive every time I get to witness it."

A shaky laugh bubbled up my throat, half sob and half pure, unadulterated joy. "Funny. Because I was just thinking the same thing about you."

He grinned, the boyish, lopsided smile that never failed to melt me into a puddle. "Guess we'll just have to agree to disagree on who the lucky one is, then."

"Guess so."

For half an hour, we moved together, going through all the sequences, stopping and starting until Lewis got it. Our boots scuffed against the polished wood while our laughter mingled with the music and chatter of the other patrons on the other side of the partition.

How was I supposed to hold onto my heart when he kept pulling out all the stops for me? No way would I survive six months on tour without falling so hard I'd never find my way out.

If I'm not careful, I might just start believing in fairy tales again.

Lost in my thoughts, I stumbled, my boot catching on the smooth wood. But before I could even let out a yelp of surprise, Lewis's arms wrapped around me, saving me from an embarrassing tumble. He straightened, taking me with him, his arms tightening around me as he held me against his chest.

"You alright?"

I stared into his eyes, my heart doing a little two-step of its own at the concern in his hazel gaze. "Yeah, I'm… I'm fine. Just got a little lost in my head for a second."

His brow furrowed, his thumb rubbing soothing circles on my hip. "Anything you want to talk about?"

Oh, sugar, if you only knew.

My gaze dropped to his lips. They were so close, just a whisper away, and part of me wanted nothing more than to close the distance and sink into him… while distracting him from his question.

But instead, I took a deep breath and let the truth spill out. "I was just thinking… about how different you are. From anyone I've ever met."

His breath hitched, his eyes darkening with an intensity that made my knees weak. "Different how?"

"In every way that matters," I whispered, my fingers curling into the fabric of his shirt. "You're kind and generous, patient and understanding. You make me feel seen, Lewis. Really, truly seen. Like I don't have to hide or pretend or be anything other than exactly who I am."

"Liv…" His voice was rough, choked with emotion. "That's all I want, cariad. For you to be yourself, always. Because the real you? She's bloody brilliant. And I feel like the luckiest man in the world every time I get to see her shine."

How does he always know just what to say to turn my insides to molasses?

I rose up on my toes, my lips parting, needing to taste him, to show him what his words meant to me. But before I could close the distance, a pointed cough sounded from behind us.

"Hate to interrupt, lovebirds, but I come bearing one last taste of Southern sweetness," Sawyer drawled, a knowing grin on his face as he lifted the silver dome with a flourish.

I groaned, dropping my forehead against Lewis's shoulder. "A bell. He needs a bell."

Lewis chuckled, the sound rumbling through me like distant thunder. "I'll get right on that."

Sawyer walked over to our table and placed the dome down. He hovered, waiting with a slightly impatient pinch to his lips for us to join him. Unfortunately for him, Suze clapped her hands to get our attention.

"Alright, y'all, this looks like a mighty fine place to call it a night. Liv, you aced it of course. Lewis, keep practising. I expect you to be a pro by the time you get back."

"Yeah, right." He shook his head but then released me and tugged her into a hug. "I can't thank you enough for coming out on such short notice. I owe you one."

She slapped him on the back and stepped away, her eyes twinkling. "Hush now, it was my pleasure. You just make sure you treat this one right, ya hear? She's a keeper."

"Don't I know it." He wrapped his arm around my waist again, holding me close as he pressed a kiss to my temple. "She's the best thing that's ever happened to me."

He said it so easily, so matter-of-factly. Like it was a given, a universal truth.

How could he be so sure? We'd only known each other for a handful of weeks, had only been together for a fraction of that.

But god, it felt right. It felt real, and true, and meant to be.

Suze said goodnight and slipped away, leaving us alone on

the candlelit rooftop. We joined Sawyer at our table and sank back into our seats. When he had all of our attention, he removed the cover with a flourish.

If he'd said he was hiding a deconstructed cobbler I would have been in my seat the instant he appeared.

Flaky bits of crust jutted up from a bed of Bourbon-soaked peaches and vanilla bean ice cream, a drizzle of caramel sauce tying it all together. It was nothing short of edible art. Too beautiful to destroy, but my mouth didn't care.

"Sawyer, honey, you've outdone yourself," I breathed, shaking my head in disbelief. "How did you even know…?"

The chef winked. "Let's just say a little birdie might've clued me in that you were craving a little sweet taste of home. And by little birdie, I mean this smitten fella over here." He nodded towards Lewis.

"Just when I think you can't possibly top yourself," I said to Lewis, my heart doing a giddy flip in my chest, "you go and pull something like this. A girl could get used to being spoiled within an inch of her life, you know."

He ducked his head, a boyish grin tugging at his lips. "Good thing I don't plan on stopping anytime soon, then. I want you to know, beyond a shadow of a doubt, just how special you are to me. Whatever it takes, for as long as you'll let me."

And Lord, if that wasn't a declaration, I didn't know what was.

I took a bite of the cobbler before my mouth could spit out all of my unprocessed feelings. The first burst of sweetness exploded on my tongue and I groaned. "Oh my lord, Sawyer. This is…" I shook my head, momentarily at a loss for words. "This is like a little slice of heaven right here."

Sawyer grinned, his chest puffing out with pride. "Don't. You're making me blush."

"I mean it," I said, pointing my spoon at him. "This might give Hattie a run for her money."

Lewis chuckled, his eyes warm as he watched me savour another bite. "High praise indeed."

"What's your secret?" I rested my chin on my upturned palm and grinned up at him.

"Oh no. I'll take my recipes to the grave."

"Fair." I laughed and took another toe curling bite. "Whatever it is, you've outdone yourself. I'm half-tempted to lick the plate clean."

"You just enjoy every last bite, darlin'. There's plenty more where that came from." With a final nod and a smile, Sawyer left us.

I dug into the cobbler with gusto, savouring each decadent mouthful. The peaches were perfectly tender, the bourbon adding a warm, smoky depth to their natural sweetness. And the ice cream, oh lord, the ice cream. Creamy and rich, flecked with fragrant vanilla bean, it melted into the warm pastry, creating a heavenly contrast of temperatures and textures.

I couldn't help the little noises of appreciation that escaped me as I ate, each bite sending me further into a state of blissful contentment.

Lewis watched me, his eyes dancing with amusement and affection. "Should I give you two a moment alone?" he teased.

I swatted at him playfully, my cheeks warming. "Hush, you. When something's this good, it deserves to be properly appreciated."

"I couldn't agree more," he murmured, but the way he was looking at me made it clear he wasn't talking about the cobbler.

My skin prickled with awareness. The air between us felt charged, electric, like a storm about to break.

I cleared my throat, trying to regain my equilibrium. "You're not going to try it?"

He blinked, seeming to come back to himself. "Oh, I am. I just…" He shook his head, a wry smile tugging at his lips. "I got a bit distracted by the view."

I ducked my head, warmth flooding my cheeks. "Sweet talker."

"Only for you, songbird. Only for you."

He dug into his own serving then, and our roles reversed. A

look of pure bliss crossed his face at the first taste. His eyes slid shut, a low hum of appreciation rumbling in his chest.

"Damn," he breathed after a moment, his eyes opening to meet mine. "That's... I don't even have words."

"Right?" I grinned, taking another bite. "Michelin Star well earned."

We polished off the rest of our cobblers in comfortable silence, punctuated by the occasional appreciative moan or contented sigh. By the time my spoon scraped the bottom of the dish, I was pleasantly full and slightly drowsy, the combination of good food, good wine, and even better company leaving me in a state of utter relaxation.

"I don't even know what to say. This whole night, everything you've done... it's like something out of a dream."

He reached across the table, tangling his fingers with mine. "It's no less than you deserve, Liv."

Lord, how does he do that? How does he make me feel like the only girl in the world with just a few simple words?

I swallowed hard, emotion rising in my throat. "I'm not sure I'm ever gonna be able to top this."

"You don't have to," he said softly, his thumb stroking over my knuckles. "Just being with you, seeing you smile... that's enough for me."

I had to face the facts. I was already gone. Hook, line, and sinker. Tumbling headfirst into something vast and terrifying and unutterably beautiful.

CHAPTER FOURTEEN

OLIVIA

*S*aturday morning hit far too fast.

It could have been any other day and other than my neatly packed suitcase, nothing had changed. I lay in bed with Lewis's furnace-like body wrapped around me, his leg hooked around mine, one arm beneath my pillow and the other draped over my waist. The steady in and out of his breathing, the tickle of it against my neck – this had become my normal. It kept me grounded, tethered me to the present.

But even as I soaked in his nearness, the jitters started to stir in my belly, growing with each tick of the clock.

The big day, the opening night of the tour, had arrived. My first real chance to show I deserved to be on that stage.

My chest tightened at the thought. I knew I belonged there, I knew I'd worked my ass off to earn the privilege, but still…

I was human, right?

Everyone got nervous.

It was acceptable to be a little jittery before something as huge as this.

I breathed deep, trying to calm the butterflies turning me inside out.

I mean I'd have thousands of eyes on me.

The concert capacity for the Rose Bowl is over sixty-two thousand people.

Oh hell.

Careful not to wake Lewis, I slipped out from under the covers. He mumbled something I couldn't make out but didn't open his eyes, his handsome face all peaceful in sleep.

I paced the room, forcing myself to breathe.

My gaze fell on my suitcase.

Why did you pack your yoga leggings? You'll want those on the bus. Or the cream sweater…

Groaning, I sank to my knees and started pulling everything out. Clearly, I needed to start again.

"Liv? What are you doing?" Lewis's sleepy voice floated over from the bed.

I kept my eyes on what I was doing, smoothing out a stubborn wrinkle in my favourite sundress. "Just packing. Go on back to sleep now."

For a couple of seconds, the only sound came from me unzipping packing cubes and I sank into it, blocking out everything else at last. Then the sheets rustled and the mattress creaked.

I blinked and his arms were around me, pulling me to my feet and holding me against him, his bare chest warm against my back.

"Didn't you finish packing last night?" His voice was gentle, but he couldn't hide the worry underneath.

"I did, but I just wanted to double check…" I squeezed the pair of jeans in my hands. Even to my own ears, it sounded weak as dishwater.

Lewis's grip tightened, turning me around to face him. He stared into my eyes, his hazel gaze still soft with sleep but searching. "Liv, what's really going on? Talk to me."

"I'm scared spitless. What if I freeze up out there? What if I forget the words to my own dang songs? Lord almighty, what if my costume goes all haywire and I flash the whole arena?" Once I got started, it was like I couldn't stop; all these fears just poured out of me. "And then it lives on forever on social media and no record label ever takes me seriously again…"

Lewis listened patiently, his thumbs rubbing soothing circles on my shoulders. When I finally ran out of steam, he cupped my face in his hands, his expression all earnest.

"Cariad," he sighed. "None of that's going to happen. You've got talent coming out of your ears, and you'll be a natural out there. Lily wouldn't have picked you if she didn't believe in you."

I wanted to believe him, I truly did. But the doubts just kept churning inside me. "But what if—"

He cut me off with a kiss, his lips warm and insistent against mine. For a moment, I forgot everything else, lost in the slide of his mouth, the teasing flick of his tongue. When he pulled back, we were both breathless.

"You're gonna be incredible," he murmured against my lips. "Let me show you."

His fingers made quick work of the buttons on my pyjama top. "Lewis, what in the Sam Hill are you…"

"Shh, just trust me." He dropped a kiss to my collarbone as he slid the top off my shoulders.

Even as desire started to hum through my veins, the nerves wouldn't quite let go. His hands skimmed down my sides as he tugged down my shorts.

Before I could ask him what he meant, I was naked as a jaybird, goosebumps rising on my skin. He took my hand and led me to the full-length mirror on the wall. Positioning me in front of it, he stood behind me, his hands settling on my hips.

I stared at our reflection—me, bare and vulnerable, him solid and sure at my back, fully clothed. "Lewis…"

"Shh. I'm proving a point here," he murmured, his breath hot against my ear. "That you're the perfect person to open for my band. That you can captivate an audience no matter what happens."

His right hand skimmed down my belly, coasting over my mound and continued lower. He parted my folds, and I sucked in a sharp breath.

"I want you to sing for me. Sing like you're up on that stage, pouring your heart out."

"What? But I—" My protest turned into a gasp as his fingers found my sweet spot, circling it with maddening slowness.

"Sing," he commanded, his voice low and rough with want. "And don't stop, no matter what I do."

No matter what he—

He tapped my clit when I didn't start, the jolt sending a spark of want through me.

"Oh," I breathed.

"Now, Liv."

And so, with my eyes locked on our reflection, I started to sing. The opening lines of my first song, the one I'd written late at night in my Nashville apartment, dreaming of moments like this.

But as Lewis's fingers worked their magic, stroking and teasing, I faltered. Quick as a wink, he stilled his hand.

"I didn't say you could stop," he said.

I took a shuddering breath and started again, my voice wavering but getting stronger with each note. And as I sang, Lewis matched his rhythm to mine, his fingers dancing over my most sensitive flesh.

It was a strange kind of duet, my voice and his touch, both building in intensity. Each time I stumbled over a lyric, he would pause, silently challenging me to keep going. And each time, I pushed through, the words pouring out of me with more and more confidence.

Higher and higher he drove me, stoking the fire inside me until I was singing as sure and clear as I hoped I would on the stage tonight, my hips rocking against his hand. The pleasure crested and broke over me, but still I sang, my voice ringing out as pure bliss shook my frame.

As the final note faded, I sagged back against Lewis, my chest heaving. He wrapped his arms around me, holding me up, anchoring me.

"Do you get it now?" he whispered, pressing a reverent kiss to my temple. "You're unstoppable. No matter what happens out there, you've got this."

And looking at our reflection, seeing the satisfied glow on my face, the pride shining in his eyes, I started to believe him. The nerves were still there, fluttering around the edges, but they felt manageable now. Like fuel, instead of a roadblock.

I could do this. I would do this.

Turning in his arms, I looped my arms around his neck, rising up on my tiptoes to brush my lips over his. "Thank you," I said. "For believing in me, even when I don't believe in myself."

"Always." He kissed me, soft and slow.

CHAPTER FIFTEEN

LEWIS

*F*or all her worries, Liv had the crowd eating out of the palm of her hand. She was crushing it. My foot tapped along to the music, my eyes glued to the live feed. The camera couldn't do her justice, but even through the digital filter, I was mesmerised.

Her voice soared over the screaming crowd; her smile was electric under the lights. My chest ached with a mix of pride, admiration, and more than a little desire.

And she thought she'd screw it up.

The mere idea was laughable to me. She had something special, and I intended to spend every moment I could reminding her of it until she believed me.

"Oi, Lewis!" Tom's voice cut through my reverie. "Quit drooling and come have a beer with us. We're meant to be celebrating and preparing, not mooning over a screen all night."

I rolled my eyes but tore my gaze away, grabbing the offered bottle.

Around me, the room buzzed with barely contained energy, the air thick with pre-show jitters and booze-fuelled laughter. Between my bandmates, the Rhiannon guys, their partners, and a couple of dancers, the green room was packed.

"How's she doing out there?" Andy asked, nodding towards the screen.

"Bloody brilliant." My voice deepened, giving away far too much emotion. "She's got the crowd in the palm of her hand."

"I'm not surprised." He tapped his bottle against mine. "Lily knows how to pick 'em."

I chuckled. That she did. I just don't think our lead singer and oldest friend intended to find my perfect match at the same time.

"So when are you gonna stop drooling and actually talk to her, mate?" Tom nudged me, waggling his brows.

I shoved him off, heat creeping up my neck. "Sod off. It's not like that."

But that was a lie. One that stuck in my throat the more I said it.

"Could've fooled me," Alex muttered as he joined us. He took a long pull of his beer.

Dan and Mel's daughter's giggles broke the awkward moment as she darted between us, her little hands sticky with what looked suspiciously like chocolate. Mel followed close behind, her scowl a mix of exasperation and barely concealed amusement.

"Which one of you lot snuck her sweets again?" She snatched the munchkin up and settled her on her hip. "I've told you, she's hyper enough without the sugar rush!"

Tom held up his hands, warding her off. "Don't look at me, love. I learned my lesson last time."

James and Jared snickered from the sofas. Mel rounded on them.

"Aw, c'mon Mel, she's just excited." Jared laughed, popping open his own beer. "It's a big night for all of us."

"She's five, Jared. She doesn't need to be bouncing off the trucking walls."

A burst of cheers from the live feed drew my attention away from them, just in time to catch Liv hitting a particularly impressive high note, her face alive with joy.

God, she was something else. I couldn't take my eyes off her, the way she commanded the stage, the way her voice seemed to reach right into my chest and—

Alex chucked a balled-up napkin at my head. "You're doing it again."

I flipped him off good-naturedly, but my face still burned. Was I that obvious? I sneaked a glance at the guys, but they were back to ribbing each other and laughing. Only Tom met my gaze, a knowing smirk on his lips.

I looked away quickly, hoping they would let it go. Fat chance of that happening.

The green room door opened, and a familiar tall figure stepped in.

"Rhys!" Lily shrieked, launching herself into his arms before he'd taken more than three steps. "What are you doing here?"

A very good question.

Rhys laughed, spinning her around. "Couldn't miss opening night, could I?"

She pulled back, smacking his chest lightly. "You could've told me you were coming!"

"And ruin the surprise?" He grinned, leaning down to kiss her softly. "Never."

I watched them, a pang of envy mixing with the happiness I felt for my friends. They made it look so easy, being together. No secrets, no hiding. Just love, plain and simple.

Tom sidled up to me, smirking. "See? That's how it's done. Take notes."

I rolled my eyes, shoving him away. "Sod off."

But he wasn't deterred. "Seriously, if you don't make a move soon, one of us might have to." His voice was laced with amusement. "Can't let a bird like that slip away, can we Andy?"

Andy shook his head. "It'd be a right shame. Girl's got pipes and looks to boot."

"Lay off, will you? I'm working on it," I said, feigning irritation.

"Working on what? Boring holes into the screen with your eyes?" Tom laughed. "Liv deserves better than your longing stares."

"I know that," I managed, struggling to keep a straight face. "I just… I don't want to screw it up, alright?"

It wasn't a total lie. I was constantly terrified of mucking it up somehow. She meant too much to me.

Andy clapped a hand on my shoulder. "You won't. Anyone with eyes can see she's just as gone on you."

I ducked my head, hiding a smile. A particularly raucous burst of laughter from the corner drew our attention. A group of dancers were huddled together, giggling and shrieking over something on one of their phones. Alex glared at the dancers. I knew that look. That rigid set of his jaw, the white-knuckled grip on his beer bottle. Ceri wasn't with them, but I had no doubt she was the reason for his foul mood.

"Reckon we should say something?" I murmured to Tom and Andy.

Tom sighed. "Doubt he'd listen. You know how he gets when Ceri's involved."

Andy shook his head. "Still, it might be worth a shot. Can't have him moping about all tour. It'll throw off the whole vibe."

I opened my mouth to agree, but before I could get a word out, the door burst open. Kevin stormed in, his face like a thundercloud.

"Jack!" he barked, making a beeline for Lily's dad. "A word. Now."

Jack, who'd been happily chatting with Rhys and Lily, looked up in surprise. "Everything alright, Kevin?"

"No, everything is not alright." Kevin's voice was tight with barely contained fury. "We need to talk. In private."

A hush fell over the room, everyone's eyes darting between

Kevin and Jack. I exchanged a worried glance with Tom and Andy. This couldn't be good.

Jack's brow furrowed, but he nodded. "Alright. Let's step outside then."

As they moved towards the door, I strained my ears, trying to catch snippets of their conversation.

"... can't just change things last minute..." Kevin hissed.

"... my daughter's wellbeing..." Jack's reply was muffled as the door swung shut behind them.

Lily watched them go. Rhys rubbed her back soothingly, murmuring something in her ear that made her relax slightly.

"What do you reckon that's about?" Andy asked in a low voice.

I shrugged, unease settling in my gut. "No idea. But it can't be good."

Tom frowned. "You don't think it's about..." He trailed off, but we all knew what he was implying.

The discrepancies in the books. The sneaking suspicion that Kevin was up to something dodgy. Just a gut feeling that something wasn't right.

"Maybe," I said slowly. "But let's not jump to conclusions. Could be anything."

Even as I said it, I knew I was just trying to convince myself. If Jack was getting involved, stepping in where he usually left the day-to-day management to Kevin, it had to be serious.

"Has anyone seen my picks?" James patted his pockets, his brow furrowed. "I swear I had them a minute ago."

Ryan smirked, producing a fistful of colourful triangles from his own pocket. "You mean these? You'd lose your head if it wasn't screwed on."

"Har, bloody, har." James snatched the picks.

I tried to block them out, to focus on Liv's voice pouring from the speakers. But it was like trying to meditate in the middle of a riot. Every time I felt myself slipping under her spell, another shout or cackle would jolt me back.

Sod it.

I slipped out of the room, letting the door click shut behind me. In the hallway, I broke into a jog, dodging roadies and techs as I made my way towards the stage.

"Where's the fire, Davies?" Mason, our head roadie, called after me, his arms full of coiled cables.

I didn't answer, just flashed him a grin and kept running, Liv's voice growing louder with each step.

Backstage was a hive of activity, a whirlwind of bodies and equipment and barely controlled chaos. I pushed through, my eyes fixed on the wings, on the sliver of stage visible beyond.

I reached the side stage just as Liv launched into her final song. Lovers Knot huddled nearby, whooping and clapping along, ready to take the stage after her.

But I only had eyes for Liv. Her hair gleamed under the lights, her smile incandescent as she poured her heart into every note. She was magnificent, a star ascending before our eyes.

As if sensing my presence, she turned, glancing into the wings. Her gaze caught mine and her face lit up. My breath hitched, my skin prickling with awareness, with the unspoken connection that had sparked between us from the moment we met.

The rest of the world fell away. It was just us, just the music and the connection crackling between us like a live wire.

Her performance took on a new intensity, every lyric, every chord imbued with unspoken promise.

When the last note faded, the roar was deafening. Liv took her bow, blowing kisses to the crowd before bounding off stage. Her cheeks were flushed and her eyes bright with triumph and a heat that set my blood humming.

I can't wait to get her alone.

I wanted nothing more than to go to her, to pull her into my arms and tell her how incredible she'd been. But I held back, mindful of the curious eyes watching our every move.

So instead, I settled for a smile. A small, secret thing that said everything I couldn't put into words.

Her answering grin was radiant, her eyes bright with joy and understanding. She knew. Of course she knew.

Mia appeared at her elbow, shepherding her towards the dressing rooms.

CHAPTER SIXTEEN

OLIVIA

*B*ackstage devolved into utter chaos the second the stage lights went dark. The Brightside and the dancers rushed off, instantly disappearing into the sea of roadies diving in to dismantle the equipment. We had an hour before the buses rolled out for San Diego. The crew would keep working after the bands left, but it looked like they had no interest in waiting around either.

I couldn't match their enthusiasm. I just wanted to sit and soak it in a little longer. Convince myself that yes, a few hours ago, I was standing on that stage singing to thousands of people.

It felt like a dream. One I never wanted to wake up from.

Between the sets, some people went back to the green room but I wasn't going to miss a second of my first stadium tour hiding backstage while people got drunk. No, I needed to be right in the thick of it and I'd happily spent the rest of the show glued to the side of the stage.

"Move, Liv," Mason, the head roadie, said, his tone authoritative. He stopped in front of me, eying up the amp I stood in front of. "You're holding up my guys."

My gaze cut to two roadies standing nearby frowning at Mason's back. They were built like linebackers, all broad shoulders and bulging biceps straining against their black t-shirts. Sweat glistened on their brows, their faces set in a scowl at the delay.

I instantly stepped out of the way with an apologetic grimace.

"Why didn't they ask me?"

"They're too chicken shit to ask talent to move on the first day of the tour."

"That's ridiculous." I'd hardly call myself scary. These two could bench press two of me.

Mason shrugged and went back to the load out. I didn't stop him. I needed to find my bassist before he slipped onto The Brightside's bus and I lost my chance for a celebratory kiss.

My bassist.

The idea of it brought a deranged smile to my lips. The roadies backed away from me but I ignored them. Not my fault they couldn't recognise a woman in love.

I stood on my tiptoes, trying to scan the area for Lewis. There were plenty of dark haired giants, just not the one I wanted.

Before I could think too much about the fact he hadn't waited for me, my phone vibrated in my pocket. I fished it out, my breath held with some silly hope.

Yes, I wanted him to need to see me as much as I did him, but this was his tour. He probably had press to deal with and any number of other commitments that I thankfully didn't have to worry about yet.

LEWIS

I'm waiting for you.

I frowned at the text. That was great and all but where?

Then another text loaded, a picture of a napkin with a crudely drawn map.

Despite the absurdity of it, a shiver of anticipation raced down my spine at the thought of seeing him, being alone with him.

Jesus, you're a goner, girl.

I followed his instructions, weaving through the chaotic maze of crew members, dancers rushing to the dressing rooms, and musicians from the other opening acts riding high on the adrenaline of their performances. The air buzzed with chatter and laughter, a palpable energy that sent electricity dancing across my skin.

"Olivia!" Nia shouted from somewhere in front of me. She pushed through a knot of roadies, her blonde hair plastered to her forehead with sweat. The woman had worked overtime to get the absolute best shots of the night. "You killed it out there! The crowd loved you."

I grinned, the enticing weight of utter joy burning in my chest. "Thanks."

"Which bus are you riding to San Diego?" she asked as I passed her. "Dan's threatening to break out the monopoly board on our bus. You should join."

"I'll think about it, yeah? There's something I need to take care of first."

Her brow quirked, a knowing smirk tugging at her lips. "Something, or someone?"

I shrugged and turned away before she could recognise the pleased smile fighting at the edges of my lips or the heat rushing to my cheeks.

Her laughter trailed after me as I hurried down the hallway, consulting my phone for the next set of directions. Left at the second junction, then right at the water cooler.

What did he have planned? Why all the secrecy? A thousand possibilities swirled through my mind, each more thrilling than the last.

"Olivia!" Another voice called out and I groaned.

Could they not see I had places to be?

I turned to see Tommy, the lead singer of Lover's Knot, jogging towards me. His bleached blond hair stood up in wild spikes. "You were incredible tonight! You ever want to jam, let me know."

"Thanks." I smiled, genuinely touched by his enthusiasm even as I itched to keep moving. How could I be annoyed when the delay was for praise? "And anytime, just say the word."

He disappeared back into the throng, his voice rising above the din as he called out to someone else.

I shook my head, amused but also kind of relieved. The camaraderie amongst the bands on this tour was like nothing I'd ever experienced. It felt like family, like belonging.

But as much as I loved it, as much as I was grateful for it, it wasn't what I needed right now.

Right now, I needed him.

Needed to see his face, to feel his arms around me, to hear his voice telling me that I'd done well. That he was proud of me.

I quickened my pace, dodging past a gaggle of giggling dancers and sidestepping a harried-looking tech with an armful of cables. The further I went, the more the bustle slipped away.

I turned the final corner and ended up in a dimly lit corridor lined with nondescript doors. Before I could second-guess myself or check my phone again, a hand shot out from one of the doorways, pulling me into a darkened room.

My breath caught on a startled scream. I bit it back, releasing a pathetic squeak instead.

Jesus, woman. If someone ever decides to kidnap you, you'll be an easy target.

The door clicked shut behind me and I stumbled into a firm chest. Strong arms encircled my waist while a familiar scent tickled my nose, Lewis's cologne. It mingled with the faint smell of cleaning supplies.

A janitor's closet.

He'd pulled me into a janitor's closet of all places. Were we that couple now?

"Lewis, what—"

"Shh," he murmured, his breath warm against my ear. "I just needed a moment alone with you. You were incredible out there, Liv." He squeezed me against his chest, hugging me tight and burying his face in my neck. "I knew you would be. I'm so proud of you."

His words washed over me, soothing the last of my jangling nerves. I melted into his embrace, my hands sliding up his chest to loop around his neck. "Thank you. It means so much to hear *you* say that."

"I mean every word." He pulled back. In the dim light filtering through the cracks around the door, I could just make out the curve of his smile, the heat in his gaze. "Watching you up there, seeing you shine… it was breathtaking."

To have him believe in me so fiercely, to know that he saw me—really saw me—it was overwhelming in the best possible way.

"I was so nervous," I whispered, my fingers toying with the soft hair at his nape. "But then I thought about your training…"

He chuckled. "Did you now?" His voice dropped, taking on a gravelly note that dragged deliciously against my skin. He drew me closer, his forehead resting against mine. "Which part in particular?"

I smirked. "You know which part."

I surged forward, capturing his mouth in a searing kiss before he could push me to dig deeper. He responded instantly, his lips moving against mine with a fervour that stole my breath. It was like every nerve ending in my body had been set alight, every sensation heightened and electric.

His hands roamed my back, slipping beneath the hem of my shirt to skim along the heated skin beneath. I arched into him, a soft moan escaping into the sliver of space between our mouths. He swallowed the sound, his tongue sweeping along my bottom lip before delving deeper, tasting me with a thoroughness that made my toes curl.

"Maybe we shouldn't have sex right now," Lewis said, suddenly pulling back, his breathing ragged.

I frowned. "Why not? I thought that was why you chose a janitor's closet for this illicit meeting."

"It was, but now that I'm thinking straight, I don't know." He grimaced. "Someone could walk in at any moment."

I grinned mischievously. "That's part of the fun, isn't it?" I nipped at his earlobe, soothing the sting with my tongue. "Knowing we could be caught any second, but not being able to keep our hands off each other."

He shuddered, his eyes fluttering shut as I worked my mouth down his neck.

"We're two consenting adults. It might be a little embarrassing, but it's not the end of the world."

"But your reputation..." he started, concern etched on his face.

I silenced him with a finger to his lips. "My reputation will be just fine. Now, are you going to keep worrying or are you going to kiss me?"

A crash from the hallway made us both freeze up, our breathing harsh in the sudden silence. I strained to hear any signs of someone approaching, my heart pounding against my ribs.

After a moment, Lewis relaxed, his hands resuming their leisurely exploration of my sides. "No one's coming," he murmured, his lips finding my collarbone. "And even if they did... I guess it wouldn't be the worst thing."

The words, low and rough, sent a bolt of pure desire straight to my core. This man would be the death of me, and what a way to go.

LEWIS

Liv's hands slid down my chest, her fingers dipping below the waistband of my jeans, and I nearly lost all semblance of control. This woman, this brazen, beautiful creature, was going to be my undoing. Seeing her like this, bold and confident, it was the sexiest damn thing I'd ever seen.

"Liv…" Her name fell from my lips, half prayer, half warning.

If she kept touching me like that, I wouldn't be responsible for my actions.

She silenced me with her hot and demanding lips, and any thoughts of slowing down evaporated. I met her kiss for kiss, my hands roaming her body, desperate to feel every inch of her.

It had only been twelve or something hours since we'd woken up in her hotel room. Logically, I knew that. But it had still been too damn long since I had my hands on her.

Even on the stage with thousands of fans screaming at me—some of them throwing lingerie and begging for things they had no business wanting—all I could think about was her.

She consumed me, owned me in a way no one else ever had.

The world narrowed to her in my arms, her taste on my tongue, her soft sighs filling my ears. Everything else fell away—the distant sounds of the crew, the lingering roar of the crowd.

In that moment, nothing existed but her and me and the electricity arcing between us. Time lost all meaning—minutes or hours could have passed in a haze of wandering hands and stolen gasps, in the slick slide of tongues and the sharp sting of teeth. The closet grew hot, the air heavy with the scent of our combined arousal.

Clothes hit the floor and the first press of her bare skin against mine nearly brought me to my knees. My fingers danced along the edge of her bra, teasing the sensitive skin.

"Lewis, please…"

With a groan, I walked her backwards until her back hit the storage shelves. "I want to touch you," I rasped against her neck. "Taste you." My fingers found the clasp of her bra. "Let me make you feel good, Liv. Let me immortalise today in your mind so that every time you think of your first time on an arena stage, you think of me."

She nodded, dragging her lips along my jaw. "Yes, please."

The clasp gave way and I drew the lace down her arms, letting it fall to the floor. Even in the dim light, she was exquisite —all soft curves and smooth skin just begging to be explored. I dipped my head, drawing one pebbled nipple into my mouth as my hand sought the heat between her thighs.

She cried out, her head falling back against the door as I stroked her through the damp fabric of her knickers.

"I have a better idea," she said before I could slip my fingers beneath the lace. She sank to her knees, surprising me while her fingers made quick work of my belt.

"Liv, what are you—"

"I think," she murmured, her breath ghosting over my aching cock as she freed me from the confines of my jeans, "it would be more memorable if I was the one giving, don't you?"

Fuck.

"You don't have to…"

"I want to."

A groan tore from my throat as her clever fingers wrapped around me, stroking from root to tip.

My head fell back and I stared at the patchwork ceiling, my heart pounding and all of the blood in my body rushing south. This had not been a part of the plan. I lured her into the empty bowels of the stadium to make her come so hard she'd still feel me inside her on the drive to San Diego.

I was so used to doing the surprising, I hadn't anticipated it being turned back on me.

At the first flick of her tongue, my hands fisted in her hair and my gaze fixed on her as she licked up a bead of pre-cum.

The way she stared up at me through her lashes, so intent and determined, made me want to lose myself in her.

I closed my eyes, trying to cool the raging inferno between

my legs. My cock throbbed in her hands, begging for release. She teased me, licking me again before taking me deep into her mouth.

"Fuck, Liv," I groaned, my voice rough with need. Her fingers wrapped tighter around me, drawing out a groan. "You're killing me."

"Is that a bad thing?" she asked, voice just as husky as mine, but filled with mischief.

I shook my head, trying to clear my thoughts. "No, god, no. It's… fantastic." I panted, my hips bucking involuntarily as she continued to stroke me. "But we don't have much time."

"Pretty sure I won't need long, rock star."

She sealed her lips around me, sucking hard in a way that drove me wild. My stomach bottomed out and my hands clenched in her hair. Then she deep throated me and any restraint I'd held on to evaporated. I thrust into her mouth, enjoying the sight of her pretty pink lips stretched around my cock.

God, the way she looked… the way she felt… it was almost too much. I could have happily let her finish me off right then and there, spilling down her throat with her name on my lips.

But then a faintly nagging thought crossed my mind: I'd lured her to the back of this stadium for her pleasure, not mine.

"Wait," I managed, my voice strangled. "Liv, wait…"

She ignored me, twisting her grip instead. With my teeth gritted, I grabbed her shoulders and pushed her back, freeing myself from her mouth.

"What's wrong?" she asked as I hauled her to her feet and spun her around to face the shelving unit. "Didn't you like it?"

"Fuck, Liv, I loved it."

"Then I don't understand." She tried to turn around and my hands clamped down on her hips holding her still.

Taking her hands in mine, I guided them to the smooth metal surface of the shelving unit in front of her. I curled her fingers around the metal edge, squeezing with a silent command to stay.

"Believe me, there is nothing in this world I want more than your gorgeous mouth on me. But..." I pressed my foot against her ankle until she widened her stance. "Tonight's your night," I whispered, my lips grazing her ear. "It's your first stadium opening, and I've had a million of 'em. You can suck me off any time you want, but right now, I want—no, need—to prolong that euphoric feeling for you."

She let out a breathy little laugh, wiggling her hips against me in a way that had me seeing stars.

"Well then, by all means... ravish me, rock star."

I chuckled as I pressed a kiss to the nape of her neck, my hands skimming down her sides to hook into the waistband of her knickers. "Your wish is my command."

In one smooth motion, I divested her of that last scrap of lace, letting it flutter to the floor. She braced her hands on the shelves, arching her back in wordless invitation. I dragged my hand down her stomach, gliding lower and lower until I found her wet, eager pussy. She trembled beneath my touch, her breath coming in quick, shallow gasps.

"Do you see how wet you are?" I murmured, leaning in to tease her earlobe with my lips. "Is this just from sucking me off?"

She hummed an agreement, and I bit my lip, willing myself to find some patience as I teased her clit. When she trembled against me, I moved my hands to her hips, gripping tight as I notched myself at her entrance, the heat of her scorching me even through the barrier of the condom.

I drove into her, inch by glorious inch, groaning against the soft skin of her neck. My hips snapped forward, finding a rhythm that had us both moaning and gasping.

"That's it," I murmured, nipping at her earlobe. "Take me, Liv. Take all of me."

She cried out, arching her back into me. I gripped her hips tighter and slammed into her faster, harder.

"Oh fuck!" she screamed, clinging to the shelving unit.

I slowed down just enough to feel every exquisite tremor that shook her body.

"Look at me," I growled against her heated skin.

She turned her head slightly, meeting my gaze with a look that made my heart race. I pumped into her harder now, my pace matching the rapid beat of our hearts.

"This is what you do to me," I said, my voice rough with desire. "You make me lose control."

She threw her head back and cried out as she came, her body bucking wildly, driving back against mine. Her walls clenched tight around me, sending shocks of pleasure straight to my cock. I gritted my teeth, willing the impending orgasm to go away. I wasn't ready for this to be over yet.

"Oh god," she panted, her body shaking.

I pulled out slowly, unable to resist one last look at how wet she was for me. Then I turned her around and gathered her in my arms. She stared up at me, her lips parted and her eyes glazed with bliss.

I kissed her, slow and drugging. She moaned against my lips, her hands running up my chest and into my hair. Her hips rolled against my rock solid erection, grinding any control I still possessed to dust.

I lifted her leg, hooking it over my arm and holding her open. I pulled back just enough to watch as I dragged the head of my cock through her lower lips.

"Tell me what you need." I asked as the tip slipped inside and her head lolled back against the shelf.

She rolled her hips again, but didn't answer. I slid in an inch more.

"Tell me, Liv," I panted against her neck.

"You," she gasped out. "I need you. I don't care how or who knows, I just need you."

"Good answer."

Smirking, I drove into her, deeper and harder than before. Her nails dug into my shoulders, undoubtedly leaving marks. The thought of her marking me sent me straight over the edge, I slammed into her over and over again, her walls clenching around me with each thrust.

Her breathy moans grew louder, more desperate. I reached between us, finding her clit and rubbing in tight circles.

"Come on, Liv," I panted, my rhythm growing erratic as my own climax approached. "Come for me."

She buried her face against my chest as she shattered, muffling a scream. The sensation of her pulsing around me, combined with the sharp sting of her nails, was more than I could take. With one final thrust, I buried myself to the hilt and let go with a hoarse shout.

For a long moment, we stayed like that, locked together, gasping for air.

Imagine ending every show like this.

I'd unwittingly unlocked a new ritual.

She slumped in my arms, humming her satisfaction and I pushed the idea to the back of my mind. Plenty of time to figure that out.

I pressed a kiss to her sweaty temple, a wave of affection surging through me.

Who would have thought I'd be starting the biggest tour of my career with a woman who lit me up in every way imaginable?

CHAPTER SEVENTEEN

OLIVIA

"God, I love this," Tommy shouted over the roar of the crowd.

He stood beside me, bouncing on his toes, his face split into a manic grin while his sweat soaked hair clung to his forehead. We were only two shows into the tour but this was a routine I could get used to. I had just as much fun watching Tommy dance around like a man possessed by the music as I did witnessing Rhiannon pump up thousands of fans.

We were tucked just out of sight in the wings, close enough to feel the heat of the lights, to see the sweat glistening on Ryan's brow as he gripped the mic. While the band lost themselves in their music and the crowd, Nia wove around the stage, shadowing all of the guys with a camera in hand and another hanging from a harness strapped to her chest.

She'd given me a peek at her shots from last night and I couldn't wait to see what she did tonight.

The crew shuffled around us with an almost eerie synchronicity, checking wires, signalling cues, preparing instruments. It was chaos, but a carefully orchestrated sort of chaos that I would never get tired of experiencing.

Alys joined us, bumping me with her shoulder to get my attention. I smiled at her and she took my hand, just as the tempo notched up and Ryan started jumping.

We jumped with him while Alys sang along to the songs, her blue eyes bright with delight and a huge smile stretching her lips. I couldn't help but grin back, caught up in her infectious joy.

"Can you believe we get to do this every night?" I shouted over the music, my voice giddy.

"It never gets old!" She laughed, squeezing my hand. "I feel like the luckiest girl in the world."

Would Lewis and I still be like this, two years down the line? Would the music still set our souls on fire, or would the pressures of fame and fortune slowly erode the magic?

I hoped I never got so used to this that I couldn't feel the joy of it, the rush of adrenaline, the pulse of the bass in my chest.

My gaze drifted back to Nia, darting along the back of the stage, camera glued to her face. She moved like she was part of the music, her shutter clicking in perfect time.

She passed James and he winked at her. Dan walked over to him, grinning and raising his eyebrows in silent communication. James's smile grew and the pair of them started showing off for the camera, lining up to play a riff in time, leaning against each other's backs.

Nia shook her head but never lowered her camera, capturing every second until the song changed and something else caught her attention.

Ryan moved towards an amp and she sprang into action, rushing towards him and the edge of the stage with a determined furrow to her brow.

Unease prickled along my spine as I watched her navigate the narrow space. The stage was slick with sweat and spilled beer, the lights disorienting in their intensity. One wrong step, one moment of distraction...

She'd barely crouched down when Ryan leapt atop the amp, teetering precariously as he belted out a high note.

Several things happened at once, too quick to process or predict.

The crowd surged forward, security gathered beneath him and girls in the front row screamed, their arms outstretched, desperate to touch him.

Nia leaned out, the stage lights glinting off her lens. Then I don't know what happened. Did her foot catch a cable? Did she lean too far? Was the stage wet?

My imagination, I know, but time seemed to slow to a crawl as I watched in growing horror.

"Nia!" The scream tore from my throat as she fell, plummeting out of sight.

James swore, the sound catching on his mic. He rushed forward, but no one was fast enough to catch her.

"No, no, no," I chanted under my breath, my feet moving before my brain could catch up. "Please be okay, please be okay."

I ran, shoving past the roadies working at the side of the stage. I jumped down the steps and rounded the speakers, pushing a security guard out of my way, my heart in my mouth.

Blood roared in my ears, my pulse a deafening drumbeat. I hit the barricade and a distant part of me startled when Tommy and Alys shoved it out of the way for me. We continued on, pushing through more security guards.

"Medical emergency in front of the stage security barrier," one of them shouted into a radio.

On stage, Ryan faltered, the song dying on his lips. For a suspended second, his eyes met mine, wide with fear. Then he was moving again, but never away from the edge of the stage. He might have been the consummate showman, but I could see the tension in his shoulders, the way his gaze kept flitting to the spot where Nia had fallen.

We pushed our way through until we reached her side.

"Oh lord." The words left me in a breathless rush, my belly turning at the sight of her crumpled form.

"Fuck. Nia." Tommy sank down by her side and took her hand, a look of absolute devastation in his eyes. "I told you not to pull that shit."

She lay on the floor, her eyes shut, a gash on her forehead that bled so profusely it dyed her platinum blonde hair red. Her broken lenses were scattered around her.

"Is she...?" Alys's voice trembled, the question hanging unfinished in the air.

Her eyelids fluttered. A low moan escaped her lips. Relief crashed through me, dizzying in its intensity. She was alive. Hurt, but alive.

"What happened?" she asked, groaning as she tried to sit up.

I sank to my knees and helped Tommy hold her down. "That's a really bad idea, right now, Nia."

"Yeah, just wait for the paramedics, okay?" Tommy squeezed her shoulder. "They'll be here, any second."

"Guys, I'm fine." Her eyelids drooped as she said it.

Alys snorted, a choked sound caught between a laugh and a sob. "Sure you are, babe. Just totally fine, bleeding on the floor. Nothing to see here."

In a blink, we were surrounded by paramedics and a security guard who I vaguely remembered being the man in charge. We moved out of the way, giving them room to work. Questions flew, orders were barked, and I bit my tongue hard enough to taste blood, swallowing back my fury at his useless security team who'd let this happen.

The more they talked the deeper the pit of worry grew inside of me. I could barely hear them over the music, catching snippets that didn't alleviate my concerns.

"Possible concussion."

"Need a neck brace."

"Get a stretcher."

Their voices were clipped, professional, but the urgency in

their movements, the tension in their shoulders spoke volumes. Was it that bad?

Through it all, Nia stirred fretfully, her hands groping at the ground. "My cameras," she mumbled. "Are... are they okay?"

A hysterical bubble of laughter caught in my throat. Trust Nia to worry about her gear. I clasped her searching fingers, my voice cracking.

"Don't worry about the cameras. Just stay still, alright? Let them help you."

"But the show," she protested weakly, trying to push herself up again. "I have to... I need to..."

"Shh, no you don't." I brushed her hair back from her face, my fingers trembling. "The only thing you need to worry about right now is you."

I glanced up and found James hovering above us. His guitar hung forgotten at his side but for the white-knuckle grip he kept on it, his jaw clenched so hard I feared he might break a tooth. He looked seconds away from diving off the stage himself.

Heedless of the show, of the thousands of eyes upon him, he paced the edge of the stage, never taking his eyes off Nia's prone form. Ryan cast him a worried look but kept singing, the show going on around this pocket of drama.

My heart ached for him, for the helpless fury and fear etched into every line of his body. I couldn't imagine being in his place, forced to perform while the person I loved lay broken.

I caught James's eye, trying to pour reassurance into my gaze. Jerking my head towards the stage, I mouthed, "I've got her."

He hesitated, indecision warring on his face. I could practically see the gears turning in his head, the desperate calculations. How fast could he get off the stage? Would he reach her before security stopped him? What would happen to the show, to the band, if he abandoned his post?

For a moment, he looked mutinous, his grip tightening on his guitar. But then, with a visible effort, he repositioned his guitar and started playing. The professional mask slipped back into place, but it lacked his usual enthusiasm. The man had turned into a robot, letting muscle memory take over.

I exhaled a shaky breath, some of the tension easing from my shoulders. One less crisis to manage.

As the paramedics eased Nia onto a stretcher, I scrambled to my feet. "I'm coming with her."

"Sorry, miss. It's not going to happen." The head honcho of the guards shook his head, grim-faced. "Family only in the ambulance."

"But I'm—" The protest died on my tongue. He was right. I wasn't family, not in the way that mattered.

Disappointment sat bitter on my tongue, mingling with the coppery taste of fear. I wanted to argue, to demand they let me stay by her side. But I knew it would be futile. These weren't people to be reasoned with, not in an emergency.

Frustration burned in my throat, but I nodded. That didn't mean I was giving up. Alys and I followed them out to the loading bay where an ambulance waited.

"What are we going to do?" she asked, her voice tight with frustration. "We can't just let her go alone."

"We won't," I said firmly, pulling out my phone. "We're going to that hospital, even if we have to hitchhike." My fingers flew over the keys, my thoughts racing ahead. "I'm texting James. He needs to know what's happening."

Alys nodded, wrapping her arms around herself while they loaded Nia into the ambulance. She looked so small, so fragile against the white sheets. Every instinct screamed at me to go with her, to not let her out of my sight.

But I couldn't. So I did the only thing I could. I ordered a taxi and kept James updated.

*T*he ride to the hospital passed in a blur of streetlights and honking horns. I fidgeted in my seat, my knee bouncing, my nails digging into my palms. Every red light felt like a personal affront, every slow driver an enemy conspiring to keep us from getting there.

Beside me, Alys was a mirror image of nervous energy, her foot tapping an anxious rhythm on the floor.

"How much longer?" she asked for the dozenth time, craning her neck to see out the window. "It feels like we've been in this cab for hours."

"Too long," I muttered.

The driver met my eyes in the rearview mirror, his expression a mix of sympathy and exasperation.

"Almost there, ladies," he said. "Just a couple more blocks."

She'll be fine, I told myself over and over, a desperate mantra. *She's tough. She has to be fine.*

But I couldn't wipe the memory of Nia lying on the stadium floor, the blood on her face, the unnatural stillness.

What if it had been Lewis? The thought hit me like a punch to the gut. If he was the one in the ambulance, would I be in this same position? Helpless, shut out, with no legal right to information or to be by his side?

The idea made me feel sick. Legally, we were nothing to each other. Even to our friends we were nothing more than colleagues.

By the time the taxi pulled up to the hospital entrance, I was coiled tighter than a spring. I thrust a wad of bills at the driver, not bothering to wait for change before Alys and I were out the door, our boots pounding against the pavement.

We rushed through the hospital, following signs to the ER without saying a word to each other. Harsh fluorescent lights and the pungent smell of antiseptic assaulted us.

The corridors seemed to stretch on forever, a maze of white walls and squeaky linoleum. Orderlies pushed gurneys, nurses hurried past with clipboards, and everywhere, that smell—a mix of bleach and sickness that turned my belly.

I'd made it a point to avoid hospitals ever since my grandmother died. It didn't matter how much time had passed, the reminders were too stark.

But I couldn't think about that now. Nia needed us. I pushed the memories down, locking them away. Later, I could fall apart. But not now. Not yet.

To my credit, I didn't even flinch while walking into the waiting room. My attention was fixed on the nurses station ahead and the people in colourful scrubs bustling around it. The air hummed with a mix of murmured conversations, crying, phones pinging and ringing, and the distant beeping of monitors.

I shouldered my way to the desk, my palms sweating and my heart in my throat. The nurse behind the counter looked up, her expression politely detached.

"I'm here for Nia Thomas," I said in a rush. "She was just brought in, head injury from a fall. Can you tell me where she is? How she's doing?"

The nurse's fingers flew over her keyboard, her eyes scanning the screen. "Are you family?" she asked without looking up.

"No, we're her friends," Alys said. "We work together. Please, I just need to know if she's okay."

"I'm sorry." The nurse's voice was kind but firm. "I can only release information to immediate family members. Hospital policy."

"But…" Desperation clawed at my throat. "Please. I saw her fall. I just need to know…"

The nurse sighed, her eyes softening a fraction. "Look, I understand you're worried. But my hands are tied. The best I can tell you is that she's being evaluated."

I fired off a text to James, updating him on the situation and then sat on my hands for I don't know how long. It might have been minutes, it might have been hours. In this place, time lost all meaning.

I checked my phone obsessively, willing it to buzz with an update from anyone. But the screen remained dark and silent, mocking me.

"Alys! Liv!" a familiar voice called out, tight with urgency.

My head snapped up and Alys leapt to her seat, nearly tripping in her haste. James stood in the doorway, his hair wild, his eyes haunted. He still wore his stage clothes, his shirt sweat-soaked and clinging to his chest.

"Oh thank lord." I rushed over to him, crossing the room in a few quick strides. "They won't tell us anything, they said only family—"

"I know." He dragged a hand through his hair, his gaze darting to the nurses station. "I called her mam on the way over. She's given permission for them to release information to me."

"That's a relief," I breathed. "So you can find out how she is? What's happening?"

He nodded, his jaw tight. "I'll talk to the nurses. Wait here, okay? I'll be right back."

And then he was gone, striding towards the reception desk with purpose. I watched him lean in close, his voice low and intense as he spoke to the nurse. She nodded, her fingers once again flying over the keys.

"What's taking so long?" she muttered, more to herself than to me. "Why won't they just tell us something, anything?"

I didn't have an answer. All I could do was shake my head, my throat too tight for words. After what felt like a lifetime, he returned with an unreadable expression. I searched his eyes, my heart in my throat.

"She's okay," he said, and it was like all the air rushed back into the room. "She has a concussion, and they want to keep her overnight for observation. But she's awake and talking."

The relief hit me like a physical force, so strong it nearly brought me to my knees. Beside me, Alys let out a shaky breath, her hand finding mine and squeezing tight.

"Can we see her?"

"They're getting her settled in a room now. The nurse said she'd come get us when we can go back."

I nodded. I lifted my hand, intending to swipe my hair back but the sight of it shaking gave me pause. When had I started shaking?

"Hey, it's okay." James wrapped an arm around my shoulders, steadying me. "She's going to be fine. We all are."

I believed him, but that didn't stop the adrenaline draining from my body. I leaned into him, grateful for the support.

"C'mon, let's sit down while we wait." He guided me back to the chairs, his hand warm on the small of my back. We collapsed into the hard plastic, shoulder to shoulder, knees bumping.

Alys sank down on my other side, her body just as tense as mine.

"I can't believe this happened," I whispered, my voice raw. "One second she was doing what she loves, and the next…"

"I know." James's voice was thick with pain. "It all happened so fast. I saw her fall and I just… I couldn't think. Couldn't breathe. All I knew was I had to get to her."

I stared at him and wished I could look away. It was disconcerting, seeing my own fear and helplessness reflected back at me.

In that moment, the reality of what we did, the risks we took, crashed over me with sickening clarity.

"It's not right," Alys said quietly, her voice tight with anger. "We're her family. We should be able to be there for her, no matter what."

James nodded, his jaw clenched. "When I propose to Nia, it'll mean more than medical access, but fuck," he released a frustrated breath and dragged a hand across his face. "I regret not having popped the question already and that's not right."

A throat cleared, snapping me out of my thoughts. I looked up to see a nurse standing before us, a gentle smile on her face.

"You can see her now," she said. "She's been asking for you."

James and I were on our feet in an instant, Alys half a step behind us. We followed the nurse down the winding hallway to a small room that smelled of lemon disinfectant and reminded me far too much of an almost identical room in Jasmine Bay where my grandmother had spent her final days, wasting away.

Only it wasn't my grandmother in the bed and Nia wasn't going to leave us any time soon.

She was propped up against stark white pillows, her face pale but her eyes open and aware.

"Hey, music man," she croaked, her lips quivering with a tired smile. "Heard you finished the set without me. I'm hurt."

Up close, the bruising on her temple stood out in vivid relief, a mottled canvas of purples and reds. The stitches stood out against her pale skin. But her gaze was clear and her grip strong as she reached for my hand.

"You scared the hell out of us, Nia," I whispered, blinking back tears. "Don't ever do that again, you hear me?"

"I'll try to limit my stage dives from now on," she said, but there was a quaver in her voice.

"How are you feeling, shutterbug?" James sank down onto the mattress at her side, his hand coming up to smooth her hair back from her forehead with aching tenderness. "And don't say 'fine,' because I can see that you're not."

"My head hurts." Her smile slipped a notch. "And everything's a bit fuzzy. The doctor said that's normal with a concussion. But I'll be okay. I'm tougher than I look."

"That you are." James pressed a kiss to her knuckles, his eyes suspiciously bright. "But you're going to need to take it easy for a while. We'll get someone to fill in for you with the band for a few weeks."

She frowned. "But—"

"No arguments."

"Fine," she muttered with a dark look. Then her expression cleared and her eyes seemed to dance with an idea. "You gonna play nurse for me?"

A surprised laugh huffed out of James. "I think I could be persuaded. As long as you promise to actually rest and not try to sneak off to edit photos the second my back's turned."

"No promises," Nia said. But then her gaze softened, her fingers tightening around James's. "Thank you. For being here. All of you."

My heart clenched. "Of course. There's nowhere else we'd be."

Alys squeezed her foot through the blanket, her eyes shining. "We love you, you daft git. You're stuck with us, remember?"

Nia's smile wobbled, her eyes suspiciously shiny. "I remember."

I settled into the chair on her other side.

Watching James and Nia, I made a silent promise to myself. I needed to find a way to ensure that Lewis and I would never be in their position, needing a parent an ocean away to give permission for my partner to see me.

Taking that leap into forever, signing the papers that would bind us in the eyes of the law… I would do it. I would do whatever it took to make sure that we could always be there for each other.

That's what love was, right?

A promise, a commitment, a choice to face the world together, come what may. And I was ready to make that choice, with all my heart.

But was Lewis on the same page?

CHAPTER EIGHTEEN

OLIVIA

*W*hen the hotel room door clicked shut behind me, something close to relief skittered through me. The smile I'd forced to my lips fell, leaving my cheeks aching. I'd enjoyed the bus rides so far, especially when I got to ride with The Brightside.

I couldn't enjoy it tonight. After the hospital, all I'd wanted to do was launch myself into Lewis's arms and never let go. But I couldn't. Especially not on a bus with his bandmates already eying us with rightful suspicion. The man was delusional if he thought his friends hadn't figured us out.

San Diego had been a whirlwind that I wouldn't forget any time soon. My nerves felt like they'd been caught up in a never ending roller coaster. I'd gone from the high of performing to the terror of watching Nia fall, to the long wait to find out if she was okay. All while I itched to grab Lewis and shake him before either of us could be flung into James and Nia's positions.

The drive to Glendale had passed in a blur of dark highway and darker thoughts. All I'd wanted to do was curl up next to

Lewis and reassure myself. Instead, I sat there with that painful smile, nodding and laughing where necessary.

Even at a careful distance, I'd been able to feel his concern. One look, and I knew he wanted to be next to me, giving me exactly what I needed. Unfortunately, he hadn't acted on it. Couldn't risk the others noticing.

And that was the crux of it, wasn't it? The razor's edge we walked every fucking day. The constant, exhausting vigilance of maintaining a facade, of pretending we were nothing more than colleagues, friends at a stretch.

When all I wanted, with a desperation that frightened me, was to fall into his arms and let the rest of the world fade away. To bury my face in the crook of his neck and breathe him in, to feel the steady thrum of his heartbeat against my cheek and know, bone-deep, that I was safe. Cherished. Loved.

Lord, I was trying to be careful. But every stolen kiss, every secret touch, felt like a ticking time bomb. A held breath, a wish cast into the void.

How long could we keep this up? How long before the weight of it all came crashing down on us?

How long before I collapsed beneath the pressure? Because the day would come. I was exhausted, tired of hiding. Of pretending. Of living in constant fear of a slip-up.

A gentle knock at the door startled me out of my spiralling thoughts. It was late, well past midnight, but I knew who it was without having to open the door.

I crossed the room on silent feet, pulse fluttering wildly as I pressed my eye to the peephole. Lewis stood on the other side, his dark hair tousled, his eyes shadowed with fatigue and something else, something rawer. Something that tugged at my soul and made my breath catch.

I opened the door, just a crack. Just enough for him to slip through. He eased the door shut behind him and flipped the lock with a soft snick.

And then he was on me, his hands cupping my face, his mouth finding mine with a desperation that stole my breath and my reason in one fell swoop. I melted into him, into the solid heat of his body and the way he gripped me like he was afraid I might disappear if he let go.

He walked me backward into the room, still kissing me like a man drowning, until my calves hit the edge of the bed. We tumbled onto it, graceless and heedless of the squeak of protesting springs.

He broke away only to strip off his shirt, to fumble with the button of his jeans. I watched him through heavy-lidded eyes, my own hands clumsy on the hem of my oversized sleep shirt. The one I'd bought just before we left LA, a cheeky black number with "I'm with the band" emblazoned across the front in neon letters.

It seemed funny at the time. A private joke, a wink at the secret part of my life I couldn't share with the world.

I am with the band. And it's slowly killing me.

But I shoved the thought down, buried it under the rush of sensation as Lewis's hands found my bare skin, as his weight settled over me, heavy and perfect. This was what I needed. What I craved like air, like sunlight.

Him. Us. This.

Even if it was only in stolen moments.

"How's Nia?" he asked, the words a hot rush against my collarbone. "Is she…"

"She'll be okay," I said, threading my fingers through his hair, marvelling at the silk of it. "Concussion. Bad one. But she'll recover."

He exhaled, a shaky gust of relief that skittered over my skin and raised goosebumps in its wake. "Thank Christ." He pressed a kiss to the hollow of my throat, a benediction. "And James? He's staying with her?"

I hummed an affirmative, arching into his touch as his hands skimmed my sides, my hips, removing my panties. "Yeah. Taking a week off tour. His bandmates are cool with it."

"Good. That's good." Another kiss, this one open-mouthed

and hot against the hinge of my jaw. "I was worried. About both of them."

"Me too. Lord, me too. When I saw her fall, I…"

But I couldn't finish, couldn't voice the fear that something worse had happened, that I couldn't stop imagining us in that position.

Lewis sensed my hesitation, my unspoken distress. He pulled back just enough to meet my eyes, his own dark and fathomless in the muted light filtering through the hotel room curtains. "She's okay, cariad. You said it yourself." He smoothed a thumb over my cheekbone, his touch achingly tender. "It was an accident. One we'll all learn from, but she'll be back before you know it, and it'll never happen again. We'll make sure of it."

I wanted to believe him. Wanted to let his words, his conviction, wash over me like absolution. But I couldn't. The seeds of doubt had taken root too deeply.

What if it did happen again and it was him next time? How would I get any information on his condition? I didn't have any way of contacting his mother or sister. What if it were serious and no one could help him?

The thoughts chased themselves round and round my head, a dizzying, sickening spiral. But I couldn't voice them. Couldn't lay that at Lewis's feet. Not when he was looking at me like that. Like I was something precious, something worth risking everything for.

So I did the only thing I could. I kissed him, hard and desperate, pouring everything I couldn't say into the press of my lips, the slide of my tongue. Begging him without words to make me forget, to chase away the shadows and the doubts and the gnawing, relentless guilt.

Just for a little while. Just for tonight.

And Lord bless him, he understood. He met me kiss for kiss, touch for fevered touch, his hands and mouth worshipping me with a reverence that bordered on the divine. He mapped every inch of my skin like he was committing it to memory.

Like this stolen moment might be our last.

His talented fingers stroked me until the thoughts quieted and nothing but him reduced me to aching, shivering need. The orgasm tore through me faster than I expected, but he was ready for it. His body hovered above me, hard and ready and perfect.

"Missed you," he rasped, eyes burning into mine as he notched himself against my entrance. "Missed you so fucking much."

A choked laugh escaped me, disbelieving and thick with unshed tears. "How?" I asked, breathless and unravelling. "We were together all night. On the bus, backstage…"

"Not like this," he growled, flexing his hips in a slow, devastating grind. Sparks burst behind my eyelids, pleasure searing me from the inside out. "Never like this. I could be standing right next to you, close enough to touch, and it's never enough. I need you like this, bare and open and mine. Need to feel you, taste you, be inside you so deep there's no telling where I end and you begin."

His words shattered me, swept me under like a riptide. I clung to him, nails biting into the flexing muscles of his back, anchoring myself to the only solid thing in a world gone soft and hazy with sensation.

"Show me. Show me how much you missed me."

And he did. Oh lord, did he. With every thrust of his hips, every drag of his cock against my inner walls, he branded me, claimed me, ruined me for anything and anyone else. The pleasure built and built, a tidal wave cresting, threatening to pull me under.

But even lost to the magic and madness of his touch, even drunk on the taste of him and the broken sounds of need he breathed into my skin, I couldn't fully surrender. Couldn't shake the nagging feeling that this was all too good to be true, too perfect to last.

That every moan, every sigh, every whispered endearment was a countdown to the inevitable end.

Because it had to end, didn't it? I couldn't tell if he truly wanted the alternative—me, wholly and publicly his.

Even loving him as I did, I knew myself too well. I couldn't be his secret forever.

LEWIS

I pulled Liv close, revelling in the feel of her warm body pressed against mine. These quiet, intimate moments were a precious rarity on tour. I wanted to freeze time, to live in this bubble where nothing existed but her and me, just like this.

She nestled into my side, her head resting on my chest, directly over my heart. Did she know she held that, too? That she'd burrowed so deep into my soul, I couldn't imagine my life without her in it?

"Can I ask you something?" she asked, voice soft, almost hesitant.

"Anything, cariad." I pressed a kiss to her hair, breathing her in.

She was quiet for a moment, her fingers tracing idle patterns on my skin. Each brush of her fingertips sent sparks dancing through my veins and teased my semi-hard cock. We needed to sleep, but if she kept it up, I'd gladly wear her out until she passed out from exhaustion.

She shifted, propping herself up on one elbow to look at me. There was something in her eyes, a flicker of uncertainty that made my heart clench.

She bit her lip, a tiny furrow appearing between her brows. "Where do you see us in a year? Two years? Five?" The words came out in a rush, like she'd been holding them back. "Can you… can you imagine a future with me?"

The question hit me like a punch to the gut, stealing my breath. Not because I didn't know the answer—God, I knew it down to my bones—but because of the vulnerability, the raw need in her eyes.

"Of course I can imagine a future with you. It's all I think about, dream about." Sitting up, I cupped her face in my hands and pressed my forehead to hers, trying to pour every ounce of certainty, of love, into the words. "You're it for me, Liv. The endgame. I've never been more sure of anything in my life."

Her breath hitched, a shaky exhale gusting over my lips. But there was still a shadow in her eyes, a hesitation. "Then why does it feel like we're stuck in limbo? Hiding, pretending, always looking over our shoulders?"

I closed my eyes, a dull ache blooming in my chest. She was right. Of course she was right. What we had, this incredible, life-altering thing... it deserved better than stolen moments and secret meetings after the rest of the band disappeared into one of the suites to party the night away.

It deserved everything. Sunlight and laughter, hand-holding walks down busy streets, red carpet kisses and fuck-the-world declarations.

But the cold, insidious tendrils of fear kept me rooted, kept the words locked behind my teeth. Fear of exposure, of scrutiny, of watching something so precious wither under the harsh glare of the spotlight.

"I know." The words felt like glass in my throat. "I know it's not ideal. There's nothing I want more than to shout from the rooftops that you're mine. That I'm the luckiest bastard alive." I drew in a shuddering breath, steeling myself. "But the world we live in... the industry, the media... it's a fucking shark tank. And I'm terrified of what they'll do to you, to us, if they catch even a hint of blood in the water."

Liv pulled back, searching my face. The understanding in her eyes, the compassion gutted me.

"I get that. I do. But we can't live in fear forever. We can't let them control us, dictate how we live our lives." She took a deep breath. "When I was sat in that hospital waiting room tonight not knowing if Nia was okay and not even her boyfriend could walk in there and demand answers without getting permission first, it hit me like a fucking freight train. The fact that if something happened to you, if you were the one in that hospital bed… I'd have no rights. No say. I'd be just the girlfriend, the secret lover, with no legal standing." Her voice wavered, tears welling in those green eyes I adored.

I smoothed her hair back and tried to see beyond the fear clamping down on my lungs.

"And I can't live like that. I won't. I need to know that if the worst happens, if one of us gets hurt or sick… I'll be able to be there. To make decisions, to take care of you. And vice versa."

The pain in her words was a knife to my gut. I gathered her close, burying my face in her hair, breathing her in. "I'm sorry," I whispered, over and over. "I'm so fucking sorry, Liv. I didn't… I hadn't thought about that."

And I hadn't. Too caught up in my own fears, my own hang-ups, to consider the very real, very practical implications of keeping our relationship a secret. The fact that if something happened to me, if I ended up in the hospital or worse… Olivia would have no legal rights. No say in my care, my treatment, my fucking life.

The thought made my blood run cold and my stomach twist with nausea. Because the reverse was true too. If something happened to her, if she needed me… I'd be powerless. A bystander, a nobody in the eyes of the law. And that was a gamble I wasn't willing to make.

Not with her life. Not with her heart.

I pulled back, just enough to cradle her face in my hands, to let her see the raw truth in my eyes. "You're right," I said, the words ringing with conviction. "You're absolutely fucking right, Liv." I swallowed hard, the next words terrifying and true in equal measure. "I want forever with you. I want marriage and babies and matching rocking chairs on a porch somewhere when we're old and grey. I want the world to know that you're mine and I'm yours, in every way that matters."

Her breath caught, her eyes wide and shimmering with fresh

tears. But this time, I could see the hope in them. The love, so vast and deep it stole the air from my lungs.

"You really mean that?" she whispered, wonder and joy trembling in her voice. "You really see a future for us, a real one?"

"I do," I said, catching her lips in a fierce kiss. "I fucking do, Liv. You're my forever. And I'll do whatever it takes to make sure the whole damn world knows it. Just give me a little time, yeah? Let me figure out how to do this right and keep you safe."

She nodded, a wobbly smile breaking through the tears. "Okay," she breathed, winding her arms around my neck. "Okay. I can wait." Her smile turned impish, a flicker of her usual fire. "But not forever, mind. A girl's got needs, and a very real desire not to be a secret baby mama."

I laughed. "Duly noted." I kissed her again, slow and sweet, pouring every ounce of love and gratitude into the press of my lips. "I promise, cariad. It won't be forever. Just long enough to make sure we're bulletproof in every way that counts."

She smiled against my mouth, her fingers threading through my hair. "I like the sound of that."

CHAPTER NINETEEN

LEWIS

"*H*oly shit, this place is insane!" Tom shouted over the music, his eyes wide.

"What?" Lily yelled back, cupping a hand to her ear. "I can't hear a fucking thing!"

Andy grinned, slinging an arm around her shoulders. "I think that's the point, Lil. If your ears aren't ringing, you're not doing Vegas right."

The bass thrummed through my body as we walked deeper into Club Phoenix, following a chatty, black-suited manager and a gang of burly security guards. He cut a path through the crowd, the sea of people parting before him like he was Moses and they were the Red Sea.

Strobe lights flashed in dizzying patterns, painting the writhing bodies in neon hues. Go-go dancers in glittering, barely-there costumes gyrated in elevated cages, their lithe forms silhouetted against the pulsing lights. The air was thick with the scent of sweat, perfume, and the unmistakable tang of alcohol.

It was quintessential Vegas—a sensory overload of light and sound that left me feeling buzzed before I'd even had a drink.

Rich, jewel-toned fabrics draped from the walls, and intricate mosaics glittered underfoot. The furniture was all plush velvet and gleaming chrome, oozing luxury and excess. It was like stepping into a modern-day pleasure palace, a hedonistic wonderland designed for indulgence and escape.

But the real spectacle was just beginning. As word of the band's arrival spread, a crowd began to gather near the VIP section stairs. Mostly women, they jostled for position, their eager faces turned towards us like flowers seeking the sun.

Security fanned out, holding them back and creating a path for us.

"Oh my god, it's them!"

"Lewis, over here!"

"I'll marry you, Alex!"

Their shrieks and pleas blended with the pounding music while camera flashes nearly blinded us. If not for Anderson's tight grip on my shoulder, I'm not sure I would have found my way through.

"Damn, it's good to be a rock star," Tom said as we mounted the stairs, surveying the scene below like a king overlooking his kingdom.

I barely heard him, my attention snagged by a flash of chestnut hair on the balcony above. Liv. She was dancing with Tommy from Lover's Knot, her body undulating to the relentless beat, her shirt riding up to reveal a strip of tanned skin at her waist.

Something hot and prickly unfurled in my gut as I watched Tommy's hands skim down her sides, coming to rest on her hips.

I had no right to feel jealous.

Watching her with someone else, seeing the casual intimacy of their bodies moving together… it cut like a knife, swift and unexpected, making me momentarily forget why it mattered that we stay a secret.

Then the fancy thoughts faded and my sister's tear stricken

face filled my mind. The press had twisted her words in ways she'd never meant. She cried for hours on the phone to me, begging me to make it stop. But nothing I or our publicist did eased the pressure or the vicious chatter of teenagers.

A month later, she was gone.

I remembered all too well the damage the press could do. I never wanted Liv to look at me like that. Or to mirror my sister's path in any way.

"You keep staring like that, your face is gonna stick that way," Lily shouted in my ear, jolting me from my brooding.

I schooled my features into something resembling nonchalance. "Don't know what you're talking about."

She snorted. "Please. You look like you're about five seconds away from punching Tommy in the dick."

I opened my mouth to protest, but she cut me off with a knowing look.

"Lewis. I've known you since we were thirteen. I can read you like a book." Her expression softened, her hand coming to rest on my forearm. "Why don't you just tell her how you feel?"

I sighed, scrubbing a hand over my face. "It's not that simple, Lil. You know what it's like, living in the spotlight. I don't want to drag her into all that."

"Maybe. But it's not your choice to make." She gave my arm a squeeze. "Olivia's a big girl, she's going to be in the spotlight with or without you. And I've seen the way she looks at you."

"Oi!" a familiar voice bellowed from across the VIP section. Jared, Rhiannon's drummer, waved us over. "Get your asses over here, you wankers! The drinks are flowing, and the night is young!"

Beside him, the rest of Rhiannon and the guys from Lover's Knot were sprawled across the plush sofas, bottles and glasses littering the table, already well on their way to properly sloshed.

"You heard the man." Andy laughed, clapping me on the shoulder. "Can't let them down, can we?"

"Absolutely not. Lead the way." I grinned, letting him steer me towards the group. As we approached, a cheer went up, hands reaching out to pull us into the fray.

"About bloody time!" Nick, Lover's Knot's drummer, crowed. "Thought you lot had gotten lost. Or worse, sober!"

"Not a chance," Tom scoffed, snagging a bottle of vodka from the table. "The night's just getting started, boys. And we've got some catching up to do."

As the banter and laughter flew around me, I found my gaze drawn back to the dance floor. To Liv. She was in her element, lost in the music, her body moving with a fluid grace that took my breath away. As if sensing my stare, she looked up, our eyes locking across the crowded room.

Her smile, slow and secret, sent a jolt of heat straight through me. She crooked a finger, beckoning me closer, and it took every ounce of willpower I had to stay put.

"Mate, you still with us?" Tom's voice cut through the haze, his hand waving in front of my face.

I blinked, dragging my focus back to the group. "Yeah, sorry. Just… distracted."

Tom followed my gaze. "I'll bet. That girl of yours is a right firecracker, isn't she?"

I bristled, my jaw tightening. "She's not 'my girl', Tom. We're just… it's complicated."

"Right," he drawled, clearly unconvinced. "Well, while you're sorting out your 'complications', get a drink. We haven't got long before they bundle us up on the bus again." He nodded to the waiting server. "They need your card to put on the tab."

"Maybe we should take it easy tonight. We've got an early start tomor—"

"Oh, come off it!" Andy cut in, slinging an arm around my shoulders. "We just played the best fucking show of our lives. If that's not cause for celebration, I don't know what is. Get a drink, Lew."

He had a point. And honestly, what was the harm? A few drinks… it was nothing in the grand scheme of things. And maybe, just maybe, it would take my mind off the growing ache in my chest, the longing to be out there with Olivia.

"Alright, fuck it," I relented, fishing my wallet from my back pocket. I handed it over, muttering a drink order to the server and went right back to staring at the dance floor and the singer owning it.

"Holy shit, lads!" Nick's eyes were wide. "Is that what I think it is?"

Tom grinned, holding up the amber-filled bottle like a trophy. "Macallan '26, aged to perfection. Smooth as silk and twice as expensive."

A low whistle went around the table. I felt my stomach drop.

"Where the hell did you get that?" I asked, my voice carefully even. "And more importantly, who paid for it?"

Tom's grin turned sheepish. He tipped the bottle towards me in a mock salute. "You said you wanted whiskey. I just gave the bar a little direction."

The table erupted in cheers and laughter.

"Damn, Davies!" Andy crowed, his grin stretching from ear to ear. "When you decide to splash out, you don't fuck around, do you? What's the damage on that beauty, a couple grand?"

"Ten, actually," Tom supplied helpfully, already pouring generous measures into the waiting glasses. "But who's counting, right? Not like our boy here can't afford it."

I forced a smile, my teeth gritted so hard my jaw ached. "Right. What's a few grand between friends?"

Just you wait. Payback's a bitch, dickhead.

I stared at Tom, communicating the threat with my eyes. He just grinned at me, unrepentant.

"Well, go on then." I gestured at the bottle. "Pour us a dram of that liquid gold. Let's see if it lives up to the hype."

I didn't need to tell him twice. He popped the top and started pouring. The whiskey flowed, the laughter and conversation picking back up. I knocked back my drink in one swallow, relishing the burn, the way it momentarily quieted the gnawing in my gut.

Half an hour and a few too many Tequila shots later, the club was in full swing. The VIP area was packed, celebrities and hangers-on jostling for space, for a chance to brush shoulders with rock royalty.

And I still couldn't tear my gaze from Liv.

I watched her move, her body swaying to the beat, her hair a wild cloud around her face. Even sweaty and drunk, she was magnetic, mesmerising. A siren's call I was powerless to resist.

Before I could think better of it, I was on my feet, weaving through the crowd with single-minded focus. All I could think about was getting to her, feeling her body against mine, consequences be damned.

I reached her just as the music kicked into high gear, my hands finding her hips, pulling her back against my chest.

"Lewis," she breathed, her voice husky and low. "What are you doing? Someone might see…

"They're all too drunk to see a foot in front of their faces." My lips grazed the shell of her ear. She melted into me, her head falling back onto my shoulder, her ass grinding in a slow, dirty circle against my crotch. "They aren't going to see a thing and even if they did, they wouldn't remember tomorrow."

For a moment, she just stared at me, her bottom lip caught between her teeth. Then, slowly, a smile spread across her face. A real smile, bright and blinding and full of promise.

"Well then…" Her arms wound around my neck. "I guess you'd better shut up and dance with me. Before I change my mind."

I grinned, wide and reckless and so fucking in love I could barely breathe. "Yes ma'am."

And with that, I spun her around, pulled her close, and lost myself in the music, in the feel of her body against mine. The rest of the world tunnelled away until there was only this. Only us. Her arms looped around my neck, my hands mapping the dip of her waist. Her breath hot against my ear.

"I've been thinking about this all night. About you."

My fingers flexed on her hips, heat licking down my spine. "Fuck, Liv. You can't just say things like that."

She grinned wickedly, her nails scratching lightly at my nape. "And why not? Afraid you won't be able to handle it?"

"More like afraid I won't be able to keep my hands to myself." The words came out lower, rougher than I intended. Reckless in a way I rarely let myself be.

But Liv had a way of undoing me, of making me want to throw caution to the wind and damn the consequences. With her, I felt drunk on more than just whiskey and Tequila. Drunk on possibility, on the promise of her skin against mine, on the future I could see unspooling before us, dizzying and bright.

She held my gaze, her green eyes molten in the strobing lights. When she spoke, her voice was a rough purr I felt all the way to my toes.

"Who says I want you to?"

If I had been a better man, a stronger man, I would have pulled back. Would have put some distance between us before I did something stupid, like kiss her senseless in the middle of this crowded club, with our friends and half the music industry watching.

But tonight, with the bass thudding in my bones and Liv pressed against me, I was weak. Weak and wanting and so bloody tired of denying myself the only thing I'd ever really wanted.

So when she fisted her hands in my hair and pulled my mouth down to hers, I didn't resist.

I sank into the kiss, into her, losing myself in the hot slide of her lips, the flick of her tongue, the gentlest graze of her teeth. She tasted like tequila and lime and something undeniably Olivia. An addictive flavour I already knew I'd never get enough of.

My hands roamed her back, slipping under her shirt to find the warm skin beneath. She shivered, arching into me, a breathy moan lost to the pounding music. It was a siren's song, calling me to ruin, and I followed willingly, eagerly, until the need for air forced us apart. We stared at each other, chests heaving, pulses racing.

Her lipstick was smudged, her hair even wilder than before. She looked thoroughly, devastatingly kissed, and the knowledge that I had wrecked her so completely, sent a dark thrill through me.

She leaned in close, her lips brushing the shell of my ear. "I have a crazy idea," she whispered, her voice a husky purr that sent shivers down my spine. "Let's get married."

I pulled back, my eyes widening. "What?"

"You heard me." She grinned, her eyes sparkling with mischief and something deeper, something that made my heart skip a beat. "Let's get married. Right now, tonight. That little chapel next door... it's perfect."

I stared at her, my mind reeling. This was insane. We'd only known each other for a few weeks. Getting married, here, now, on a drunken whim in Vegas... it was the epitome of recklessness, of irresponsibility.

But as I gazed into her eyes, saw the love and certainty shining there... I couldn't remember why that was a bad thing.

There'd be no more risk of another man catching her eye, no more need for jealousy. We'd still be able to keep our relationship quiet, but she'd be mine and I'd be hers. That was all that mattered, wasn't it?

"Okay," I breathed, a giddy laugh bubbling up my throat. "Okay, yes. Let's do it."

CHAPTER TWENTY

OLIVIA

The chapel was a riot of kitsch, a neon fever-dream of hearts and cherubs and twinkling fairy lights. Or maybe that was just the tequila. Lewis and I stumbled through the doors, clinging to each other and giggling like lovesick teenagers, and it seemed like the most romantic place in the world.

"Oooh, look at the little cupids!" I cooed, pointing at the chubby cherubs adorning the walls. "Aren't they just the cutest? I want to pinch their little cheeks!"

"I think they're judging us." Lewis squinted, his brow furrowing in concentration. "They know we're insane."

"Shh, don't say that!" I swatted at his arm, dissolving into another fit of giggles. "This isn't insane. It's... it's fate. Kismet. Meant to be!"

The words tumbled out, slightly slurred, but I meant them with every fibre of my being. I had never been more certain of anything in my life.

Lewis and I were supposed to be together. This wedding, impulsive and wild as it might be, was just the universe's way of making it official. I mean, what were the odds? Us, picking a club right next door to a 24-hour wedding chapel? If that wasn't a sign from the big man upstairs, I didn't know what was.

Right now, our friends were still partying next door, none the wiser that we were about to commit ourselves to each other. The thought of their shocked faces when we walked into sound check tomorrow with rings on our fingers filled me with absolute delight.

Maybe we should have a wedding reveal party?

"Welcome to Serendipity Chapel!" a cheerful voice said before I could figure out what that thought meant. A woman in a pink sequinned dress approached us, her smile wide and knowing. "I'm guessing you two lovebirds are here to tie the knot?"

"Yes!" I threw my arms around Lewis's neck and nearly toppled us both over. "We want to get married. Right now. Tonight. The full Vegas experience. Elvis, glitter... give us the whole shebang!"

The chapel lady chuckled, clearly used to dealing with drunk, impetuous couples. "Of course. Let's get started on the paperwork, shall we? While you fill out the licence, you can browse our selection of rings and choose your ceremony package."

She led us to a small table where she laid out the necessary forms. I stared at the lines and boxes, the legalese blurring before my eyes. This was really happening. In a matter of minutes, Lewis and I would be husband and wife.

"I love you," I blurted out, the words tumbling from my lips before I could stop them. "I know it's fast and it's crazy but I do, Lewis. I love you so much. Like, so much. So, so much. More than... more than tequila. And you know how much I love tequila."

His smile could have lit up the entire Strip. "I love you too, Liv. More than all the tequila in Mexico." He leaned in, capturing my lips in a kiss that tasted like whiskey, promises, and a hint of lime.

We filled out the forms in a haze of laughter and sloppy kisses, our handwriting a drunken scrawl. Then we moved on to the fun part—picking out our rings. After much deliberation and a lot of giggling, we settled on a matching set of thin silver bands. They glinted under the fluorescent lights, a tangible symbol of our commitment. Our beautiful, alcohol-fuelled commitment.

"Alright, lovebirds," the chapel lady called out, waving us towards an altar that looked like Cupid had thrown up all over it, a riot of plastic flowers and twinkling lights. "It's showtime!"

An Elvis impersonator stood waiting for us, his rhinestone-studded jumpsuit catching the light. He greeted us with a crooked grin and a wink, launching into a rendition of 'Can't Help Falling In Love' as we wobbled towards him.

"Dearly beloved," Elvis began, his voice a perfect imitation of that iconic drawl. "We are gathered here today to join this man and this woman in holy matrimony."

I blinked up at Lewis, my vision blurring with happy tears. He stared back at me, his expression a mirror of the love and joy I felt.

"And now, I believe y'all have written your own vows?" Elvis prompted, a smirk playing at his lips.

We had—scribbled on the backs of cocktail napkins from the club, the words smudged and barely legible.

Lewis went first, clearing his throat dramatically. "Liv Monroe, from the moment I first saw you on that stage, I knew you were special. Your voice, your spirit, your beauty… you captured my heart in an instant. And now, I know I never want to let you go."

His voice cracked with emotion and I squeezed his hands in reassurance, swaying slightly on my feet.

"I vow to love you," he continued, "to cherish you, to support you in everything you do. I vow to be your partner, your friend, your family. I vow to rock out with you, to dance with you, to make beautiful music with you, in every sense of the word."

The Elvis impersonator fanned himself dramatically, pretending to wipe away a tear. "Those are some mighty fine vows, son. And now, the bride?"

I took a deep, shaky breath. My head was swimming and my tongue felt clumsy, but I pushed through. "I had a crush on you when I was sixteen years old. It was silly." A nervous giggle bubbled up my throat. "I used to dream about meeting you, about telling you how much your music meant to me. But I never imagined... I never dared to hope that we'd end up here. That you'd see me, really see me, and that you'd love me the way I love you. That you'd want to claim me in the most important way you could."

I swallowed hard, my voice thick with tears.

"I, Olivia Monroe, take you, Lewis Davies, to be my lawfully wedded husband, to have and to hold, to support through all the highs and lows whether backstage or on stage, from this day forward, for better, for worse, for richer, for poorer, in sickness and in health, until death do us part. Or until the tequila wears off."

A ripple of laughter went through our small audience—the Elvis and the random chapel employee serving as our witness. But I barely heard them. All I could see was Lewis, his eyes shining with love and laughter and unbridled joy.

"By the power vested in me by the King of Rock and Roll and the great state of Nevada," Elvis declared grandly, "I now pronounce you husband and wife. You may kiss your bride!"

Lewis didn't need to be told twice. He swept me into his arms, dipping me low as his lips claimed mine. I clung to him, pouring every ounce of love and joy and pure, incandescent happiness into that kiss.

It was messy and off-centre and absolutely perfect. Just like us. Just like this wild, wonderful, once in a lifetime night.

We were married. Actually, legally married. The man of my teenage dreams was now my husband and this, this wild, wonderful, unexpected journey we were on together… it was only the beginning.

When we finally came up for air, both of us flushed and breathless and giddy, Elvis was holding out a pen and a piece of paper. "Alright, kids. Just need your John Hancocks here and here and you'll be official."

We signed with a flourish, our names a messy tangle on the paper.

Mr and Mrs Lewis and Olivia Davies.

It had a nice ring to it. It looked right. It felt right. Like it was always meant to be.

We stumbled out of the chapel, hand in hand, giddy newly-weds ready to take on the world. The Vegas night enveloped us, all flashing neon and pulsing music and shimmering, drunken magic.

And that's when it hit me. The buses. The tour.

I gasped, the thought hitting me like a bucket of ice water. "Oh shit, what time is it?"

Lewis fumbled for his phone, his brow furrowing as he tried to focus on the screen. "Fuck, I can't… it's all blurry. Too many numbers."

"Gimme that." I snatched the phone, squinting at the display. "2:55… the buses leave at 3!"

"Fuck, we have to go. Now."

We took off running, a mad dash across the crowded Strip. Lewis grabbed my hand, pulling me along as we wove through the throngs of tourists and partiers. The world tilted and spun around us, a dizzying whirl of lights and pounding feet on pavement.

With seconds to spare, we practically fell into the bus, breathless and dishevelled and grinning like a couple of love-drunk fools.

Which, of course, is exactly what we were.

The driver just shook his head, clearly used to this kind of last-minute insanity. But Anderson… oh, if looks could kill, we'd have been sent to the morgue instead of the honeymoon suite.

"Well, well, well," he drawled, his voice deceptively calm. "Look what the cat dragged in. You two have a nice little adventure, did you? A little Vegas sightseeing, maybe some souvenir shopping?"

Lewis, still high on the rush of it all, just grinned sheepishly. "Something like that."

Anderson stepped closer, his hulking frame looming over us. "I'm your bodyguard, not your bloody babysitter. It's my job to keep you safe, but I can't very well do that if I don't know where the fuck you are, now can I?"

I cringed, guilt twisting in my gut. He was right. We'd been so caught up in our own little bubble, we hadn't stopped to think about the people we'd worried, the risks we'd taken.

"I know we shouldn't have run off." Lewis collapsed onto the sofa, his eyes starting to droop. I wasn't faring much better, on account of needing to hold myself up with the bus dashboard. "It was stupid and irresponsible, and I'm sorry."

His eyes narrowed, his scarred face twisting into a scowl. "Stupid and irresponsible doesn't even begin to cover it. You can't keep pulling this disappearing act shit."

"It won't happen again," Lewis said, his voice slurred and his head lulling back. "From now on, I'll stick to the schedule and keep you in the loop. Scout's honour."

"Scout's honour." Anderson snorted, shaking his head. "You wouldn't know a schedule if it bit you in the ass."

Despite the severity of his words, there was a hint of affection in his tone.

"Won't happen again, Savage. Promise." Lewis lifted his head and threw a sloppy salute, his grin turning cheeky. "Permission to retire to our bunks and sleep off this tequila haze, sir?"

Anderson rolled his eyes, but I swore I saw the ghost of a smile twitching at the corner of his mouth. "Permission granted. But if you even think about sneaking off again, I will personally handcuff you to your bunk. And not in the fun way, mind."

"Kinky," Lewis quipped, winking at me. "But I think I prefer my current bunk mate, thanks all the same. No offence, big guy. You're just not my type."

With that, he tugged me towards the back of the bus, the world tilting and spinning with each stumbling step, leaving a grumbling Anderson in our wake.

CHAPTER TWENTY-ONE

LEWIS

*S*omebody needed to crank the AC. Heat blanketed my side in a comforting yet overwhelming way in the small space of my bunk. My body always went into overdrive after a night of hard drinking, but this was intense.

I shifted restlessly, trying to escape the smothering heat, but there was nowhere to go.

My head throbbed, a vicious drumbeat pounding behind my eyes. Fragments of memories danced at the edges of my consciousness, taunting me with their hazy, disjointed images. Flashes of light, snatches of music, the taste of whiskey on my tongue. And through it all, a constant, pulsing awareness of her. Olivia. My...

I tried to turn over, my sleep dazed mind trying to escape it. Pain splintered through my head, but still I couldn't move.

What the fuck?

My eyes opened. Liv lay tucked into my side, her soft curves and sleep-warm skin moulded to my body while her head rested on my shoulder, her leg thrown haphazardly over mine.

Between the tangle of the sheet and the death grip she had on me, no wonder I couldn't move.

For a moment, I let myself sink into the drowsy contentment of holding her close. In the cocoon of my bunk, with the curtains drawn against the world, it was easy to pretend that this was all there was. Just her and me, skin to skin, the way it was meant to be. But as the cobwebs slowly cleared from my mind, little details began to filter in, chipping away at the edges of my peace.

The air was too still, the gentle rocking motion that usually lulled me to sleep conspicuously absent. The muted light seeping through the curtain was too bright, too steady, lacking the strobing quality of passing streetlights as we travelled from city to city.

Something wasn't right.

We should have been moving, the low thrum of the engine a constant background noise. But the bus was silent, stationary, the air heavy with a stillness that set my teeth on edge.

I shifted slightly, dislodging the hook of her foot around my knee, trying to get my bearings without disturbing her.

If we aren't on the road, then where the hell are we? And more importantly, what time is it?

The thought sent a fresh jolt of anxiety through me, a sickening lurch in my gut as the pieces started to fall into place.

If the bus was parked, if the sun was already high in the sky… then we'd slept far later than we should have. And if we were still in my bunk, tangled together like lovers with nowhere else to be…

Oh shit. *Oh shit shit shit.*

The band.

They would have seen us… it would all come out.

Fuck.

Why had I been so stupid, so careless?

I squeezed my eyes shut, trying to force back the panic so I could think clearly and find a way out before… it was too late for that now. The damage was done. All I could do was try to minimise the fallout.

But how?

Bile rose in my throat, hot and acrid. This couldn't be happening.

I'd spent years helplessly watching relationships get torn apart, watching the press degrade people, reducing them to nothing more than the lies that sold papers or drove website traffic. The constant scrutiny, the relentless pressure, the voracious hunger of a public that felt entitled to every last shred of our lives… it was a meat grinder, chewing up and spitting out anything good or pure or real.

Like my sweet, innocent sister who they drove to suicide.

I couldn't let that happen to Liv. To us. I'd sworn to myself that I would protect this precious thing between us. That I would shield her from the worst of it, the soul-deep scars that never really healed. Protect her from becoming like…

No. Inside, I cringed away from the thought, shutting it down instantly. I never went there. I couldn't.

I squeezed my eyes shut, trying to calm the rising tide of dread. I shifted carefully, trying not to wake her as I craned my neck to peek through the gap in the curtain. The narrow hallway was empty, the other bunks silent and still. No sign of movement, no clinking of glassware or the murmur of voices from the living area downstairs.

Hope flared in my chest, cautious but persistent.

Maybe we'd gotten lucky.

And that's when I saw it.

A glint of silver on my left hand, catching the thin beam of sunlight as I reached to pull back the curtain.

A ring.

A fucking wedding ring, sitting on my finger like it had every right to be there.

The world tilted, my stomach lurching with it. Memories came flooding back, snapshots and sensations tumbling through my mind in a dizzying cascade. Liv's smile, radiant under the neon lights. The press of her body against mine as we danced, so close I could feel her heartbeat. The electric brush of her lips on my skin as she whispered in my ear, giddy and giggling and so fucking beautiful.

"I have this crazy idea. Let's get married."

Oh god. What had we done?

My hand shook. The ring gleamed mockingly in the sun, a tangible reminder of the insanity, the sheer fucking madness of what we'd done.

We were married. Actually, legally married.

A grin spread across my face, a disbelieving laugh escaping my lips. It was insane, completely and utterly insane. But it was also the most incredibly perfect thing I could imagine.

Married. To Olivia. My Liv.

A rush of warmth flooded through me, chasing away the last vestiges of my hangover. This was real. It wasn't just a drunken fantasy or a fleeting whim. We'd actually gone and done it.

I stared down at her in awe. She was mine now, truly and completely mine. My wife.

The word sent a thrill through me, a burst of possessive pride. I'd never get tired of saying it.

I brushed a gentle kiss across her forehead and pulled her closer, now able to savour the warm weight of her against me. She stirred, her lashes fluttering, a sleepy little hum vibrating through her as she nestled closer.

"Mmm, morning handsome," she mumbled, her lips brushing my skin in a drowsy kiss. "What time's it?"

Her voice was hushed and honeyed, rough with sleep but sweet with affection. "Liv," I murmured, my voice thick with emotion. "Wake up. We did something amazing last night."

She stiffened slightly, the note of awe in my voice catching her attention. Slowly, her head lifted from my chest, her eyes blinking open in curiosity.

"What is it?" she asked, her brow furrowed as she took in my expression. "You look like you snuck out and jammed with Slash without telling me."

I barked out a joyful laugh, the sound ringing out in the still air. "It's even better than that." I held up my hand so she could see the ring. "We got married last night."

There was a beat of silence, a heartbeat that stretched into an eternity. I watched the emotions play across her face like clouds across the sun—shock, disbelief, a flicker of something that might have been wonder or terror or both.

Then, slowly, a smile began to bloom. It started at the corners of her mouth, a tiny upward tilt that gradually spread into a grin so wide it crinkled the corners of her eyes.

"Holy shit," she breathed, her gaze locked on the ring. "We did. We actually fucking did it!"

A disbelieving laugh bubbled up from her throat, half shock and half pure, unadulterated joy. She scrambled to sit up, the sheets falling away to reveal miles of bare skin that I wanted to explore all over again.

"I can't wait to tell the band. Lily is going to be so furious that we got married without her." She grinned, her eyes sparkling with amusement. "And Ash, oh she'll never let me hear the end of it."

Reality came crashing down, the icy fingers of dread wrapping around my heart and squeezing until I could barely breathe.

Tell the band? Make it public?

No. No, no, no. We couldn't. *I* couldn't.

This had to be the punchline of a cosmic joke I was too fucked in the head to appreciate.

The panic must have shown on my face because Liv's smile faltered, confusion and concern creeping into her eyes.

"What's wrong?"

I shook my head, trying to find the words to explain the sheer fucking terror coursing through my veins. What the fuck had we been thinking? How could we have been so stupid, so reckless, so blindly, naively romantic?

"We can't tell anyone. Not yet. Maybe not ever."

She frowned, hurt and bewilderment warring across her

features. "What? Why not? This is amazing. This is everything we wanted."

I swallowed hard, my throat suddenly bone dry. "I know. Fuck, Liv, I know. But the press, the public scrutiny… it'll tear us apart. It'll destroy us."

Her mouth opened, a protest forming on her lips, but I barrelled on, desperate to make her understand.

"You don't know what it's like. The constant invasion of privacy, the lies and speculation and fucking *entitlement* people feel to every aspect of your life. It's suffocating. It's toxic. And I can't… I *won't* let that touch us. I won't let it taint this." My voice cracked, the raw edge of desperation bleeding through.

I cupped her face in my hands, my thumbs brushing over the delicate arch of her cheekbones. I released her and removed a silver necklace from around my neck. I removed the ring and threaded it through the chain. She lifted her own hand, staring at the matching band on her finger with a sort of dazed awe. I placed the ring around my neck and stared at her, struggling to get a clear read. Her eyes were shining, her cheeks flushed with emotion.

"Please, Liv. I need you to trust me on this. I need you to understand why we have to keep this quiet, at least for now. Can you do that? Can you give me that, just for a little while?"

livia

The words hit me like a slap.

His expression screamed sheer, unadulterated panic, maybe even horror.

He threw back the curtain and scrambled out of the bunk, his body almost shaking. He started pacing and I slid to the edge of the bed, letting my legs dangle in the air as I watched him with dread choking me.

My belly churned, a sickening sense of foreboding stealing the air from my lungs. This wasn't how it was supposed to go.

He was supposed to be happy, elated, as dizzy with love and possibility as I was.

Not... this.

Not looking at me like I was a mistake, a regret, a problem to be solved.

"What..." I swallowed hard, trying to find my voice past the sudden lump in my throat. "What... what do you mean? I thought... last night, you were so happy. You said you wanted this."

My mind raced back to the chapel, to the way he'd looked at me as we'd exchanged vows. The love, the certainty, the pure fucking elation shining in his eyes. Had I imagined it all?

"I was drunk, Liv!" He snapped, his voice rising. "We both were! Drunk and high on adrenaline and... and fucking caught up in the moment." He tugged at his hair, the words falling from his lips rapid-fire. "But this... this is reality. Cold, hard reality. And the reality is that we fucked up, big time."

"Fucked up?" I pushed myself off the bunk and landed on the floor in front of him, glaring up at him. "Is that what you think this is?"

"No, that's not... shit." He scrubbed a hand over his face. "I love you," he said, his voice softer now but no less desperate. "You know I do. But this... it's too much, too fast. We don't have the luxury of living in denial, we have to face the reality of what we've done."

Reality.

The word lodged in my chest like a shard of ice. Because the reality was this: I loved him. Loved him with a fierce, all-consuming intensity that I'd never known before. Loved him in a way that made me certain, down to my very marrow, that this was right. That he was it for me, my once-in-a-lifetime, written-in-the-stars soulmate.

As unexpected as it all was, I still wanted it with every fibre of my being. For him to claim he loved me and then... I couldn't fathom how it could be true.

How could he look at me with such fear, such regret, when all I wanted to do was pull him close and never let go?

I couldn't speak for a second. My eyes burned and my heart twisted in my chest.

"So that's it then?" I asked, hating the way my voice shook. "Was it all just a drunken mistake to you? Something to undo and sweep under the rug as quickly as possible?"

He flinched, his eyes squeezing shut as if in pain. "That's not… fuck. That's not what I'm saying."

"Then what are you saying?" I demanded, the hurt morphing into something hotter, sharper. Anger, bubbling up from some deep, wounded place inside me. "Because from where I'm standing, it sounds a whole lot like 'sorry Liv, but this was a huge mistake and I can't wait to get out of it.' Is that really how you feel?"

"I'm saying we need to be realistic!" He shouted, flinging his hands out in frustration. "We're in the middle of a fucking tour, under a microscope every second of every day. If the press gets wind of this…"

"Oh, well, heaven forbid the press finds out," I mocked, the words bitter on my tongue. "Imagine the scandal. Rock star marries girlfriend in Vegas. Stop the fucking presses."

"You don't get it." His jaw clenched, a muscle ticking in his cheek. "You don't know what it's like, to have every aspect of your life dissected and splashed across the tabloids. To have your privacy, your relationships, your fucking soul bared for public consumption."

I softened slightly. "We can figure this out," I said softly, reaching for his hand. "Together. That's what marriage is, isn't it? Facing the world as a team, no matter what comes our way."

He stared at our joined hands, his thumb brushing over my knuckles in a feather-light caress. The touch sent shivers down my spine, even now.

"I want to believe that."

I could hear the 'but' even though he stopped short of voicing it. I shook off his grip, the fight draining from me the longer I stared into his pleading eyes. Did I actually stand a chance of convincing him to give this a shot?

"So what, then?" I asked quietly, my fingers twisting the ring on my finger. The metal was warm from my skin, the weight of it already feeling like a part of me. "We just pretend this never happened? Go back to stolen kisses in supply closets and clandestine hookups in hotel rooms?"

If it meant not losing him, I could do it. *I think.* It was better than the alternative—him not wanting me.

It turned my stomach, but I took off my own necklace and removed my rings, copying him. He didn't answer immediately, his gaze fixed on the ring with a glint of fascination that relit my hope.

"Lewis!" Anderson called out from below. "If you're still up there, Liv's sound check is in thirty minutes. Maybe you could pass the message along."

Sound check. The show. The tour. The reality of our lives, crashing back in with all the subtlety of a wrecking ball.

I patted myself down, my mind scrambling into business mode, working up a list of things I had to do before I could get to sound check.

First, find my purse. I fished it out of the bunk sheets and took off down the row of bunks, aiming for the small stairwell. I dragged my fingers through my hair, trying desperately to make myself look presentable for my mad dash into the stadium outside.

Get my bus bag. Take the fastest shower of my life. Sound check. Stop Lewis tearing my heart out and drawing up annulment papers. Easy peasy.

"You can't just walk away from this!" Lewis called after me, his voice tight with frustration. "We have to deal with it, Liv. We can't just ignore it and hope it goes away."

"You deal with it," I snapped.

"It's not—"

"Stop!" I got to the bottom and whirled on him, glaring at

the stupid lug. I didn't care that Anderson was right behind me, hearing every word.

I stared up at him, my heart a raw, aching wound in my chest. The urge to crumple, to fall into his arms and beg him not to do this, was almost overpowering. But I couldn't.

I wouldn't.

If he wanted out of this marriage, he was going to have to say it straight to my face, not hide behind excuses and fears.

"I'm going to go do my job. You go do whatever the fuck it is cowardly musicians do before a show."

His mouth snapped shut and his jaw shifted, tensed. He stared at me with a fire in his eyes that would have made me tingly a few hours ago. Hell, I'd be a liar if I claimed it didn't still. But that didn't matter now.

"I'm not a coward," he gritted out, his hands clenched into fists at his sides. "I'm trying to be smart about this. Trying to do what's best for both of us."

"What's best for both of us?" I shook my head, a disbelieving laugh falling from my lips. "No, Lewis. You're trying to do what's easiest, what's safest, what doesn't force you to take a risk or face your fears." I stepped closer, tilting my chin up to meet his gaze head-on. "But you know what? I don't want safe. I don't want easy. I want you, for better or worse, in sickness and health, all that jazz. I want us. So you need to decide, right here and now, if that's what you want too."

"We'll talk after the show."

I crossed my arms. "So you can force me to divorce you or so we can talk like adults and leave our fears at the door?"

He nodded, the movement jerky and pained.

My brows rose and my patience frayed to threads. "Which is it?"

"The last one."

Which meant I had eight hours to come up with a game plan. Because Lewis Davies had another think coming if he thought I'd roll over so easily.

"Fine."

CHAPTER TWENTY-TWO

LEWIS

I stood on the stage, my bass slung around my shoulders, but I might as well have been a thousand miles away. It should have been another normal day. The stage was the same, the same people surrounded me. Only the venue and city had changed.

Come off it.

I was fucking married.

To Olivia.

Beautiful, brilliant, larger-than-life Liv, who I'd known for a handful of weeks and yet somehow felt like the missing piece I'd been searching for my entire life.

My fingers fumbled over the strings of my bass, the notes coming out all wrong, discordant and jarring. I winced, trying to focus, to lose myself in the music like I always did. But every time I closed my eyes, all I could see was her face. The hurt, the confusion, the barely-masked devastation when I'd panicked, when I'd called our marriage a mistake.

"Fuck," I muttered under my breath, my fingers slipping

again. The sour note echoed through the stadium, earning me a raised eyebrow from Tom at the drums.

"Alright there, Enrique?" he called out, his voice tinged with equal parts amusement and concern. "You're playing like you've never held a bass before, mate."

I forced a smile, shaking my head. "Sorry, sorry. Just… got a lot on my mind."

Understatement of the fucking century.

"Well, get it off your mind and into the music, yeah?" Alex said from the other side of the stage. "We've got a show to put on tonight, in case you forgot."

I took a deep breath, trying to centre myself.

I launched into the opening riff of our fifth song, the notes flowing from my fingers on pure muscle memory. For a moment, it worked. For a moment, I was lost in the music, in the familiar rush of adrenaline that came with playing, with losing myself in the beat.

But then I caught a flash of chestnut hair out of the corner of my eye, and my heart stopped.

It wasn't Liv.

My fingers faltered, the notes dying on the strings. Tom threw his drumsticks down.

"Dude, what the actual fuck?" he groaned.

"Sorry, I…"

"Hey!" Ben, the sound engineer, called out from the sound booth, his voice tight with frustration. "You guys planning on finishing sometime today? We've got a lot of work to do!"

I flinched, guilt churning in my gut. I was fucking this up for everyone, not just myself. Not just Olivia. The whole band, the whole crew, everyone was counting on me to get my shit together.

"Lew?" Andy's voice cut through the haze, softer now, laced with concern. "Everything alright?"

"I… yeah. Yeah, I'm good." I shook my head, like I could physically dislodge the confusion and fear swirling in my brain. "From the top, yeah?"

We launched into the song again, and this time, I held it together. Barely. The notes were right, the rhythm steady, but the soul was gone. I was just going through the motions, a robot in a leather jacket, while my heart beat a brutal tattoo against my ribs.

"*A*lright, that's it!" Ben threw his hands up in exasperation five minutes later. "Let's take five, yeah? Lewis, mate, go take a walk or something. Clear your head. We'll pick this up in a bit."

I nodded, just as frustrated at myself as everyone else. I needed air. I needed space. I needed...

"Lewis." Andy's voice stopped me in my tracks, his hand landing on my shoulder. "Talk to me, man. What's going on with you?"

I shrugged him off, not meeting his eyes. "Nothing. I'm fine. Just... didn't sleep well, that's all."

It wasn't a lie. I hadn't slept well. I'd been too busy getting hitched to the woman of my dreams in an alcohol-fuelled haze, then waking up to the cold, harsh reality of what that meant.

Andy snorted, clearly not buying it. "Bullshit. This is more than a rough night. You've been off since we started." His eyes narrowed, a knowing glint sparking in their blue depths. "This is about Olivia, isn't it?"

My heart lurched at the sound of her name, a physical ache forming in my chest. "No. Why would you think that?"

"Oh, I don't know," Andy drawled, crossing his arms over his chest. "Maybe because you have developed a habit of always having eyes on her? Or because she couldn't get off the stage fast enough after her sound check, and refused to so much as look in your direction?"

I winced. "We're just... it's complicated." I sighed, dragging a hand through my hair.

"You forget I know you, man." Andy's voice softened, his

hand coming to rest on my shoulder again. Gentler this time, a grounding touch. "I've never seen you like this over a woman before."

I let out a humourless laugh, the sound scraping my throat raw. "She's not just any girl, Andy. She's… fuck. She's everything."

The words slipped out before I could stop them, the truth of them rattling me to my core. Because she was. In the space of a few short weeks, Liv had become everything to me. My muse, my motivation, my North Star in the unstable, ever changing, high emotion whirlwind of this life.

And I was terrified of losing her before I even really had her.

"Okay." Andy nodded slowly, understanding dawning on his face. "Okay, so she's special. That's a good thing, right? I mean, how long have we been talking about you needing to find someone who gets it, who gets you? And now you have."

I shook my head, frustrated not at Andy but at the situation, at my own tangled mass of fears and doubts.

"It's not that simple. You know what this life is like, the scrutiny, the fucking circus. And I'm already in too deep to hide the way I feel about her."

The confession tasted bitter on my tongue, the ugly truth of it staring me in the face. I was so far gone for this woman, I couldn't see straight. Couldn't think past the desperate need to protect her, to shield her from the shit storm that came with loving someone like me.

"I've seen what that does to people, Andy. What it did to… to Tegan." The name caught in my throat, the old wound throbbing beneath my ribs. My little sister, the bright-eyed girl I'd tried so hard to protect from the dark side of fame.

I'd failed her. Failed to save her from the vicious cycle of tabloid fodder and public meltdowns. I couldn't do that again. I couldn't watch another person I loved get chewed up and spat out by the machine.

Especially not Liv.

Beautiful, vibrant, fiercely talented Olivia, with her sunshine smile and her heart on her sleeve. She deserved better than that. Better than me, and the baggage that came with my name, my face.

"I get it, okay?" Andy's grip tightened on my shoulder, forcing me to meet his gaze. "I do. What happened with Tegan... it was a fucking nightmare. For all of us, but especially for you. You've been through hell, mate."

I swallowed hard, blinking back the sudden sting of tears. "But Olivia isn't Tegan," he said softly, his gaze searching mine. "No, listen. I'm not saying it'll be easy. God knows this life is fucking hard on relationships. But Lew..." He paused, his expression softening into something achingly sincere. "If you've found something real with her, something that makes you feel like this? That's worth fighting for, man. That's worth a little risk."

Risk. The word lodged in my throat, sharp and bitter.

Hadn't I risked enough already? Risked my heart, my sanity, my fucking soul on this rollercoaster of a career?

Maybe he was right and she wasn't Tegan, but that didn't mean this would be any different. I had to protect her at all costs. Even if that meant annulling our marriage.

Carly, our publicist, would know how to keep a lid on it and then maybe we could go back to normal.

CHAPTER TWENTY-THREE

OLIVIA

*T*he stadium hallway stretched out either side of me, cold and empty. My footsteps echoed off the concrete walls as I paced with my phone clutched in my hand.

The digital clock ticked over to 11:05 PM. Five minutes since the final encore. He should be here by now. Unless he was tied up with the band, or the fans, or…

I shook my head, trying to dislodge the doubt swirling in my brain. He'd come. He had to come. We couldn't keep avoiding this, avoiding each other.

My phone buzzed in my hand and I nearly jumped out of my skin. But it wasn't Lewis's name lighting up my screen. It was Ashley's.

I frowned, doing a quick mental calculation. It had to be well past 2 AM back in Jasmine Bay. What was she doing up so late?

I swiped to answer, pressing the phone to my ear. "Ash? Everything okay?"

"There you are!" Her voice was too loud, straining to be

heard over the muted thump of bass and chatter in the background. "I've been trying to reach you for hours, sugar!"

I winced, pulling the phone away slightly. "Are you at a club? It's the middle of the night back home."

"Just blowing off some steam." She laughed, the sound more carefree than I had any hope of achieving right now. "I wanted to check in on you before I head home. Have you talked to him yet about…?" She trailed off, like she couldn't quite say the word. Like saying it out loud would make it too real.

Marriage.

The happy buzz that had come with that word a few hours ago had long shrivelled up and faded. I hadn't taken the ring off. I couldn't bear to. Too scared that that would mean we really were done.

"He's avoiding me." I slumped against the concrete wall, hating how small my voice sounded, how defeated. "He didn't come to the side stage during my set tonight, like he usually does. Didn't text me good luck before the show. It's like he can't stand to be around me, Ash."

She made a sympathetic noise, the club sounds fading with the slam of a car door. "Oh honey. I'm so sorry. He's being a real ass, isn't he?"

I laughed, but it came out more like a sob. "I just don't get it. Last night, it was like… like magic. It felt so right, you know? Like it was meant to be. And now…"

Now I was standing in a cold, empty hallway, waiting for a man who might never come. Waiting for answers I wasn't sure I wanted to hear.

"Have you considered that maybe…" Ashley hesitated, like she didn't want to say it. "Maybe it was too much for him? Too soon?"

Too soon. The words hit like a punch to the chest, stealing my breath. Because isn't that exactly what Lewis had said that morning, his eyes wide and panicked, his voice shaking with regret?

But I had been so ready, so sure. Sure of him, of us, of this wild, wonderful thing brewing between us.

Had I been wrong? Had I let the fantasy of it all, blind me to reality? To the fact that a few weeks of whirlwind romance didn't erase whatever baggage had driven him to keep us secret in the first place?

Hell, even that should have clued me in. You didn't fall in love with someone and then keep it to yourself. I'd barely managed to hold in my excitement these last few weeks and even trying, I'd failed to mask the deliriously happy look people in love got. The girls all knew. They'd just chosen to overlook it for now.

I bit my lip, fighting back the tears I refused to let fall. Not here, not now. Not when I had to walk out of this stadium and stay on The Brightside's tour bus for the ten hour drive to Eugene.

It took a strong person to say no to Lily Tyler and when she'd caught me after my sound check this afternoon, it had taken everything I had not to break down crying in front of the entire crew. I didn't have it in me to beg off hanging out with the band like I normally would.

She thought she was being helpful. Instinct told me tonight would be the most painful night of my life.

"Maybe you're right," I whispered finally, the words like ashes on my tongue. "Maybe it was a mistake. Maybe I… maybe I'm not enough for him."

"Olivia Monroe, you stop that right now." Ashley's voice cut through the spiral of my thoughts, hard and fierce. "You are more than enough. You are everything. And if Lewis Davies is too much of a fool to see that, then that's his loss."

I smiled despite myself, a rush of gratitude and love for my best friend warming the cold, numb places in my chest. "Thanks Ash."

She blew out a breath. "You want me to come out there? Give him a piece of my mind?"

The thought of Ashley storming into the bus, all five feet

four inches of Southern fire and fury, made me laugh for real this time.

"That's sweet, but no. I need to handle this myself." I glanced at my phone again. 11:35. Half an hour since the show ended. Half an hour of standing here like a fool, waiting for a man who clearly wasn't coming. "I have to go. The bus will be leaving soon."

She sighed but didn't argue. "Alright. But promise me you'll call if you need anything, okay? Anything at all. I don't care what time it is."

"I promise. Love you, Ash."

I hung up, the ghost of a smile still playing about my lips. But as I slipped my phone back into my pocket, the smile faded, replaced by a cold, sinking certainty.

He wasn't coming. He'd left me standing here, waiting, hoping, like a fool. Like the naive small-town girl I was starting to feel like again.

CHAPTER TWENTY-FOUR

OLIVIA

*A*n hour after we arrived in Eugene, I stood in the quiet hallway outside Lewis's hotel room. My hand hovered over the door, poised to knock. Part of me wanted to turn tail and run, to avoid the confrontation to come.

But I couldn't.

He owed me answers and I owed it to myself to force them out of him. I couldn't keep waiting, hoping that one day soon he'll stop pretending it wasn't the most real, visceral connection either of us had ever felt. Married or not, drunken Vegas decisions be damned, Lewis and I were meant to be together. And I was going to make him see that, even if it killed me.

I rapped my knuckles against the door, three sharp knocks that echoed in the stillness.

For a moment, nothing happened. I held my breath, anxiety coiling in my gut.

Maybe he wasn't here. Maybe he'd gone out, avoiding me just like he'd been doing for days…

The door swung open, revealing a very startled Lewis. His

eyes went wide when he saw me, a flash of something—Panic? Guilt?—flickering across his face before he could hide it.

"What are you doing here?"

I tried not to let his reaction sting but I failed. I crossed my arms, trying to project a confidence I didn't really feel. "We need to talk. Can I come in?"

He hesitated for a split second.

"Yeah, of course." Lewis stepped back, gesturing me inside with a tight smile.

I brushed past him, my skin prickling with awareness. The click of the door closing behind us sounded unnaturally loud, sealing us into our own private bubble.

"It's like you can't stand to be around me ever since…" I gestured vaguely to my left hand, to the slim band of silver on my finger. "Ever since Vegas."

His eyes followed the movement, something unreadable flickering in their hazel depths. He was silent for a long moment, the tension stretching taut between us.

"How did you know which room I was in?"

I blinked, thrown by the sudden change in topic. "What?"

"My room number. How did you know?" There was an edge to his voice now, a hint of suspicion that made my hackles rise.

Heat crept up my neck. "Lily told me."

His eyes went wide, alarm flashing across his features. "Lily knows? Fuck, Liv, did you tell her about Vegas?"

Anger flared hot in my chest, quick and bright as a struck match. I gaped at him, hurt and indignation warring for dominance.

"Unbelievable. You're more concerned about who might know about us than you are about us." I shook my head, a humourless laugh escaping my lips. "Do you even hear yourself right now? It's like you're ashamed of me. Of this."

"I'm not ashamed. How could you even think that?" He took a step towards me, his hands coming up to grip my shoulders. His touch burned even through the fabric of my shirt. "I want to be with you. I lo—"

"Don't." I cut him off, my voice shaking. "Don't you dare say you love me when every action, every word out of your mouth since that morning screams the opposite."

He flinched like I'd slapped him. "I do love you. More than... more than I even have words for."

"Then why are you acting like this?" My voice rose, frustration and hurt bleeding into every syllable. "Hiding me away, avoiding me, treating me like some dirty little secret..."

I blinked back the hot sting of tears, refusing to let them fall. I wouldn't cry. Not now, not in front of him.

"If you loved me—really, truly loved me—you wouldn't be able to stay away. You wouldn't want to." I stared at him, willing him to contradict me, to offer some explanation that would make this all make sense.

But he just looked at me, his eyes anguished, his jaw working like he was physically biting back words. The silence stretched between us, heavy and suffocating.

"Say something," I whispered finally, hating the way my voice broke. "Please, Lewis. Just... tell me what's going on in that head of yours. Make me understand."

He scrubbed his hands over his face, a shuddering sigh escaping him. When he looked at me again, there was a raw, desperate edge to his expression that I'd never seen before.

"You want to know why I'm acting like this? Why I'm so fucking terrified of the world finding out about us?" His voice was low, rough with emotion. "It's because I've seen firsthand what that kind of scrutiny can do to a person."

I frowned, confusion and concern warring in my chest. "What are you talking about?"

He was silent for a long moment, his gaze distant, like he was looking at something I couldn't see. When he spoke again, his voice was barely above a whisper.

"My sister, Tegan... she was like you, once. Kind, talented and so fucking eager to take on the world." A ghost of a smile touched his lips, there and gone in a flash. "But then The Brightside became a household name and the press and public were clamouring for more and more of us. They set their sights on our family, on my fifteen-year-old sister. They hounded her."

My breath caught, my heart twisting painfully in my chest. "Lewis…" I reached for him, my fingers grazing his arm. He flinched but didn't pull away.

"She was fifteen and they tore her apart for entertainment. Kids in school bullied her, the public bullied her. It shattered her in ways I didn't even know a person could break."

Tears burned the back of my throat, hot and bitter. I swallowed them down, forcing my voice to remain steady.

"I… I'm so sorry. I had no idea."

I vaguely remembered seeing interviews and press on his sister years and years ago.

He shook his head, his eyes finding mine. There was a plea in them, a raw, aching desperation.

"I can't watch that happen to you. Can't bear the thought of you getting caught in the crosshairs, of the media sinking their claws into you because of me." His voice cracked, a single tear tracing down his cheek. "It would destroy me, Liv. Seeing you hurt like that… I couldn't take it."

And just like that, I understood. The distance, the avoidance, the desperate need for secrecy… it all clicked into place with a horrible sort of clarity.

He wasn't ashamed of me. He was trying to protect me. Protect us.

I cupped his face in my hands, forcing him to meet my gaze. His skin was warm beneath my palms, his scruff rasping against my fingers.

"I understand your fear, but I'm not Tegan. I'm not a teenager." I held his gaze, refusing to let him look away. "I know you're scared. I know you want to protect me. And I love you for that, more than you can possibly imagine."

His breath hitched. The words had slipped out unrehearsed, unplanned. But I didn't regret them. Not even a little.

"But you have to trust me. Trust us." I stroked my thumbs over his cheeks, wiping away the dampness. "I'm not some delicate flower. I'm an adult and I knew what I was getting into when I got into this business. I knew a relationship with you might put the spotlight on me, but that would have happened with or without you. I can handle the press, the scrutiny. It's part of our job."

I took a shaky breath, pouring every ounce of certainty, of love, into my next words.

"But I can't handle you shutting me out. Can't handle feeling like I'm alone in this, like you're already half out the door." My voice wavered but I pushed on, needing him to hear me. To really hear me. "I need you to be all in."

For a long, suspended moment, he just stared at me. I could practically see the gears turning behind his eyes, the war raging between his fear and his love.

"You don't understand, Liv. The media, they're relentless." His voice was strained, his fingers flexing against my hips like he didn't know whether to pull me closer or push me away. "They tore my sister apart, and I can't bear the thought of them doing the same to you."

"So we don't let them." I slid my hands down to his chest, feeling the thunder of his heartbeat beneath my palm. "I know you're scared. What happened to Tegan… it's unimaginable. But she was just a kid. She wasn't prepared for that kind of attention. We are. We control the narrative. We go public on our own terms, in our own way."

"It's not that easy," he said, staring at me with a deep, hopeless sadness.

"Yes, it is," I bit out, trying to temper my frustration. "I'm not saying it'll be a walk in the park, but I'm an adult. I've been building my career, my public image, for years. I know how to handle myself."

He bit his lip, still unconvinced.

An idea bloomed to life in my mind, bright and shining with possibility. "Tomorrow, we'll go to the market together, just like we planned ages ago. We'll act like any other couple. Hold hands, laugh at the terrible street acts... maybe even share an ice cream cone, if you're feeling extra daring."

A surprised laugh huffed out of him, his eyes crinkling at the corners. "An ice cream cone? How daring."

He closed his eyes, his forehead coming to rest against mine. For a moment, he just breathed, his chest rising and falling in tandem with my own.

"Okay," he whispered finally. "Okay, you win. We'll go to the market. We'll let ourselves be seen."

I smiled, relief and love flooding through me. "Thank you. Thank you for trusting me."

He pulled back, his gaze searching mine with an intensity that made my heart stutter. "I do trust you. It's the press I don't..." He grimaced. "I'll try to stop doing that. It's just... the thought of losing you, of seeing you hurt..."

"You won't lose me."

I pressed a soft, reassuring kiss to his lips. He pulled me into his arms, hugging me close and I melted into his embrace, confident that he'd finally heard me.

CHAPTER TWENTY-FIVE

LEWIS

*M*orning came far too quickly. I buried my face in the pillow, willing myself to fall back asleep and delay the day from starting. With Liv's delectable, naked body pressed against my chest and my semi-hard erection nudging her ass, sleep unsurprisingly eluded me.

A better idea hit me when she shifted, teasing me in her sleep.

I let my fingers trail down her side, over her hip and between her legs. When I reached the apex of her thighs, I found her already wet, her body responding to my touch even in sleep.

A groan rumbled in my chest, my cock hardening further at the evidence of her desire.

I slid down the bed, gently pushing her onto her back and settling between her sprawled legs. She murmured something unintelligible, her brow furrowing adorably, but didn't wake. Not yet.

I dipped my head, pressing a soft kiss to her inner thigh. Her skin was like nectar under my lips, sweet and addictive. I trailed a path of open-mouthed kisses higher, higher, until I reached her needy pussy.

The first touch of my tongue against her slit had her gasping, her hips bucking up into my face. I pressed my elbows down on top of her thighs, holding her open and steady as I lapped at her, savouring her sleepy, uninhibited sounds.

Her fingers sank into my hair, her nails scraping deliciously against my scalp as she surfaced from sleep straight into red hot need. I doubled my efforts, focusing my attention on her clit, circling and flicking and sucking until her moans turned to cries, until her thighs started to shake and tremble around my ears.

"Lewis," she gasped, my name a prayer and a plea on her lips. "Oh lord, don't stop…"

As if anything in the known universe could tear me away from the heaven between her legs, the perfect satisfaction of bringing her closer and closer to the edge with every stroke of my tongue.

I slid two fingers into her tight, clenching heat, curling them just the way I knew would make her see stars. Her back bowed, her cry strangled and desperate as her orgasm crashed over her, her walls seizing and pulsing around my fingers.

I worked her through it, murmuring praise and endearments into her slick flesh, drawing out her pleasure until she was limp and boneless beneath me, spent and sated.

But I was far from done.

If I had my way, we wouldn't leave this bed until dinner with the band.

I crawled up her body, fumbling for a condom from the pile we'd strewn over the bedside table in our rush last night. She watched me through heavy-lidded eyes, her smile lazy and content as I rolled the latex over my aching cock.

"Good morning," I whispered, settling into the cradle of her hips, the head of my erection nudging against her still-fluttering entrance.

"Good morning, indeed." She looped her arms around my

neck, pulling me down for a kiss that was deep and filthy and perfect. "That was quite the wake-up call."

"Oh, I'm not finished with you yet." I punctuated the words with a slow, deliberate press of my hips, sheathing myself inside her inch by delicious inch.

Her breath caught, her nails digging into my shoulders as I stretched and filled her.

"But we were supposed to go to the market this morning." She gasped when I hitched her legs higher around my waist, sinking deeper.

"What would you rather do, Liv?" I pulled out almost entirely before slamming back in, relishing her sharp gasp, the way her eyes rolled back. "Spend the morning wandering around stalls and trying fucking blueberry chutneys?" I set a deep, purposeful rhythm, each thrust angled to hit that spot inside her that made her mindless. "Or spend it in this bed, coming on my cock over and over again until you forget your own name?"

She made a sound somewhere between a laugh and a moan, her fingers tangling in my hair as I mouthed at her neck, her collarbone. "Well, when you put it like that…"

I grinned against her skin, nipping at her pulse point. "That's what I thought."

And then there were no more words. There was only the slap of skin on skin. The mingled sounds of our pleasure. The urgent, perfect slide of our bodies as I made good on my promise, wringing climax after shuddering climax from her until she was an incoherent, trembling mess beneath me, and my own release barrelled through me like a freight train, whiting out my vision and short-circuiting my higher brain functions.

*T*he Eugene Saturday Market was in full swing by the time we arrived, the stalls and booths packed with locals and tourists alike. The smell of cooking food and handcrafted candles filled the air. The sounds of laughter, haggling and street musicians surrounded us.

It should have been idyllic, the perfect summer day. But with every step we took, every friendly smile aimed our way, tension wound tighter and tighter inside of me, the anxiety buzzing like angry hornets in my blood.

I tried to shake it off, tried to focus on Liv's sunny enthusiasm as she pulled me from stall to stall, exclaiming over handmade jewellery and quirky art prints. But my eyes kept darting to the crowds around us with suspicion.

"Ooh, look at these!" Liv tugged me towards a stall draped in a rainbow of woven scarves, her eyes alight with excitement. She fingered a gauzy blue one shot through with metallic thread, holding it up to catch the light. "Isn't it gorgeous?"

I made an appreciative noise, but I barely glanced at it. My eyes were fixed on her.

"What about this one?" She held up a black scarf, the fabric smooth and dark. "It matches your aesthetic, Mr Tall, Dark, and Brooding."

I laughed, some of the tension leaking from my shoulders. "Excuse you, I think you mean Mr Tall, Dark, and Devastatingly Handsome."

"Eh, it's a fine line." She grinned, tossing the buttery-soft scarf around my neck and using it to tug me closer. "Luckily, I happen to love brooding."

I dipped my head, brushing a kiss across her smiling mouth. I kept it brief, chaste. If I lingered, if I let myself sink into her the way I was dying to, I'd end up getting us arrested for public indecency and definitely draw the press to us.

"I love you," I murmured against her lips, too low for anyone but her to hear. "And I love that you put up with my broody ass."

"Mmm, I more than put up with it. I quite enjoy your ass." She nipped at my bottom lip, soothing the sting with her tongue.

Heat bloomed low in my gut, a surge of want so intense it nearly brought me to my knees. Christ, the things this woman did to me. The way she could undo me with a word, a touch, a kiss.

I wanted nothing more than to haul her against me, to lose myself in her right there in the middle of the market. Consequences be damned.

But I'd never do it.

Even after all my promises, my shoulders tensed and the nape of my neck itched with the phantom touch of eyes.

"Behave," I gritted out, even as my hands flexed on her hips, itching to drag her closer. "We're supposed to be keeping things G-rated, remember?"

At the reminder, Liv rolled her eyes, taking a pointed step back. "Please. As if you've ever cared about ratings."

I tensed, my fingers clenching around hers as my gaze darted from stall to stall. Did that woman in the floppy sun hat seem a little too focused on her phone? Was that teenager with The Brightside t-shirt pointing us out to his friend?

Paranoia crawled up my spine like icy fingers, a clammy, clawing dread that made it hard to breathe. Everywhere I looked, every face in the crowd, every fucking phone winking in the sun... they all felt like a threat. Like a ticking time bomb just waiting to blow my world apart.

On some level, I knew I was being irrational. Knew, logically, that not every glance in our direction was nefarious, not every shutter click spelled doom. But logic had no place in the fevered, panicked mess of my mind.

The fear was a living thing inside me, wrapping around my lungs, my heart. It whispered that this was all too good to be true. That our bubble of happiness was nothing more than a glass globe, waiting for the press to shatter it.

I shook my head, trying physically to dislodge the paranoia. They were just people, for fuck's sake. Normal, everyday people going about their normal, everyday lives. Not every smartphone was a weapon lying in wait, not every glance in our direction was accompanied by dollar signs and delusions of tabloid fame.

But the fear wouldn't abate. It sank its claws deeper.

I couldn't shake the feeling that it was all a dream. A beautiful, fragile bubble just waiting for the first pinprick of reality to burst it.

Liv's hand on my arm startled me out of my rapidly swirling thoughts. "Hey. Where'd you go just then?"

"Just got distracted for a second." I straightened my shoulders and pasted on my best attempt at a carefree grin. "So, those scarves. You want to get them? Start our collection of tour souvenirs?"

She narrowed her eyes like she wasn't buying the subject change for a second. But she allowed it and I fell a little more in love with her.

"Definitely. And we have to find something for the rest of the band. And for our families!"

The click of a camera shutter was like a gunshot, freezing me in place. My head snapped up, a coldness seeping into my bones that had nothing to do with the weak Oregon sunshine.

I stepped in front of Liv, shielding her from the camera.

"Lewis, what—" Liv started, but I was already moving, my hand finding hers and tugging her away from the stall, away from the prying eyes.

I bolted, dragging Liv behind me as I wove through the throngs of shoppers, putting as much distance as I could between us and that damning phone camera.

Anderson hung back, probably dealing with the photo.

But even as I walked faster, my legs eating up the ground in long, tense strides... I knew there was no escaping this. Not really.

Because the worst of it, the part that made my lungs seize up and my blood turn to ice in my veins...

It wasn't the threat of discovery, the awfulness of having our most private moments splashed across Page Six.

It was the stark betrayal that flashed across Liv's face when I blocked her from that godforsaken camera.

We made it to the far edge of the market before Liv finally dug in her heels and breathlessly demanded that I stop. I stumbled to a halt, my chest heaving, an apology on the tip of my tongue.

"What the fuck was that?"

I scraped a hand through my hair, trying to force air past the bands constricting my lungs. "There was... a camera... "

Understanding dawned on her face, chased by something fiercer.

"You panicked." It wasn't a question.

"I– Yeah. I fucking panicked." All the air left my lungs in a rush, leaving me feeling hollowed out. Empty. "You don't understand what it's like, living under that kind of scrutiny."

Her eyes flashed, anger and hurt warring in their green depths. "Don't I?"

She stepped back, crossing her arms over her chest like a shield. "I knew what I was signing up for when I agreed to date you. I knew it wouldn't be easy, that one day our every move would be dissected and splashed across the tabloids." Her jaw clenched, a muscle ticking in her cheek. "But I thought we were in this together."

"I'm trying. I'm fucking trying, okay? But it's not a switch I can just flip. This fear has been hardwired into me since before I even knew your name... it doesn't just disappear because I want it to."

Liv's expression softened, the anger draining away to leave something sadder, more resigned in its wake. She stepped closer, laying a gentle hand on my arm.

"I know you're trying." Her thumb rubbed soothing circles into my skin, her touch an anchor in the maelstrom of my emotions. "But this level of reaction, it's not healthy. It's not sustainable."

I flinched, shame and defensive pride welling up in equal measure. I wanted to pull away, to insist that I was fine, that I could handle this on my own. But the plea in her eyes, the quiet desperation... it cut through the bullshit, through the bravado.

"You need to talk to someone," she said softly, her gaze

holding mine. "A professional. Someone who can give you the tools to deal with this, to work through it in a healthy way."

I stared at her. "What, like a shrink? Are you serious?"

She nodded, worrying at her bottom lip. "I think it's time for you to face these demons head-on, with someone who actually knows what the fuck they're doing."

A bark of laughter ripped from my throat, too sharp and brittle to be mistaken for humour. "Right. Because that's just what I need. Some head doctor rummaging around in my fucked up psyche, picking apart all the broken bits."

I could see the headlines already—'The Brightside Bassist Seeks Help for Secret Struggle.'

They'd paint me as some kind of unstable head case, too fucked up to handle the pressures of fame.

And what would that do to the band?

No. It was too big a risk. My baggage was mine to carry. Liv was shaking her head, face pinched with a disappointment that cut straight through me.

"I can't do this. I can't keep watching you tear yourself apart because you're too fucking stubborn to admit you need help."

And with that, she walked away. Slipped into the crowd and disappeared, leaving me standing there. Alone.

CHAPTER TWENTY-SIX

OLIVIA

*T*he roar of the crowd pulsed through me as I stepped off the stage, my heart pounding in rhythm with their cheers. For twenty blissful minutes, everything else faded away and I revelled in the crowd's joy.

But reality came crashing back and the high faded quickly as I made my way into the dark wings. The noise of the crowd dulled, replaced by the organised craziness of backstage—roadies shouting instructions, equipment clattering, the low thrum of generators. My ears rang with the sudden absence of chatting and bass.

I swiped a water bottle from a passing tech, chugging it greedily. My throat was raw, my body buzzing with spent energy. I needed a minute. Just a minute to breathe, to process before diving into the post-show madness.

Alys materialised at my elbow, her face uncharacteristically serious. "Liv, there you are. I've been trying to catch you."

I grinned at her, still riding the wave of euphoria. "Hey! Did you see that crowd tonight? They were insane! I swear, Vancouver topped Pasadena."

She didn't return my smile. She held out my phone, her brow creased with concern. "Your mom's been calling. A lot. I didn't want to bother you before the show, but... I think you need to call her back. Like, now."

The giddy balloon in my chest deflated, a cold sense of foreboding taking its place. My mama knew never to call before a show unless it was an emergency. With shaking hands, I took the phone, staring down at the missed call notifications lighting up the screen.

Three missed calls. All from Mama.

"Thanks," I said, my throat suddenly dry despite the water I'd just gulped. "I... I'll find somewhere quiet to call her back."

Alys squeezed my shoulder, her blue eyes filled with understanding. "Take your time."

I nodded, already heading for the maze of hallways that snaked through the stadium's backstage. I needed privacy for this. Whatever it was.

My heart hammered against my ribs as I wound my way deeper into the concrete labyrinth, the sounds of the crew fading behind me. Roadies and techs rushed past, barely sparing me a glance. Everyone was in their own world back here, focused on the million tasks that needed doing to keep a tour of this scale running smoothly.

I finally found a relatively secluded corner, tucked between a rack of cables and a stack of instrument cases. With trembling fingers, I hit the call button, raising the phone to my ear. It rang once. Twice.

"Olivia?" My mother's voice was thick, strained in a way I'd never heard before. "It's so nice to hear from you."

I couldn't process her attempt at pleasantries. If something was wrong, I needed it ripped off like a band-aid so I could figure out how to fix it.

"Mama, what's wrong? Are you okay?" The words tumbled

out in a rush, my free hand clenching at my side. "Is it Dustin? Did something happen at the shop?"

There was a long pause, broken only by a shuddering breath on the other end of the line. "I need you to be strong right now, okay? Can you do that for me?"

Ice slid down my spine, my stomach plummeting to my toes. "Mama, you're scaring me. What's going on?"

Another pause. Another ragged breath. Then, "I'm sick, Livvie. Real sick. The doctors, they... they found a tumour. Cancer. Stage four."

The world tilted, my knees going weak. I braced a hand against the rough concrete wall, trying to keep myself upright. This couldn't be happening. It had to be a mistake, a terrible dream I could wake up from.

"No," I whispered, my voice cracking. "No, that's not... Mama, are they sure? Maybe it's a mistake, maybe—"

"It's not a mistake, baby." Her words were gentle but firm, laced with a resigned sort of sadness that shattered my heart. "I've known for a while now. Been going through treatments, but... it's not responding like we hoped."

Hot, stinging tears blurred my vision. I blinked them back furiously, refusing to break. Not now. Not when she needed me to be strong.

"What do you mean 'a while'?" I demanded, anger and fear warring in my chest. "How long have you known? Why didn't you tell me?"

She sighed, the sound heavy with weariness and regret. "A few months. I didn't want to worry you, not with the tour and everything. I thought... I thought I had more time."

Months. She'd been fighting this battle for months. Guilt and grief crashed over me in nauseating waves.

Terminal. She was terminal. The doctors had given her an expiration date.

Bile rose in my throat, hot and acrid. I swallowed it down, forcing my voice to remain steady.

"I'm coming home. Today. As soon as I can get a flight."

"No, Livvie, you can't," she said, her tone riddled with steel, the infamous Monroe backbone showing through. "You've got obligations, people counting on you. I won't let you throw that away, not for me."

"To hell with obligations!" The words burst out of me, too loud in the echoing hallway. "You're my mama. You're more important than any tour or album or... or anything."

Her breath hitched and her muffled sniffles rattled the phone as she tried to hide it. It broke me in ways I couldn't begin to comprehend.

"Please don't do this. Don't make me the reason you give up on your dreams."

I needed to be there for her. In whatever way I could, for however long I had left.

"You listen to me, Mama." My voice shook but my resolve was iron-clad. "There is nothing, nothing in this world more important to me than you. Not the tour, not my career, not a damn thing. I'm coming home and that's final."

She was silent for a long moment. I could practically feel her resistance, her stubborn desire to put everyone else's needs above her own. But this time, I wouldn't let her.

Couldn't let her.

Finally, she let out a shuddering sigh. "Okay. If that's what you need to do... then I understand. I don't like it, but I understand."

Relief and grief tangled in my chest, a bittersweet knot. "There'll be other tours."

I hoped.

"Right." She didn't sound so convinced, but I didn't stop to question it.

"I'll call you as soon as I have a flight. I love you, Mama. So much."

"I love you too, Livvie. More than all the stars in the sky."

The tears came then, hot and blinding. I let them fall as I ended the call, great silent sobs wrenching through me.

It wasn't fair. It wasn't right. She was too young, too fucking necessary. The world couldn't take her yet. I couldn't lose her yet.

But I was losing her. Had already lost her, in the ways that mattered most. Lost her to this disease eating her up from the inside out.

Anger and helplessness twisted within me, raging and impotent. I wanted to scream, to rage, to tear the whole fucking stadium down with my bare hands. But I couldn't. I had to keep it together. Had to hold on, just a little longer.

I had to tell Lily. They needed to know I was leaving, that I wouldn't be there to open tomorrow's show in Vancouver or any of the shows after that.

It was going to be a shitstorm. I knew that. Knew there would be consequences, fallout I couldn't even begin to predict. But I didn't care.

None of it mattered. Not in the face of this.

I pushed off the wall, swiping at my tears with the back of my hand. I needed to find Lily. Needed to rip the band-aid off, to set this all in motion before I lost my nerve.

My feet carried me through the maze of hallways, past startled roadies and curious glances. Let them look. Let them wonder. It didn't matter.

Nothing fucking mattered except getting home to my mama.

But no matter where I looked, I couldn't find Lily. She didn't answer her phone, either.

Frustration and urgency clawed at my throat. I didn't have time for this. Didn't have time to play hide-and-seek while my mother was... was...

"You alright there, Olivia?"

I spun around to find Kevin, the band's manager, eyeing me with a mix of concern and annoyance. I must have barged past him but I couldn't remember it.

"No." The word came out choked, strangled. "I... I have to go. I'm leaving the tour."

"What?" His jaw slackened for a second. "Why?"

"My mother..." My voice cracked, grief welling up like

blood from a wound. "She's sick. Really sick. I have to go to her."

For a moment, his expression softened, a flicker of sympathy breaking through the blustering outrage. But it was gone as quickly as it came.

"I understand that, Olivia. I do. But we have commitments. Contracts. You can't just walk away from those."

Red-hot fury surged through me, momentarily burning away the pain. How dare he? How fucking dare he try to guilt me, to hold me hostage with legalese and fine print when my world was crumbling?

"I can and I will." Each word was ice, smooth, cold and brittle. "My mother is dying. So frankly, I don't give a fuck about commitments or contracts. I'm going home. Today. And if you try to stop me, I swear to god I will raise holy hell the likes of which you've never seen."

We glared at each other, a battle of wills played out in the scuffed concrete hallway. But I refused to bend. Refused to break.

Not now. Not for this.

Finally, Kevin sighed, raising his hands in grudging surrender. "Fine. Go. I'll… I'll figure something out."

"Thank you." The words were hollow, meaningless. What did I care for his permission? I was going either way.

But I needed one last thing from him.

"I need you to tell Lewis." My voice wavered, just slightly. "I can't… I don't have time to find him. To explain."

It was too much. Too fucking much on top of everything else.

Kevin nodded, his expression unreadable. "I'll tell him. I can't promise he'll understand, but I'll tell him."

CHAPTER TWENTY-SEVEN

LEWIS

I stumbled off the stage, sweat dripping down my back and the roar of the crowd still deafening me. At one point in my career, that sound was enough. It fuelled me, gave me the energy to get back up there night after night, to roll into the studio between tours, eagerly lay down our next hit.

It should have been the same tonight. The show had been incredible, easily one of our best.

Yet all through it, I couldn't stop my gaze from scanning the side of the stage.

I'd gotten so used to seeing Liv there, dancing and singing along that it was jarring without her.

My own fault, I know.

I wove through the heaving backstage area, roadies and techs rushing past with purposeful strides, barely sparing me a glance. I needed air. Space. A moment to just breathe and process the shit show that the last few days had been without someone interrupting me.

My eyes scanned the dimly lit corridor, searching for an escape of any kind. A dark corner would do.

Spotting a small alcove, tucked away from the main traffic paths, I ducked into it and leaned heavily against the cool brick wall, my damp t-shirt clinging to my skin.

I dragged a hand down my face, my wedding ring startlingly cold against my heated skin. I'd thought about taking it off, but every time I tried, I couldn't do it. I'd never wished to be just a normal guy, but caught in this screwed up situation, I couldn't help but think life would have been much easier.

If I hadn't joined The Brightside, I wouldn't have developed this anxiety-inducing fear of people knowing that I loved a woman. I would have drunkenly married Liv and shared in her joy the next day, called my mother and let her berate us for stealing her dreams of watching me get married.

I would be a different person because...

My sister wouldn't have been harassed by the press and the public.

She wouldn't have committed suicide and I wouldn't have spent the last eleven years letting guilt eat away at me for my failure. I'd been so wrapped up in the spectacle of fame that I'd missed all of the signs. Too busy partying and living it up in LA, to notice that my baby sister was struggling with the increased attention from not only her classmates but the entire world.

But there was one unavoidable hitch in this dream.

Without the band and the fame that came with it, I never would have met Liv.

And fuck didn't that just tie me up in a whole new kind of knot because I didn't know which I would choose.

My spiralling thoughts scattered as the sharp click of foot-steps approached. I straightened, expecting to see Tom or Andy, ready with a post-show debrief or a half-hearted scolding about going AWOL.

But my bandmates didn't round the corner. Instead, a weedy looking man in a rumpled suit appeared, a press badge dangling from his neck and a hungry glint in his eye. He zeroed in on me like a shark scenting blood, his thin lips curling into a triumphant grin.

"Lewis! Just the man I was hoping to see." He sidled closer, invading my space, his voice dripping with false friendliness.

"Sorry mate, no interviews tonight." I tried to brush past him, but he stepped into my path, blocking my escape.

"Just a quick comment. Won't take more than a minute." His grin sharpened, a glint of something predatory in his gaze. "Word on the street is you and your opening act, Ms. Monroe, tied the knot in Vegas. Care to confirm or deny?"

Ice slid down my spine. How? How did he know? "We aren't married. We're just friends and co-workers."

The words burned like acid, the betrayal of them searing my gut. But I pushed through, my fear overriding the sickening guilt.

"Whatever you think you know, you're mistaken. There's no story here."

The reporter's eyes glittered with malice, his smile razor sharp and a retort on the tip of his tongue. A large hand clamped down on the reporter's shoulder before he could get it out, spinning him around.

"Alright, that's enough." Anderson's deep baritone cut through the tension, his scarred face set in a scowl. "This area is off limits to press. I'm going to have to ask you to leave."

The reporter sputtered, indignation colouring his weaselly features. "I have every right to be here! The public has a right to know—"

"The public has a right to fuck all, and particularly not from trespassing reporters who stick their noses where they don't belong," Anderson growled, his grip tightening on the man's shoulder. "You can walk out of here on your own, or I can personally escort you out. Your choice."

For a moment, the reporter looked like he might argue. But one glance at Anderson's thunderous expression and bulging biceps seemed to change his mind. With a final, venomous glare in my direction, he shrugged out of Anderson's grip and slunk away, disappearing into the shadows of the corridor.

I sagged against the wall, my legs suddenly weak, my head spinning. Anderson watched me, his hard gaze softening a fraction.

"You alright, Lewis?"

I nodded, not trusting my voice. He studied me for a long moment, then sighed, shaking his head.

"I know you want to keep it hush, but your time is running out. Once the vultures start circling, they won't stop until they've picked you clean."

With that cheerful bit of wisdom, he turned on his heel and stalked off, no doubt to shout at security for letting the smarmy git slip through in the first place.

Alone again, my words echoed in my mind, slapping me in the face.

Christ, what had I done?

I'd panicked. I'd let my fear, my doubts, my stupid bloody pride get the best of me. And in doing so, I'd betrayed the one person who mattered most.

※

I burst through the door of Carly's makeshift office, the flimsy plywood rattling on its hinges. She looked up from her laptop, her perfectly arched brows climbing to her hairline at my abrupt entrance.

"Lewis? What's wro—"

"I fucked up." The words tumbled out of me in a rush, my voice raw and ragged. "I fucked up so bad and I need your help."

She straightened in her chair, her expression shifting from surprised to alert in the space of a heartbeat. "Okay, close the door and sit down. Tell me everything."

And so I did.

I spilled everything, from our first meeting at Rhymes to our impulsive wedding. I told her about the morning after, the doubts and the fear that had gripped me, the way I'd panicked and pushed Liv away. I told her about the argument at the farmers' market and the fans.

And then, with shame burning hot on my cheeks, I told her about the reporter. About the story he threatened to run. About the denial that had spilled from my lips in a moment of blind panic.

Through it all, she listened. She didn't interrupt, didn't judge, though I could see the wheels turning behind her cool blue gaze. When I finally fell silent, grimacing, my eyes stinging with unshed tears, she leaned back in her chair and laced her fingers together.

Anger bled into her expression and I braced myself.

"Are you a complete idiot?"

Apparently I wasn't the only one asking that question.

"Marriage licences are a matter of public record. You should have told me the second a ring slipped onto your finger, because this confrontation was inevitable."

I shook my head once, shame stealing my voice.

"I taught you better than this." She pinched the bridge of her nose.

I opened my mouth, an apology on my lips, but she held up a hand to silence me.

"Save it." She glared. "Right now, my priority is minimising the fallout. But you and I are going to have a serious conversation about communication and trust, because this?" She waved a hand between us. "This cannot happen again. Understand?"

"What do I do? How do I fix this?"

She tapped her manicured nails against the desk, her brow furrowed in thought. "First things first, we need to get ahead of this story. I'll reach out to my contacts at the major outlets, see if I can get a handle on what they've got and how far it's spread."

I nodded, my throat tight. "And then?"

"And then..." Carly sighed. "Then we do damage control. We release a statement, confirming the marriage but stressing

the private nature of the ceremony. We paint it as a sponta-
neous, romantic gesture, not a drunken mistake."

I flinched at the word "mistake," guilt churning in my gut.
Because that's what I'd made it seem like, wasn't it? A regret, a
lapse in judgement. Something to be ashamed of.

But it wasn't. It was the best fucking thing I'd ever done,
even if I'd been too much of a coward to see it until now.

"I just… I can't let what happened to Tegan happen to Liv. I
can't watch another person I love get destroyed by this fucking
circus."

Understanding dawned on Carly's face, tinged with sorrow.
"Oh, Lewis. What happened to your sister… it was tragic, and
awful, and completely unfair. But Olivia isn't Tegan."

"Isn't she?" I laughed, the sound bitter and broken. "A
small-town girl thrust into the spotlight, into a world she never
asked for? Tegan was strong too. Until she wasn't."

She sighed, leaning forward to rest her elbows on the desk.
"Look, I can't promise you that it'll be easy. That there won't be
challenges, and scrutiny, and assholes with cameras looking for
their next headline. But I can promise you this: Olivia is tougher
than you think."

I wanted to believe her. Wanted it so badly my chest ached.
But the fear, the doubt, they were insidious fuckers, and they
had their claws in deep.

Her expression softened, a touch of sympathy breaking
through her professional mask.

"I know this is hard. I know you're scared and overwhelmed
and probably questioning every choice that led you here. But
you need to be honest with yourself, and with Olivia. Do you
love her?"

"Yes." The word left me in a rush of breath, a bone-deep
certainty that settled over me like armour. "God, yes. More than
anything."

"Then fight for her." She stared at me. "Don't let fear or
pride or the fucking tabloids come between you. Go to her, tell
her everything you just told me. Beg for her forgiveness and then

spend every day proving that you meant those vows, that she's it for you."

I swallowed hard, a lump forming in my throat. She made it sound so simple, so straightforward. But the chasm of hurt and betrayal that yawned between Liv and me felt vast, unbridgeable.

"What if…" My voice cracked, the words sticking in my throat. "What if she can't forgive me? What if I've ruined everything?"

Her lips quirked in a sad, knowing smile. "Then you live with the consequences and learn from your mistakes. But… I don't think it'll come to that. I've seen the way that girl looks at you. Like you hung the moon and stars just for her."

A shaky laugh bubbled up my throat, half sob and half relief. Because God, I wanted to believe her. Wanted to believe that the love I'd seen shining in Liv's eyes, the love I felt burning in my own heart, was strong enough to weather any storm."

"I need to go." I pushed to my feet, my chair scraping harshly against the floor.

❄

I turned the corner, my long strides eating up the distance. Couple more minutes and I'd be late for our departure and the guys would start blowing up my phone. Even knowing that, it didn't feel like I was rushing towards the bus.

More like I was running from a spectral image of the press circling Liv. The need to put as much distance between me and the suffocating weight of my fears as possible rode me.

I'd barely made it halfway down the hall when a familiar voice stopped me dead in my tracks.

"Lewis! Wait up, man."

Kevin. Fucking perfect. Just what I needed, more bad news and bullshit from my self-serving prick of a manager.

I briefly considered ignoring him, pretending I hadn't heard and making a break for the nearest exit. But something in his tone, in the uncharacteristic urgency lacing his words, made me pause.

Slowly, reluctantly, I turned to face him. My stomach dropped to the vicinity of my toes at his expression. The tightness around his eyes, the grim set of his mouth. Unease pricked at my spine, a sinking feeling in my gut telling me that whatever had put that look on his face, it wasn't good.

"What's going on?"

He sighed, rubbing the back of his neck. A tell, one I'd seen a hundred times before. Usually right before he delivered news that would fuck up our carefully laid plans.

"It's Olivia."

My heart stopped, my blood turning to ice in my veins. No. No, no, no.

"What about her?" The words came out strangled, barely audible over the roaring in my ears. "Is she okay? Did something happen?"

A dozen scenarios, each worse than the last, played out in my mind in rapid fire succession. Liv hurt, Liv scared, Liv in danger. Christ, if anything happened to her...

"She's fine. Physically, at least." Kevin's voice cut through the spiral of my panic, but his words did little to ease the knot of dread in my stomach.

Had the story already broken? Were the press hounding her while he held me up?

"What the hell does that mean? Spit it out, for fuck's sake!"

"She quit." He held up his hands, a placating gesture that only served to ratchet up my agitation. "Packed up her stuff and left without a word to anyone. Well, anyone except me. I caught her on the way out the door."

I stared at him, uncomprehending. The words made sense individually, but strung together, they were nonsense. White noise. Static in my head, because surely, surely I'd heard him wrong.

"I'm sorry, she what?"

Kevin pressed his fingers into his temples like he could physically ward off an impending headache. "She quit the tour. Olivia's gone."

Olivia's gone.

This couldn't be happening. It couldn't be real. She wouldn't just leave, not without a word, not without…

Not without a damn good reason.

And suddenly, with a clarity that made me want to vomit, I knew. I knew exactly why she'd left, why she'd run as far and as fast as she could.

Because of me.

"Did she…" My voice cracked, my throat closing around the words. "Did she say anything? Leave a note, a message, anything?"

Kevin shook his head, a sardonic smile playing at the corners of his mouth. "Tough break, man. She said she was leaving because of you. Didn't give specifics, but it doesn't take a genius to read between the lines, if you know what I mean." He leaned in closer and whispered, "Guess she finally got tired of being your dirty little secret, huh? Can't say I blame her. It must've been exhausting."

"I have to… I need to…" I fumbled for my phone, my hands shaking so badly I nearly dropped it twice. I had to call her. Had to explain, to apologise, to make her see that I hadn't meant it, any of it. That I loved her, that I would fix this, fix us.

But when I finally managed to dial her number, it went straight to voicemail.

She wasn't going to pick up. Not now, maybe not ever again.

I'd broken us. Shattered the beautiful, fragile thing we'd been building with my own clumsy fucking hands. And now…

Now I had no idea how to put us back together again.

CHAPTER TWENTY-EIGHT

OLIVIA

The taxi pulled up outside Mama's house, the same one she'd lived in since before I was born. My hands shook as I fumbled with the latch, swinging the car door open. I hadn't been this nervous coming home since the summer after I graduated high school and I'd decided to move to Nashville and chase my dreams.

My stomach churned as I stumbled out of the cab. The driver popped the trunk and I grabbed my guitar case, the one thing I'd made damn sure not to leave behind, and my hastily packed suitcase. He peeled away from the kerb, leaving me standing there like an idiot, staring up at the weathered white siding and the faded blue shutters like I'd never seen them before.

"Well, well, well. Lookee what the cat dragged in."

I spun around to find Gertrude Finkle leaning over the porch railing next door, her bright blue housecoat flapping in the breeze. She eyed me up and down, her lips pursed like she'd just bit into a lemon.

Subtly, I hid my hand behind my back. I should have taken the ring off before I got to town, but no matter how I'd tried on the plane, I just couldn't. Now, I had no choice unless I wanted the entire gossip brigade spreading it around town that the goodie goodie musician had come home married without a husband.

"Hey, Miss Gert," I called out, pasting on a smile that felt as brittle as one of Hattie's stale biscuits. I slipped the ring off and slotted it into my pocket, squashing my guilt. "Long time no see."

"Didn't expect to see you back so soon," she said, her voice dripping with pointed curiosity. "Thought you were off galli-vanting around the country with that fancy-pants band of yours."

"Just taking a little break," I said lightly, hoping she couldn't hear the wobble in my voice. "Thought I'd come home and check on Mama."

Gertrude's eyes narrowed. "Just as well. Poor thing's been lookin' a bit peaked lately if you ask me. Could use some company." She sniffed. "Well, I won't keep you." Gertrude waved a dismissive hand. "Best get on in there. And Olivia?" Her voice softened, just a touch. "It's good to have you home, sugar."

Tears pricked at the backs of my eyes. I blinked them away, refusing to fall apart under Gertrude's hawkish gaze. "Thanks, Miss Gert. It's good to be back."

With a final nod, she disappeared back into her house, the screen door slamming behind her. I took a deep, shuddering breath and started up the walk, my legs feeling like lead weights with every step.

The porch boards creaked under my feet, a familiar sound that echoed through my bones. How many times had I bounded up these steps, eager to tell Mama about my latest song or some boy who'd caught my eye? How many lazy afternoons had I spent on that old porch swing, strumming my guitar and dreaming of the day I'd make it big?

I raised a trembling hand and opened the door.

"Mama?" I called out as I stepped into the house and dropped my bags in the foyer.

"In here, baby!" Mama's voice drifted from the kitchen, followed by the clanging of pots and pans.

I kicked off my boots and padded down the hallway, drinking in the familiar sights and smells of home. The faded floral wallpaper, the slightly crooked family photos lining the walls. It all wrapped around me like a warm hug, soothing the ragged edges of my heart.

I stepped into the kitchen and spotted her standing at the stove with her back to me. Her brown hair was pulled up in a messy bun. She turned, a bright smile already curving her lips.

"There's my baby girl." She opened her arms wide. "Get over here and give your mama a hug."

I didn't hesitate. I crossed the room in two quick strides and threw my arms around her, burying my face in her shoulder.

She felt thinner than I remembered, more fragile somehow. But she still smelled the same, like vanilla and cinnamon and home.

"Oh, Livvy," she murmured, rubbing soothing circles on my back. "Wish you hadn't come but I'm so glad you're here." She pulled back and swiped at the tears that had escaped to trickle down my cheeks. "Is that selfish of me?"

"Of course not. I need to be here."

She cupped my face in her hands, her green eyes, so much like my own, shining with love and understanding. "I know. But I still hate that you had to leave your tour for this. For me."

I shook my head vehemently. "No. Don't you dare apologise. There is nowhere, *nothing* more important than being here with you right now."

She smiled, but it was tinged with sadness. "I just don't want you putting your life on hold for me, Livvy. You've worked so hard for this."

"Stop it," I said firmly, gripping her hands in mine. "You and Dustin and this family are more important. Everything else is just… details." She looked like she wanted to argue, but I cut her off with a fierce hug, holding her as tightly as I dared. "I love you, Mama," I whispered, my throat tight with tears. "I love you so much."

"I love you too," she murmured into my hair.

We stayed like that for a long moment, just holding each other, soaking in the comfort of being together again. But as I breathed in her familiar scent, I couldn't help but notice how much sharper her bones felt beneath my hands, how much more pronounced her collarbone was above the collar of her shirt.

I pulled back, really looking at her for the first time since I'd walked in. She was still beautiful, still the same Mama I'd always known. But there was no denying the toll her illness had taken. The shadows beneath her eyes, the pallor of her skin, the way her clothes hung a little looser on her frame.

It hit me then, really hit me, the reality of what we were facing. This wasn't just some bad dream or distant fear. This was happening, right here, right now. She was slipping away. And there wasn't a damn thing I could do to stop it.

"Mama…" I started, my voice cracking on the word.

But before I could continue, the front door slammed, followed by the thud of heavy footsteps. "Hey Ma, you home?"

"In here, Dustin," Mama called, her eyes never leaving mine. "You got a surprise visitor."

My brother lumbered into the room, all six-foot-two of him, his chestnut hair sticking up in wild tufts. He stopped short when he saw me, his mouth falling open.

"Well, damn. If it ain't Miss Nashville herself, gracing us with her presence." His shock quickly morphed into a teasing grin. "To what do we owe this honour, your highness?"

I rolled my eyes, but I couldn't stop my own grin from spreading. "Shut up, twerp."

I crossed the room and threw my arms around him, squeezing tight. He hugged me back just as fiercely, nearly lifting me off the ground.

"Missed you, Liv," he mumbled into my hair, so low only I could hear.

"Missed you too, Dusty," I whispered back, using the childhood nickname I knew he hated.

He set me down, ruffling my hair like he used to when we were kids. "Not that I'm not thrilled to see you, but what gives? Thought you were living the high life out on the road with The Brightside."

My smile faded, and I glanced at Mama. Did he know? One look at her expression told me everything I needed to know.

"Why don't you sit down, Dustin? We need to talk." She gestured to the kitchen table with a sad smile.

Dustin's brow furrowed, confusion and concern etching lines into his boyish face. "What's going on, Ma?"

I swallowed hard, my stomach twisting into knots. This was it. The moment of truth, the awful, unavoidable reality we had to face head-on.

Mama sighed, sinking into one of the kitchen chairs. She suddenly looked so small, so tired. It made my heart clench painfully in my chest.

"I'm sick, Livvie," she said softly, reaching out to take Dustin's hand in hers. "Real sick. I got diagnosed with cancer a few months back. Stage four ovarian cancer."

Dustin's face went slack, the colour draining from his cheeks. "What? No, that's not... Ma, are you sure?"

She nodded, her eyes shining with unshed tears. "I'm sure, honey. I've been going through treatments, but... it's not looking good."

"How long have you known?" His voice was tight, strained with the effort of keeping his emotions in check.

"A while now." She glanced at me, apology written all over her face.

"And you're just telling me now?" Dustin turned to me, hurt and accusation burning in his eyes. "Did you know about this, Liv?"

I flinched at the betrayal in his tone. "I only found out yesterday."

"But she told you before me?" he demanded, his hands balling into fists at his sides. "What the hell, Liv?"

"Don't you take that tone with your sister," Mama cut in sharply. "I didn't tell either of you because I didn't want you worrying about me. I wanted you both to focus on your own lives, your futures."

"Screw our futures!" Dustin exploded, slamming his hand down on the counter. "You're our mother. You don't think we deserve to know that you're... that you're..."

He couldn't say it. None of us could.

Dying. Our mama was dying.

Her eyes filled with tears, her lip trembling. "I never meant to hurt you. I just... I didn't want to be a burden. Didn't want to get in the way of your dreams."

"We're adults," Dustin cut in, his voice rising with each word. "You don't get to decide what's a burden for us and what's not!"

Her lips firmed and her expression hardened, that stubborn Monroe streak coming out.

"I'm sorry," she said, meeting each of our gazes in turn. "I truly am. But I stand by my decision. You both have so much ahead of you, so much life to live. I didn't want this to derail everything you've worked for."

"But Mama..." My voice cracked, the fight draining out of me as quickly as it had come. "None of that matters without you. Don't you get that? You're everything to us."

Dustin nodded, swiping roughly at his eyes. "Liv's right, Ma. Fuck the shop, fuck Nashville. If you're sick, then we're gonna be right here."

Mama smiled then, a wobbly, tearful thing that somehow still managed to light up the room. "I know you will, babies. And Lord knows I'm gonna need you. But I don't want this to become your whole life, you hear? I want you to keep living."

I shook my head, a laugh that was more of a sob bubbling

up my throat. "Only you could be facing down cancer and still be worried about everyone else."

She reached out again and this time, I let her take my hand. Let her pull me into her arms and hold me close while the tears came, hot and fast and relentless.

We stayed like that for a long time, the three of us huddled together in her warm kitchen, crying and holding each other like the world outside had ceased to exist. In a way, it had. Because in that moment, in the circle of my mother's embrace, everything else fell away. The tour, the fact Lewis didn't want me enough, my own selfish worries and wants... none of it mattered. Not in the face of this.

When Mama's sobs had quieted to sniffles, I pulled back, searching her face. "Tell me everything. What did the doctors say? What kind of treatment are you getting?"

She sighed, wiping at her eyes. "They caught it late, after it had already spread. I've been doing chemo, but..." She shook her head, her face pinching with resignation. "It's not looking good. They're saying six months, maybe a year if I'm lucky."

The bottom dropped out of my stomach. Six months. A year. I swallowed hard against the bile rising in my throat. "Okay. Okay, so we fight. We get second opinions, we look into clinical trials. There has to be something—"

"Olivia." Mama cut me off gently, her hand coming up to cup my cheek. "I appreciate your fighting spirit, I do. But I've made my peace with this. I don't want to spend whatever time I have left chasing false hope and putting my body through hell. I want to live. Really live, while I still can."

Fresh tears burned my eyes. I wanted to argue, to rail against the unfairness of it all. But the quiet acceptance in her gaze, the serenity in her smile...

How could I deny her that?

"Okay, Mama." I managed a wobbly smile, leaning into her touch. "Then that's what we'll do. We'll live. We'll make every moment count."

"That's my girl." She patted my cheek, her eyes shining with love and pride. "Now, enough of all this heavy talk. I want to hear everything about the tour. Did anything develop with that handsome bassist?"

My face flushed, my gaze dropping to my hands. I couldn't quite bring myself to meet her knowing eyes, not when the mere mention of Lewis sent a pang of longing and confusion spearing through my heart.

"It was amazing," I said, trying for a smile. "Everything I ever dreamed of. Like nothing I've ever felt before."

And it was true. Being on that stage, feeling the roar of the crowd, the thrum of the music in my bones… it was a high unlike anything I'd ever known.

"But?" Mama prompted gently, seeing right through me as always.

"It's… complicated," I hedged, my heart giving a painful squeeze. "Lewis and I, we're… I don't really know what we are right now."

"Ah." Understanding dawned on her face. "So that's part of the reason you're home."

"No." I shook my head hard, ignoring the little voice in the back of my head that called me a liar. "I'm here for you."

Dustin, who had been unusually quiet through all of this, cleared his throat awkwardly. "I hate to break up the girl talk, but uh… what bassist are we talking about here? Because if some wannabe rock star is sniffing around my sister, I'm gonna need *details*."

I couldn't help it. I burst out laughing, the tension and the tears and the sheer absurdity of it all bubbling up and out of me in great, gulping guffaws. Mama joined in and soon even Dustin was chuckling, shaking his head at the picture we made.

CHAPTER TWENTY-NINE

LEWIS

Please answer me, Liv. We need to talk.

i know I should've fought harder for you. I keep replaying Eugene over and over, thinking of all the ways I could've handled things differently. I'm so sorry for how I acted at the market, for panicking. If you just give me another chance, come back, I'll do better. I swear.

LEWIS

We made it to Edmonton. The bus ride up was strange without you humouring the guys bullshit. God, I miss your teasing, your laughter, your smile...

They wanted to go out after we got to the hotel, hit up some bars before tomorrow's show. I begged off. Didn't feel much like partying. Tom tried giving me shit for being a miserable bastard and Andy keeps telling me to open up more and lean on the band. But how can I do that when the one person I want to lean on is gone?

LEWIS

I miss you so fucking much. The bed feels empty without you, the whole world feels dimmer. Tell me what I need to do so you can come back. Please, Liv. I'll do anything.

LIV

There's nothing for you to do. I didn't leave because of you.

LEWIS

I know that's not true. I wish you'd stayed so we could figure out our next step together.

Answer my call. Please.

CHAPTER THIRTY

OLIVIA

*T*he little bell over the door at Mayfield's Bakery jingled cheerfully as I walked in, immediately enveloped by the warm, sugary air. It smelled like vanilla and apples and childhood and every good thing I could think of. My mouth watered, my stomach grumbling impatiently even though I'd just had breakfast.

I'd promised Mama I would get out for a bit, give myself a break from the endless hovering and obsessive Googling of cancer treatments. She'd all but shoved me out the door after two days of my pestering, insisting she was fine, just tired. That a nap and some alone time would do her a world of good.

I didn't like it, leaving her alone. But I couldn't deny the itch beneath my skin for something to do other than re-reading Lewis's texts over and over again, questioning my every choice. So I'd texted Ash, asking her to meet me for coffee and some much-needed catching up.

"Well, bless my stars! If it isn't Livvy Monroe, back in the flesh!" Hattie bustled out from behind the counter, wiping her flour-dusted hands on her apron. She grinned at me and I couldn't stop myself from reciprocating.

"Hey, Hattie." I accepted her hug, breathing in the familiar scent of cinnamon and sugar. "Long time no see."

"I'll say!" She held me at arm's length, giving me a once-over. "Look at you, all grown up and fancy. Guess that rock star life agrees with you!"

I winced, forcing a laugh. "Oh, I don't know about that. It was... an experience, that's for sure."

I could see the questions burning in her eyes—what was it like? Why was I back so soon? But to her credit, she didn't voice them. Just gave me a gentle smile and a pat on the cheek.

"Well, we're surely glad to have you back, sugar. Even if it's just for a little while."

Guilt squeezed my heart. I knew she meant well, but her words just reminded me of the mess I'd made. The bridges I might have burned. Would Lewis and the band ever trust me again, after I'd bailed on them without a word?

I wished his texts would answer that question, but I didn't have the guts to ask.

I pushed the thought away, pasting on a bright smile. "It's good to be home. I've missed your baking something fierce."

Hattie chuckled. "Well, then you just sit yourself down and I'll fix you right up. Coffee and a baklava, on the house."

"You don't have to do that. I'm happy to pay—"

She waved me off, already heading back behind the counter. "Don't you even think about it, missy. It's the least I can do for our very own rising star."

Tears pricked at the back of my eyes. Rising star.

I was saved from having to respond by the jingle of the bell, followed by a familiar squeal. "Liv!"

I spun around, my face breaking into a genuine grin at the sight of Ashley, all chestnut hair and bright brown eyes as she darted across the bakery and threw her arms around me.

"Oof!" I laughed, hugging her back just as fiercely. "Easy. I still need to breathe."

"Sorry, sorry!" She pulled back, her cheeks flushed with joy. "I'm just so damn happy to see you! And here, of all places!" She glanced around, her nose wrinkling.

A pang of guilt speared me. So maybe I'd forgotten to so much as text my best friend in the last two days. And maybe I'd only left the house because Mama had forced me out the door...

"Oh hush, you." We slid into a booth by the window and tried not to wince as the lie tripped off my tongue. It was true. Usually. "You know you're the first person I'd come running to. Besides Mama, of course."

Her gaze softened and she reached across the table to squeeze mine. "How's she doing?"

I swallowed hard, my gaze dropping to the chipped table. "She's hanging in there. Stubborn as ever, insisting she's fine and that we shouldn't worry." I shook my head, blinking back the ever-present tears. "But I can see it, Ash. The toll it's taking. She's so thin, so tired all the time..."

"I'm so sorry." Her voice was gentle, full of shared sorrow. "I can't even imagine what you're going through."

I managed a wobbly smile. "It's been... a lot. I feel like I'm barely keeping my head above water most days."

She grinned, giving my hand another squeeze. "I'm here for you, whatever you need. Shoulder to cry on, trashy magazines to distract you..."

I laughed, the tightness in my chest easing just a little. "Speaking of trashy magazines... catch me up! What's the latest gossip around here? I need something to take my mind off of... everything."

A sly smile tugged at her lips. "Well... you didn't hear it from me, but word on the street is that Christopher Harris is back in town."

My eyebrows shot up. "As in my high school sweetheart Christopher?"

"The very same." She leaned in, lowering her voice conspiratorially. "Apparently he's taking over his daddy's law practice. And let me tell you, that boy has only gotten finer with age."

Christopher Harris. Now there was a name I hadn't thought about in years. We'd been the golden couple back in high school, the quarterback and the choir girl. Everyone had thought we'd get married straight out of school, pop out a couple of babies and settle down in a nice little house on Jasmine Lane.

But I'd had bigger dreams, and when graduation rolled around, I'd packed my bags, kissed Christopher goodbye and set off for Nashville without a backwards glance, leaving him and Jasmine Bay in my rear-view mirror. Last I'd heard, he'd gone off to some fancy law school up North, chasing his own ambitions.

"Huh. Never thought I'd see the day he came back to town." I sat back, sipping my coffee thoughtfully. "Guess the big city lost its shine for him too."

"Well, well, well. If it isn't Olivia Monroe." A syrupy-sweet voice dripped from behind me, making the hair on the back of my neck stand up. "I heard a rumour you were back in town, but I just couldn't believe it. Thought you'd gotten too big for your britches, what with all your gallivanting off to Hollywood."

I closed my eyes briefly, sending up a silent prayer for strength before plastering on my best beauty queen smile and turning to face the devil herself.

"Sadie-Mae! What a surprise." I let my eyes widen innocently. "I almost didn't recognise you without your pom-poms and a football player on each arm."

Her mouth tightened, a muscle ticking in her jaw before she recovered, her smile saccharine-sweet. "Oh sugar, I hung up my pom-poms years ago. Figured I'd leave the cheering to the professionals, you know?"

"How thoughtful of you," I simpered. "I'm sure the squad appreciated not having to compete with your... enthusiasm."

Ashley smothered a snort into her napkin, her shoulders shaking with repressed laughter. Sadie-Mae shot her a venomous look before turning her attention back to me, her eyes narrowed.

"So tell me. What brings you back to our humble little town? Last I heard, you were opening for some big-shot band, living the high life." Her lips curved in a smirk. "Don't tell me you've given up on your little pipe dream already."

Red-hot rage surged through me, my fingers curling into fists beneath the table. I opened my mouth, ready to let her have it, to tell her exactly where she could stick her snide little comments—

But I was saved by the bell. Literally. The door chimed again, and we all turned to see who had interrupted our little showdown.

And there, standing in the doorway like a vision straight out of my high school fantasies, was Christopher Harris.

He'd filled out since I last saw him, his shoulders broader, his jawline sharper. But his eyes were the same blue, his hair the same jet black. He scanned the bakery, gaze landing on our little group.

"Well, look what the cat dragged in!" His voice was deeper than I remembered. He strode over to us, eyes crinkling at the corners. "Olivia Monroe. Aren't you a sight for sore eyes."

I rose to accept his hug. He smelled the same, like fresh air and laundry detergent and something uniquely Christopher.

"Hey there, stranger. Long time no see."

"Too long." He pulled back, holding me at arm's length as he looked me over. "Guess that rock star life is treating you well. You look great, Liv."

My face heated while I shrugged off the compliment. "Oh, it's not all it's cracked up to be. But thanks." I glanced at Sadie-Mae, noting with no small satisfaction the way her smile had gone tight and brittle. "I hear you're back to take over your daddy's practice."

"Yeah. It feels good to be home."

Sadie-Mae cleared her throat pointedly, breaking the moment. "Speaking of home, Christopher... I've been meaning to ask. Are you free for dinner sometime this week? I'd love to catch up, fill you in on all the goings-on around here." She batted her lashes, pressing a hand to his arm. He glanced down at it, then back up, his brow furrowing.

"Ah, thanks Sadie-Mae, but I'm pretty swamped this week. Lots of cases to catch up on." He extracted himself gently from her grip, taking a subtle step back. "But you girls enjoy your coffee. Liv, it was great seeing you." He flashed me another grin that once upon a time would have weakened me at the knees. Now it just made me think of Lewis. "Don't be a stranger, alright?"

And with a final wave, he was gone, striding up to the counter to place his order. Sadie-Mae stood there gaping after him.

Ash caught my eye, waggling her brows suggestively. "Well. That was interesting."

I bit back a laugh, sliding back into my seat as Sadie-Mae huffed and flounced away, her heels clacking angrily on the tiles. "Oh, hush you. That was nothing. Just two old friends saying hello."

"Mmhmm." She smirked knowingly. "Two old friends who used to swap spit behind the bleachers."

I groaned, burying my face in my hands. "That was a million years ago. Ancient history."

"Maybe." Her eyes went sly.

I shifted uncomfortably, my stomach twisting. She wasn't entirely wrong. We had been close. Once. But all we shared now were memories that had long grown stale.

My heart still very much belonged to Lewis.

Because I never knew when my big break would come, I'd always kept my hopes for the future pretty loose. Unfortunately, they'd started to solidify in the time I spent with him. Thinking about how we'd never get to do our wedding over again with our loved ones, never travel together, walk a red carpet, or anything normal couples do, it made my eyes burn.

I swallowed hard, fiddling with my napkin while I willed the tears away. Ashley didn't need me dissolving into a blubbering mess on her.

Ash sobered immediately, her teasing grin fading. "Hey, what's going on in that head of yours? You look like you're about to either burst into tears or punch something."

I shrugged, trying for a casual smile that felt more like a grimace. "It's nothing. Just… a lot on my mind, you know?"

She raised a brow, calling my bluff. "Uh-huh. And would any of that 'a lot' have to do with a certain tattooed bassist?"

I sighed, my shoulders slumping. Ash always could see right through me. "Maybe."

"Spill, girl. Did you talk to him before you left?"

I winced. "Yes and no."

Her eyes narrowed. "What does that mean?"

"We talked about us and it was good. For a few hours. He agreed to try and be more open about our relationship. Even said he'd go to the market with me, let us be seen together."

Ash's eyes widened, a grin splitting her face. "Liv, that's great! That's progress!"

"It was." I swallowed hard, the memory of that day, of the hopeful flutter in my chest, stinging like salt in a wound. "But it all went to hell pretty fast."

Her brow furrowed. "What do you mean?"

"We were at this market in Eugene, just walking around, holding hands. It felt so right. Like we were just a normal couple, you know?" I blinked back the sudden sting of tears. "But then some fan spotted us. Snapped a picture. And he freaked."

"Freaked how?"

"He basically dragged me out of there. Started going on about how it was too risky, how we needed to keep our distance. Like he was ashamed of me or something."

Ash's face softened with sympathy. "Oh, honey…"

"And the worst part?" I laughed, the sound harsh and bitter. "He refuses to get help. To even try and work through his issues with the press and the public scrutiny. It's like I'm not enough for him to face his fears. Like he'd rather hide me away than risk the world knowing we're together."

"Liv, I'm sure that's not—"

"But it is!" I cut her off, my voice rising with each word. "He's so terrified of what people will think, of what they'll say... it's like he can't see past it. Can't see that I'm going to be in the spotlight too, with or without him. That I'm going to have to deal with the press and the gossip and all of it, no matter what."

The words poured out of me in a rush, All the fear and hurt and anger I'd been bottling up, spilling over in an unstoppable tide.

"And maybe he's right. Maybe I can't handle it. Maybe I'm not cut out for this life, for this level of scrutiny. Maybe I should just... just give up. Go back to singing in honky-tonks and pretending I never had these big, stupid dreams in the first place."

"Okay, stop. Just... stop." Ash held up a hand, her expression fierce. "You're catastrophising again, Liv. Spinning yourself into a worst-case spiral that has no basis in reality."

I opened my mouth to argue, but she barrelled on.

"No, listen to me. You're talented and brilliant and brave as hell. You didn't claw your way out of this town, didn't pour your heart and soul into your music, just to let some man's issues derail everything you've worked for."

I stared at her, my throat tight. "But—"

"But nothing. Look, I'm not saying Lewis's fears aren't valid. I'm sure growing up in the spotlight, dealing with all that pressure... it messes with your head. And maybe he does need help." She reached across the table, gripping my hands in hers. "But that's on him, Liv. That's his journey, his responsibility. You can't fix him. Can't love him into being ready for what you need."

Tears blurred my vision, my chest aching with the truth of her words. Because she was right. As much as I loved Lewis, as much as I wanted to be with him... I couldn't force him into being someone he wasn't. Couldn't make him confront his demons if he wasn't willing.

"I know," I whispered, my voice thick. "I know you're right. I just… I love him. So fucking much. And the thought of losing him, of walking away…"

"I know, babe. I know it hurts like hell." She squeezed my hands, her touch grounding me. "But you've gotta put yourself first. Gotta do what's right for you, for your career and your sanity. And if he can't get on board with that, if he can't step up and be the partner you need… then maybe it's not meant to be. At least not right now."

I nodded, swiping at my damp cheeks. It felt like ripping out my own heart, the idea of letting Lewis go. But Ash was right. I couldn't dim my own light just because he was afraid of the glare.

CHAPTER THIRTY-ONE

LEWIS

*F*our days. It had been four bloody days since Liv left, and the gaping hole she'd left behind hadn't gotten any smaller. If anything, it felt like it was growing, swallowing me whole with each passing mile.

I lay in my bunk, staring at the ceiling as the tour bus rumbled down the highway towards Winnipeg. The gentle sway and the low hum of the engine did nothing to ease the ache in my chest.

I could hear the guys downstairs, their laughter and banter filtering up through the thin walls. Normally, I'd be down there with them, shooting the shit and enjoying a well-earned beer after the show. But not tonight.

Not when Liv still hadn't called me back or answered my texts since that first day.

I scrolled through the endless stream of texts I'd sent her. Some of them filled with pure desperation and others a thinly veiled attempt to pretend that nothing had changed.

But everything had changed.

I'd pushed her away and somehow I had to fix it. How I'd do that still eluded me. I couldn't just abandon the tour and my bandmates. They were relying on me. The fans would be devastated.

I just needed to bide my time. Wait for the right moment and sneak away for a long break. Surely all I needed was a couple of days to convince her that I was serious about us.

Serious enough to go to therapy?

I winced at the thought. That was still a sticking point for me. If I had some guarantee that the person I'd be spilling my soul to would keep their lips zipped, maybe. But I didn't have the faintest idea how to go about finding that person.

The curtain of my bunk twitched, startling me out of my misery. Lily appeared, her brow furrowed with concern.

"Hey," she whispered, her voice barely audible over the rumble of the bus. "You alright? We missed you at dinner."

I forced a smile, the muscles of my face feeling stiff and unnatural. "Yeah, I'm good. Just feeling a bit under the weather, that's all."

She studied me, her blue eyes sharp and knowing. I could practically see the gears turning behind them, piecing together the clues I'd unwittingly left in my wake.

My sudden change in demeanour. The way I'd been isolating myself, spending hours locked away in my bunk or staring blankly out the window. The dark circles under my eyes, the beard I hadn't bothered to shave.

And of course, the glaring absence of a certain brunette singer-songwriter who'd been attached to my hip since before the start of the tour.

"Lewis…" She sighed, her expression softening. "I know something's going on. Something more than just a bug or a bad day."

I looked away, my throat tightening. I couldn't do this. Couldn't put into words the mess I'd made, the ache that was eating me alive.

"Lily, please. I just… I need some space, alright? I promise, I'm fine. Just need to sleep it off."

She hesitated, clearly wanting to push, to demand the truth. But to her credit, she didn't. Just nodded, her hand coming to rest briefly on my shoulder.

"Okay. But I'm here, yeah? When you're ready to talk. We all are."

I managed a nod, not trusting my voice. She gave me one last searching look before disappearing, the curtain swishing shut behind her.

I let out a shaky breath, the silence of the bunk pressing in on me. My fingers itched for my phone, for the lifeline I'd been clinging to like a drowning man.

I'd texted Olivia every day since she'd left. Little things, snippets of my day, the random thoughts that popped into my head. Things I would've shared with her in person, if she'd been here.

If I hadn't fucked it all up.

LEWIS

Please, just let me know you're okay.

My breath froze as the dots started to bounce.

LIV

I'm okay.

Two words. Two measly words that simultaneously eased the tightness in my chest and ripped the wound wider.

She was okay. Thank fuck for that. But what did it mean? Was she okay without me? Okay with leaving me behind, with walking away from everything we'd started?

My fingers hovered over the screen, a thousand questions burning on my tongue. But I couldn't make myself type them out. Couldn't bear to see them go unanswered, to face the reality that she might not want to answer.

❄

"*I*'ve managed to keep the story about your marriage under wraps for now," Carly said two days later, her voice crisp and businesslike even through the phone. "But it's only a matter of time before someone else comes sniffing. If you want to keep this out of the tabloids, you need to consider getting that annulment sorted."

I stood backstage at Winnipeg Arena, my mind a million miles away from the rush of the load out around me. Roadies and techs rushed by, shouting orders and hauling gear, but they might as well have been ghosts. I couldn't focus on anything but the phone clutched in my white-knuckled grip and the voice on the other end of the line.

The word hit me like a punch to the gut. Annulment. The erasure of the worst and best mistake I'd ever made.

"Carly, I…" My voice cracked, the words sticking in my throat. "I don't know if I can do that. If I can just… erase what we have."

"Lewis." She sighed, and I could picture her pinching the bridge of her nose, the way she always did when one of us was being particularly difficult. "I know this is hard. I know you have… feelings for Olivia. But you have to think about the bigger picture here."

"I am thinking about it," I snapped, frustration and heartache sharpening my tone. "Every bloody second of every bloody day. It's all I can think about."

"Then you know what's at stake." Carly's voice softened, but there was steel beneath the silk. "If this gets out, if the press gets wind of your hasty Vegas wedding… it'll be the opposite of what you want for Olivia."

If our marriage became public fodder, if the tabloids and the gossip rags sank their teeth into Liv the way they had with Tegan…

A vision of me in a suit, standing in some Southern cemetery staring down at a pit in the ground filled my head. It turned my blood to ice.

Maybe you should believe her when she says she can handle it.

"I don't..." My voice shook, barely audible over the roaring in my ears. "I don't want to lose her, Carly."

"I know, love." The endearment, so rare from our usually unflappable publicist, nearly undid me. "But you can't have privacy and stay married. It's just not possible. So you need to make up your mind."

I closed my eyes, the arena fading away until there was nothing but the crackles of static on the line and the sickening thud of my heart.

She'd never forgive me.

I knew her well enough to know I wasn't exaggerating. Liv wanted—had wanted this.

I twisted the ring I still hadn't taken off. I'd started to hate the thought of being without it. Had Liv taken hers off?

"I'll think about it," I said, the words like ashes on my tongue.

*T*hree bloody days had passed since my conversation with Carly, and the word still haunted me.

Annulment.

It clung to me like a second skin. It whispered in my ear as I lay in my bunk, staring at the ceiling, my phone clutched to my chest, hoping that tonight would be the night she called. It taunted me from the stage, the faces of the crowd blurring into a sea of accusation and pity.

It was in every breath, every heartbeat, a constant reminder of what I'd had... and what I was about to lose.

I hadn't slept more than a handful of hours since that call. Couldn't seem to shut off my brain, to quiet the voices that warred in my head. One minute, I was resolute, determined to do what was best for Olivia, no matter the cost. The next, I was drowning in doubt, in the aching certainty that letting her go would be the biggest mistake of my life.

But through it all, one truth remained, stubborn and unshakeable.

I needed her. Needed her like air, like sunlight, like the music that flowed through my veins. She was a part of me now, as vital and necessary as the beat of my own heart.

And God help me, I couldn't let her go. Not without a fight, not without one last desperate plea.

While the bus sped through the night, my fingers flew over my phone screen. Pouring out my heart, my hopes, my dreams in a tangle of digital words.

LEWIS

> We're on the way to St. Paul. Remember I was going to take you to see that comedian after the show? I still have the tickets. You could still come.

I stared at the words, barely breathing while I waited for those dots to move. They didn't.

LEWIS

> There's a flight out of Charleston. You'd have plenty of time to get there. We could talk, hang out with no pressure. I just want to see you, cariad.

Seconds ticked by and still nothing.

LEWIS

> Please, Liv. I just need to hear your voice. Please, pick up.

I hit dial before I could second guess myself. It rang once, twice, the sound echoing in the confines of the bunk. I prepared myself for it to go to voicemail and that I'd have to face the reality that she didn't want to talk to me, that she might actually be done with us.

"Lewis?" Her voice filled my ear.

"Liv." It came out choked, strangled.

"Yeah." She sounded exhausted, wary, like she was bracing herself for something. For me, for the conversation we'd been avoiding for days. "It's me."

"I... God, Liv. I've missed you so much." The words tumbled out, raw and unfiltered, the dam inside me finally cracking under the pressure. "I know things are a mess, I know I fucked up, but I... I can't do this without you. I can't imagine my life without you in it."

Silence. A beat, two, three. Each second an eternity, an agony of uncertainty.

"It's not that simple."

"But it can be." I sat up, my free hand fisting in the sheets, desperate to make her understand. "We can figure this out. I know we can. You just need to come back."

CHAPTER THIRTY-TWO

OLIVIA

"*I* can't." My voice caught, tears pricking at the back of my eyes. "Not right now."

"Why?"

I swallowed hard, steeling myself. This conversation was inevitable, but that didn't make it any easier. "Didn't Kevin give you my message?"

Lewis's scoff crackled through the phone. "He said you left because of me. Because I'd driven you away."

"What?" Shock lanced through me, followed swiftly by a flare of anger. "That's not true at all! I didn't leave because of you and I didn't tell him that."

"Then why?" The desperation in his voice was a palpable thing, a living echo of the ache in my own chest. "Please, Liv. I need to understand."

I closed my eyes, the words like shards of glass in my throat. "It's my mama. She's sick, Lewis. Really sick. Terminal."

A sharp intake of breath, then a beat of stunned silence. "Fuck, I'm so sorry."

A sob caught in my chest, the reality of it still too raw, too overwhelming to fully comprehend. "I got the call right after I finished my set in Vancouver. I couldn't... I had to come home. I had to be with her."

"Of course you did." Lewis's voice was gentle, achingly soft. "If you'd told me, I would've been on that plane with you in a heartbeat. You shouldn't have had to deal with this alone."

Tears spilled down my cheeks, hot and fast. He meant it, I knew he did. But it wasn't that simple.

Silence stretched between us, heavy with unspoken emotion. I could practically hear the gears turning in Lewis's head, searching for a solution.

"I'm sorry," I whispered, fresh tears welling. "For not calling, for not explaining. I've read every one of your messages, I just... I didn't have the words. Didn't have the energy to try and make sense of any of this."

"It's okay," he murmured, a catch in his voice. "I understand. I really do. I just miss you. So bloody much."

My heart clenched, a physical pain in my chest. "I miss you too."

"I uh..." He cleared his throat. "I've been seeing someone. A therapist."

My breath caught, shock and tentative hope warring in my chest. "You have?"

"Yeah." He exhaled slowly. "Jared referred me to his guy. Said he was discreet, that he could help me work through some of my shit."

"And?" I hardly dared to breathe. "How's it going?"

A humourless chuckle. "It's been bloody awful, if I'm honest. Digging up all that old pain..." He sighed, heavy and weary. "But I'm trying, Liv. I'm really fucking trying. Because I want to be better. For you, for us. For myself."

Tears blurred my vision. "I'm so proud of you."

And I really was. Even if the stars didn't align for us again, at least he would get better.

"I'd do anything for you." The conviction in his voice, the

raw sincerity, sent a shiver down my spine. "I know I've got a long way to go. I know I've still got so much to prove. But I'm in this, cariad. All the way."

I bit down on my lip, an ocean of emotions threatening to drown me. I wanted to believe him, wanted it with every fibre of my being. But the timing... it couldn't have been worse.

"Come to the Grammys with me."

I blinked, certain I must have misheard. "I'm sorry, what?"

"The Grammys," Lewis repeated, his voice gaining strength, conviction. "Come with me, Liv. As my date. My real, public, no-more-hiding date."

My heart stuttered, skipped, then kicked into overdrive. "Are you serious?"

"Deadly." I could hear the smile in his voice, the excited tremble. "I'm done hiding. Done letting fear dictate my choices. I want the world to know what you mean to me. What we mean to each other."

Tears sprang to my eyes, hope and love and overwhelming emotion crashing over me in waves. "I want that too."

"Is that a yes, then?" The boyish hope in his voice, the barely contained excitement, made me want to laugh and cry in equal measure.

"It's a maybe," I said gently, hating to dim his enthusiasm but needing to be realistic. "The Grammys are still months away. A lot could change."

He was quiet for a moment, processing. "What are you saying, Liv?"

I took a deep breath, gathering my courage. "I'm saying... let's take it one step at a time. You focus on the tour, on your therapy. I'll focus on my family and being here for my mama. And if, after the North American leg wraps, we still feel this way... then we can talk about next steps. About the future."

"The future. I like the sound of that."

A smile tugged at my lips, a flicker of warmth amidst the chaos. "Me too."

We lapsed into silence, the weight of all we'd said, all we'd promised, settling over us like a blanket. It was scary and exhilarating and so full of potential I could hardly breathe.

I probably should have reined in my hope just in case it didn't pan out. But I needed something to look forward to right now. With Mama's health declining faster than the doctors anticipated, I needed a glimmer of hope to keep me upright and moving.

Lewis groaned. "I really don't want to mention this while you're actually talking to me, but there is something we should discuss."

"What is it?" Dread settled heavy in my stomach, chasing away the tentative warmth of moments before.

Lewis sighed, the sound heavy with reluctance. "Carly suggested we file for an annulment. She's been on my case about it. Thinks we need to get it sorted before the press catches wind."

"Oh." My breath caught, a sharp pain lancing through my chest.

"I don't care what Carly wants," Lewis cut in, fierce and unequivocal. "The only opinion that matters here is yours. So tell me, honestly… is that what you want? Do you want to undo what we did?"

I closed my eyes, tears burning hot behind the lids. "You're my husband. For better or worse, in sickness and in health. I meant those vows, even if I was too drunk to remember making them."

Silence filled the line for a moment before his breath rattled the phone. "Just so we're on the same page, we're married and staying married, right?" Relief dripped from his tone.

"Yes. This is just us testing out the 'or worse' part of our vows sooner than I hoped."

He chuckled and I smiled, absorbing every second of this temporary high. Later, I'd go back to worrying about my mother, but right now, I just wanted to lay here and bask in his happiness.

"What if I helped you relax?" he asked, his voice dropping until it vibrated against my ear in the most delicious manner.

"What?"

"You said you're emotionally exhausted. You're probably stressed too. So let me help."

"How?"

"Tell me what you're wearing," Lewis drawled, his voice dropping to a low, intimate rumble.

My breath hitched, arousal and amusement warring for dominance. "Are you seriously trying to initiate phone sex right now?"

"Maybe." I could practically hear his shrug, picture the mischievous glint in his hazel eyes. "Is it working?"

I bit my lip, fighting a smile even as heat pooled low in my belly. "It might be. If you play your cards right."

His low chuckle resonated through the line, through my body, igniting every nerve ending. "Well then. Tell me, Mrs Davies... what are you wearing?"

I glanced down at my threadbare sleep shorts and ratty old band tee, a wicked idea taking root. "Who says I'm wearing anything at all?"

Lewis groaned, the sound shooting straight to my core. "Fuck, Liv. You can't just say things like that."

"Oh no?" I sunk down into the pillows, letting my free hand drift over my chest, my stomach, teasing the hem of my shirt. "And why's that?"

"Because," he growled, the rough timbre of his voice making me shiver. "It makes me want to do very, very wicked things to you."

Heat licked up my spine, pooling molten in my veins. "Like what?" I breathed, already squirming with anticipation. "Tell me."

"Like kiss my way down your gorgeous body," he rumbled, low and dark. "Taste every inch of your sweet skin. Run my tongue over your pretty pink nipples until you're writhing and begging for more."

I whimpered, my fingers slipping beneath the worn cotton to play over the sensitive peaks. They pebbled instantly, aching for his touch, his mouth. "Don't stop," I pleaded, breathless and needy. "Please."

"Greedy girl," Lewis purred, smug and aroused. "You want more? Want me to tell you how I'd worship those perfect tits with my mouth, my hands, until you're dripping wet and desperate for me?"

"Yes," I moaned, pinching and rolling my nipples, sparks of pleasure shooting to my core. "God, Lewis, yes."

"I'd take my time with you," he promised darkly, the implied threat making me shudder. "Kissing down your stomach, nibbling on your hip bones. Avoiding where you need me most, until you're a writhing, pleading mess."

I could picture it perfectly, could feel the phantom brush of his lips, his stubble against my skin. My free hand drifted lower, teasing along the edge of my shorts.

"Tell me you're touching yourself," Lewis said, a stark, wrecked edge to his voice. "Tell me you're fucking soaked and aching, just from the sound of my voice."

"I am," I panted, shoving my shorts down to shimmy out of them. "I'm dripping."

He made a guttural sound, almost pained. "Christ. Wish I could taste you, bury my face between your thighs until you're screaming for me."

I moaned brokenly, fingers dipping into the wet heat of my sex. I was slick and swollen, my clit throbbing for attention. "I'm so close already." I circled the sensitive nub. "Just from your voice."

"That's it, cariad," Lewis whispered, a tremor in his words hinting at his own unravelling. "Make yourself feel good. Plunge those pretty fingers inside, fuck yourself like I would. Hard and deep and so fucking perfect."

I obeyed with a sob, sinking two fingers knuckle-deep into my channel. My head thrashed on the pillow. "Lewis, god. Wish it was you. Your fingers, your cock, splitting me open."

"Soon," he promised, raw and ragged. "Soon I'll fuck you so hard and sweet, you'll be ruined for anyone else. Only ever want my cock, stretching that needy little cunt."

"Yes." I pumped faster, grinding my clit against my palm. "Only you, always you."

"Come for me, Liv. Scream my name, let me hear you fall apart."

I did. Explosively, back arching off the bed as I clamped down on my fingers, inner muscles spasming almost violently. Lewis's name tore from my throat, a broken, blissful moan as waves of ecstasy crashed over me again and again.

In my ear, Lewis groaned long and low, the unmistakable sounds of his own release spurring my pleasure higher. We rode it out together, gasping and shaking.

Slowly, I floated back to myself, boneless and sated in the tangled sheets. Lewis's heavy breathing filled my ear, a soothing lullaby I never wanted to end.

"That was…" I sought for words, my sex-drunk brain struggling to string together coherent thought.

"I think you broke me, Liv."

I giggled, giddy and luminous. "Ditto, Mr Davies. Ditto."

We lapsed into comfortable silence, basking in the afterglow, in the renewed sense of connection thrumming between us. I could've stayed like that forever, suspended in this perfect, peaceful moment.

But reality, as it always did, came knocking.

"I should let you go," I murmured, regret already seeping in. "It's late, and we both have big days tomorrow."

Lewis sighed, heavy and resigned. "I know. I just… I miss you. So fucking much."

Tears stung my eyes, the ache in my chest throbbing anew. "I miss you too, Lewis. More than anything."

"We'll talk again soon, yeah?" The forced cheer in his voice, the stubborn optimism, made me smile through the tears.

"Yes. I'll get better at checking in. Promise."

A few more murmured endearments, promises to talk soon, and then we reluctantly rang off. I clutched the silent phone to my chest, tears of sorrow and joy, grief and hope, spilling down my cheeks.

CHAPTER THIRTY-THREE

LEWIS

*a*s I stepped out of the air-conditioned rental car, the South Carolina humidity wrapped around me like a suffocating blanket. I'd never experienced a southern summer. All I had for comparison was TV shows and who knew how realistic they had been.

Anderson stopped next to me as I surveyed the quaint, picture-postcard Main Street of Jasmine Bay, searching for Mayfield's Bakery.

"I don't know if this is a good idea, Lewis."

He'd said the same thing before we got on the plane in Toronto. Then again when the car rental employees stared at me, starstruck, while we picked up the car in Charleston.

"It'll be fine." I hoped.

He grunted. "At least you had enough sense to bring me."

"Like I'd get on a plane without you. I know my limits."

"If you actually knew your limits, you and your band of delinquents wouldn't have evaded your entire security team for two days and fucked off to the woods in Toronto."

I smirked. "Chill, man. It all worked out."

He glowered at me, but I ignored him. Instead, I took a deep breath, and squaring my shoulders, I started down Main Street, scanning the shops and cafes for the ones she'd mentioned. My hands were clammy, my stomach a roiling mess of nerves, but I couldn't back down now.

I needed two things: her address, and the entire town gossiping about our marriage before I got to her house.

Anderson fell into step beside me, his gaze scanning every face we passed. "The first words out of my mouth when this all goes to hell and I'm done rescuing you are going to be I told you so, you know that, right?"

"Yes, but it's not going to happen."

Had never happened in fact. For all my rebellious moments, I'd never gotten into a situation I couldn't escape. It helped that I'd always been careful with the locations, only skipping out on him when it was somewhere I knew well with owners I trusted impeccably. Like Rhymes. I'd spent a good five years frequenting that bar and I'd never drawn more than a friendly nod.

"Can you at least put a cap and glasses on?" he asked when someone pulled out their phone.

"Nope."

Thankfully, I spotted the bakery before he could overreact some more. I crossed the street, heading towards the cheerful but faded green awning.

I needed to show her that she wasn't alone, that I would always put her first. I'd failed until now and I couldn't live with her believing I would again.

All that had held me back was the band and my commitment to the tour. Then we'd all skipped town after Toronto, ditched our security detail and spent a night in the woods, drinking, laughing and enjoying two nights surrounded by nature. We'd shared some shit, opened up to each other in a way we hadn't in a long time.

By the time we pulled up in Montreal and rejoined the tour,

they had it all figured out. Lily handed me plane tickets and shoved me into a waiting taxi.

The bell above the door jingled merrily as I stepped inside the bakery, announcing my arrival to the gaggle of locals gathered around mismatched tables, sipping sweet tea and trading juicy gossip.

The moment I crossed the threshold, a hush fell over the room, like someone had hit the mute button on a TV. Anderson tensed. The weight of their curious stares settled on me as they sized me up. The whispers started, my name bouncing around the room like a ping pong ball at a church social.

"Is that…?"

"It can't be."

I shifted uncomfortably, suddenly feeling like a sore thumb in my designer jeans. I'd faced crowds of thousands, their screams shaking stadiums, but somehow, the scrutiny of these people made me pause.

Anderson sniggered at my frozen state. "Still think this is a good idea?"

"Well, I'll be." A gruff voice cut above the whispers. A robust, flour-dusted woman behind the counter beckoned me over with a wave of her rolling pin. "Don't just stand there catching flies! What can I do you for, sugar?"

The woman behind the counter eyed me with a mix of curiosity and calculation. Her hair was streaked with grey, wisps escaping the messy bun atop her head, and her apron was dusted with flour. But the look in her eyes was sharp, assessing.

I approached the counter, grateful for the reprieve from the stares boring holes in my back. "I'm looking for Hattie."

The woman let out a hearty laugh, warm and rich as black-strap molasses. "Well, you found her." She looked me over, her keen eyes missing nothing, like she could read my entire life story in the creases of my vintage band tee. "Now, what brings a famous rock star like you to my humble little slice of heaven?"

Something about her warmth and kindness sucked all of the nervous energy out of me.

I leaned in. "I'm here for my wife. I want to surprise her, sweep her off her feet, but I don't know where she lives. I was hoping you might be able to point me in the right direction."

A hush fell over the bakery. Somewhere, a teacup clattered against its saucer.

Hattie's eyebrows shot up so high, they nearly disappeared into her hairline. "Your wife, you say? And who might the lucky lady be?"

"Olivia Monroe."

The moment the words left my mouth, the dam broke. The bakery erupted into a frenzy of chatter, the volume rising. Despite my nerves, a smile tugged at the corner of my mouth as the whispers fixated on that particular detail.

"Livvy Monroe got hitched and didn't breathe a word?"

"And to a genuine celebrity, bless her heart!"

"I wonder if her mama knows."

Two older women in the corner, their heads bent together like conspiring hens, gathered up their handbags and hustled out the door, no doubt off to spread the news. Just like I wanted.

Hattie let out a low whistle. "Well, paint me purple and call me a plum. Our little Livvy, married to a bona fide rock star." She fixed me with a look that managed to be both warm and warning. "You sure you're ready for the whirlwind that comes with a secret like that in a town like this?"

I met her gaze head-on, my jaw set with determination. "I'm ready for anything as long as it means I get to be with Liv."

Before Hattie could respond, the bell jingled again. A tall, dark-haired guy walked in, his grin wide as he returned greetings from the still shellshocked patrons.

His gaze fell on me and his eyes widened for a second before a charming smile slid into place. "I can hardly believe it. Lewis Davies in Jasmine Bay." He strode up to the counter, offering his hand. "Chris Harris. I've caught your band in concert a time or two. What brings you to our charming little corner of the world?"

Hattie chuckled. "Oh, this is going to be fun." She crossed

her arms and grinned at me. "Well, go on then, don't dither. Tell him why you're here."

Puzzled by her amusement, I shook his hand. "I'm looking for my wife, actually. Olivia Monroe."

His grin faltered, slipping for a heartbeat before he hitched it back into place. "Liv? You two tied the knot?" He let out a low whistle. "Did not see that coming. I was hoping…" He grimaced. "I mean, with both of us back in town, I thought maybe she and I could take a walk down memory lane. We were high school sweethearts, you know? But if she's—"

"Married." I felt a flare of possessiveness lick up my spine. "Sorry, man. She's off the market. Permanently."

Chris held up his hands in surrender, his grin turning a touch rueful. "Message received, loud and clear." He clapped me on the shoulder, his grip bordering on painful. "You treat her right, you hear? She's one of a kind."

"I'm aware," I agreed with a small smile. "Which is why I'm not letting her go without one hell of a fight."

Especially now that I had somewhat of a handle on my fears. I couldn't have done it without nearly two weeks of daily sessions with Jared's therapist. I still had a long way to go, but at least now I could recognise the source of my reactions and think through them before acting impulsively. It wasn't foolproof, but baby steps.

The words hung between us, heavy with implication. Christopher inclined his head, expression inscrutable.

"I can see that." A muscle ticked in his jaw. "If you'll excuse me, I should be going. My morning just got… unexpectedly busy."

I watched him go, feeling a strange mix of triumph and guilt. Hattie clapped her hands together, her expression filled with glee. "Well, then. I'm guessing you're here for Liv's favourite baklava as much as an address." She bustled around the counter, packing up a generous helping of Liv's favourite dessert.

"You'd be right."

"Of course I'm right, daft boy." She shook her head, clucking her tongue at me. "Now, I can't rightly go giving out her address willy-nilly. Wouldn't be proper. But I can send you in the right direction, get you pointed straight as an arrow."

She leaned across the counter, her voice dropping to a conspiratorial whisper. "You'll want to mosey on over to Jazzy Blooms. Daisy Hawthorne, the gal who runs the flower shop, she's got a soft spot for grand gestures and love stories. Might be she can hook you up with a clue."

I accepted the box of baklava. "Thanks, Hattie. For the baklava and the wisdom."

"You know you're being led on a wild goose chase, right?" Anderson asked once the bakery door closed behind us.

"Yup."

His scowl deepened as he surveyed the growing crowd of onlookers. "Let's keep this moving. The longer we linger, the more attention we draw."

$\mathcal{T}$he walk from Mayfield's Bakery to Jazzy Blooms Florist was a short one, just a few storefronts down. Already I could see a rainbow of colourful blooms spilling out onto the sidewalk.

The moment we stepped into the flower shop, the fragrant perfume of all the flowers crammed into the small space assaulted me. Blooms of every hue spilled from buckets and vases, turning the small space into a lush, vibrant garden. I half expected a hummingbird to come buzzing by my ear, drunk on nectar.

Behind the counter, a willowy blonde with wildly curling hair and a flowing, floral-print dress looked up from an arrangement of sunflowers, a smile playing at the corners of her rosepetal lips.

"Well, well, well. If it isn't the man of the hour, the talk of the town." She glided around the counter, her dress swishing around her ankles like a summer breeze. "Lewis Davies, I presume?"

"I am." I smiled. "News travels fast around here."

She threw her head back and laughed, the sound as bright and tinkling as wind chimes. "Oh, honey. You've been the hottest topic on the gossip grapevine since Flossie Pendergast's prized peach pie went missing at last year's church social. I'm Daisy, by the by. What can I do for you?"

"I'm looking to woo my wife, make a grand romantic gesture. I was hoping you might be able to help me pick out the perfect bouquet, something that says, 'I'm a damned fool, but I'm your fool, now and forever'."

Daisy's smile turned sly, a mischievous twinkle in her blue eyes. "I reckon we can cobble together something that'll make her weak in the knees." She set to work, flitting among the blossoms, plucking stems with an expert eye. "I'm glad you're here. Our Liv, she's been through the wringer lately, what with her mama getting sick and all. That girl could use a double dose of happiness right about now."

I leaned against the counter, watching as she artfully arranged a medley of sunflowers, pink roses, and sprigs of lavender. "That's the goal."

Daisy tied off the bouquet with a flourish. "Well, sugar, you're sure as shooting on the right track." She pressed the bouquet into my hands, the silky petals whispering against my skin. "Now, if I were a betting woman and I never bet against love I'd say your next stop ought to be Mama Jo's Diner. Liv's been known to seek solace in a slice of Jo's famous pecan pie, the kind that'll make your eyes roll back in your head."

"Then I guess that's my next stop. Thanks. For the flowers and the guidance."

As I turned to leave, bouquet in hand, I nearly collided with a blonde in a sundress, her smile as bright and artificial as a plastic daisy.

"Oops. I'm so sorry." Her voice dripped with a saccharine sweetness, cloying as spun sugar. She eyed me with a critical eye.

"Wait, don't I know you? Yes, I do. I don't think I've ever seen someone famous in Jasmine Bay."

"Well that's about to change." I sidestepped her, keeping a polite bit of distance between us. "I'm just picking up some flowers for my wife."

Her perfectly arched brows shot up, disappearing into her hairline. "Wife? From Jasmine?"

I nodded. "Liv Monroe."

Her laugh tinkled like breaking glass. "My, my. And here I thought she'd end up an old maid, pining after Christopher Harris 'til the day she died."

A muscle in my jaw ticked, irritation simmering in my gut. "Well, lucky for me, Liv's got better taste than that. If you'll excuse me…"

I brushed past her, the cloying cloud of her perfume clinging to me like a bad memory.

Anderson laughed as he followed me. "I don't think I've ever seen you shoot someone down before they can break out the flirting. I'm impressed."

I rolled my eyes. "Get used to it. I'm all in."

"You said, but I don't think I believed it until now." He clapped me on the shoulder. "Good for you, man. Does this mean you're going to be pulling less disappearing acts?" He side-eyed me, smirking.

"Maybe. We'll see."

*A*nderson and I slid into a vinyl booth at the local diner. He reached for the laminated menu while I rested the box of baklava and the bouquet on the tabletop. He'd barely cracked the menu open when a woman in a pink gingham uniform descended upon us, a fresh pot of coffee in hand.

"You must be Liv's Lewis." She stopped in front of us, placed two mugs on the table and started pouring. "The name's Jo, but you can call me Mama. Everyone does."

Before I could utter a word, she bustled off, only to return a heartbeat later with two slabs of pecan pie the size of my head.

"Pie's on the house, sugar. You could use it after the morning you've had. Move over, handsome." She waved her hand at Anderson but didn't bother waiting for him to respond before she slid into the booth.

"That obvious, huh?" I took a gulp of coffee.

All around us, phones hovered in the air and hushed voices filled the small diner. By now they probably had my movements marked on a map.

Mama Jo chuckled, the sound warm and knowing. "Honey, you're wearing your heart on your sleeve. And in a town like Jasmine Bay, that's like waving a steak in front of a pack of starving dogs. Everybody's just dying to take a bite out of your business."

I smiled, enjoying this quirky little town more than I probably should. "I just want to find Liv, make things right. Show her that I'm in this for keeps, gossip be damned."

Mama Jo reached across the table, patting my hand with a touch as comforting as a worn quilt. "I've known that girl since she was knee-high to a June bug. She's got a heart as big as the Lowcountry sky, but preparing to lose her mama, that kind of grief, it can make a body want to curl up small and shut out the world."

I leaned forward, the worn vinyl creaking beneath me. "I want to be her world. I want to hold her through the hard times and celebrate the good ones. I just need her to know I'm serious first, and then I need to find her, tell her face-to-face."

A slow grin spread across Mama Jo's face. "Why, you sly dog, you're playing us all."

I smirked. "Just a little."

"Well, if there's one thing this town excels at, it's spreading gossip. You don't need to worry about keeping secrets here. There's nothing these people can't sniff out." Mama Jo studied me for a long moment, her cornflower blue eyes seeing clear to my soul. "You really do love her, don't you?"

I nodded. "More than music."

She smiled, a slow, sweet thing that crinkled the corners of her eyes. "Well, then. I suppose I ought to put you out of your misery." She reached into her apron pocket, pulling out a slip of paper and sliding it across the table. "The library. Our Liv's been spending an awful lot of time there lately, reading to her mama, keeping her company."

I accepted the slip of paper and turned it over to find a map. She winked when I stared at it with shock.

"My friends might enjoy sending you all over town without the foggiest idea where you're going, but I'm a little kinder than that." She slid out of the booth and stood. "Besides, I'd say they've all gotten their fill of you now. Your work's done, just find your girl."

"Thank you, I will. And thanks. For the pie, the coffee, and the tip."

She dismissed my thanks with a flick of her wrist. "Just promise me one thing, sugar. When you find that girl, you hold on tight and never let go. Love like yours is rarer than a blue moon."

"I intend to. I'm not letting her slip away again."

With a final nod of thanks, I slid out of the booth, Anderson trailing behind me. I consulted my mental map of the town, trying to remember if I'd seen a library on our drive in.

"The library's just a couple blocks down," Anderson said, reading my mind in that uncanny way of his. "But are you sure you want to keep playing this game? Why not just ask for her address and be done with it?"

I shook my head, a wry smile tugging at my lips. "Where's the fun in that? Besides, I want to give the gossip mill time to work its magic. By the time I reach Liv, I want there to be no doubt in her mind that I'm serious about us."

Anderson snorted, but fell into step beside me as we made our way down the sun-baked street. The heat and humidity were oppressive, but I barely noticed. My mind was focused on

Liv, on the moment I'd finally see her again, hold her in my arms and never let go.

Lost in my thoughts, I almost didn't notice the figure stepping out of the mechanic's shop up ahead. "Does my sister know you're in town?"

I turned to see a young man in grease-stained coveralls leaning against the shop's doorframe, his arms crossed over his chest. He had Liv's same brown hair and a face that was all sharp angles and suspicion.

"Not yet, but I'm trying to remedy that."

Of all the people I wanted to run into before I found Liv, I'm not sure her brother would have made the list. The way she'd always described him was protective. Despite being younger, he'd always tried to look out for her.

"Dustin," I said, injecting as much calm into my voice as I could muster. "It's good to meet you. I've heard a lot about you from Liv."

His eyes narrowed, his gaze raking over me like he was trying to peel back my skin and see the truth beneath. "Funny, I haven't heard a damn thing about you. Imagine my surprise when I'm elbow deep in an engine and I overhear Myrtle Hawkins yammering on about how Liv went and got herself hitched to some rock star."

I winced, guilt spiking through me. "I know it's a lot to take in. Liv and I, it all happened so fast."

Dustin took a step closer, his jaw clenched tight. "And that's why you thought it was okay to let my baby sister come back here alone?"

The accusation hit like a punch to the gut. I swallowed hard, meeting his gaze head-on. "You're right. I should have been here. I should have dropped everything and been by her side. But I'm here now. I'm here to make things right."

Dustin studied me for a long moment, the seconds ticking by painfully slow. Finally, he sighed, some of the tension leaching out of his frame. "You love her? Like, really love her?"

"Yes," I said without hesitation. "She's everything to me, Dustin. I just want a chance to prove it to her."

He ran a hand through his hair, leaving streaks of grease in the blond strands. "Alright, rock star. I'll give you a chance. But I swear, if you hurt her…"

"I won't," I said fiercely. "I'd rather smash up my favourite bass than cause her more pain."

Dustin's lips twitched, like he was fighting back a smile. "Good. Because if you do, I've got a wrench with your name on it."

I huffed out a laugh, some of the tension easing out of me. "Duly noted."

He jerked his chin towards the end of the street. "She's at the doctor's office. She should be done soon."

"Thank you. Truly." I grinned, clapping him on the shoulder as I passed. "I'll catch you later."

"That you will," he muttered as we walked away.

"Well that could have been worse."

"Yeah, it could have." Anderson shook his head. "Liv definitely wouldn't have forgiven you if I'd had to put her brother in the hospital. Jesus." He dragged a hand across his face. "Babysitting you just gets harder and harder."

"Just keeping it interesting for you."

"Well, make it less fucking interesting, will you?"

"I'll get right on that."

Chuckling, I quickened my pace, the bouquet clenched tightly in my hand and the bakery bag swinging on my arm. I was close, so damn close. And this time, I wasn't letting go. Not for anything.

CHAPTER THIRTY-FOUR

OLIVIA

"The latest test results show that the cancer has progressed more rapidly than we anticipated." Dr. Honeysuckle's voice was gentle, but each word felt like a blow.

Mama's hand tightened around mine, her weathered skin soft and familiar. I swallowed hard, my heart hammering against my ribs.

"I'm so sorry, but… we're looking at a matter of weeks now, not months."

Weeks?

Had I not been sitting down, I might have fallen. I couldn't breathe, couldn't think. This couldn't be happening. Not now. Not ever.

The sterile, antiseptic smell of the doctor's office faded away as my mind spiralled. "How many weeks?" Mama's voice was steady. She stared at the doctor, her face perfectly composed while tears started to burn in the back of my eyes.

"It's hard to say exactly, but based on the aggressive nature of the cancer… I'd estimate four to six weeks, at most."

Four to six weeks.

How could a lifetime be reduced to mere weeks? How could I say goodbye to the woman who had raised me in such a cruelly short time?

A lump formed in my throat and I pressed my lips together, willing myself not to cry. I couldn't fall apart, not now. Mama needed me to be strong.

"What can we do?" I asked, my voice barely above a whisper. "There must be something…"

Dr. Honeysuckle shook his head, a sad smile on his lips. "At this stage, our focus should be on keeping your mother comfortable." He leaned back in his chair, his gaze compassionate. "I know this is a lot to process. Take your time, ask any questions you may have. I'm here to support you and your family in any way I can."

Questions? I had a thousand, but they all stuck in my throat, trapped behind the lump of grief and fear. Mama squeezed my hand, drawing my attention to her. She looked at me, her green eyes filled with a love and serenity that took my breath away. "It's going to be alright, Livvy."

I wanted to believe her, but in that moment, with the weight of Dr. Honeysuckle's words pressing down on me, all I could feel was a suffocating sense of loss. How would we tell Dustin? How could I go back to Nashville after she… and leave him alone in this town?

"Mama…" My voice broke, the tears I'd been holding back spilling down my cheeks.

She pulled me into her arms, comforting me. Our roles should have been reversed. I buried my face in her neck, inhaling the familiar scent of her lavender perfume. She stroked my hair, murmuring soothing words I couldn't quite make out over the roaring in my ears.

How was I supposed to do this? How could I watch the woman who had been my everything fade away, powerless to stop it?

"Shhh, baby girl. It's okay. Let it out."

And so I did. In that sterile, impersonal doctor's office, with the weight of our new reality pressing down on us, I let myself shatter in my mother's arms. I cried for the future we would never have, for the memories we'd never get to make. I cried for the hole that would be left in my heart, a void that could never be filled.

"I'm here, Livvy. I'm right here." Her words were a lifeline, a promise. "We'll take this one day at a time, one moment at a time. And we'll make every second count."

Dr. Honeysuckle, who had been quietly observing our exchange, cleared his throat softly. "I'll give you two a moment. When you're ready, we can discuss the next steps, the support services available to you. There's no rush."

No rush. The irony of those words, in the face of the ticking clock that now governed our lives, was not lost on me.

*a*shley's smiling face greeted us as we exited the doctor's office. She took one look at my red, puffy eyes and pulled me into a warm hug.

I clung to her. "It's all fucked," I whispered.

Ashley gasped, faking outrage. She pulled back and grinned at me. "Liv Monroe, did you just cuss?"

"Yes, and I stand by it."

My mother chuckled, the sound so happy while the heavy weight of grief pressed down on my chest. How could she find humour in anything right now? How could she smile and laugh when we'd just been told she had mere weeks left to live?

A flare of anger sparked in my gut, hot and irrational. I wanted to shake her, to question how she could be so cavalier about her own impending death. But as quickly as the anger came, it fizzled out, replaced by a sickening wave of guilt.

What right did I have to wallow, to rage against the unfairness of it all, when she was the one living on borrowed time?

"Liv, honey?" Ashley's gentle voice pulled me from my

spiralling thoughts. "Why don't we get your mama settled in the car? We can talk more on the way home."

Home. The word felt hollow, empty. What would home be without Mama's warm presence, her infectious laughter? And Dustin... my heart clenched at the thought of my baby brother, left alone in this gossipy little town, with no one to lean on.

Mechanically, I helped Ashley manoeuvre Mama's wheel-chair towards the car, my mind a million miles away. Could I really go back to Nashville after all this?

As we made our way outside, a grin overtook Ashley's expression. "You'll never guess who Myrtle Hawkins saw sneaking out of the Johnson's barn last night."

Mama chuckled, a spark of her old mischief flickering in her eyes. "Let me guess... Sadie-Mae and that no-good Christopher Harris?"

Ashley gasped, a hand flying to her chest in mock scandal. "Why, Mrs Monroe! How ever did you know?"

Their laughter, warm and familiar, washed over me like a soothing balm. For a moment, the weight on my chest eased, the knot of grief and fear loosening just a fraction.

As we turned the corner into the clinic parking lot, a familiar figure caught my eye. My breath hitched, my step faltering.

For a second, I thought I was imagining things. But Lewis kept coming towards me, striding down the street towards us with purpose. His bodyguard trailed after him, a perplexed look. Then Lewis started running. Concern etched on his handsome face.

"Liv? What's wrong, cariad?" His rich, lilting voice washed over me. He pulled me into his very real arms and the dam broke.

Tears spilled down my cheeks in hot, unrelenting streams. A sob tore from my throat, raw and guttural. All I could focus on was the solid warmth of Lewis's arms as they wrapped around me, pulling me into his embrace.

I buried my face in his chest, my fingers clutching at his shirt as if he were my only lifeline in a stormy sea of grief. He held me tight, one hand stroking my hair, the other rubbing soothing circles on my back.

"Shh, cariad. I've got you. Let it out," he murmured, his lips pressed against my temple.

And so I did. In the middle of a parking lot, with my mother and my best friend looking on, I fell apart in Lewis's arms. Great, heaving sobs wracked my body, my tears soaking into his shirt. All the fear, the anger, the overwhelming sense of loss poured out of me in a torrent of anguish.

Through it all, he held me. He didn't try to shush me or tell me it would be alright. He just let me cry, his strong arms anchoring me, his steady heartbeat soothing against my cheek.

I'm not sure how long we stood there, but eventually, my sobs subsided, tapering off into shuddering-breaths and hiccupping sighs. Reluctantly, I pulled back, swiping at my tear-stained cheeks with the back of my hand.

"I'm sorry," I whispered, my voice hoarse and small.

Lewis cupped my face, his thumbs gently brushing away the last of my tears. "You have nothing to apologise for, Liv. I'm here for you, always."

"But the tour, the band... won't they be furious?"

"None of that matters, Liv. Not compared to you." He shook his head, a small smile playing at the corners of his mouth. "The band understands. They practically pushed me onto the plane themselves."

I searched his face, looking for any hint of hesitation or regret. But all I saw was love.

"My tech is going to step in for a couple of shows, and we'll play it by ear from there. But Liv, listen to me..." He took my hands in his, his gaze intense and serious. "You're my top priority right now. Nothing else comes close. So don't worry about the tour, okay?"

How could I not worry about it? But what if he regretted this? What if he resented me for pulling him away from the tour? What if the band blamed me for his absence? I couldn't bear the thought of being the reason for any friction between them.

"I don't know if I can handle it if you change your mind again." My voice trembled and I hated it. "I'm barely holding it together as it is, and if you leave…"

"I'm not leaving, Liv." He shook his head vehemently, his grip on my hands tightening. "Not unless you tell me to go. I'm in this, all the way. I know I've given you reason to doubt me in the past, but I swear to you, I'm done running from us."

I searched his eyes, wanting desperately to believe him. "What if the press finds out? What if they start hounding me and you freak out?"

Lewis sighed, his thumb rubbing soothing circles on the back of my hand. "I won't lie to you, I'm nervous. They will find out, and they will make a big deal out of it. But I'm not going to let the fear of them come between us, not again."

"I want to believe you. I do. But I'm scared that it'll all be too much, and you'll realise that I'm not worth the trouble."

The words burned in my throat, the vulnerability of the admission making me feel raw and exposed. But he merely pulled me closer, his forehead resting against mine.

"You are worth everything, Liv. Everything. I'm not going to run, not this time. I'm here, and I'm yours, for as long as you'll have me."

"Lewis…" I swallowed hard, my heart too full for words.

Before I could say more, a voice called out from across the parking lot. "Well, if it isn't the happy couple!" Hattie Mayfield walked towards us, a beaming smile on her face. "I see you found her."

What on earth?

"I just had to come and offer my congratulations, you two," Hattie said.

"But how…"

"How did I know?" Hattie grinned at my nod. She hooked a thumb at Lewis. "This one has been all over town calling your name and telling anyone who'd listen that you're his wife."

A crowd started forming, full of familiar faces who had watched me grow up. They stood across the road, keeping a respectful distance, but most definitely listening to every single word we said.

I stared at all of them, my eyes widening as it sunk in. "You... you told people, the entire town we're married?"

He nodded, a sheepish grin on his face. "I might've been a bit overzealous, but I needed them to know. I needed *you* to know, without a doubt, that I'm all in. That I'm not hiding or holding back anymore."

"But what about the press?"

"I already told you, cariad. I'm doing everything I can to not care about the press." He reached for my hand and pulled me back into his arms. "I just want you. All of you. Publicly."

The crowd awwed and whooped, making me chuckle, but Lewis grimaced.

"I'm sorry I went and outed us to the whole town without consulting you but I needed you to believe me." He pulled me closer, his forehead resting against mine. "I love you, Liv. I love you so damn much. And I don't care who knows it."

Tears pricked at my eyes again, but this time, they were tears of joy, of love so fierce it stole my breath.

"Well, if that isn't the sweetest thing I've ever seen," Mama Jo said, her voice thick with emotion. "You two are gonna make it, I can feel it in my bones."

A chorus of agreement rose from the small crowd who beamed at us. I looked around at the faces of my friends, my family. At the man who held my heart in his hands, who had travelled across the country just to do the one thing that scared him the most.

Hattie's gaze dropped to my ringless finger. "Best fix that if I were you. There are far too many people in this town who'd gladly sweep him out from under you."

I caught sight of Sadie-Mae at the edge of the crowd, her eyes fixed on Lewis with a predatory gleam. Lewis followed my line of sight, his body tensing as he spotted her.

He leaned in close, his breath tickling my ear. "I don't trust that woman not to try something."

A laugh bubbled up in my throat, despite the gravity of the moment. "Worried she's going to steal you away?"

He huffed, pressing a kiss to my temple. "Hardly. I just don't want there to be any doubt in anyone's mind that I'm yours, completely and utterly."

I smiled, my heart aching with love for this man. "Well then, I guess we better make it official. But let's do it at home, just you, me, and my family."

His eyes softened, a tender smile playing at his lips. "I like the sound of that." Then he sighed. "And while we're at it, I'll call Carly and give her the heads up before she tries to castrate me for blindsiding her again.

"You didn't tell your publicist that you were coming here? That you were going to out our relationship to the town and by default the world?"

He grimaced, rubbing the back of his neck. "I didn't want her to try and talk me out of it. You know how she is, always worrying about optics and media narratives."

"She's going to be furious."

He took my hands in his, his gaze unwavering. "I know. And I'm sorry for any chaos this might bring to your doorstep. But I'm not sorry for doing it. I meant what I said—I'm all in, consequences be damned."

The sincerity in his words, the determination in his eyes... it stole my breath. This was a side of Lewis I'd never seen before, a man so certain of his love, so ready to fight for it.

"You really mean it, don't you? This isn't just some fleeting moment of madness?"

He cupped my face, his thumbs stroking my cheekbones. "I've never meant anything more in my life. I love you, Liv Monroe. I love you in a way I didn't know was possible. And I'll spend every day proving it to you, if that's what it takes."

Tears pricked at my eyes, my heart so full it felt fit to burst.

"I love you too, Lewis. More than I ever thought I could love anyone."

He smiled, a bright, beautiful thing that made my knees weak. "Then that's all that matters."

"Well, I'd say there's one more thing," I smirked when his smile fell.

"What?"

Despite all the pain swirling about inside of me, a smile curled my lips. "Whether Carly lets you live once she finds out. Please can I be in on that call?"

He shook his head at me, but he couldn't stop his smile. "Anything you want." He pressed a soft kiss to my forehead before pulling back, a mischievous glint in his eye. "Now, I believe we have a ring to retrieve and a publicist to call. I expect we'll have a pack of press vultures camped out on your lawn by morning."

I groaned. "I suppose that's a small price to pay for winning all of you."

His grin widened, his arms tightening around me. "The smallest."

We stood there for a moment, wrapped in each other's embrace, the rest of the world fading away. But there was one last thing niggling at the back of my mind, one last doubt that needed to be voiced.

"Can I ask you something?"

"Anything, cariad."

I took a deep breath, steeling myself. "What happens when the day comes that you're ready to hang up your guitar? When the rock star life loses its lustre and you're ready to settle down? Will you still love me then, when I'm the one on stage and you're the one at home, waiting for me to return?"

His expression softened, a tender smile playing at his lips. "I'll love you until my last breath, no matter where life takes us. Whether I'm by your side on stage or cheering you on from the front row, my heart is yours. Always and forever."

My vision blurred with unshed tears. "You promise?"

"With everything I am." He brushed a kiss across my knuckles, his eyes never leaving mine. "I'm in this for the long haul, Liv. Through the good times and the bad, the ups and the downs. I'm yours, in whatever capacity you'll have me."

I surged forward, capturing his lips in a searing kiss. He responded instantly, his arms banding around me, his mouth moving against mine with a fervour that left me breathless.

In that moment, with the man I loved in my arms, and this newfound certainty that no matter what happened in the next few weeks, I would always have him, I felt invincible.

EPILOGUE

 *ix weeks later*

OLIVIA

I stood in Mama's room just staring at it, hovering near the door, for the millionth time. The emptiness pressed in on me from all sides. The once vibrant space now felt like a shell. Her clothes, her treasures—the dresses she'd worn to church every Sunday, the aprons she'd tied around her waist as she baked— were all gone, donated or sold off in the weeks since her passing. Only the memories remained, clinging to the walls like faded wallpaper.

One month. It had been one month since we'd lost her, since the world had tilted off its axis and left me reeling.

Some days, it felt like an eternity. Others, like no time at all. Like she'd just stepped out for a moment and would breeze back through the door any second, filling the space with her light once more.

But she wouldn't. I knew that. She was gone, and all the wishing in the world wouldn't bring her back.

I closed my eyes, breathing in deep, searching for some

lingering trace of her. The air still held a hint of her perfume, the floral scent she'd loved and I'd always associated with her. I remembered the day I'd accidentally knocked over the bottle on her dresser. The fragrance soaked into the carpet. We'd laughed as we'd tried to mop it up, the scent clinging to our hands, our clothes.

Now, it was all I had left of her. That, and the aching hole in my chest.

A soft knock startled me, and I spun around to find Dustin hovering in the doorway.

"Lewis is ready to go." He stepped into the room, his gaze casting over it almost hesitantly. "Anderson has the car all packed up."

I swallowed hard, a lump rising in my throat. "I don't know if I can do this, Dustin."

He sighed, crossing the room to pull me into a hug. I leaned into him, breathing in the familiar scent of motor oil. My little brother, all grown up and strong.

When did that happen?

"I know it's hard, Liv," he whispered into my hair. "I know you're hurting. We all are. But you can't put your life on hold forever."

I squeezed my eyes shut against the sting of tears. "I just… I feel like I'm abandoning her. Abandoning you. Running off to chase my dreams while you're left here to pick up the pieces."

"We've gone through this." He pulled back, his hands firm on my shoulders. "You're not abandoning anyone, you hear me? This is what Ma would want. What I want. For you to get back out there, to sing your heart out and show the world what you're made of."

A wobbly laugh escaped me, half sob, half amusement. "When did you get so wise, little brother?"

He grinned, the crooked, impish smile that always made him look like an overgrown child. "I've always been wise. You just never listened."

I shoved at his chest, sniffling. "Jerk."

"Brat," he shot back, the old, familiar banter a balm to my battered heart.

But the moment was short-lived. I'd put off leaving for weeks and Lewis, bless him, had nodded every time I delayed us. The band was understanding but I knew we couldn't put it off forever. Still, the thought of leaving this house, this town, my family... it crashed over me anew, stealing my breath.

"I can't," I whispered, fresh tears welling. "I'm not ready. I thought I was, but... maybe I should stay another week. Just to make sure you're okay, to help get everything settled with the house, the estate..."

He sighed, exasperated but fond. "You said one more week last week. And the week before that. If you keep putting it off, you'll never leave."

I opened my mouth to argue, but he cut me off with a look. "I'm a big boy, sis. I can handle things here. And Ashley's just a phone call away if I need anything. You're not leaving me high and dry."

He gripped my shoulders, his gaze intense. "But if you stay, if you keep putting your life on hold because you're worried about me... that's not what Ma would want. That's not what any of us want."

His words hit home, a bittersweet truth I couldn't deny. Mama had been my biggest cheerleader, my fiercest supporter. She'd believed in me, in my music, with a faith that never wavered. The thought of disappointing her, even now...

But still, the idea of walking out that door, of leaving her behind...

Dustin must have seen the hesitation, the conflict, in my eyes. He huffed a laugh, shaking his head. "Alright, you asked for it. Don't say I didn't warn you."

Before I could process his words, he'd scooped me up, throwing me over his shoulder like a sack of potatoes. I yelped, flailing and pounding on his back as he carried me out of the room, down the stairs.

"Dustin Monroe, you put me down right this instant!" I shrieked, torn between laughter and outrage.

He ignored me, his grip firm as he marched us through the living room and out the front door. I caught a glimpse of Lewis and Ashley waiting by the car, matching grins on their faces.

"A little help here?" I called out, glaring daggers at their amused expressions.

Ashley shrugged, her eyes dancing with mirth. "Sorry, Liv. I'm with Dustin on this one. It's for your own good."

Lewis nodded. "She's right, cariad. It's time."

I huffed, going limp in my brother's hold. He set me down next to the car, his hands gentle on my shoulders.

"I don't want to go," I whispered, my voice small and child-like to my own ears. "I don't want to leave her."

Lewis stepped forward, pulling me into his arms. I sagged against him, breathing in his scent, his strength. He'd been my rock this past month. I didn't know how I would have survived without him.

"I know it feels like leaving her behind. But she's with you always. In your heart, in your memories. In the music you make and the life you live." He pulled back, cradling my face in his hands. His hazel eyes were soft, shining with love. "And we'll be back. As often as you need. Just because we're going back to the tour doesn't mean we're saying goodbye to Jasmine Bay, to your mam. Not forever."

He was right. Of course he was right.

Leaving didn't mean forgetting. It didn't mean I loved my mother any less, that I was abandoning her memory.

It just meant... living. Moving forward.

I took a deep, shuddering breath, leaning my forehead against Lewis's. "Okay," I whispered, the word a shaky exhale. "Okay. You're right. It's time."

A smile broke over his face, bright and beautiful. He leaned in, brushing a soft kiss over my lips. "That's my girl."

I turned to Ashley and Dustin, my heart clenching at the sight of them. My best friend, my brother. Leaving them behind, even for a little while… it was a physical ache, more so than it had ever been before.

But they were smiling, their eyes shining with affection and the sheen of tears. They knew, better than anyone, how much this meant to me. How much I needed to do this, for myself.

For the little girl who'd first picked up a guitar and dreamed of something bigger than this small town, this sheltered life.

"Go on, then," Ashley said with a shaky but fierce smile. "Go show the world what Olivia Monroe is made of."

Dustin nodded, his grin crooked and bright. "And don't you worry about us. We'll hold down the fort here. You just focus on knocking 'em dead out there."

I swallowed hard, my throat tight. "I love you both. So much."

"We love you, too." She pulled me into a fierce hug. "More than anything."

Dustin wrapped his arms around us both, squeezing tight. "What she said," he mumbled, his voice gruff with emotion.

We held each other for a long moment and I closed my eyes, relaxing into them, committing the moment to memory. When we finally pulled apart, my cheeks were wet, my heart full to bursting.

"Okay," I said, my voice steadier now. Stronger. "Let's do this."

I hugged Ashley and Dustin one last time, whispering promises to call, to visit, to keep them close even from a distance. Then, with a deep breath and a resolute nod, I turned to Lewis.

"Ready, husband?" I asked, the word still new and thrilling on my tongue.

His smile was blinding, his hand warm and strong as it enveloped mine. "Ready, wife."

As Anderson pulled away from the kerb, I watched my childhood home recede in the rearview mirror, the porch swing where Mama and I had spent countless hours swaying in the breeze.

My heart ached, the loss still so fresh, so raw. But with Lewis by my side, with the love and support of my family, I knew I could face whatever lay ahead.

Mama was with me, just like Dustin said. In my heart. In my music. And as long as I kept singing, as long as I kept reaching for those stars… she'd never truly be gone.

LEWIS

"Holy shit, it's true!" Tom shouted when Liv and I stepped into the green room in Jacksonville, his grin stretching from ear to ear. "The newlyweds have landed!"

The familiar chaos of the green room washed over me as Liv and I stepped through the door. Half-empty water and beer bottles and scattered sheets of set lists covered every available surface. The air buzzed with pre-show adrenaline, the electric anticipation that never failed to set my blood humming.

Heads turned, faces lighting up as the rest of the band and crew registered our presence. In seconds, we were surrounded, engulfed in a sea of hugs and back slaps and welcome backs.

"Oh, honey. I'm so sorry about your mam." Lily pulled Liv into a fierce hug. "How are you holding up?"

Liv leaned into the embrace, her shoulders loosening just a fraction. "I'm… I'm getting there," she whispered. "Taking it day by day. But it's good to be back, to be here with all of you."

Lily squeezed her tighter, a wordless offer of support.

"I can't even imagine what you two have been through." Andy clapped me on the shoulder. "But we're here for you, yeah? Anything you need, just say the word."

I nodded, my throat tight with emotion. "Thanks. That means a lot."

When Lily released Liv, she turned to me with a gentle but mischievous smile. "And you. Looks like married life is treating you well."

I grinned, tugging Liv closer to my side. "Better than well. I'm the luckiest man alive."

"Damn right you are!" Alex chimed in, clapping me on the shoulder. "Never thought I'd see the day you settled down."

I rolled my eyes, shoving him away. "Like you're one to talk, Al."

Alex grinned, his arm snaking around Ceri's waist as she joined us. "What can I say? When you know, you know. And I knew from the moment I met this one." He pressed a kiss to Ceri's temple, his eyes soft with adoration and not even a glint of frustration. "She's got me wrapped around her little finger, and I wouldn't have it any other way."

Ceri laughed, leaning into his side. "Oh, please. You're still a handful, Alex Thomas. But you're my handful."

Laughter rippled through the room, warm and easy.

"In all seriousness, though, I'm so happy for you both." Ceri threw a warm smile at Liv and me. "You deserve all the love and happiness in the world."

A chorus of agreement echoed through the room, each member of our little family offering their own heartfelt congratulations and well-wishes.

For a moment, I just breathed it in. Let the feeling of home, of family, wash over me. It had only been a month since we'd last been together, but god, I'd missed this. Missed them.

And from the way Liv's hand tightened in mine, the way she leaned into my side… I knew she felt it too.

One by one, they came to us. Offering hugs, condolences, congratulations. Gentle ribbings and heartfelt words of support. Each gesture, each smile or clasped shoulder, seemed to ease something in Liv. A tension I hadn't even realised she'd been carrying.

With every passing minute, I watched a little more of the grief, the weight, slip from her shoulders. Watched her come back to herself, piece by fractured piece.

It hit me then, standing there amidst the chaos and the laughter, just how far we'd come. Two months ago, the idea of walking into this room, hand in hand with my wife, had seemed impossible. I wasn't capable of doing it, let alone enjoying the moment.

But now… things had changed.

I had changed.

It hadn't been easy. Those first few weeks in Jasmine Bay, watching her mother decline and a piece of Liv fracture day by day. Dealing with the press camped out on our doorstep, soaking up all of the drama, spinning their tales with any little snippet they could glean from watching us or talking to people who didn't know us.

Then laying her mother to rest, having to hold Liv through the ceremony while she sobbed into my suit jacket, needing me to be strong.

They were some of the hardest weeks of my life. Of both our lives.

Grief was a funny thing. It snuck up on you when you least expected it. One moment, you were fine. Coping. Moving forward. And the next it whacked you in the knees and set you back.

I'd watched Liv battle that tide, day after day. Watched her rage and weep, retreat into herself and push everyone away. Even me.

There had been moments I'd feared I was losing her. Not because of the press as I'd always thought, but the devastating weight of her grief.

I hadn't given up. Hadn't let her give up, either. I'd been her rock even when she tried to disappear into herself, hiding beneath the duvet and refusing to come out. Even when she'd screamed and cursed and beat her fists against my chest, demanding to know why.

Why her mother? Why now? Why, when everything had finally been falling into place?

I didn't have answers. I just kept holding her through her worst and loving her more and more each day.

And little by little, it had been enough to return a little piece of normal to us.

Therapy helped. I smiled to myself, remembering those first few sessions. The way we'd both fidgeted in our seats, holed up in her grandfather's old study in her mother's house, staring at the laptop, defensive and raw and so bloody terrified of cracking open our chests, of letting another person peer inside.

But my therapist had been patient. He'd given us the tools, the safe space, to peel back the layers and understand our feelings.

It hadn't been pretty. There had been tears, harsh words. Painful truths dragged into the light, kicking and screaming.

But fuck, it was worth it. Every gut-wrenching moment, every soul-deep confession.

Because here we were. Together. Whole and healed and ready to face whatever came next.

I let my gaze drift over the room, over the faces of these people I loved. My bandmates, my best friends. Liv was still raw, but I knew a week in the company of these loveable assholes would lift her spirits even more.

My attention snagged on a face I hadn't seen in years. Alex's sister, Leah, sat on one of the sofas, sipping a drink and chatting to Daphne, our new band manager's girlfriend.

But her presence wasn't the reason I did a double take.

No, it was Andy. The man had a fucking death wish.

He crossed behind the sofa, his fingers grazing the nape of Leah's neck in a touch that lingered just a beat too long to be casual. She turned, watching him walk away with a secret smile playing about her lips, her eyes soft and heated.

I leaned down, my mouth close to Liv's ear. "Is it just me," I whispered, "or did you see that too?"

She followed my gaze, her own eyes widening. "Andy and Leah? No way."

"That was not a 'just friends' touch. That was an 'I've seen you naked and I'd like to again' touch."

Liv muffled a snort against my shoulder. "You would know."

I grinned, unrepentant. "Damn right I would."

One thing was for sure. If Alex found out, if he got even a whiff of his baby sister shacking up with his bandmate... there would be hell to pay.

World War III in the green room. Blood on the walls and chunks of guitarist all over the floor.

I blew out a breath, pushing the thought away. That was a problem for another day. Another tour stop.

Today, I had more important things to focus on. Like holding on to Liv, putting on a brave face for all our friends.

Like getting her through this first day back. This first step into the crazy, chaotic, wonderful world we'd chosen.

"Are you ready for this?" My hands came up to cup her jaw, my thumbs stroking over the delicate skin beneath her eyes. "We can take it slow. Ease back in. We've seen everyone, we can leave now. You don't have to be 'on' right away."

Liv leaned into my touch, her eyes fluttering shut for a moment. "I know. And I love you for worrying." She pressed a quick, sweet kiss to my palm. "But you were right, I need to be here. I want to be here."

When she opened her eyes, they were clear. Determined.

Despite her confidence, we moved slowly. The Candle-makers had her slot covered for the next two weeks, and Lily had given me until New Orleans to settle back in. So that night, we enjoyed the show from the side of the stage like two fans without a care in the world.

Tonight, all that mattered was the woman at my side. The way she leaned into me, her head on my shoulder as we watched our friends, our chosen family, set the stage on fire.

"I love you." My arms tightened around her waist. "So fucking much."

She turned in my embrace, her eyes finding mine in the shadows. "I love you too. More than anything."

I'd lost the ability to resist her weeks ago. So I kissed her. Kissed her like I'd done countless times before, like I would do countless times again. I didn't care who saw us. Didn't care if they got photos or texted some bullshit to their friends.

I just held her close, enjoyed that I could, that I got to call her my wife. My heart. And I let the music wash over us, through us while I quietly admitted the truth to myself.

Marrying Olivia had been the best mistake I'd ever made, and I'd do it again in a heartbeat.

Not ready to say goodbye to The Brightside?

Don't worry, this lot's not done yet. There's plenty of tour left to make things interesting for your favourite Welsh band.

Next up is Craving Leah. What's Alex going to do when he finds out his bandmate's been secretly dating his sister?

Preorder now on your favourite retailer or direct from the author to be the first to know

ALSO BY MORGANA BEVAN

True Platinum Series (Rock Star Romance)
(Rhiannon)
Chasing Alys–Ryan (Resistant to Love)
Charming Daphne–Matt (Force Proximity)
Winning Nia–James (Second Chance)
Enticing Mel–Dan (Secret Baby)
Needing Emily–Emily (Accidental Marriage/Runaway Bride)
Defying Ella - Jared (Close Proximity / Snowed-in)

(The Brightside)
Braving Lily - Lily (Opposites Attract)
Daring Ceri - Alex (Second Chance)
Marrying Olivia - Lewis (Accidental Marriage)
Craving Leah - Andy (Best Friend's Sister) - Coming 2025

Kings of Screen Series (Hollywood Romance)
Between Takes (Enemies to Lovers)
Married Blind (Marriage of Convenience)
Acting Counsel (Close Proximity, Forbidden)
Fashionably Fake (Fake Dating)
Lights, Camera, Baby! (Accidental Pregnancy) - *Coming August 2024*

Sign up for Morgana Bevan's mailing list.

ABOUT MORGANA

Morgana Bevan is a sucker for a rock star romance, particularly if it involves a soul-destroying breakup or strangers waking up in Vegas. She's a contemporary romance author based in Wales. When Morgana's not writing steamy celebrity romances with gorgeous British rock stars and movie stars, she's travelling the world, searching for inspiration.

She enjoys travelling, attending gigs, and trying out the extreme activities she forces on her characters.

Find Morgana online at morganabevan.com.

Morgana's Facebook Reader Group: facebook.com/groups/498919364708263

Made in the USA
Coppell, TX
28 August 2024

36562365R00184